Brother Grimm

ALSO BY CRAIG RUSSELL
FROM CLIPPER LARGE PRINT

Blood Eagle

Brother Grimm

Craig Russell

W F HOWES LTD

This large print edition published in 2006 by
W F Howes Ltd
Unit 4, Rearsby Business Park, Gaddesby Lane,
Rearsby, Leicester LE7 4YH

1 3 5 7 9 10 8 6 4 2

First published in the United Kingdom in 2006
by Hutchinson

A CIP catalogue record for this book is available
from the British Library

ISBN 1 84632 764 4

Typeset by Palimpsest Book Production Limited,
Grangemouth, Stirlingshire
Printed and bound in Great Britain
by Antony Rowe Ltd, Chippenham, Wilts.

For Wendy

ACKNOWLEDGEMENTS

I had a lot of fun spinning this dark yarn. I would like to thank everyone who both helped me and made the experience even more fun:

First and foremost, my wife, Wendy, who was a great enthusiast of *Brother Grimm* from the start, and whose support and comments on the first draft helped make this a better book. My children, Jonathan and Sophie, my thriller-fan mother, Helen, and my sister Marion. I owe special thanks to Bea Black and Colin Black, to Alice Aird and Tony Burke, and to Holger and Lotte Unger for their friendship, support and invaluable advice.

I am enormously grateful to my agent, Carole Blake, whose energy, commitment and drive has made the Jan Fabel series an international success, as well as Oli Munson and David Eddy of Blake Friedmann Literary Agency. Paul Sidey, my editor, has always been a great champion of my work and I thank him for all of the time, effort and thought he has devoted to this book. Thanks also to my accountants, Larry Sellyn and Elaine

Dyer, who have offered such key advice and support throughout my writing career.

Again, I owe great thanks to the excellent Dr Bernd Rullkötter, my German translator, who worked closely with me on the English as well as the German version of *Brother Grimm*. Thanks, Bernd, for caring so much, and for all your help.

I have to make very special mention of the following people who offered their help and support freely and enthusiastically. I offer my deepest gratitude to: *Erste Hauptkommissarin* Ulrike Sweden of the Polizei Hamburg for reading my first draft and correcting technical inaccuracies as well as for all of the information, help and contacts she supplied; the journalist Anja Sieg who read my manuscript to ensure I got the East Frisian details right, and made a host of other invaluable comments; Dr Anja Lowit, who likewise read and commented on the first draft; Dirk Brandenburg and Birte Hell, both of the Hamburg murder squad; Peter Baustian of the Davidwache police station and Robert Golz of the Hamburger Polizeipräsidium; Katrin Frahm, my German language tutor, who has done a wonderful job in taking my German to new levels; Dagmar Förtsch, of GLS Language Services (and Honorary Consul of the Federal Republic of Germany in Glasgow) for her enthusiastic support and help; Udo Röbel, former editor-in-chief of *BILD* and now, himself, a crime author, for his enthusiasm and friendship; Menso Heyl, editor-in-chief of *Hamburger Abendblatt*, for his interest in my work and for sending me an airmail copy every day to help me keep totally up-to-date with events in Hamburg.

And very special thanks to my German publisher, Marco Schneiders for his enthusiasm for and commitment to my work.

I gratefully acknowledge everyone at my publishers in the UK, in Germany and around the world, who has made a positive contribution to the Jan Fabel series.

And, of course, to all of the people of Hamburg: *ich bedanke mich herzlich.*

For more information about Craig Russell and his books, please visit www.craigrussell.com.

CHAPTER 1

9.30 a.m., Wednesday, 17 March:
Elbstrand beach, Blankenese, Hamburg

Fabel stroked her cheek gently with his gloved hand. A stupid gesture; probably an inappropriate gesture, but one that he felt was somehow necessary. He saw his finger tremble as it traced the curve of her cheek. He felt something tight and panicky in his chest when he realised just how much she reminded him of his daughter Gabi. He smiled a small, tight, forced smile and felt his lips tremble as the muscles of his face strained under the effort. She looked up at him with her large eyes. Unblinking, azure eyes.

The panic grew in Fabel. He wanted to wrap his arms around her and tell her that it was all going to be all right. But he couldn't; and it wasn't going to be all right. She still held him with her unblinking, unwavering azure gaze.

Fabel felt Maria Klee's presence beside him. He withdrew his hand and stood up from his squatting position.

'How old?' he asked without turning to Maria, keeping his eyes locked with the girl's.

'Difficult to say. Fifteen, sixteen, I'd guess. We don't have a name yet.'

The morning breeze scooped up some of the fine sand of the Blankenese beach and swirled it like a drink stirred in a glass. Some of the grains blew into the girl's eyes, settling on the whites, but still she did not blink. Fabel found he could not look any more and tore his gaze away. He shoved his hands deep into his coat pockets and turned his head, looking, for no good reason except to fill his eyes with something other than the image of a murdered girl, up towards the red and white striped spindle of Blankenese lighthouse. He turned back to Maria. He stared into her pale blue-grey candid eyes that never told you much about the person behind them; that sometimes suggested a coldness, a lack of emotion, unless you knew her well. Fabel sighed as if some great pain or sadness had forced the breath from him.

'Sometimes I don't know if I can do this any more, Maria.'

'I know what you mean,' she said, looking down at the girl.

'No . . . I really mean it, Maria. I've been doing this job for nearly half my life and sometimes I feel like I've had more than a bellyful of it . . . Christ, Maria – she's so like Gabi . . .'

'Why don't you leave this one to me?' said Maria. 'For now, at least. I'll deal with forensics.'

Fabel shook his head. He had to stay. He had to look. He had to hurt. Fabel was drawn back to the girl. Her eyes, her hair, her face. He would remember every detail. This face that was too young to wear death would remain in the galleries of his memory, along with all those other faces – some young, some old, all dead – from years of murder inquiries. Not for the first time Fabel found himself resenting the one-way relationship he was forced to have with these people. He knew that, over the coming weeks and months, he would get to know this girl: he would talk with her parents, her siblings, her friends; he would learn her routines, the music she was into, the hobbies she enjoyed. Then he would delve deeper: he would tease solemn secrets from closest friends; he would read the diary she had kept hidden from the world; he would share the thoughts she had chosen not to share; he would read the boys' names she had doodled in secret. He would build a complete picture of the hopes and dreams, the spirit and personality of the girl who had once lived behind those azure eyes.

Fabel would know this girl so totally. Yet she would never know him. His awareness of her began with the total extinction of her awareness of anything. Her death. It was Fabel's job to know the dead.

Still she gazed at him from the sand. Her clothes were old: not rags, but drab and worn. A baggy sweatshirt with a ghost of a design on its front, and faded jeans. And when the clothes had been new they had been cheap.

She lay on the sand with her legs partly pulled up under her, her hands folded and resting on her lap. It was as if she had been kneeling on the sand and had toppled over, her posture frozen. But she hadn't died here. Fabel was sure of it. What he wasn't sure about was whether her posture was an accidental arrangement of limbs or a deliberate pose struck by whoever had left her there.

Fabel was snapped back from his bitter thoughts by the approach of Brauner, the head of the Spurensicherung forensics team. Brauner walked across the wooden planking, elevated on bricks, that he had assembled as the sole ingress and egress to the crime locus. Fabel nodded a grim welcome.

'What have we got, Holger?' Fabel asked.

'Not a lot,' said Brauner, bleakly. 'The sand is dry and fine and the wind shifts it about a bit. It literally blows away any forensic traces. I don't think this is our primary locus . . . you?'

Fabel shook his head. Brauner looked down at the girl's body, his expression clouded. Fabel knew that Brauner too had a daughter and he recognised the gloom in Brauner's face as a shade of the dull ache he felt himself. Brauner drew a long breath.

'We'll do a full forensic before we pass her on to Möller for the autopsy.'

Fabel watched in silence as the white-overalled

forensic specialists of the Spurensicherungsteam processed the scene. Like ancient Egyptian embalmers wrapping a mummy, the SpuSi technicians worked on the body, covering every square centimetre in strips of Tesa tape, each of which was numbered and photographed, then transferred to a polythene sheet.

Once the scene had been processed, the girl's body was carefully lifted and zippered into the vinyl body bag, hoisted on to a trolley and half pushed, half carried across the yielding sand by two mortuary attendants. Fabel kept his gaze focused on the body bag, an indistinct smudge against the pale colours of the sand, the rocks and the uniforms of the mortuary men, until it disappeared from view. He then turned and looked back along the clean, blond sand towards the slender Blankenese lighthouse, out across the Elbe towards the distant green shores of the Altes Land, then back up at the manicured green terraces of Blankenese, with its elegant, expensive villas.

It occurred to Fabel that he had never viewed such a desolate scene.

CHAPTER 2

9.50 a.m., Wednesday, 17 March:
Krankenhaus Mariahilf hospital,
Heimfeld, Hamburg

The *Oberschwester* chief nurse watched him from the hall. She felt a leaden sensation coalesce in her heart as she did so. He sat, unaware of observation, leaning forward in the bedside chair, his hand resting on the grey-white wrinkled topography of the old woman's forehead. Occasionally his hand would run gently and slowly through the white hair; and all the while he spoke into her ear in a low, gentle murmur that only the old woman could hear. The chief nurse became aware of one of her subordinates standing behind her. The second nurse also smiled with a bitter sympathy as she took in the scene of middle-aged son and elderly mother wrapped in their own exclusive universe. The chief nurse indicated the scene with a small thrust of her chin.

'He never misses a day . . .' She smiled joylessly. 'None of mine will bother their backsides about me when I'm that age, let me tell you.'

The other nurse gave a small knowing laugh. The two women stood in silence for a moment, each taking in the same picture, each wrapped up in their individual, dully terrifying thoughts about their own distant futures.

'Can she hear anything he says to her?' asked the other nurse after a moment.

'No reason to believe she doesn't. The stroke has all but paralysed her and struck her dumb, but, as far as we know, her faculties are still in order.'

'God . . . I'd rather die. Imagine being imprisoned in your own body.'

'At least she's got him,' said the chief nurse. 'He brings in those books of his each and every day and reads to her and then spends an hour just sitting there, stroking her hair and talking quietly to her. At least she's got that.'

The other nurse nodded and gave a long, sad sigh.

Inside the room the old woman and her son were both oblivious to the fact that they were being observed by others. She lay unmoving, incapable of moving, on her back, presenting her son, who sat hunched forward in the bedside chair, with her faintly noble profile of high arched brow and aquiline nose. Every now and then, a trickle of saliva would dribble from the corner of the thin lips and the solicitous son would dab it away with a folded handkerchief. He smoothed the hair back from her brow once more and leaned in close again, his lips almost touching her ear and his breath, as he spoke low and soft and gentle, stirring the silver strands of hair on her temple.

'I spoke to the doctor again today, mother. He told me that your condition has stabilised. That's good, isn't it, *Mutti*?' He didn't pause for the answer that he knew she was incapable of giving. 'Anyway, the doctor says that after your big stroke, you had what they call a series of 'stuttering' strokes . . . like tiny little strokes that did the damage. He also said that these are over now and you won't get any worse if I make sure your medication is maintained.' He paused and let his breath out slowly. 'What that means is it would be possible for me to look after you at home. The doctor wasn't too keen on the idea to start with. But you don't like strangers looking after you, do you, *Mutti*? I told the doctor that. I told him that you'd be much better off with me, with your son, at home. I told him I'd be able to arrange for your care when I'm at work, and the rest of the time . . . well, the rest of the time you'd have me to look after you, wouldn't you? I told him that the nurse can visit us in the cosy little apartment I've bought. The doctor says I might be able to take you home towards the end of the month. Isn't that great?'

He let the thought sink in. He scanned the pallid grey eyes that moved sluggishly in the immobile head. If there was any emotion behind the eyes, it could not break through to be read. He drew even closer, eagerly tugging the chair in tighter to the

8

bed, making it squeak on the polished hospital floor. 'Of course, we both know that it won't be like I told the doctor, don't we, mother?' The voice remained gentle and soothing. 'But there again, I couldn't tell the doctor about the other house . . . *our* house. Or that what I'll really do is leave you to lie in your own shit for days on end, could I? Or that I will spend hours exploring what capacity you have left to feel pain. No, no, that wouldn't do at all, would it, *Mutti*?' He gave a small, childlike laugh. 'I don't think the doctor would be too keen on me taking you home with me if he knew that, would he? But don't worry, I won't tell him if you don't . . . but of course you *can't*, can you? You see, mother, God has gagged and bound you. It's a sign. A sign for me.'

The old woman's head remained motionless, but a tear oozed from the corner of her eye and sought out the creases in the skin of her temple. He dropped his voice even lower and infused it with a conspiratorial tone. 'You and I will be together. Alone. And we can talk about the old days. About the old days in our big old house. About when I was a child. When I was weak and you were strong.' The voice was now a hiss: venom breathed into the ear of the old woman. 'I've done it again, *Mutti*. Another one. Just like three years ago. But this time, because God has bound you up in the prison of your own hideous body, you can't inter-fere. This time you can't stop me, and I'll keep on doing it and doing it. It will be our little secret.

You will be there at the end, mother, I promise you that. But this is just the beginning . . .'

Out in the hall, the two nurses, neither of whom could have guessed the nature of what had passed between son and mother, turned away from the hospital room and the pathetic tableau within it of a deteriorating life and a constant filial devotion. In that instant, the intrusion through a window on to a sadder life ended and they returned to the practicalities of rotas, charts and the medication-dispensing round.

CHAPTER 3

4.30 p.m., Wednesday, 17 March:
Polizeipräsidium, Hamburg

The crisp bright cold of the morning had yielded to a damp sodium-coloured sky that had indolently shouldered its way in from the North Sea. A faint drizzle now freckled the panes of Fabel's office windows and his view out towards the Winterhuder Stadtpark seemed to have had the life and colour sucked from it.

Two people sat across the desk from Fabel: Maria and a stocky, hard-looking man in his mid-fifties, whose scalp gleamed through its black and grey bristle covering.

Kriminaloberkommissar Werner Meyer had worked with Fabel for longer than anyone else in the team. Junior in rank but senior in years, Werner Meyer was not just Fabel's colleague: he was his friend, and often his mentor. Werner shared the same rank as Maria Klee and together they represented Fabel's immediate support in the team. Werner, however, was Fabel's number two. He had much more practical experience as a police officer than

11

Maria, although she had been a high-flyer at university, where she had studied law, and then later at the Polizeifachhochschule and Landespolizeischule police academies. Despite his tough look and considerable bulk, Werner's approach to police work was typified by a methodical thoroughness and an attention to detail. Werner was 'by-the-book' and had often reined in his *Chef* when Fabel had wandered too far down one of his 'intuitive' routes. He had always seen himself as Fabel's partner and it had taken time, and dramatic events, to accustom him to working with Maria.

But it had worked. Fabel had teamed them because of their differences: because they represented different generations of police officer, and because they combined and contrasted experience with expertise, theory with practice. But what really made them work as a team was that which they shared: a total and uncompromising commitment to their roles as Mordkommission officers.

It had been the usual preliminary meeting. Murders took two forms: there was the hot pursuit, where a body was found quickly after death, or there was a strong and clear evidential direction to be pursued; then there was the cold trail, where the killer had already distanced himself or herself in chronology, in geography and in forensic presence from the murder event, leaving the police only scraps to piece together: a process that took time and effort. The murder of the girl on the beach was a cold-trail case: its form was nebulous, amorphous. It would take them a long time and a lot of investigative toil before they made any defined shape of it. The afternoon's meeting had therefore been typical of initial case meetings: they had reviewed the scant facts that were available and timetabled further meetings to examine the awaited forensic and autopsy reports. The body itself would be the starting point: no longer a person but a store of physical information about time, manner and place of death. And, on a molecular level, the DNA and other data retrieved from it would begin the process of identification. The major part of the meeting had been devoted to allocating resources to the various investigative tasks, the first of which was to get almost everyone on to the job of identifying the dead girl. The dead girl. Fabel was steadfastly committed to uncovering her identity, but it was that moment he dreaded most: when the body became a person and the case number became a name.

After the meeting Fabel asked Maria to hang around. Werner nodded knowingly at his boss and, in so doing, succeeded in further highlighting the awkwardness of the situation. So now, Maria Klee, dressed in an expensive black blouse and grey trousers, her legs crossed and her long fingers interlocked in a cradle around her knee, sat impassively and somewhat formally, waiting for her superior officer to speak. As always, her posture was one of restraint, confinement, control, and her blue-grey eyes remained impassive under the questioning arch of her eyebrows. Everything about Maria Klee exuded confidence, self-control and authority. But now there was something between Fabel and Maria that was awkward. She had been back at work for a month now, but this was their first major case since her return and Fabel wanted them to say what had been left unsaid.

Circumstances had forced Fabel and Maria into a unique intimacy. An intimacy closer than if they had slept together. Nine months before, they had spent several minutes alone, under a starry sky in a deserted field in the Altes Land on the southern shore of the Elbe, their breaths mingling, the self-assured Maria Klee transformed into a little girl by her very real and reasonable fear that she was about to die. Fabel had cradled her head and maintained a constant eye contact with her, talking soothingly all the time, not allowing her to drift into a sleep from which she would not wake, never allowing her to take her gaze from his and down to where the hideous haft of a thick-bladed knife jutted from under her ribcage. It had been the worst night of Fabel's career. They had closed in on the most dangerous psychopath Fabel had ever had to deal with: a monster responsible for a series of particularly vicious, ritualistic murders. The pursuit had left two policemen dead: one of Fabel's team, a bright young officer called Paul Lindemann, and a uniformed SchuPo from the local Polizeikommissariat. The last officer the fleeing psychotic had encountered had been Maria: instead of killing her, he had left her with a potentially fatal wound, knowing that Fabel would have to make a choice between continuing his pursuit or saving his officer's life. Fabel had made the only choice that he could.

Now both Fabel and Maria bore scars of different kinds. Fabel had never before lost an officer in the line of duty, and that night he had lost two, and damned near a third. Maria had lost a vast amount of blood and had come close to death on the operating table. Then there had been two tense weeks in intensive care, in which Maria had inhabited that precarious no man's land between awareness and unconsciousness; between life and death. Seven months of a slow return to full health and strength had followed. Fabel knew that Maria had spent the final two months of her recovery in the gym, rebuilding not only her physical strength but something of the iron resolve that had characterised her as an efficient, determined police officer. Now she sat before Fabel, the same old Maria with her flinty, unwavering gaze and her fingers locked around her knee. But as Fabel took in her robust body language, he still found himself looking beyond it, to a night when he had held her chilled hand and listened to her small breaths as she begged him, in a small child's voice, not to let her die. It was something they had to find their way past.

'You know why I want to talk to you, don't you, Maria?'

'No, *Chef* . . . is it about this case?' But the earnest blue-grey gaze faltered and she made a show of brushing away some invisible speck on her immaculate trousers.

'I think you do, Maria. I need to know that you're ready for a full case.'

Maria started to protest but Fabel silenced her with a gesture of his hand.

'Look, Maria, I'm being straight with you. I could very easily say nothing and allocate you duties on the fringes of any investigation that comes up until I'm convinced you're ready. But that's not the way I operate. You know that.' Fabel leaned forward, resting his elbows on the desk. 'I value you too much as an officer to do you that disrespect. But I also value you too much to jeopardise your long-term well-being – and your effectiveness within this team – by pushing you to the forefront of an investigation that you're not ready for.'

'I'm ready.' A steel frost crackled in Maria's voice. 'I've dealt with everything I need to deal with. I wouldn't have come back to work if I thought I was going to compromise the effectiveness of the team.'

'Dammit, Maria, I'm not challenging you. I'm not questioning your abilities . . .' Fabel returned her gaze with equal frankness. 'I nearly lost you that night, Maria. I lost Paul and I nearly lost you. I let you down. I let the team down. It's my responsibility to make sure you're all right.'

The chill in Maria's glacial expression began to thaw. 'It wasn't your fault, *Chef*. To begin with I thought it was mine. That I didn't react quickly enough, or react in the right way. But he was something that we've never encountered before. He was a unique kind of evil. I know that it's highly unlikely that I'll ever encounter someone – some*thing* – like him again.'

'What about the fact that he's still out there on the loose?' said Fabel, and immediately regretted it. It was a thought that had cost him the sleep of more than one night.

'He's far away from Hamburg by now,' said Maria. 'Probably far out of Germany or even Europe. But if he isn't, and if we were to pick up his trail again, I'd be ready.'

Fabel knew she meant what she had said. He didn't know if he was ready to face the Blood Eagle killer again. Now or ever. He kept that thought to himself.

'There's no shame in easing back into things, Maria.'

She smiled a smile that Fabel had not seen before: the first signal that something had, indeed, changed within Maria. 'I'm fine, Jan. I promise you.' It was the first time that she had used his first name in the office. The first time she had ever used it was as she lay somewhere between life and death in the long grass of a field in the Altes Land.

17

Fabel smiled. 'It's good to have you back, Maria.'

Maria was about to say something when Anna Wolff knocked on the door and entered without waiting to be invited.

'Sorry to bust in,' said Anna, 'but I've just had forensics on the phone. There's something we need to look at right away.'

Holger Brauner didn't look like a scientist, or even vaguely academic. He was a man of just medium height with sand-blond hair and a rugged, outdoor appearance. Fabel knew that Holger had been some kind of athlete in his youth and had retained a powerful, stocky frame. Fabel had worked with the head of the SpuSi scenes-of-crime unit for a decade and their mutual professional respect had developed into genuine friendship. Brauner was employed by LKA3, the division of the Hamburg Landeskriminalamt responsible for all forms of forensic investigation. He spent much of his time working out of the Institut für Rechtsmedizin, but also had an office by the forensics labs in the Präsidium. When Fabel entered Brauner's office, Brauner was bent over his desk, examining something through a combined light and magnifying glass that was swung over on an articulated arm. When Brauner looked up he did not greet Fabel with his customary broad grin. Instead he beckoned for Fabel to come over.

'Our killer is communicating with us,' he said

grimly and handed Fabel a pair of surgical gloves. Brauner stepped back to allow Fabel to examine the object on the desk. Set on a small sheet of plastic was a rectangular slip of yellow paper; it was about ten centimetres wide by five long. Brauner had laid a clear perspex sheet over the note to protect it from contamination. The hand-writing, in red ink, was tight, regular, neat and very small.

'We found this in the girl's fist. I am guessing that it was placed in her hand and the fingers closed around it post-mortem but before rigor set in.'

Although the writing was tiny it was legible to the naked eye. But Fabel examined the note through Brauner's illuminating magnifier. Through the lens the writing became more than words on paper: each tiny red stroke became a sweeping band across a textured yellow landscape. He pushed the magnifier to one side and read the message.

Now I am found. My name is Paula Ehlers. I live at Buschberger Weg, Harksheide, Norderstedt. I have been underground and now it is time for me to return home.

Fabel straightened up. 'When did you find this?'

'We took the body over to Butenfeld this morning for Herr Doktor Möller to carry out the autopsy.' Butenfeld was the name of the road in Eppendorf on which the Institut was located and had become police shorthand for the morgue there. 'We were doing our usual pre-autopsy examination of the body when we found this squeezed into her hand. As you know, we place separate bags around the hands and feet to ensure that no forensic evidence is lost in transit, but this note had remained stuck to the palm of her hand even after rigor had worn off.'

Fabel read the note again. There was a sluggish, vaguely nauseating sensation in his gut. *Paula*. She now had a name. The azure eyes that had stared up at him had belonged to *Paula*. He took a notebook from his pocket and noted down the name and address. Fabel had no doubt that it had been the killer and not the victim who had written this message. If the killer had forced the girl to write it, Fabel could not imagine her being able to compose herself sufficiently to write with such neat precision. He turned back to Brauner.

'"*I have been underground . . .*" Does that mean she's been buried somewhere before being dug up, moved and dumped on the beach at Blankenese?'

'I thought of that when I read that in the note . . . but no, I can say for sure that this body has not been interred previously. Anyway, from the post-mortem lividity and the easing of rigor, my rough reckoning is that she's only been dead just over a day. Maybe it's a reference to her being kept in a cellar or something before death. We're checking her clothing for any dust or other contaminants that might give us an idea of the environment she's been kept in for the last twenty-four hours.'

'Could be,' said Fabel. 'Did you find anything else?'

'No.' Brauner picked up a file from his desk and glanced through it. 'Of course, Herr Doktor Möller will be furnishing full pathological details, but our initial findings were that the beach was not the primary locus – that the victim was killed somewhere else and brought to the beach later to be dumped.'

'No, Holger . . .' Fabel replayed the images from the beach in his mind. 'Not dumped. *Posed*. It's been bothering me since this morning. She looked as if she was resting. Or waiting. It was no random abandonment of a corpse. It was a statement of some kind . . . but I just don't know what it was supposed to say.'

Brauner considered Fabel's words. 'I suppose so,' he said eventually. 'I have to admit that I don't quite see it the same way. I agree there was some care in the way she was left. But I didn't see a deliberate pose. Maybe he felt remorseful for what he had done. Or maybe he's so psychotic that he doesn't fully appreciate that she's dead.'

Fabel smiled. 'You could be right. Anyway, I'm sorry, you were saying . . . ?'

Brauner returned to the file. 'Not much more to say. The girl's clothes were not of good quality and quite old. What's more, they weren't fresh . . . I'd say she'd been wearing the same clothes, and underclothes, for at least three or four days prior to death.'

'Was she raped?'

'Well, you know Möller would have my guts for prejudging his findings – and, to be fair, only he can give you a definitive answer on that – but no ... I saw no evidence of any sexual trauma on the body. In fact I didn't see any marks of violence other than the ligature marks around the neck. And there were no traces on her clothes.'

'Thanks, Holger,' Fabel said. 'I take it that you're going to look into the type of paper and ink used on the note?'

'Yes. I've already scanned it for a watermark. Nothing. I'll be able to give you a weight and type match, et cetera, but it will take time to pin it down to a particular make.' Brauner sucked the air in through his teeth. 'I have a funny feeling that we're looking at a mass-market generic paper, which means it will be difficult to trace to a specific outlet.'

'It also means that our friend has thought this through and is covering his tracks,' Fabel sighed. Then he slapped Brauner on the shoulder. 'See what you can do, Holger. While you deal with the medium, I'll deal with the message . . . Can you arrange for some photocopies to be sent up to the Mordkommission? Ideally blown up to three times the original size?'

'Not a problem, Jan.'

'And I'll make sure you get a copy of the autopsy

report Möller sends me.' Fabel knew that Möller's abrasive manner rankled with Brauner even more than it did with him. 'Just in case there's anything in it that leaps out at you as significant . . .'

When Fabel got back to the Mordkommission, he stopped off at Anna Wolff's desk. He handed her the name and address listed on the note that the killer had pressed into the girl's hand. Anna's smile faded as she read the note.

'This the dead girl?'

'That's what I need you to find out,' said Fabel grimly. 'The killer hid a note in the victim's hand. It claimed this is the girl's identity.'

'I'll get on to it right away, *Chef*.'

Fabel closed the door behind him when he entered his office. He sat down behind his desk and looked out through the glazed partition that separated him from the open-plan main Mordkommission office. He had never fully settled into the new Polizeipräsidium; he had much preferred the old headquarters, down on Beim Strohhause near the Berliner Tor. But much was changing with the Polizei Hamburg. And most of the change did not appeal to Fabel much. They were now in a brand new building that radiated out as a five-storey-high star shape around a central atrium. It hadn't all gone as smoothly as planned. Originally the atrium had been home to a pond feature, which had become home to clouds of mosquitoes. When the Präsidium had, in turn, become infested with spiders

23

prospering on the pond's bounty, it was decided to fill the water feature with gravel. There were other changes too: the uniforms of the Hamburg police's SchuPo branch were being changed away from the mustard and green that was the standard across all of Germany's police forces to blue and white. But the change that Fabel had most difficulty with was the militarisation of parts of the Hamburg police: the MEKs, the Mobile Einsatz Kommando surveillance and special-weapons response units, were a necessary evil, so Fabel's superiors assured him. Fabel himself had called on MEK units for back-up, particularly after his experience of losing one of his own team, but he had grave reservations about the attitudes of some MEK officers.

Fabel watched his team through the partition. This was the machine that would be brought to bear on hunting down Paula's killer. These were the people who would be sent off in different directions, to perform their separate allocated tasks, until they were all brought together in the final moment of resolution. It fell to Fabel to maintain the overview, to see beyond the detail. It was his judgement, his arrangement of the disparate investigative elements, that would determine whether they found Paula's killer or not. It was a responsibility that he tried not to dwell on, because when he did he found it almost unbearable. It was at such times that he questioned the choices he had made. Would it have been so bad to settle for a life as an academic in some provincial university?

Or as a teacher of English or history in a Frisian school? Maybe if he had, his marriage to Renate would have survived. Maybe he would have slept through each night without dreams of the dead.

Anna Wolff knocked at the door and entered. Her pretty face with its dark eyes and too-red lips was clouded with a gloomy expression. She nodded gravely in response to Fabel's unspoken question.

'Yep. Paula Ehlers went missing on her way home from school. I searched the database and then spoke to the Norderstedt Polizeidirektion. Her age fits as well. But there is something that really doesn't fit.'

'What?'

'Like I say, her age would fit with the dead girl . . . now. Paula Ehlers went missing three years ago, when she was thirteen.'

CHAPTER 4

7.50 p.m., Wednesday, 17 March:
Norderstedt, north of Hamburg

It normally only took about half an hour to drive from the Präsidium to Norderstedt, but Fabel and Anna Wolff stopped on the way to get something to eat. The Rasthof café was all but empty, apart from a couple of drivers who, Fabel assumed, belonged to the lorry and large panel van parked outside. The truckers sat together at the same table, silently and gloomily eating their way through a mountain of food. Fabel idly observed the two drivers, both of whom had the sag-belly builds of lethargic middle age; but, as he passed them, Fabel noticed that one of the drivers could only have been in his late twenties or early thirties. There was something about such a waste of youth that depressed Fabel. He thought of what lay ahead of him and Anna: of a life and youth not wasted but stolen, and a family left broken and lacking wholeness. Of all of the things he had to deal with as a murder detective, the thing that got to him most was the homes of the missing.

Particularly where the missing person was a child. Such households always had a sense of the incomplete; of the unresolved. More often than not, there was simply the overwhelming sense of waiting: waiting for the husband, the wife, the son or the daughter to come home. Or for someone to end the waiting by telling them that the missing was now the dead. Someone like Fabel.

Fabel and Anna Wolff took a table at the end of the café furthest from the truckers, where their conversation wouldn't be overheard. Anna ordered a Bratwurst hot dog and coffee. Fabel took an open sandwich and some coffee. When they were seated, Anna laid the file she had brought in from the car on to the table, turning it around so that it was the right way up for Fabel to read.

'Paula Ehlers. She was thirteen when she disappeared – in fact she went missing the day after her thirteenth birthday – which would make her sixteen now. Like the note said, she lived in Buschberger Weg, in the Harksheide district of Norderstedt. She lived about only ten minutes' walk from her school, and according to the report from the Norderstedt KriPo, she disappeared at some point during that ten-minute walk.'

Fabel flipped open the file. The face that smiled out at him from the photograph was that of a freckled, smiling girl. A child. Fabel frowned. He thought back to the body on the beach; to the face that had stared blankly at him from the cold sand. He compared the pre- and post-puberty

Paulas. There was a common architecture to the faces, but the eyes seemed different. Was it just the difference between the androgyny of childhood and the near-womanhood of a sixteen-year-old? Were they the changes wrought in a face by three years of God knows what kind of hardship? The eyes. He had stared so long into the dead girl's eyes as she had lain, dead but as if alive, on the beach at Blankenese. It was the eyes that bothered Fabel.

Anna took a mouthful of Bratwurst before continuing. When she spoke she tapped the file with the finger of one hand while holding the other hand before her mouth as if to shield the file from crumbs.

'The Norderstedt police did all the right things. They even carried out a re-enactment of her walk home. When they still didn't find her after a month they gave the case dual status as a missing person and possible murder.'

Fabel flipped through the rest of the file. Brauner had sent up half a dozen enlarged photocopies of the note. One was now pasted to the incident board in the main Mordkommission office; another lay in the file before Fabel.

'After a year, they relaunched the case,' Anna continued. 'They stopped and questioned everyone walking or driving through the area on the anniversary of Paula's disappearance. Again, despite their best efforts, nothing. It was a Kriminalkommissar Klatt, from the Norderstedt KriPo who ran the investigation. I phoned him this afternoon . . . he's basically put himself at our disposal, even given us his home address if we want to call in after we've spoken to the Ehlers. According to Klatt, there were no real leads at all, although Klatt said he did look very closely at one of Paula's teachers . . .' Anna turned the file partly back towards her and flicked through the pages of the report that the Norderstedt police had faxed to the Präsidium. 'Yes . . . a Herr Fendrich. Klatt has admitted he had nothing on Fendrich, other than an uneasy gut feeling he had about the relationship between Fendrich and Paula.' Fabel stared at the freckled face in the photograph. 'But she was only thirteen . . .'

Anna made a 'you should know better' face. Fabel sighed: it was a naive, even stupid comment to have made. After more than a decade leading a murder squad, there was little about what people were capable of that should surprise him, least of all the possibility of a paedophile teacher becoming fixated on one of his charges.

'But Klatt couldn't find anything concrete on which to base his suspicions?' asked Fabel. Anna had taken another mouthful and shook her head.

'He questioned him more than once.' Anna spoke through her food, again shielding her lips with her fingertips. 'But Fendrich started to make noises about harassment. Klatt had to back right off. To be fair to Fendrich, in the absence of any other investigative route to follow, I get the impression there was a fair amount of clutching at straws.'

Fabel looked out of the window at the double image of the illuminated car park and his own darkly reflected face. A Mercedes pulled up and a couple in their thirties got out. The man opened the back door and a girl of about ten stepped out and automatically took her father's hand. It was an instinctive and habitual gesture: the innate expectation that children have to be protected. Fabel turned back to Anna.

'I'm not convinced it's the same girl.'

'What?'

'I'm not saying it isn't. It's just that I'm not sure. There are differences. Especially the eyes.'

Anna leaned back in her seat and pursed her lips. 'Then it's one hell of a coincidence, *Chef*. If it's not Paula Ehlers then it's someone who looks hell of a lot like her. And someone who had her name and address in her hand. Like I say, a hell of a coincidence . . . and if there's one thing I've learned not to believe in, it's a coincidence.'

'I know. Like I said, it's just that something doesn't gel.'

The B433 runs straight through Norderstedt on its way north into Schleswig-Holstein and into Denmark. Harksheide lies to the north of the town centre and Buschberger Weg is to the right of the B433. As they approached the turn-off for Buschberger Weg, Fabel noted that the school

Paula attended lay further up the main road, ahead and to the left. Paula would have crossed this busy thoroughfare to get home, and might have walked along its length for a while. This was where she had been taken. On one side or the other: more than likely on the Hamburg-bound carriageway.

It was as Fabel had expected. There was a dark electricity in the Ehlerses' household: something between anticipation and dread. The house itself was the most ordinary of dwellings: a single-storey bungalow with a steep red-tiled roof: the type of home you see from the Netherlands to the Baltic coast, from Hamburg to the northern tip of Danish Jutland. An immaculate, well-stocked but unimaginative garden framed the house.

Frau Ehlers was in her early forties. Her hair had clearly been as blonde as her daughter's, but the decades had muted its lustre by a tone. She had the pale Nordic look of a Schleswig-Holsteiner, the people of Germany's slender northern neck: light blue eyes and skin that had been prematurely aged by the sun. Her husband was an earnest-looking man whom Fabel placed at around fifty. He was tall and a touch too lean: *schlaksig*, as they say in Northern Germany. He too was fair, but a further tone duller than his wife's colouring. His eyes were a darker blue and shadowed against the pale skin. In the moment of introduction, Fabel processed the images before him with the images in his memory: the Ehlers, the girl in the file photograph, the girl in the sand. Again something snagged in his brain: some barely perceptible inconsistency.

'Have you found our little girl?' Frau Ehlers searched Fabel's face with an urgency and intensity he found almost unbearable.

'I don't know, Frau Ehlers. It's possible. But we need you or Herr Ehlers to make a positive identification of the body.'

'So there's a chance it isn't Paula?' There was a hint of defiance in Herr Ehlers's tone. Fabel caught Anna's glance out of the corner of his eye.

'I suppose so, Herr Ehlers, but there's every indication that it may well be Paula. The victim is taller than Paula was when she went missing, but her height is well within the growth you would expect over the last three years. And there was some evidence that seemed to link her with this address.' Fabel did not want to tell them that the killer had tagged his victim.

'How did she die?' asked Frau Ehlers.

'I don't think we should go into that until we make sure it really is Paula,' said Fabel. The desperation in Frau Ehlers's expression seemed to intensify. Her lower lip trembled. Fabel relented. 'The victim we found was strangled.'

Frau Ehlers's body was racked with silent sobs. Anna stepped forward and put her arm around her shoulder, but Frau Ehlers drew back. There was an awkward silence. Fabel found himself sweeping his gaze around the room. There was a large photograph framed on the wall. It had obviously been taken with an ordinary camera and had been enlarged more than it should have been. The texture was grainy and the girl at the centre of the picture gazed out with flash-reddened pupils. It was Paula Ehlers; she was smiling up at the camera from behind a large birthday cake that was emblazoned with the number thirteen. Fabel felt a chill as he realised that she looked out at him from the day before she was snatched from her family.

'When can we see her?' asked Herr Ehlers.

'We've arranged for the local police to take you down tonight, if that's okay.' It was Anna who answered. 'We will meet you there. A car will pick you up about 9.30 p.m. I know it's late . . .'

Herr Ehlers cut her off. 'That's all right. We'll be waiting.'

On the way back to the car, Fabel could sense a tension in Anna's movements. And she was silent.

'You okay?' he asked.

'Not really,' She looked back at the sad little house with its tended garden and its red roof. 'That was tough. I don't know how they have stood it so long. All that waiting. All that hope. They have depended on us to find their little girl and, when we do, we can't even bring her back alive.'

Fabel bleeped off the alarm and locks and waited until they were both in the car before answering. 'I'm afraid that's the way it works out. Happy endings belong in movies, not in real life.'

'But it was as if they hated us.'

'They do,' said Fabel resignedly. 'And who can blame them? Like you say, we were supposed to bring her back alive, not tell them we found her body abandoned somewhere. They were depending on us to deliver the happy ending.' Fabel started the engine. 'Anyway, let's stay focused on the case. It's time we called in on Kriminalkommissar Klatt.'

Norderstedt has an officially split personality. It is part of Greater Hamburg, its phone numbers share the Hamburg 040 prefix, and when Fabel and Anna drove up through Fuhlsbüttel and Langenhorn into Norderstedt there had been a sense of an unbroken metropolitan continuum. Yet the Polizei Hamburg has no jurisdiction here: it is the Landespolizei of Schleswig-Holstein that operate in Norderstedt. However, because of their close proximity and the continual overlapping of cases, the Norderstedt police had more contact with the Polizei Hamburg than with their own force in the gentle landscapes and small towns of Schleswig-Holstein. Anna had phoned ahead to arrange for Kommissar Klatt to meet with them at the Polizeirevier Norderstedt-Mitte in the town's Rathausallee.

When they arrived at the Polizeirevier, they were not conducted, as they expected, to the main Kriminalpolizei offices; instead a young female uniformed officer led them to a stark, windowless interview room. The female SchuPo asked them if they would like some coffee, to which they both said yes. Anna glanced gloomily around the room and, after the SchuPo had left, she and Fabel exchanged meaningful glances.

'Now I know what it must be like to be a suspect,' said Anna.

Fabel gave an ironic smile. 'Quite. Do you think we're being told something?'

Anna didn't get a chance to answer: the interview-room door swung open and a man in his early thirties entered. He was shortish but powerfully built and had a big, friendly but forgettable face fringed with dark hair and a stubbly beard. He smiled broadly at both Hamburg officers and introduced himself as Kriminalkommissar Klatt. He placed the file he had brought under his arm on the interview-room table and indicated that Anna and Fabel should be seated.

'I'm sorry we've been stuck in here,' said Klatt. 'I'm afraid this isn't my usual location. I'm actually stationed at the Europaallee Revier, but I thought it would be easier for you to find your way here. They are doing me a favour . . . but I'm afraid our accommodation is a little more modest than I expected.' He sat down. The geniality on his face was washed away by a more sombre expression. 'I believe you've found Paula . . .'

'The truth is, Kommissar Klatt, we won't know for sure until the parents make a positive ID of the body . . . but yes, it looks like it.'

'It was always just a matter of time.' There was a resigned sadness on Klatt's broad face. 'But you always hope that this is the one you'll bring back alive.'

Fabel nodded. Klatt's sentiments echoed his own. The only difference was that Klatt had a chance: on the whole, he dealt with the living, while Fabel's job as a murder detective meant that someone had to die for him to become involved. For a fleeting moment Fabel wondered what it would be like to transfer back to a general KriPo office. The female officer returned with the coffee.

'Did you think there was a chance you'd find her alive?' asked Anna.

Klatt thought for a moment. 'No, I suppose not. You know the statistics. If we don't find them within the first twenty-four hours, then the chances are that they're never coming back. It's just that Paula was my first missing kid. I got involved. Maybe too involved. It was tough to see a family in so much pain.'

'She was an only child?' Anna asked.

'No, there's a brother . . . Edmund. An older brother.'

'We didn't see him at the Ehlerses' home,' said Fabel.

'No. He's about three years older. He's nineteen or twenty now. He's doing his national service in the Bundeswehr.'

'I take it you checked him out thoroughly.' Fabel made it a statement, not a question. Whenever there's a murder, the first rank of potential suspects is the victim's immediate family. Fabel was being careful not to suggest that Klatt didn't know his job. If Klatt was annoyed, he showed no indication of it.

'Of course. We got a full account of his movements that day. All corroborated. And we went over them again and again. What's more, he was truly worried sick about his sister. You just can't act as well as that.'

Yes, you can, thought Fabel. He had seen countless genuinely distressed lovers, friends or relatives of a victim who had turned out to be their killer. But he had no doubt that Klatt had examined Paula Ehlers's family thoroughly.

'But you did suspect Paula's teacher . . .' Anna checked through her own copy of the file.

'Fendrich. He was Paula's German teacher. I wouldn't go so far as to say he was a suspect . . . it's just that there was something about him that didn't gel. But again he was pretty much in the clear as far as an alibi is concerned.'

Klatt went through the report with Fabel and Anna. It was clear that much of this investigation had etched itself into Klatt's brain. Fabel knew what it was like to have a case like that: nights where he had desperately sought sleep yet was doomed to gaze up at the dark ceiling, unanswered questions swirling with images of the dead, the distraught and the suspected in the vortex of a restless, exhausted mind. When Klatt was finished and Fabel and Anna could think of no more questions, they rose and thanked him for his time.

'I'll see you later this evening,' said Klatt. 'I take it you'll be there when the Ehlerses identify the body?'

Anna and Fabel exchanged glances. 'Yes,' said Fabel, 'we'll be there. You too?'

Klatt smiled sadly. 'Yes, if you don't mind. I'll bring the parents down to Hamburg. If this is the conclusion of the Paula Ehlers case, then I'd like to be there. I'd like to say goodbye.'

'Of course,' said Fabel. But, he thought, this isn't the conclusion of the Paula Ehlers case: this is just the beginning.

CHAPTER 5

10.10 p.m., Wednesday, 17 March:
Institut für Rechtsmedizin, University Hospital
Eppendorf, Hamburg

The Universitätsklinikum Hamburg-Eppendorf, housing the main medical functions and facilities of Hamburg university, stretches back from Martinistrasse like a small town. The sprawl mixes high-rise and low-rise buildings of all ages and is woven through with a web of roadways. The largest of the meagre parking spaces lies right at the heart of the complex, but, because of the lateness of the hour, Fabel knew that he would be able to park close to the Institut für Rechtsmedizin – the Institute of Legal Medicine. Fabel knew the Institut well. It had become the focus for every form of science that had a legal application: serology and DNA testing, forensic medicine and a dedicated forensic-psychiatric experts service. It was not just through work that Fabel had contact with the Institut: for the last year he had been in a relationship with a criminal psychologist, Susanne Eckhardt. Susanne, who was officially based at the thirteen-storey-high Psychiatry and Psychotherapy Clinic, spent most of her time working out of the nearby Institut.

Fabel did not take the turn into the main entrance; instead he continued along Martinistrasse and turned up Lokstedter Steindamm and on to Butenfeld. As he had suspected, there were a number of free spaces in the car park outside the Institut's wide, two-storey pavilion. The Institut had a global reputation and the building had been radically extended recently to accommodate courses run for budding forensic pathologists and chemists from around the world. Three thousand bodies were forensically examined and one thousand autopsies were carried out here each year. It was here that the dead girl's body lay, in the dark, in a chilled steel cabinet, waiting to be identified.

Fabel noticed that one of the other parked cars was Susanne's Porsche: for once he and Susanne seemed to be working roughly the same hours which, hopefully, would mean that they might manage to see a little more of each other.

Fabel and Anna were admitted to the Institut by an older security officer whom Fabel recognised as a former Obermeister in the uniformed division. When they entered the main reception, they found a uniformed Hamburg police officer waiting with Klatt and Herr and Frau Ehlers. Fabel greeted them and asked Klatt if they'd been waiting long, to which he replied that they'd only arrived ten minutes before Fabel. An orderly arrived and led the small party to the identification room. The mortuary trolley on which the body lay had been dressed in a deep blue covering and a clean white sheet lay over the face. Fabel let Klatt lead the Ehlerses across to the body. Anna stepped forward and placed an arm around Frau Ehlers and spoke soothingly to her before signalling to the orderly who drew back the sheet. Frau Ehlers gave a sharp gasp and swayed a little in Anna's grasp. Fabel saw Herr Ehlers tauten, as if a small electric current had caused all of his muscles to lock simultaneously.

It was the smallest of silences. Not even a second. But in that tiny, crystal quiet Fabel knew that the girl on the trolley was not Paula Ehlers. And when Frau Ehlers shattered the silence with a long, low, pain-filled cry, it was not a cry of mourning or loss, but of a desperation renewed.

Afterwards, they all sat in the reception area, drinking coffee from a dispensing machine. Frau Ehlers sat with her gaze not focused on anyone or anything in the here and now, but as if locked on to some far-distant moment in time. In total contrast, there was a wild, confused and angry expression on her husband's face.

'Why, Herr Fabel?' Ehlers's eyes searched Fabel's. 'Why do this to us? She looked so like Paula . . . so like her. Why would someone be so cruel?'

'You're positive it isn't your daughter?'

'It's been a long time. And like I say, she's so much like Paula, but . . .'

'That girl is not my daughter.' Frau Ehlers cut across her husband's answer. Her eyes were still glazed and dreamy, but her voice was edged with a hard, uncompromising determination. It was more than an opinion: it was an incontrovertible, indisputable certainty. Fabel felt the steel of her will penetrate him and leave something of itself embedded. He felt a fury and hatred rise in him like a bitter bile. Someone had not only taken a young life, he had twisted a long-buried knife viciously in the heart of another family. And that was just the beginning: there was now every reason to suppose that the killer of the girl on the beach had, indeed, abducted and murdered Paula Ehlers three years before. Why else would he – or she – have involved the Ehlers family in his sick game? One body, two murder cases. He turned back to the refreshed, raw hurt of Paula Ehlers's parents: a family returned to the renewed torture of uncertainty and unreasonable, unfounded hope.

'We are obviously dealing with a very disturbed and evil personality here.' Fabel's voice held a paler reflection of Ehlers's frustration and fury. 'Whoever killed this girl wanted us to be sitting here as we are now, angry and hurting and asking why. This is as much a scene of his crime as the beach where he left the girl's body.'

Herr Ehlers simply stared uncomprehendingly at Fabel, as if he had just addressed him in Japanese. His wife fixed Fabel with a searchlight gaze. 'I want you to get him.' She switched the beam of her gaze from Fabel to Klatt and back again, as if distributing the burden of her words equally on both men. 'What I really want is for you to find him and kill him. I know I can't ask that of you . . . but I can demand that you catch him and punish him. I can expect at least that.'

'I promise you that I will do everything I can to find this monster,' said Fabel, and he meant it.

Fabel and Anna accompanied Klatt and the Ehlers out into the car park. The Ehlers climbed into the back of Klatt's Audi. Klatt turned to Fabel; the sadness that Fabel had noticed in Klatt's expression had returned, but this time it was keener, honed to a sharper edge by anger.

'This dead girl is your case, Herr Kriminal-hauptkommissar. But there is clearly some kind of correlation between her death and the Paula Ehlers case. I would be obliged if you could keep me up to date on all developments that may have a bearing on the Ehlers case.' There was an almost defiant tone in Klatt's voice: he had a stake in this and he clearly wasn't going to let Fabel forget it. Fabel looked at the younger man: a junior officer in another police service; not too tall and a little too overweight. Yet there was a quiet determination and a sharp intelligence in the unassuming, forgettable face. Standing there in the car park of the Institut für Rechtsmedizin, Fabel made a decision.

'Kommissar Klatt, it could well be that the killer

of this girl simply picked Paula Ehlers's identity because he knew about the case. Maybe he read about it at the time. The only connection between the cases may well be that we have a psychotic who reads the newspapers.'

Klatt seemed to weigh up Fabel's words. 'I doubt it. But what about the amazing similarity between the two girls? At the very least he must have made a very detailed study of the Ehlers case. But I'm pretty convinced that whoever picked this girl as a victim and branded her with Paula's identity must have seen Paula in life. I don't have your experience or specific expertise in murder inquiries, Herr Hauptkommissar, but I do know the Ehlers case. I've lived with it for three years. I just know the connection is more than a selection of a dead girl's identity.'

'So you expect us to give you every detail of our inquiry?' asked Fabel.

'No . . . just anything that you may feel is germane to the Ehlers case.' Klatt maintained a calm and relaxed manner.

Fabel allowed himself a small smile. Klatt wasn't easily rattled, nor was he intimidated by another officer's seniority. 'As a matter of fact, Kommissar Klatt, I think you're right. My gut instinct is that you and I are looking for the same person. That's why I'd like you to consider a temporary secondment to my team for the duration of this investigation.'

Klatt's broad face registered surprise for a

moment, then broke into a grin. 'I don't know what to say, Herr Fabel. I mean, I'd be delighted . . . but I'm not sure how it would work . . .'

'I'll sort out the paperwork. I'd like you to continue your inquiries into the Ehlers case and to act as a liaison between us and the Norderstedt force. But I want you to be directly involved in this case too. There may be something that comes up in relation to the girl we found on the beach that we would miss but which may have a resonance with you because of your detailed knowledge of the Ehlers case. That means I'd prefer it if you moved into the Hamburg Mordkommission for the time being. I'll arrange a desk for you. But I have to stress that this is an ad-hoc arrangement, exclusively for the duration of the inquiry.'

'Of course, Herr Kriminalhauptkommissar. I'll have to speak to my boss, Hauptkommissar Pohlmann, about getting a couple of current cases reassigned . . .'

'I'll speak to your boss to clear the way for you and take any flak.'

'There won't be any,' said Klatt. 'Herr Pohlmann will be delighted that I'm being given the opportunity to see this case all the way through.'

The two men shook hands. Klatt indicated the couple sitting silently in his Audi with a nod of his head. 'May I inform Herr and Frau Ehlers that we'll be working together? I think that they'll find it . . .' He struggled for the right word. '. . . Reassuring.'

*   *   *

Fabel and Anna did not speak until Klatt's Audi had turned out on to Butenfeld.

'So we've got a new member of the team . . .' said Anna in a flat tone positioned somewhere between a question and a statement.

'Just for the duration of this inquiry, Anna. He's not a replacement for Paul.' Paul Lindemann, the member of Fabel's team who had been shot and killed the previous year, had been Anna's partner. The wound that still lay deep and sore within Fabel's team was at its rawest with Anna.

'I know that.' Anna bristled slightly. 'You rate him?'

'Yep. I do,' said Fabel. 'I think he has all the right instincts about this case and he does have a head start on us. I think he'll be useful. But, for the moment, that's as far as it goes.' He handed Anna the keys to his BMW. 'Would you mind waiting in the car for me? I need to go back into the Institut for a moment.'

Anna gave a knowing smile. 'Okay, *Chef*.'

Fabel found Susanne at her desk in her office, gazing bleakly at a report on the screen of her computer. Her raven-black hair was tied back from her face and she was wearing her glasses, behind which her eyes were shadowed with tiredness. On seeing Fabel her smile was weary but warm. She stood up, crossed her office and kissed him on the lips.

'You look as tired as I feel,' she said, in her

Munich accent. 'I'm just about to wrap up here. What about you? You coming over later?'

Fabel made an apologetic face. 'I'll try. It might be late. Don't wait up for me.' He walked over and slumped into the chair opposite Susanne's. She took the hint and sat back down at her desk again.

'Okay . . . let's have it.'

Fabel ran through the events of the day. He spoke of a girl long lost, a girl found, a family reunited in death only to be torn apart again. When he finished, Susanne sat in silence for a moment.

'So you want to know if I think the person who killed the girl you found this morning killed this other girl who went missing three years ago?'

'Just an opinion. I won't hold you to it.'

Susanne let out a long slow breath. 'It's certainly possible. If the intervening period was not so long, I would say it was probable. But three years leaves us with a long gap. As you know, the first escalation in offender behaviour is the biggest step . . . the leap from fantasy to commission.'

'Committing their first murder.'

'Exactly. Then it just gets easier. And the offending escalates quickly. But, there again, that's not always the case. Sometimes the first murder is committed in childhood or very early adulthood and there can be decades before a second murder is committed. Three years is an odd gap.' Susanne frowned. 'That would tend to make me believe

47

that we are dealing with separate killers, but the close resemblance of the two girls and the identity of the first being given by the killer to the second really bothers me.'

'Okay,' said Fabel, 'let's assume for the moment that we are dealing with the same killer. What does the three-year gap tell us?'

'If it is the same perpetrator, then I think, given the premeditated cruelty of confusing the identities of the two girls, that it is highly unlikely that the delay has been self-imposed. I don't believe that this hiatus is the result of guilt or any inner turmoil or repulsion at what he or she has done. I think it's more likely to be an external pressure . . . some restraint or obstacle that has put a check on the escalation of his psychosis.'

'Such as?'

'Well . . . it could be a physical, geographical or personal restraint. By physical, I mean he may have been confined – in prison or by illness in a hospital. The geographical obstacle may be that he has been working and living outside the area for the last three years and has only recently returned. If that were to be the case, and if the opportunity were to have presented itself, I would have expected the subject to have committed similar offences elsewhere. And what I meant by personal restraint is that there may have been a personality in the subject's background who has been able to prevent recommission of homicidal behaviour. Someone dominant who has been able to contain the subject's homicidal psychosis . . . perhaps without even knowing about the first killing.'

'And now that person is out of the picture?'

'Perhaps. It could be a domineering parent or spouse who has died . . . or perhaps a marriage that has failed. Or it could simply be that our killer's psychosis has developed to such an extent as to be beyond any external control. If that is the case, then God help the person who was holding him in check.' Susanne slipped off her glasses. Her dark eyes were heavy-lidded and her voice drawled with fatigue, her southern accent more pronounced, swallowing the ends of her words. 'There is one other explanation, of course . . .'

Fabel was there before her. 'And that explanation is that our killer has not been inactive for the last three years . . . that we just haven't found his victims or made a connection between them.'

CHAPTER 6

8.30 a.m., Thursday, 18 March:
Polizeipräsidium, Hamburg

F abel had woken early but had lain awake, staring at the ceiling while the pallid light of morning had slowly and reluctantly bloomed across it. Susanne had been asleep when he had come back from the Präsidium. Their relationship had reached that awkward stage where they had keys for each other's apartments, and Fabel had therefore been able to let himself into Susanne's Övelgönne flat and slip silently into her bed while she slept. The exchange of keys had been a symbol of the exclusivity of their relationship and the permissiveness they allowed each other in accessing the most personal of territory – but they had not yet made the decision to live together. In fact, they had not even discussed the option. They were both intensely private individuals who had, for different reasons, dug invisible moats around themselves and their lives. Neither was yet ready fully to lower the drawbridge.

When Susanne awoke the following morning, she

smiled sleepily and welcomingly at Fabel and they made love. For Fabel and Susanne, there was a golden time in the mornings when they did not discuss work but chatted and joked and shared breakfast as if they each worked in some innocuous, undemanding career that made no intrusion into their personal lives. They had not planned it. They had not made a rule about where and when they should talk about their work in parallel fields. But, somehow, they had fallen into the habit of greeting and beginning each new day afresh. Then they would each descend, down their separate but parallel paths, into the world of derangement, violence and death that was the stuff of their professional everyday.

Fabel had left the apartment shortly before Susanne. He had arrived at the Präsidium just after eight and reviewed the case files and his notes from the previous day. For half an hour he added detail to the sketch he already had in his mind. Fabel tried to objectivise his view, but no matter how hard he tried, the stunned and weary face of Frau Ehlers crept its way back to the front of his mind. And as it did so, Fabel's anger grew anew: the embers of the fury of the previous evening rekindled and burned even more intensely in the cold, bright air of a new day. What kind of beast derived gratification from inflicting such psychological torture on a family? Especially a family whose daughter, Fabel believed, he had already murdered. And Fabel knew he must prolong their agony: he could not rely on the failed identification of a victim who had been missing for three years. There was still a remote chance that time, and whatever traumas and abuses she had suffered in the intervening period, had wrought subtle changes to her appearance.

Fabel waited until nine a.m. before he picked up his phone and pressed the dial button pre-set to the Institut für Rechtsmedizin. He asked to be put through to Herr Doktor Möller. Möller was the forensic pathologist with whom Fabel had dealt on the majority of his cases. Möller's arrogant, abrasive manner had earned him the dislike of almost every murder detective in Hamburg, but Fabel had a great deal of respect for his expertise.

'Möller . . .' The voice on the other end of the phone sounded distracted, as if answering the phone was an unwelcome interruption to some infinitely more important task.

'Good morning, Herr Doktor Möller. Kriminalhauptkommissar Fabel here.'

'What is it, Fabel?'

'You're about to do an autopsy on the girl we found on Blankenese beach. There's some confusion over her identity.' Fabel went on to explain the background, including the scene at what should have been a routine identification at the Institut the night before. 'I am concerned that there is still a chance that this dead girl *is* Paula Ehlers, albeit a very remote chance. I don't want to distress the family any further, but I need to establish the dead girl's identity.'

Möller was silent for a moment. When he spoke

his voice lacked its usual imperiousness. 'As you know, I should be able to do that from dental records. But I'm afraid the quickest and surest way would be to have cheek swabs taken from the missing girl's mother. I'll get a DNA comparison rushed through the lab here at the Institut.'

Fabel thanked Möller and hung up. He made another call, to Holger Brauner, and, knowing that he could rely on Brauner's tact, asked him if he could take the cheek swabs from the mother himself.

By the time Fabel had hung up, he could see, through the glazed partition that separated his office from the main open-plan area of the Mordkommission, that Anna Wolff and Maria Klee were now both at their desks. He buzzed through to Anna and asked her to come into his office. When she came in he pushed the mortuary photograph of the dead girl across his desk to her.

'I want to know who she really is, Anna. I'd like to know by the end of the day. How have you been getting on so far?'

'I've got a check running on the BKA database of missing persons. The chances are that she'll be listed. I've put a filter on the search for females between ten and twenty-five and prioritised any cases within a two hundred kilometres' radius of Hamburg. There can't be that many.'

'This is your thing for today, Anna. Drop everything else and concentrate on establishing this girl's identity.'

Anna nodded. '*Chef* . . .' She paused. There was

an awkwardness in her stance, as if she was unsure of what she was going to say next.

'What's up, Anna?'

'That was tough. Last night, I mean. I couldn't get to sleep afterwards.'

Fabel gave a cheerless smile and indicated that Anna should sit down. 'You weren't the only one.' He paused. 'You want to be put on something different?'

'No.' Anna's response was emphatic. She sat down opposite Fabel. 'No . . . I want to stay on this case. I want to find out who this girl is and I want to help find the real Paula Ehlers. It's just that it was pretty hard to watch a family being torn into pieces for a second time. The other thing was – and I know this sounds crazy – but I could almost sense Paula's . . . well, not her presence, more her *lack* of presence in the home.'

Fabel remained silent. Anna was tracing out a thought and he wanted her to follow it through.

'When I was a kid, there was this girl in my school. Helga Kirsch. She was about a year younger than me and a mousy little thing. She had the kind of face you never notice but would recognise as someone you knew if seen out of context. You know, if you saw her in town at the weekend or something.'

Fabel nodded.

'Anyway,' continued Anna, 'one day we were all assembled in the school hall and we were told that Helga had gone missing . . . that she'd gone out on her bike and just disappeared. I remember that after that I started, well, noticing that she wasn't there. Someone I'd never even spoken to but had taken up some kind of space in my world. It took a week before they found her bike, and then her body.'

'I remember,' said Fabel. He had been a young Kommissar at the time and had been involved at the edges of the case. But he had remembered the name. Helga Kirsch, thirteen years old, raped and strangled in a small field of dense grass next to the cycle path. It had taken a year to track down her killer, only after another young life had been snuffed out by him.

'From the moment her disappearance was announced to the day her body was found there was this weird feeling in the school. Like someone had taken away a small part of the building that you couldn't identify but you knew wasn't there any more. After she was found there was this *grief*, I suppose. And guilt. I used to lie in bed at night and try to remember if I had ever spoken to Helga, or smiled, or had any kind of interaction with her. And of course I hadn't. But the grief and the guilt were a relief after that feeling of *absence*.' Anna turned and looked out through Fabel's window at the cloud-bruised sky. 'I remember talking to my grandmother about it. She talked about when she was a girl during the Hitler time, before she and her parents went into hiding. She said that that was what it was like for them then: that someone they knew would be taken in the night by the Nazis – sometimes a whole family – and there would be this inexplicable space in the world. There wasn't even the knowledge of death to fill it.'

'I can imagine,' said Fabel, even though he couldn't. Anna's Jewishness had never been a feature in his choosing her for the team, either positively or negatively. It simply hadn't registered on Fabel's radar. But every now and then, like now, he sat across a table from her and was aware that he was a German policeman and she was Jewish, and the weight of an unbearable history seemed to descend on him.

Anna turned back from the window. 'I'm sorry. I don't have a point, really, just that it got to me.' She stood up and held Fabel in her disconcertingly frank gaze. 'I'll get your ID for you, *Chef.*'

After Anna had gone, Fabel took out the sketch pad from his desk drawer, laid it on his desktop and flipped it open. He spent a moment looking down on the wide expanse of white paper it presented. Empty. Clean. Another symbol of a new case beginning. Fabel had used these sketch pads for more than a decade of murder investigations. It was on these thick, brilliant sheets, meant for a much more creative task, that Fabel would summarise incident boards, note down abbreviated names of people, places and events, and trace lines between them. These were his sketches: his outlines of a murder inquiry into which he would invest first light and shade, then detail. First, he plotted the locations: the beach at Blankenese and Paula's home in Norderstedt. Then he wrote down the names he had encountered in the last twenty-four hours. He listed the four members of the Ehlers family and in so doing gave form to the absence that Anna had described: three members of a family – father, mother and brother – accounted for; three people you could track down and find, to whom you could talk and of whom you could form a living image in your brain. Then there was the fourth member. The daughter. To Fabel she was still a concept, an insubstantial collection of other people's impressions and memories; an image caught on film blowing out the candles on a birthday cake.

If Paula was a concept without form, then there was also the girl they found on the beach: a form without a concept; a body without an identity. Fabel wrote down the words 'blue eyes' at the centre of the sheet. There was, of course, a case number he could have used, but in the absence of a name 'blue eyes' was the closest he could get. It sounded more like a person and less like the dead thing that a case number made it. He drew a line from 'blue eyes' to Paula, making a break midway. In this space he drew a double question mark. Fabel was convinced that in this gap lay the killer of the girl on the beach and the abductor and probable murderer of Paula Ehlers. It could, of course, have been two people. But not two or more people acting independently of each other. Whether it was an individual, a pair or a larger team, whoever killed 'blue eyes' had also taken Paula Ehlers.

It was then that the phone rang.

CHAPTER 7

6.30 p.m., Thursday, 18 March:
Norddeich, East Frisia

It was a place he had called home. A place that he had always considered to have defined him. But now, standing here in a landscape that was all horizon, he knew that he belonged elsewhere. Hamburg was the place that truly defined who Jan Fabel was. Who he was now. Who he had become. Fabel's dislocation from this landscape had come in two stages: the first had been when he had moved out of the family home and travelled inland, to Oldenburg, where he had studied English and History at the newly founded Carl von Ossietzky Universität. Then, after graduating, he had moved on to the Universität Hamburg to study European History. And to live a new life.

Fabel parked his BMW at the back of the house. He got out and swung open the rear door and reached in for his hastily packed holdall. As he straightened up he paused for a moment, standing silent, absorbing all the shapes and sounds that had been his constants as a child: the continuous slow-rushing pulse of the sea hidden by the fringe of trees behind the house and the dyke and dunes beyond; the simple, earnest geometry of his parent's house, squat and resolute under its vast red-tiled roof; the pale green grasses that rippled like water in the fresh Frisian breeze; and the massive sky that fell hard on to the flat-ironed landscape. The sharp panic he had felt when he had received the call in the Präsidium had soothed to a low but constant ache during the three-and-a-half hour drive along the A28, and had been assuaged even further by seeing his mother sitting up in the hospital bed in Norden, telling Fabel to stop fussing and to make sure that his brother Lex didn't get all worked up about it either.

But now, amongst the familiarities of his childhood, the keenness of that first panic was renewed. He fumbled for the spare key in the pocket of the coat he had slung across the holdall and unlocked the heavy wooden kitchen door. The bottom of the door still showed, under its years of varnish, the dark scuff marks where Fabel and his brother, laden with schoolbooks, used to push at it with their feet. Even now, with a leather holdall and expensive Jaeger coat rather than a schoolbag on his arm, he felt the instinct to push the door with his foot as he turned the handle.

Fabel stepped into the kitchen. The house was empty, and silent. He put his bag and coat on the table and stood for a moment, taking in all that had not changed in the kitchen: the floral dishcloths draped over the chrome bar of the cooking range, the old pine table and chairs, the cork wallboard pinned with layers of notes and postcards, the heavy wooden dresser against the wall. Fabel found the child in himself resenting the few and small changes that his mother had made: a new kettle, a microwave oven, a new IKEA-style storage unit in the corner. It was almost as if, somewhere deep down, he felt that these contemporary incursions were tiny betrayals; that his childhood home should not have moved on with the years as he had.

He made himself some tea. It never occurred to him to have a coffee: he was back home in East Frisia where tea-drinking was a central part of life. His mother, although not a Frisian by birth, had enthusiastically embraced the local tea rituals, right down to the pre-noon three-cup tea break known as *'Elfürtje'* in Frysk, the impenetrable local dialect that lay somewhere between German, Dutch and Old English. He reached into cupboards automatically, every ingredient lying within expected reach: the tea, the traditional *'Kluntjes'* of crystallized sugar, the white and pale blue cups. He sat at the table and drank the tea, listening for the echoes of his father's and mother's voices buried deep in the quiet. The ringing of his cell phone split the silence. It was Susanne; her voice tight with worry.

'Jan . . . I just got your message. Are you okay? How's your mother?'

'She's fine. Well, she's had a small heart attack, but she's stable now.'

'You still at the hospital?'

'No, I'm at home . . . I mean at my mother's. I'm going to stay overnight and wait for my brother. He should arrive tomorrow.'

'Do you want me to come over there? I could leave now and be there in two or three hours . . .'

Fabel reassured her that there was no need, that he would be fine and that his mother was probably going to be home in a couple of days. 'It was just a warning shot across the bows,' he explained. But after he hung up, Fabel suddenly felt very alone. He had bought some pre-made open sandwiches but, finding he couldn't face eating, he put them in the fridge. He finished his tea and climbed up the stairs to his old bedroom under the vast expanse of the steep pitched roof. Fabel dumped his bag and coat in the corner and lay down on the single bed, not turning on the light. He lay in the dark trying to remember the voice of his long dead father shouting up the stairs for Fabel and his brother, Lex, to get out of their beds. He found that he could only recall his father's voice encapsulated in a single word. *Traanköppe*. That was what his father would call in the mornings: 'Sleepy Head' in Frysk. Fabel sighed in the dark. That's what comes with middle age: voices, once heard daily, fading from your memory until just one or two words remain.

Fabel picked up his cell phone from the bedside

cabinet and, still without turning on the light, searched through the phone's memory for Anna Wolff's home number. It rang several times and then her answering machine kicked in. He decided against leaving a message and, on a hunch, dialled Anna's direct number at the Präsidium. Anna's usually bright voice was deadened by tiredness.

'*Chef* – I didn't expect to hear from you . . . Your mother . . .'

'She's going to be okay. A minor heart attack, or so they say. I was in the hospital most of the afternoon. I'll be going back later. Did you get anywhere with the girl's identity?'

'Sorry, *Chef*, no, I didn't. I got the feedback from my BKA search. No missing persons that fit. I've widened the search: she's maybe from another part of Germany, or even somewhere else. You never know with so much traffic in women from eastern Europe.'

Fabel grunted. The trafficking of young women from Russia, the Balkans and elsewhere on the eastern fringers of the West's wealth had become a major problem in Hamburg. Attracted by promises of everything from modelling contracts to jobs as domestics, these women and girls became virtual slaves and were as often as not sold into prostitution. The birth of a new century had brought with it the rebirth of an old evil: slavery. 'Keep on it, Anna,' he told her, although he knew he didn't need to, for the same reason as he had known he would find her at the Präsidium. Once

Anna was focused on a task, she was relentless. 'Anything else?'

'Kommissar Klatt turned up this afternoon. I explained that your mother had been taken ill and you'd been called away. I gave him the grand tour of the Präsidium and introduced him to everyone. He seemed to be impressed. Other than that, nothing. Oh, wait, Holger Brauner called. He said he'd arranged the DNA tests and he'll have them with Möller at the Institut für Rechtsmedizin tomorrow morning.'

'Thanks, Anna. I'll call in tomorrow and let you know what my movements are likely to be.'

'Then I'd speak to Werner when you call. He's concerned about you. About your mother.'

'I'll do that.' Fabel hung up, breaking the connection with his new world, and sank back into the dark and silence of his old.

When Fabel arrived back at the Kreiskrankenhaus Norden, the doctor he had spoken to earlier had gone off duty, but the chief nurse was still there. She was a middle-aged woman with a round, frank and honest face. She smiled as Fabel approached and gave him an update without him having to ask.

'Your mother is doing just fine,' she said. 'She had a sleep after you left this afternoon and we ran another ECG on her. There really is nothing to worry about if she takes things easy.'

'Is she likely to have another attack?'

'Well, once you've had one, the chances of a second are always higher. But no, not necessarily. The important thing is for your mother to get up and about – and reasonably active – within the next few days. I would say she might be able to go home later tomorrow. Or perhaps the next day.'

'Thank you very much, nurse,' said Fabel and turned towards his mother's room.

'You don't remember me, do you, Jan?' said the nurse. He turned back to her. There was a tentativeness and shyness now in her smile. 'Hilke. Hilke Tietjen.'

It took a second or two for the name to register and tumble through the piles of others in Fabel's memory. 'My God. Hilke. It must be twenty years! How are you?'

'More like twenty-five. I'm fine, thanks. And you? I heard you were a Kommissar in the Hamburg police.'

'Erster Hauptkommissar now,' said Fabel, smiling. He searched the round, middle-aged face for vestiges of the younger, slimmer, prettier face he had always associated with the name Hilke Tietjen. They were there, in the structure of the face, like archaeological traces, overlaid by the years and gained weight. 'You still live in Norddeich?'

'No, I live here in Norden. My name's Hilka Freericks now. You remember Dirk Freericks, from school?'

'Of course,' Fabel lied. 'You have kids?'

'Four,' she laughed. 'All boys. You?'

64

'A daughter, Gabi.' Fabel was annoyed with himself when he realised he didn't want to admit he was now divorced. He smiled awkwardly.

'It was nice to see you again, Jan,' Hilke said. 'You must be keen to see your mother.'

'Nice to see you, too,' said Fabel. He watched her walk back down the hospital corridor. A small, broad-hipped, middle-aged woman called Hilke Freericks who, twenty-four years before, had been Hilke Tietjen and had been slim with a pretty, freckled face framed with lustrous long red-blonde hair, and who had shared urgent, breathless moments with Fabel amongst the sand dunes of the Norddeich coast. For Fabel, in those stark changes wrought by the passage of nearly a quarter of a century there lay an intolerably depressing and sad contrast. And with it came the same old urge to get as far away from Norddeich and Norden as possible.

Fabel's mother was sitting up on the chair next to her bed, watching 'Wetten, Dass . . . ?' on TV when he entered her room. The sound was turned down and Thomas Gottschalk grinned and chattered mutely. She smiled broadly and switched off the TV with the remote.

'Hello, son. You look tired.' Her voice carried an almost comical combination of her British accent and the heavy Frysk dialect with which she spoke German to her son. He bent to kiss her cheek. She patted his arm.

'I'm fine, *Mutti*. I'm not the one we should be worrying about. But it all seems to be good news . . . the nurse said your ECG was normal and you might get out later tomorrow.'

'You were talking to Hilke Freericks? You two were an item once, as I remember.'

Fabel sat down on the edge of the bed. 'That was a very, very long time ago, *Mutti*. I hardly recognised her.' As he spoke, the image of Hilke, her long red-gold hair shining and her skin translucent in the bright sun of a distant summer, collided with the image of the frumpy middle-aged woman with whom he'd chatted in the corridor. 'She's changed.' He paused. 'Have I changed so much, *Mutti*?'

Fabel's mother laughed. 'Don't ask me. You and Lex are still my babies. But I wouldn't worry about it. We all change.'

'It's just that when I come back here, I expect everything to be the same.'

'That's because here is a concept for you, a place in your past, more than a reality. You come back here to refocus the details of your memories. I used to do exactly the same whenever I went back to Scotland. But things change, places change. The world moves on.' She smiled, reached up and ran her hand gently through the hair of his temple, combing it with her fingers in the way she used to when he had been a boy going to school. 'How's Gabi? When are you going to bring my granddaughter for a visit?'

'Soon, I hope,' said Fabel. 'She's due to come for a weekend.'

'And how's her mother?' Ever since the break-up, Fabel's mother had never once referred to his ex-wife, Renate, by name; and, as she spoke, he could hear the ice crystallising in his mother's voice.

'I don't know, *Mutti*. I don't talk with her much, but when I do it's not very pleasant. Anyway, let's not talk about Renate: it only gets you annoyed.'

'What about this new girlfriend of yours? Well, not so new now. That's quite a while you've been seeing her – is it serious?'

'What . . . Susanne?' Fabel looked startled for a moment. It wasn't so much the question that had caught him off balance as much as the sudden realisation that he didn't know the answer. He shrugged. 'We get on. Really well.'

'I get on really well with Herr Heermans, the butcher, but that doesn't mean we have any kind of future together.'

Fabel laughed. 'I don't know, *Mutti*. It's early days. Anyway, tell me what the doctor said to you about what you've to do when you get out of here . . .'

Fabel and his mother spent the next two hours chatting idly. As they did so, Fabel regarded his mother more closely than he had for a long time. When did she get so old? When did her hair whiten and why hadn't he noticed? He thought about what she said about Norddeich being a concept to him; he realised that she too was a concept, a constant that was expected never to alter, to age. To die . . .

It was ten-thirty before Fabel got back to his mother's home. He got a Jever beer from the fridge and took it out into the cool night. He walked to the foot of the garden and through the low gate and the fringe of trees. Then he climbed the steep grassy embankment of the dyke and, when he reached the top, he sat down, elbows resting on knees, occasionally easing the bottle of herby Frisian beer to his lips. The night was crisp and clear and the huge Frisian sky was scattered with stars. The dunes stretched before him and, midway to the horizon, he could see the glittering lights of the evening Norderney ferry. This was another constant: this spot where he sat, elevated above the flat earth behind and the flat sea beyond. He had sat here so many times before; as a boy, as a youth and as a man. Fabel breathed in deeply, trying to sweep away the thoughts that were crowding in on him, but they continued to buzz in his head randomly and relentlessly. The image of a long-disappeared Hilke Tietjen on the Norddeich dunes collided with the image of the dead girl on the beach at Blankenese; he thought of his home changing in his absence and of Paula Ehlers's home being frozen in time during hers. The ferry, the last of the evening, drew closer to the Norddeich shore. He took another sip of the

Jever. Fabel tried to recall Hilke Tietjen as she looked now, but found that he couldn't: the teenage Hilke's image prevailed. How could someone change so much? And was he wrong about the dead girl? Could she have changed in such a short space of time?

'Thought I'd find you here . . .' Fabel jumped at the sound of the voice. He half turned and saw his brother Lex standing behind him.

'Christ, Lex, you scared the daylights out of me!'

Lex laughed and gave Fabel's back a sharp nudge with his knee.

'You spend too much time with crooks, Jannik,' said Lex, using the Frisian diminutive form of Fabel's first name. 'You must always be expecting one to creep up on you. You need to chill out.' He sat down next to his brother. He had brought another two bottles of Jever from the fridge and slapped one against Fabel's chest.

'I wasn't expecting you until tomorrow.' Fabel smiled warmly at his brother.

'I know, but I got my sous chef to do a double shift for me. Between Hanna and the staff they'll manage fine until I get back.'

Fabel nodded. Lex ran a restaurant and hotel on the North Frisian island of Sylt, close to the border with Denmark.

'How's *Mutti*?'

'Fine, Lex. Honestly, fine. She'll probably be out tomorrow. It was a very minor attack, according to the medics.'

'It's too late for me to see her tonight. I'll go in first thing tomorrow.'

Fabel looked at Lex. 'Older in years but younger in heart' was how Fabel habitually described his older brother. They looked nothing like each other: Fabel was a typical North German while Lex seemed to be a throwback to their mother's Celtic roots. He was a good deal shorter than Fabel and had thick dark hair. And the difference lay in more than appearance. Fabel had often envied Lex's easygoing good humour and irrepressible sense of fun. A smile came more quickly and more easily to Lex than to his younger brother and his good humour had left its traces in Lex's face, particularly around the eyes that seemed always to be smiling.

'How are Hanna and the kids?' Fabel asked.

'Great. Well, you know, the usual chaos. But we're all fine and we've had a good year with the hotel. When are you going to bring that sexy psychologist of yours up?'

'Soon, I hope. But I've got a swine of a case on my hands just now, and I know that Susanne has a heavy workload . . . but, with a bit of luck, it won't be too long. God knows I could do with a break.'

Lex took another mouthful of beer. He turned back to his brother and put a hand on his shoulder. 'You look tired, Jan. This has been quite a shock with *Mutti*, hasn't it? I know I'm not going to feel any easier until I see her tomorrow.'

Fabel looked into his brother's eyes. 'I got such a shock, Lex. It reminded me of when I got the call about *Papi*. It's just that I've never really contemplated life without having *Mutti* around.'

'I know. But at least we know it wasn't too serious.'

'This time,' said Fabel.

'Life's full of bridges that we have to cross when we get to them, Jan. You've always been the worrier.' Lex gave a sudden laugh. 'You were always such a serious kid.'

'And you never were serious, Lex. And you're still a kid,' said Fabel, without a hint of bitterness.

'It's not just *Mutti*, though, is it?' asked Lex. 'You're really wound up, I can sense it. More wound up than usual, that is.'

Fabel shrugged. The lights of the ferry had disappeared behind the headland and the stars had the night to themselves. 'Like I said, Lex, this case I'm on is a rough one.'

'For once, Jan, why don't you tell me about it? You never talk about the stuff you have to deal with. You never did with Renate, either. I think that was part of the problem between you.'

Fabel gave a bitter snort. 'The problem between us was that she started screwing someone else. And as a result I lost my daughter.' He turned to Lex. 'But maybe you're right. It's just that I see things, I get to know things about what people are capable of doing to each other. Things that you should be able to go through a lifetime without

71

seeing or knowing. When I don't talk about it, it's not because I'm cutting people off, it's because I'm trying to protect them. Renate never understood that. And she never understood that sometimes I have to give everything to a case, all my attention, all my time. I owe it to the victims and to their families. Maybe that's why Susanne and I are good together. As a forensic psychologist, she has to wade around in the same filth as I do. She knows what a shitty job it can be and what it can do to you. Renate used to say that it was like a game for me. Me against the bad guy. A contest to see who wins. It's not like that, Lex. I'm not pitting my wits against some cunning foe: I'm racing against the clock and against a sick mind and trying to get to him before he gets to his next victim. It's not about catching a criminal, it's about saving a life.'

Lex sighed. 'I don't know how you do it, Jan. I understand *why*, I guess, but I can't understand how you cope with all of that pain and horror.'

'Sometimes I don't, Lex. Take this case. It started with a girl . . . fifteen, maybe sixteen, strangled and dumped on a beach. A girl like Gabi. A girl like your Karin. A young life snuffed out. That's bad enough, but the sick fuck who did it left an identity on her that belonged to a different girl – a girl who has been missing for three years. It's sick. It's sick and unbelievably cruel . . . like he's deliberately planned to devastate a family that's already in pieces.'

'And it definitely wasn't the same girl?'

'We're almost certain. But I'm having to put the poor bloody family through DNA tests to make sure.'

'Christ,' said Lex, and looked out across the dunes and the dark velvet waves. 'So do you think that the killer of this girl on the beach maybe killed the other girl, the missing girl?'

Fabel shrugged. 'I think there's a good chance.'

'So you're back to your race against the clock. You have to get to him before he gets to another girl.'

'That's about the size of it.'

Lex let out a long, slow breath. 'It's getting cold out here and I need another beer.' He stood up and slapped his hand down on Fabel's shoulder. 'Let's go inside.'

Fabel cast one last long look out over the dunes and out to the sea before rising and following his brother back down the dyke, towards their shared childhood home.

CHAPTER 8

3.30 p.m., Friday, 19 March:
Norddeich, East Frisia

Fabel hadn't slept well. He had dreamt of a teenage Hilke Tietjen running along the Norddeich beach, beckoning for him to follow. She had disappeared behind a dune but, when Fabel had caught up, it wasn't Hilke who lay on the sand but another teenage girl from another beach who looked up at Fabel with an unblinking, azure gaze.

That morning he and Lex had driven into Norden to visit their mother. They had been told that she was well enough to be discharged, but that a home visit would be arranged each day for the next few days. As they had walked back to the car, Fabel had become painfully aware of how fragile his mother looked. Lex had suggested to her that Fabel should return to Hamburg, while he volunteered to stay for the next couple of days and had explained that Fabel was in the middle of a very important case. Fabel was grateful to his brother for taking the pressure off him, but felt guilty about leaving.

'Don't fuss,' she had said. 'You know how I hate a fuss. I'll be fine. You can come and see me next weekend.'

As soon as he was back on the A28 Autobahn, Fabel phoned Werner at the Präsidium. After Werner asked about Fabel's mother, they settled down to discussing the case.

'We got confirmation back from the Institut für Rechtsmedizin,' Werner told him. 'The DNA from the girl on the beach doesn't match the swabs taken from Frau Ehlers. Whoever she is, she definitely isn't Paula Ehlers.'

'Has Anna made any more progress on finding her real identity?'

'No. She's been widening her search and she picked up a couple of hopefuls, but they turned out not to match when she pursued them. She's been at it solidly since you left . . . God knows what time she left the Präsidium last night. Oh, by the way, when Möller called with the DNA results he wanted to talk to you to discuss his autopsy findings. The stuck-up bastard wasn't going to talk to me – you know what he's like. He said the report will be on your desk for when you get back. But I told him that you'd want me to pass the main points on to you.'

'What did he give you?'

Werner's tone suggested he was scanning through notes as he spoke. 'The dead girl is about fifteen or sixteen, according to Möller. There are signs of childhood neglect: bad teeth, evidence of a couple of old fractures, that sort of thing.'

'Then she could have been subject to long-term abuse,' said Fabel. 'Which could mean that the killer was a parent or guardian.'

'And that would fit with Anna finding it so hard to trace her as a missing person,' said Werner. 'If it were a parent, then they may be delaying reporting her missing, or not reporting her missing at all, to try to keep us off their trail.'

'So far it's working.' Fabel paused for a moment to process the information Werner had given him. 'The only problem is that kids exist beyond the confines of their family. There must be a school somewhere questioning her absence. She must have had friends or relatives who have missed her.'

'Anna's way ahead of you, *Chef*. She's been trawling through school attendance records. Again, nothing so far. And you can add a possible boyfriend to the list. Möller says the dead girl was sexually active, but there is no evidence of sexual contact in the last two days before her death.'

Fabel sighed. He realised that he had passed through Ammerland and a sign indicated the Oldenburg turn-off. His old university town. He was only just out of East Frisia, but already he was reimmersing in the mire of what humans are capable of doing to each other; to their children. 'Anything else?'

'No, *Chef*. Other than Möller says that the girl hadn't had much to eat in the forty-eight hours prior to death. You coming back into the Präsidium?'

'Yep. I'll be there in a couple of hours.'

After he hung up, Fabel switched the radio on. It was tuned into NDR Eins. An academic was railing against a writer who had written some kind of highly controversial literary novel. Fabel had missed a good bit of the debate, but from what he could gather the novelist had used the fictitious premise that accused some well-known historical personage of having been a child-murderer. As the debate continued, it became clear to Fabel that the personage was one of the Brothers Grimm, the nineteenth-century philologists who had collected German folk and fairy tales, legends and myths. The academic was becoming more and more incensed, while the author remained unshakeably calm. Fabel was able to gather that the author's name was Gerhard Weiss and the title of his novel was *Die Märchenstrasse – The Fairy Tale Road*. The novel had been written in the form of a fiction-alised Reisetagebuch – travelling diary – of Jacob Grimm. The host of the programme explained that, in this fictional account, Jacob Grimm accom-panies his brother Wilhelm, collecting the tales that they will eventually publish as *Children's and Household Tales (Grimms' Fairy Tales)* and *Deutsche Sagen (German Myths)*. Where the novel departed from fact was in how it described Jacob Grimm as a serial killer of children and adult women, commit-ting murders in the towns and villages he visits with his brother, each killing replicating a tale that they have collected. In the novel, the mad Grimm's rationale is that he is keeping the verity of these tales alive. The fictionalised Jacob Grimm eventually comes to believe that myths, legends and fables are essential in giving voice to the darkness of the human soul.

'It is an allegory,' explained the author, Gerhard Weiss, 'a literary device. There is not, nor has there ever been, any evidence or even suggestion that Jacob Grimm was a paedophile or any sort of murderer. My book *Die Märchenstrasse* is a story, an imagined tale. I chose Jacob Grimm because he and his brother were involved in the collection and study of the German folk tale, as well as analysing the mechanics of the German language. If anyone understood the power of myth and folklore then it was the Brothers Grimm. Today we are afraid to let our children play out of sight. We see menace and danger in every aspect of modern life. We go to the cinema to terrify ourselves with modern myths that we convince ourselves hold a mirror up to our life and society today. The fact is, the danger has always been there. The child-killer, the rapist, the insane murderer have all been constants in the human experience. All that is different is that, where we used to frighten ourselves with the spoken tale of the big, bad wolf, of the wicked witch, of the evil that lies waiting in the dark of the woods, we now scare ourselves with cinematic myths of the super-intelligent serial killer, the malevolent stalker, the alien, the monster created by science . . . All we've done is reinvent the big, bad wolf. We just have modern allegories for perennial terrors . . .'

'And that gives you the justification to malign the reputation of a great German?' asked the academic. His tone was stretched between anger and incredulity.

Again, the voice of the author remained calm. Disturbingly so, thought Fabel. Almost emotionless. 'I am aware that I have infuriated much of the German literary establishment as well as the descendants of Jacob Grimm, but I am merely fulfilling my duty as a writer of modern fables. As such, it is my responsibility to continue the tradition of scaring the reader with the danger without and the darkness within.'

It was the show's host who asked the next question. 'But what has particularly infuriated the descendants of Jacob Grimm is the way that, although you have made it clear that your portrayal of Jacob Grimm as a murderer is totally fictional, you have used this novel to promote your theory of "fiction as truth". What does that mean? Is it fictional or not?'

'As you say,' answered Weiss in the same, level, emotionless tone, 'my novel has no foundation in fact. But, as with so many works of fiction, I have no doubt that future generations will probably believe that there was some truth in it. A less educated, lazier future will remember the fiction and accept it as fact. It is a process that has been at work for centuries. Take William Shakespeare's portrayal of the Scottish king Macbeth. In reality, Macbeth was a well loved, respected and successful king. But because of Shakespeare's desire to please the then British monarch, Macbeth was demonised in a work of fiction. Today, Macbeth is a monumental figure, an icon for ruthless ambition, avarice, violence and bloodlust. But these are the characteristics of the Shakespearean character, not the historical reality, of Macbeth. We do not simply progress from history to legend to myth – we invent, we elaborate, we fabricate. The myth and the fable become the enduring truth.'

The academic responded by ignoring the author's point and repeating his condemnation of how the novel impugned Jacob Grimm's reputation and the debate was curtailed by the expiry of the programme's airtime. Fabel switched the radio off. He found himself thinking about what the writer had said. That there had always been the same evil amongst men; that there had always been the kind of random, cruel violence and death. The sick monster who had strangled the girl and dumped her body on the beach was just the latest in a long lineage of psychotic minds. Of course, Fabel had always known this to be true. He had once read about Giles De Rais, the sixteenth-century French nobleman whose absolute power over his fiefdom meant that he had been able to abduct, rape and murder young boys with impunity for years; the estimated body count was in the hundreds, and could even have been in the thousands. But Fabel had also tried to convince himself that the serial killer was a modern phenomenon: the product of a disintegrating social order, of sick minds forged by abuse and fed by the availability of violent porn in the street or on the Internet. In that belief, somehow, there lay a faint hope: that if our modern society created these monsters, then we could somehow fix the problem. To accept that it was a fundamental constant in the human condition seemed almost to give up hope.

Fabel slipped a CD into the player. As Herbert Groenemeyer's voice filled the car, and as the kilometres slipped by, Fabel tried to turn his thoughts from a perennial evil lurking in the woods.

The first thing Fabel did when he got back to his office was to phone his mother. She assured him she was still fine and that Lex was fussing over her and preparing the most beautiful meals. Her voice on the phone seemed to re-establish the balance in Fabel's universe. At a telephone line's distance, her distinctive accent and the timbre of her voice belonged to a younger mother. A mother whose presence he had always taken as an immutable, unshakeable constant in his life. After he hung up, he called Susanne and told her he was back and they agreed that she would come over to his flat after work.

Anna Wolff knocked on his door and entered. Her face looked even paler under the mop of black hair and against the dark eyeliner. The too-red lipstick seemed to flame angrily against the tired pallor of her skin. Fabel beckoned for her to take a seat.

'You don't look like you've been getting much sleep,' he said.

'Nor do you, *Chef*. How's your mother?'

Fabel smiled. 'Improving, thanks. My brother's staying with her for a couple of days. I understand you've been having an uphill struggle with the girl's identity.'

Anna nodded. 'I gather from the autopsy report that she suffered neglect and probably abuse when she was younger. She may be a long-term runaway from somewhere else in Germany, or even abroad. But I'm still on it.' She paused for a moment, as if unsure of how Fabel would take what she was about to say next. 'I hope you don't mind, *Chef*, but I've been looking at the Paula Ehlers case pretty closely as well. It's just that I have this strong instinct that we're looking for the same guy for both these girls.'

'Based on the false identity he left in the dead girl's hand?'

'That and the fact that, as you pointed out, the two girls were so alike in appearance that it would suggest he saw Paula Ehlers in life, rather than just a press photograph. I mean, when we had to get DNA tests to rule out for certain that the dead girl wasn't Paula Ehlers.'

'I take your point. So what have you been looking at?' asked Fabel.

'I've been going over the case notes with Robert Klatt.'

Fabel gave a small curse. 'Damn, I forgot all about Kommissar Klatt. How's he settling in?'

Anna shrugged. 'Fine. He's a good guy, I suppose. And he seems to be excited about working in the Mordkommission.' She flipped open the file and continued. 'Anyway, I went over this with him. We went back over the Fendrich thing. You remember? Heinrich Fendrich, Paula's German teacher?'

Fabel gave a brief nod. He remembered Anna briefing him on Fendrich in the service station café on their way to the Ehlerses.

'Well, as you know, Klatt had his suspicions. He admits that his grounds for suspecting Fendrich were slight . . . more of a combination of a gut feeling, prejudice and a total absence of other leads.'

Fabel frowned. 'Prejudice?'

'Fendrich is a bit of a loner. He's in his mid-thirties . . . well, late thirties now, I suppose, still single and living with his elderly mother. Although, apparently, he did have a kind of on-off girlfriend at the time. But I believe that broke up about the time of Paula's disappearance.'

'So Kommissar Klatt was desperate for suspects and he found a Norman Bates-type figure,' said Fabel. Anna looked puzzled. 'The character in the American film, *Psycho*.'

'Oh, yes, of course. Well, yes, I suppose he did to

a certain extent. But who could blame him? There was a girl missing, presumably dead by now, and there was this teacher with whom she seemed to have had a rapport and who, let's face it, didn't seem to have formed normal relationships. Added to that were claims by Paula's schoolfriends that Fendrich devoted a disproportionate amount of time to Paula in the classroom. To be honest, we would have pushed Fendrich a little ourselves.'

'I suppose so, but Paula's abductor and probable killer is just as likely to be a family man with a typical background. Anyway, how does Klatt feel about Fendrich now?'

'Well . . .' Anna stretched the word to emphasise her uncertainty. 'I get the feeling he now thinks he was barking up the wrong tree. After all, Fendrich does seem to have a solid alibi for when Paula Ehlers disappeared.'

'But?'

'But Klatt still maintains he has a "feeling" about Fendrich. That there was maybe something less than appropriate in his relationship with Paula. He suggested that Fendrich is maybe worth another look – although he recommends that he doesn't go along. Apparently Fendrich all but threatened Klatt with a restraining order and a harassment suit.'

'So where do we find him? Is he still at the school?'

'No,' said Anna. 'He has moved to another school. This time in Hamburg.' Anna consulted the file. 'In Rahlstedt. But apparently he still lives in the same house as he did three years ago. That's in Rahlstedt, too.'

'Okay,' said Fabel, checking his watch and rising from his seat. 'Herr Fendrich should be long home from school. I'd like to see if he has an alibi for when the girl on the beach was killed. Let's pay him a visit.'

Fendrich's house in Rahlstedt was a largish robust pre-war villa, set back from the street in a row of five similar houses. They had, at one time, aspired to a fraction of the prestige of the grander homes of Rotherbaum and Eppendorf, but now, having survived British wartime bombers and nineteen-fifties planners, they looked simply discordant, set amidst the post-war social housing of the area: Rahlstedt had been hastily planned and developed to accommodate the population of central Hamburg who had been bombed into homelessness.

Fabel parked across the street. As he and Anna approached the row of villas, Fabel realised that where the others had been converted into two or more apartments each, the Fendrich home had remained a single dwelling. There was a melancholy drabness to the building and the small garden at the front was unkempt and had attracted the unwanted detritus of passers-by.

Fabel rested his hand on Anna's arm as she started up the half-dozen stone steps to the front door. He indicated where the wall of the house met the overgrown garden: there were two small, shallow windows of grimy glass. Fabel could see the vague silhouette of three bars behind each window.

'A basement . . .' said Anna.

'Somewhere you could keep someone "underground" . . .'

They climbed the steps and Fabel pressed an old china bell push. There was the sound of ringing somewhere deep in the house. 'You take the lead, Anna. I'll ask if there's anything additional I feel I need to know.'

The door opened. To Fabel, Fendrich looked more in his late forties than late thirties. He was tall and thin, with a grey complexion. His dull blond hair was thin and lank and the scalp of his high-domed head gleamed through it under the pendant light of the high entrance hallway. He looked from Anna to Fabel and back again with an expression of indifferent curiosity. Anna held out her oval Kriminalpolizei shield.

'Hamburg KriPo, Herr Fendrich. Could we have a word?'

Fendrich's expression hardened. 'What's this about?'

'We're from the Mordkommission, Herr Fendrich. A body of a young girl was found on the beach at Blankenese the day before yesterday—'

'Paula?' Fendrich cut Anna off. 'Was it Paula?' His expression changed again: this time it was more difficult to read, but Fabel recognised something akin to dread mixed in with it.

'If we could maybe talk inside, Herr Fendrich . . .' suggested Fabel in a quiet, reassuring tone. Fendrich looked confused for a moment, then resignedly stood to one side to let them in. After he closed the door, he indicated the first room off the hall, to the left.

'Come into my study.'

The room was large and untidy and lay stark under the bleak illumination of a too-bright strip light that hung incongruously from an ornate ceiling rose. There were bookshelves on every wall except for the one with the window facing out on to the street. A large desk was positioned almost dead centre in the room; its top was scattered with more books and papers and a cascade of cables and wires tumbled from the computer and printer that sat upon it. There were piles of magazines and papers bound with string stacked, like sandbags, under the window. It looked like total chaos, but, taking in the whole room, Fabel sensed an organised disorder; as if Fendrich would probably be able to locate anything he wanted instantly and with greater ease than if everything was carefully indexed and filed. There was something about the room that suggested concentration; as if much of Fendrich's living – a bleakly functional living – was done in this room. It filled Fabel with the urge to search through the rest of this large house, to see what lay beyond this small focus.

'Sit down,' said Fendrich, liberating two chairs of their burden of books and papers. Before they were seated he asked again, 'This girl you found – was she Paula?'

'No, Herr Fendrich, she wasn't,' said Anna. The tension in Fendrich's expression eased, but Fabel wouldn't have described it as relief. Anna continued, 'But we have reason to believe that this girl's death and Paula's disappearance are linked.'

Fendrich smiled sourly. 'So you've come to harass me again. I had enough of that with your Norderstedt colleagues.' He sat down behind the desk. 'I wish you people would believe me: I had nothing to do with Paula's disappearance. I wish you would just leave me the hell alone.'

Anna raised her hand in a placatory gesture and smiled disarmingly. 'Listen, Herr Fendrich. I know you had, well, *issues* with the Norderstedt police investigation three years ago, but we're Polizei Hamburg, and we're murder-commission detectives. We're not investigating the Paula Ehlers case other than to find out if there is any connection with the dead girl. Our interest in talking to you is as background to a totally different investigation. You might hold some piece of information that could be relevant to this new case.'

'So you're telling me I am in no way a suspect in either of these cases?'

'You know we can't make an absolute statement like that, Herr Fendrich,' said Fabel. 'We don't know who we're looking for yet. But our interest in you at the moment is as a witness, not a suspect.'

Fendrich shrugged and slumped back in his chair. 'What do you want to know?'

Anna ran through the basic facts about Fendrich. When she asked him if his mother was still living with him, Fendrich looked as if he had been stung.

'My mother died,' he said, for the first time breaking eye contact with Anna. 'She died six months ago.'

'I am sorry.' Fabel looked at Fendrich and felt a true empathy with him, thinking about the scare he'd just had with his own mother.

'She had been ill for a very long time.' Fendrich sighed. 'I live alone now.'

'You changed schools after Paula's disappearance,' said Anna, as if to ensure the momentum didn't go out of the interview. 'Why did you feel the need to move on?'

Another bitter laugh. 'After your colleague – Klatt was his name – after Klatt had made it very clear that I was a suspect, the suspicion stuck. Parents, students, even my colleagues . . . I could see it in their eyes. That dark doubt. I even got a couple of threatening phone calls. So I left.'

'Didn't you think that would add to the suspicion?' Anna asked, but with a sympathetic smile.

'Didn't give a damn. I'd had enough of it. No one ever thought for a moment that I was deeply upset too. I was very fond of Paula. I thought she had enormous potential. No one seemed to take that into account. Except your colleague Klatt, who somehow managed to make it sound . . .' Fendrich struggled for the word '. . . *corrupt.*'

'You taught Paula German language and literature, is that right?' asked Anna.

Fendrich nodded.

'You say she showed particular academic promise . . . that that was the focus for your interest in her.'

Fendrich tilted his head back defiantly. 'She did. Yes.'

'Yet none of her other teachers seemed to be aware of it. And her school records show only average performance in almost all of her classes.'

'I've been through all this God knows how many times before. *I* saw the potential in her. She had a natural talent for the German language. It's like music. You can have an ear for it. Paula had a good ear. She could also express herself wonderfully when she put her mind to it.' He leaned forward, resting his elbows on the cluttered desktop and fixing Anna with an earnest gaze. 'Paula was a classic underachiever. She had the potential to become a real somebody and was in danger of becoming a nobody, of becoming lost in the system. I admit other teachers in the school missed it. And her parents were incapable of seeing it. That's why I devoted so much time to helping her. I saw a real opportunity for her to escape from the confines of her family's limited expectations.'

Fendrich leaned back in his chair and made an

open-palmed gesture with his hands, as if he'd finished his address to a court. Then he let his hands fall heavily on to the desktop, as if the last of his energy had been expended. Fabel watched him but remained silent. There had been something about the earnestness – almost the passion – with which Fendrich had spoken of Paula that disturbed him.

Anna let the subject drop and moved on to the details of Fendrich's alibi for the time of Paula's disappearance. His answers were exactly as he had given three years ago and were in the file. But, during Anna's questioning, Fendrich became increasingly impatient.

'I thought this was about a new case,' he said when Anna had finished. 'All you've done so far is go over the same old stuff. I thought this was about another girl. About a murder.'

Fabel gestured for Anna to hand him the file. He took out a large glossy photograph taken at the scene where the dead girl had been discovered. He placed it squarely before Fendrich, keeping his eyes on the teacher's face to gauge his reaction. It was a significant reaction. Fendrich muttered, 'Oh Christ . . .' and placed a hand over his mouth. Then he froze, his gaze locked on the image. He leaned forward and ranged his eyes over the photograph as if examining every pixel. Then his face relaxed in relief. He looked up at Fabel.

'I thought . . .'

'You thought it was Paula?'

Fendrich nodded. 'I'm sorry. I got a shock.' He stared at the picture again. 'My God, she's so like Paula. Older, obviously, but so very like her. Is that why you think there's a connection?'

'It's more than that,' explained Anna. 'The killer left something to mislead us about the dead girl's identity. To make us believe this was Paula.'

'Can you give us an account of your movements from Monday afternoon to Tuesday morning, Herr Fendrich?'

Fendrich pursed his lips and blew air through them as he considered Fabel's question. 'Not much to tell. I went to work as usual, both days. Monday evening I came straight home, did some marking, read. Tuesday . . . did some shopping at the MiniMarkt on my way home on Tuesday. Got home about five, five-thirty . . . Then I was here all evening.'

'Can anyone else confirm this?'

A sliver of flint entered Fendrich's eyes. 'I see . . . You couldn't get me for Paula's disappearance, so now you're trying to tie me into this.'

'It's not like that, Herr Fendrich.' Again Anna sought to placate him. 'We need to check all the facts otherwise we'd be seen not to be doing our job properly.'

The tension in Fendrich's angular shoulders eased and the defiance dulled in his eyes, but he still looked unconvinced. He looked again at the photograph of the dead girl. He looked at it for a long, silent time.

'It's the same man,' he said at last. Anna and Fabel exchanged looks.

'What do you mean?' asked Anna.

'What I mean is that you're right . . . There is a connection. My God, this girl could be her sister, they're so alike. Whoever killed this girl must have known Paula. Known her pretty well.' Pain had returned to Fendrich's dull eyes. 'Paula's dead. Isn't she?'

'We don't know that, Herr Fendrich . . .'

'Yes.' Fabel cut across Anna's answer. 'Yes, I'm rather afraid that she is.'

CHAPTER 9

9.30 p.m., Friday, 19 March:
Naturpark Harburger Berge, south of Hamburg

Buxtehude was a joke. It was a place 'wo sich Fuchs und Hase gute Nacht sagen'. A place where nothing ever happened.

For Hanna, to come from Buxtehude had a clear and unambiguous meaning. It meant to come from the back of beyond. To be a hick. To be a nobody. Hanna Grünn had come from Buxtehude, but as she sat and waited in her five-year-old VW Golf, in the middle of this creepy forest car park, she reflected bitterly that she hadn't come far from Buxtehude. Only as far as that stupid bloody bakery.

From about the age of fourteen, Hanna had always attracted the boys. She had grown tall and full-figured with long blonde hair, and had been the most sought-after girl at her school. Hanna wasn't clever, but she was smart enough to realise that and to use other resources to achieve what she wanted. And what she principally wanted was to get the hell out of Buxtehude. She had gathered clippings about Claudia Schiffer's career: how Claudia had been plucked from obscurity while at a disco, about her first modelling contracts, about the phenomenal sums she had earned, about the exotic places she had been to. So the eighteen-year-old Hanna had left Buxtehude behind and set off, with the unshakeable conviction of youth, to launch a career in modelling in Hamburg. It hadn't taken long, however, for Hanna to realise that every agent's reception she waited in was populated by other Claudia Schiffer clones. At her first interview she had shown the portfolio of shots taken of her by a local photographer before she left home. A tall, skinny queer and a woman in her late forties, who was clearly a former model, had all but sniggered as they looked through Hanna's pictures. Then they had asked where Hanna came from. When she had replied, 'I come from Buxtehude', the bastards had actually laughed.

The story had been the same at most of the other agencies. Hanna had felt as if the life she had envisioned for herself was evaporating. There was no going back to Buxtehude, but what had been, in her mind, the certainty of a modelling career now became a dream, fast on its way to becoming a total fantasy. Eventually she had worked her way through the phone books until she had found an agency in Sankt Pauli. Hanna wasn't so green that she hadn't realised the significance of the agency's offices being above a strip club. The sign on the door had confirmed that the agency specialised in 'models, exotic dancers and escorts', and the stocky, leather-jacketed Italian who ran the agency had looked more like a gangster than a figure from the fashion industry. He had, to be fair, spelled it out. He had told Hanna that she was a looker with a great body and he could get her lots of work, but it would be mainly video work. 'Real fucking – you understand?'

When Hanna had told the Italian that she wasn't interested he had simply shrugged and said, 'Okay.' But he had handed her a card and said that if she ever changed her mind she should get in touch. Back in the bedroom of her shared apartment, Hanna had bunched her pillow to her mouth to stifle the huge, uncontrollable sobs that racked her body. What had depressed her most was the businesslike, matter-of-fact way the Italian had told her that the video work would involve 'real fucking'. He hadn't been particularly seedy, he hadn't been lecherous: he had simply been laying out a job description for her, just as if he had been discussing the details of an office job. But what had got to her most was that it was clear that he thought that was all she was worth. All she should expect. It was then that she started looking around for an ordinary job; and without secretarial skills, without her Abitur, her choices had been very limited.

It was then that Hanna had got the job in the Backstube Albertus: on a production line with fat, stupid, middle-aged women who had been strangers to any kind of ambition all their lives.

Now, day after tedious day, she stood, her lustrous blonde hair gathered up under an elasticated bakery hat, her perfect body concealed in a formless white bakery coat, as she iced birthday cakes with an ever-increasing sense of doom.

But not for much longer. Soon Markus would take her away from all that. Soon she would have the wealth and lifestyle she had always wanted. Markus owned the bakery and if fucking the boss was what it took to get what she wanted, then that was what she would do. And now she was so close: Markus had promised to leave that frigid cow of a wife of his. Then he would marry Hanna.

She looked at her watch. Where the fuck was he? He was always late, mainly because of his wife. She looked around at the dense mass of trees that crowded around the car park, a darker black against a black, moonless sky. She hated meeting him here: it was so creepy. She thought she saw something move in the trees. She peered into the darkness intently for a moment and then relaxed, letting go an impatient sigh.

He had tracked her here before, but had not been able to follow her up the road to the Naturpark car park for fear of being too conspicuous: the only other vehicle on an isolated road that led just to this car park. That was why he had come back during daylight and scouted out the site. So, tonight, when he had followed her long enough to establish where she was heading, he had overtaken her and got here first. His reconnaissance of the Naturpark had revealed a narrow service track used by the foresters for maintaining the woodland. He had ridden his motorbike halfway up the track and then killed the lights and engine, letting it coast for a moment before concealing it amongst the trees. Then he had walked the rest of the way, concerned that anyone already in the car park would hear the motorcycle's approach. Now he was at the fringe of the trees, unseen, watching the whore as she waited for her married lover. He felt the thrill of a grim anticipation, a knowledge that soon the anger and the hate that ate at him like a cancer would be released. They were going to hurt. They were both going to know what it was like to experience real pain. She turned in his direction. He didn't shrink back, didn't move. She looked directly at him, peering into the dark, but the stupid bitch couldn't see him. She would see him soon enough.

The sweep of a car's headlights arced across the face of the trees and he drew back slightly. It was a Mercedes sports. Markus Schiller's car. He watched as the car pulled up alongside the Golf and Schiller put down the window and made an apologetic gesture. From his concealed vantage point in the trees he watched as Hanna got out of the Golf, slammed the door, marched ill-temperedly to the Mercedes and climbed into the passenger seat.

Now was the time.

CHAPTER 10

10.20 a.m., Saturday, 20 March:
Krankenhaus Mariahilf, Heimfeld, Hamburg

The bright spring sun, cutting through the large paned window at a slant, starkly divided the hospital room into angles of light and shade. The son had pulled up the blinds, allowing the sun to glare mercilessly into the unprotected face of his mother.

'There you are, *Mutti*. Now, that's better, isn't it?' He stepped back to the bed and drew the chair in close before sitting down. He leaned forward in his habitual posture of devotion and solicitousness. In a gesture that seemed gentle and considerate, but which hid a malevolent intent, he laid his hand on her forehead, easing it ever so slightly back towards the hairline and pulling the heavy, unresponsive eyelids up and open to let the full glare of the sun burn into the old woman's pallid eyes.

'I went out to play again last night, *Mutti*. Two this time. I cut their throats. I did him first. Then she begged for her life. She begged and she begged. It was *so* funny, *Mutti*. She just kept on saying "Oh no, oh no . . ." Then I stuck her with the knife. In the throat too. I sliced it wide open and she shut up.' He gave a small laugh. He let his hand slide off the old woman's brow and his fingers traced the fragile angles of her cheek and across her thin, wrinkled neck. He tilted his head to one side, a wistful expression on his face. Then he removed his hand suddenly and sat back in his chair.

'Do you remember, *Mutti*, when you used to punish me? When I was a boy? Do you remember how you would make me, as my punishment, recite those stories over and over and over? And if I got even one word wrong, you would beat me with that walking stick you had? The one you brought back from the walking holiday we had in Bavaria? Remember how you got a fright one time, when you beat me so badly that I passed out? You taught me that I was a sinner. A worthless sinner, you used to call me – do you remember?' He paused, as if half expecting the answer she was incapable of giving, then continued, 'And always you'd make me recite those stories. I would spend so much of my time memorising them. I used to read them over and over again, reading until my eyes began to jumble up the letters and the words, trying to make sure I didn't forget or misplace a single word. But I always did, didn't I? I always gave you an excuse to beat me.' He sighed, looked out at the bright day beyond the window and then back to the old woman. 'Soon, very soon, it will be time for you to come home with me, mother.'

He stood up, leaned over and kissed her on the forehead. 'And I still have the walking stick . . .'

CHAPTER 11

9.15 a.m., Sunday, 21 March:
Naturpark Harburger Berge, south of Hamburg

Maria had been at the scene for some time before Fabel arrived. It was more of a clearing than a car park, and Fabel suspected that it served two purposes: by day, a starting point for walkers; by night, a discreet location for illicit liaisons. He parked his BMW next to one of the green-and-white marked SchuPo cars and got out. It was a bright, breezy spring morning and the dense woods that framed the car park seemed to breathe with the breeze and the chatter of birdsong.

'"In the midst of life" . . .' he said in English to Maria as she approached him, indicating the trees and the sky with a sweep of his hand. She looked confused.

'"In the midst of life, we are in death" . . .' he repeated, translating into German. Maria shrugged. 'Where are they?' Fabel asked.

'Over there . . .' Maria indicated a small gap in the fringe of trees. 'It's a Wanderweg – a path for walkers. It goes right through the woods, but there is a small clearing with a picnic table about three hundred metres along. This is as far as you can take a car.' Fabel noticed that half of the parking area, the half next to the entrance of the Wanderweg path, had been cordoned off.

'Shall we?' Fabel indicated that Maria should lead the way. As they made their way up the uneven, slightly muddy path, Fabel noticed that the Spurensicherung forensic team had lain down protective covers at irregular intervals. Fabel looked questioningly at Maria.

'Tyre marks,' she said. 'And a couple of foot-prints that need checking out.'

Fabel stopped and scanned the path they had just come. 'Mountain bikers?'

Maria shook her head. 'Motorbike. Could be totally unconnected, as could the footprints.'

They walked on. Fabel took in the trees on either side. The spaces between them darkened as they receded, like green caves into which the bright day could not reach. He thought back to the interview on the radio. The darkness of the forest in the light of the day: the metaphor for the danger that lies in the everyday. The path took a turn and suddenly opened up into a small clearing. There were about a dozen police and forensics moving around the space. The focus of their activities was a wooden picnicking table with attached benches, set to the right of the main path. Two bodies, a man and a woman, sat on the ground, propped up against the end of the table. They both stared out at Fabel and Maria with death's disinterested glare. They sat side by side, each with an arm extended, as if reaching out to the other; their limp hands touching but not holding. Between them lay a handkerchief, carefully unfolded and laid flat. The cause of death was immediately apparent: both throats had been slashed deep and wide. The man was in his late thirties with dark hair cropped close to disguise the thinning on the top of his scalp; his mouth gaped, black-red with the blood that had frothed up from the ravaged throat in the final seconds of life.

Fabel stepped closer. He looked at the male victim's clothing. It was one of the most unsettling things at a death scene for Fabel: how death set its own agenda, how it refused to recognise the trivial subtleties that we build into our lives. The man's pale grey suit and tan leather shoes were clearly expensive: something to be noticed in life as indicators of status, of taste, of his place in the world. Here, the suit was a crumpled, mud- and blood-smeared rag. The shirt lay blood-dyed under the dark gash across the throat. One of the shoes had come off and lay discarded half a metre from the foot that pointed towards it, as if seeking to reclaim it. The grey silk sock had unfurled halfway and the mottled, pale flesh of the man's heel was exposed

Fabel turned his attention to the woman. Compared to the man, she had considerably less blood on her clothes. Death had come more quickly and more easily to her. A swathe of blood was splashed diagonally across the thighs of her jeans. She was in her early twenties and had long blonde hair, some of which had been blown by the breeze into the slash across her throat and had become matted in the blood. Fabel noted that, although the colours and cut had been carefully and tastefully chosen, her clothes were of a totally different price bracket from those of the man. She wore a pale green T-shirt and her jeans were new, but a cheaper alternative to the designer jeans whose style they copied. This was not a couple. Or at least, not an established couple. Fabel leaned forward and examined the handkerchief; there were small pieces of bread crumbled on to it. He stood up.

'No sign of the blade used?' he asked Maria.

'No . . . and no blood spatter on the ground, the table or anything around here. Hi, Jan . . .' Holger Brauner, the Präsidium's forensic team leader, joined them.

Fabel smiled. As soon as he had seen the sweeping stain of blood on the woman's jeans he had realised that this was not the primary locus: the killing had been done elsewhere.

'You got here quickly . . .' he said to Brauner.

'We got a call from a local Kommissar, who decided not to leave it to the Lagedienst to inform me. I guess the same one who called you. A Kommissar . . .' Brauner struggled for the name.

'Hermann,' Maria completed the sentence for him. 'That's him over there.' She indicated a tall, uniformed man in his early thirties. He was standing with a group of SchuPos, but when he noticed that he had become the focus of interest he made an apologetic gesture to his colleagues and strode towards the Mordkommission officers. There was an earnest purposefulness in his movements and, as he approached, Fabel noticed that his nondescript appearance, sand-coloured hair and mottled, pale skin were at odds with the keen energy that burned in his pale green eyes. His appearance reminded Fabel of Paul Lindemann, the officer he had lost, but when the uniformed officer came closer Fabel realised that the similarity was superficial.

The SchuPo nodded to Maria and extended his hand, first to Fabel, then to Brauner. Fabel noticed the single silver Kommissar star on the shoulder flashes of his short black leather uniform jacket.

Maria introduced him. 'This is Kommissar Henk Hermann, from the local Polizeidirektion.'

'Why did you call us in specifically, Herr Kommissar?' Fabel asked, smiling. The normal role of the Schutzpolizei was to secure the murder scene and keep any onlookers outside the taped perimeter, while the Kriminalpolizei took charge of the crime scene itself. The Lagedienst would be responsible for informing the KriPo, and the Mordkommission would investigate any sudden death.

An uncertain smile stretched Hermann's meagre

lips even thinner. 'Well . . .' he looked past Fabel towards the bodies. 'Well, I know that your team specialise in, well, this sort of thing . . .'

'What sort of thing?' Maria asked.

'Well, it's clearly not a suicide. And this is not the primary scene of the crime . . .'

'Why do you think that?'

Hermann wavered for a moment. It was unusual for a SchuPo to offer any form of opinion on a murder scene, and even more unusual for any KriPo, far less a Kriminalpolizei officer of Fabel's rank, to listen. He moved round the group to have clearer access to the bodies, but maintained a distance sufficient to ensure that the scene wasn't contaminated. He knelt down, balanced on the balls of his feet and pointed to the male victim's lacerated throat. 'Obviously, without moving the bodies I can't see very clearly, but it looks to me like our male victim was killed with two blows. The first caught him on the side of the neck and he started to bleed out fast. The second sliced right across his wind-pipe.' Hermann pointed to the female victim. 'It's my belief that the girl died from a single slash across her throat. This blood here –' he indicated the broad splash of blood across her thighs '– isn't hers. It's almost certain to have come from our male victim. She was in close proximity to him when he was attacked and she must have caught the arterial spray from his neck. But there is no significant amount of blood anywhere else here . . . indicating that this is not the primary scene of crime. It also suggests that they were brought here by the killer. And that, in turn, leads me to believe that our killer is maybe a big man – or, at least, physically strong. There are few signs of dragging, other than when he was putting the male victim in place and the shoe was pulled off. You can't get a vehicle up here, so that means he must have carried the victims.'

'Anything else?' asked Fabel.

'I'm only guessing, but I'd say that our killer did the guy first. Maybe a surprise attack. That way he takes the path of least resistance. His second victim doesn't have the same strength and doesn't pose the same threat as the man.'

'A dangerous assumption to make,' said Maria, with a bitter smile. Hermann straightened up and shrugged.

'You've described the modus used in this murder,' Fabel said. 'But you still haven't explained why you felt this was something for my team, specifically.'

Hermann stepped back and tilted his head slightly to one side, as if standing before some painting or exhibit that he was appraising.

'That's why . . .' he said. 'Look at it . . .'

'What?' asked Fabel.

'Well . . . This isn't just where our killer decided to dump the bodies. He could have done that twenty metres into the woods and we would maybe have taken weeks or months to find them. This is a message. He's telling us something – the choice of location, the position of the bodies, the handkerchief, the breadcrumbs. This is all for our benefit. It's all posed.'

Fabel looked across to Holger Brauner, who smiled knowingly.

'Posed . . .' repeated Hermann, clearly becoming frustrated. 'This is all carefully laid out. And that means that there is a psychotic agenda behind these killings, which in turn means that potentially we have a serial killer on our hands. And *that* is why I thought that I should inform you directly and right away, Herr Erster Hauptkommissar.' He turned to Holger Brauner. 'And the reason I contacted you, Herr Brauner, is because I felt that you might elicit something from this scene that our team might miss. I have followed your work with interest and have attended several of your seminars.'

Brauner beamed a good-natured smile and nodded in mock humility. 'And it is obvious you paid attention, Herr Kommissar.'

Fabel broadened his own smile to a grin. 'I'm sorry, Herr Hermann, I wasn't suggesting you were wasting our time. Everything you have said about the crime scene is true – including the fact that it is the secondary, not primary scene. I just wanted to hear your reasoning.'

The tense expression on Hermann's nondescript face relaxed slightly, but the flint sharpness remained in his pale green eyes.

'The question we're faced with now,' continued Fabel, 'is where the primary locus lies . . . where we find our actual murder scene.'

'I have a theory about that, Herr Hauptkommissar,' Hermann cut in before anyone else could comment. Brauner laughed.

'I thought you might.'

'As I said, I believe the bodies were carried here. We have footprints on the track. Large footprints, suggesting a tall man. They have made a deep impression on the earth which is soft but not muddy. It suggests to me that he was carrying something heavy.'

'Maybe what he was carrying was simply too much weight,' said Brauner. 'It could just be someone who's taken up walking in the woods to burn off some calories.'

'Then it's very effective,' Hermann responded, 'because we have at least two sets of tracks, one coming and one going. The ones that head back towards the parking area don't make the same deep impression. And that suggests to me that he carried something heavy to this spot, at least once, and walked back to the parking area unburdened.'

'So you're saying the murder scene was the car park?' asked Fabel.

'No. Not necessarily. He might have killed them there, but we've found no forensic evidence so far. That's why I've secured the half of the car park nearest the Wanderweg. My belief is that the victims were murdered elsewhere and brought here by car. Or perhaps they were murdered in a car while still in the car park. But if he brought them here, I would guess that he parked his car close to the path.'

Fabel nodded appreciatively. Brauner barked a laugh and slapped Hermann good-naturedly on the shoulder. It was a gesture that Hermann did not seem to appreciate too much. 'I concur, Herr Kollege. Although I have to say we have a long way to go before we identify these footprints as belonging to our killer. But this really is very good work. Very few people would have thought to preserve the scene at the car park.'

'The car park was empty when the bodies were found?' asked Fabel.

'Yes,' said Hermann. 'The only vehicle here was the blue Opel that belongs to the walker who found the bodies, about seven-thirty this morning. Which leads me to believe that the vehicle that was our murder scene or was used to transport the bodies is long gone. Maybe even dumped and burnt-out somewhere to destroy forensic evidence.' He pointed to the Wanderweg in the direction opposite that which they had taken. 'This path leads to another parking area, about three kilometres along. I sent a car to check that, just in case, but there was nothing.'

It suddenly struck Fabel that Maria had been quiet throughout the conversation. She had stepped closer to the bodies and her gaze seemed magnetically locked to the dead woman. Fabel held up a hand to the others and said 'Excuse me . . .' before moving over to join her.

'You okay?' he asked. Maria snapped her face towards him and gazed at him blankly for a moment, as if dazed. Her skin seemed pulled taut over the angular architecture of her face, like skin whitened over knuckles.

'What? Oh . . . yes.' Then, more determinedly: 'Yes. I'm fine. It's not stirring up post-trauma stresses, if that's what you mean.'

'No, Maria, that's not what I meant. What is it you see?'

'I was just trying to work out what it is that he's trying to say with this. Then I looked at their hands.'

'Yes . . . holding hands. The killer obviously posed them to appear as if they were holding hands.'

'No . . . not that,' said Maria. 'The other hands. His right and her left. They're made into tight fists. It doesn't look right. It looks like it's part of the posing.'

Fabel turned abruptly. 'Holger – come and take a look at this.' Brauner and Hermann came over and Fabel pointed out what Maria had noticed.

'I think you're right, Maria . . .' said Brauner. 'It looks like they've been closed post-mortem but ante-rigor . . .' Suddenly, Brauner looked like he'd been stung. He turned sharply to Fabel. 'Christ, Jan – the girl on the beach . . .'

Brauner reached into his jacket pocket and

pulled out an unopened surgical-glove packet. He snapped on a latex glove and pulled a probe from his breast pocket. There was an urgency about each action. He moved forward and turned the girl's hand over. The rigor made it difficult and he called Hermann across, holding out the pack of latex gloves as he did so.

'Put these on before you touch the body. I want you to keep her hand turned round.'

Hermann complied. Brauner tried unsuccessfully to use the probe as a lever to open the woman's fingers. Eventually he had to pry them open with his own. He turned to Fabel and nodded grimly, before reaching into the palm with a pair of surgical tweezers and extracting a small, tightly rolled piece of yellow paper. He slipped the paper into a clear plastic evidence bag and carefully unrolled it flat. He stood up and carefully retraced his steps back from the bodies. Hermann followed.

'What does it say?'

Brauner handed the evidence bag to Fabel. Fabel felt a chill somewhere deep in his bones. Again it was a rectangular slip of the same yellow paper, about ten centimetres wide by five long. He recognised the small, regular, red-ink handwriting as the same on the note recovered from the hand of the dead girl on Blankenese beach. This time there was just one word written: 'Gretel'. Fabel showed the paper to Maria.

'Shit – it's the same guy.' She looked down again

at the bodies. Brauner was already prying open the clenched fist of the male victim.

'And this, apparently, is "Hänsel",' said Brauner as he stood up, slipping another piece of yellow paper into an evidence bag.

Fabel felt a tightness in his chest. He looked up at the pale blue sky, down the path that led back to the parking area, into the green sepulchre of the woods and then back to the man and woman lying with their throats slashed to the spine, sitting with their hands touching and a large, breadcrumb-scattered handkerchief spread on the grass between them. *Hänsel and Gretel.* The bastard thought he had a sense of humour.

'You were right to call us in, Kommissar Hermann. You may have just shortened the distance between us and a serial killer whom we know has killed once, maybe twice before.' Hermann beamed with satisfaction: Fabel didn't return the smile. 'What I need you to do now is to get all of your team back to the parking area for a briefing. We need this whole area fingertip-searched. And then we've got to find the primary locus. We have to know who these people are and where they were murdered.'

CHAPTER 12

10.00 a.m., Sunday, 21 March:
Blankenese, Hamburg

She sat in her chair and grew older.

She sat straight and unmoving, listening to the clock ticking, aware that every measured second was a wave that eroded her youth and her beauty. And her beauty was great. Laura von Klosterstadt's refined grace transcended passing fashions for the waiflike or for the voluptuous. It was a true beauty: a timeless, glacial, cruel perfection. Hers was not a look to be 'discovered' by a photographer: it had been formed from true nobility, bred over generations. It had also proved to be highly marketable, an asset for which fashion houses and cosmetics companies had paid vast sums of money.

The scale of Laura's beauty was matched by that of her loneliness. It is difficult for the plain and the ordinary to imagine how beauty can repel as much as ugliness. Ugliness inspires disgust; great beauty such as Laura's inspires fear. Laura's looks threw a fence around her that few men were brave enough to breach.

She sat and felt herself age. It was her thirty-first birthday in a week's time. Heinz, her agent, would be here soon. He was coming to help her prepare for the birthday party. Heinz would make sure that everything went well: he was an extravagant, ebullient gay who combined limitless energy with steely determination and efficiency. He was a good agent; but, much more, he was also the closest thing Laura had to a real friend. She knew Heinz's concern for her went beyond 'looking after the talent': he had been the only person to see through Laura's defences and understand the extent of her sadness. And soon the villa would be filled with Heinz's flamboyance. But for now it was still.

The room in which Laura sat was one of the two places to which she would retreat. Both were in her vast Blankenese villa: there was this large, over-bright and deliberately functionless room with its uncompromisingly hard chair, hard wooden floor and white walls; and there was the pool room that projected from the side of the house, out over the terraces and, when one swam towards the vast picture windows at the pool's end, the feeling was of swimming out into the sky. These were the places where Laura von Klosterstadt met with herself.

This room, however, was empty other than for the unyielding chair in which she sat and a single cabinet along one wall. The CD system on the drawer unit was the only comfort or amenity she had allowed into this space.

It was a bright room. It had been this room that had persuaded her to move here. It was large, with a high plaster ceiling framed with ornate cornicing and filled with light from the vast bay window. Ideal for a nursery, she had thought, and at that moment had decided to buy the villa.

But it wasn't a nursery. She had left it stark and white, turning its brightness into something uncompromisingly sterile. It was here that Laura sat and thought about a ten-year-old child who didn't exist. Who never really did exist. Laura would sit in the comfortless chair in the sterile white room and think of how it might have looked with bright colours, with toys. With a child.

It was better this way. Laura's experience of her own mother had led her to believe that having a child would simply pass down to another generation the misery she had herself experienced. It was not that Laura's mother had been cruel. She had not beaten her nor deliberately humiliated her. It was simply that Margarethe von Klosterstadt, Laura's mother, had clearly never felt anything in particular for her. Sometimes Margarethe would look at Laura in an unsettling and vaguely disapproving way, as if trying to assess her; to work out who and what exactly Laura was and where she should fit in to her life. Laura had always been very aware that, in some way that was apparent only to her mother, she must have been a bad girl. A naughty child. Margarethe had clearly identified all of Laura's flaws as a child and had highlighted them with the glacial spotlight of her disapproval. Her mother had also, however, recognised Laura's extraordinary beauty – in fact, she isolated it as Laura's sole virtue. She had even, at the start, managed Laura's career, before Heinz had been appointed. She had worked tirelessly, even obsessively, to promote Laura's career and to ensure that she became a prominent part of the social circle to which the von Klosterstadts belonged. But Laura had no childhood memory of her mother playing with her. Caring for her. Smiling at her with a genuine warmth.

Then there had been the problem.

Almost exactly ten years before, when Laura's beauty was in its very first bloom and the modelling contracts had started to come in, someone had somehow slipped through the barbed defences that Margarethe von Klosterstadt had cast around her daughter. That Laura had cast around herself.

Laura's mother had taken charge; had arranged everything. Laura hadn't told her mother she was pregnant: she had only just found out for sure herself, but through some near-mystical means that Laura could not attribute to maternal instinct, her mother had come to know about the pregnancy. Laura had never seen her boyfriend again, and had never mentioned him again or even thought of him again. She knew that her mother had made sure he would never reappear: the von Klosterstadt family had the power to bend others to its will, and it had the wealth to buy those who did not bend. A week before her twenty-first birthday, a short holiday was arranged: a private clinic in London. Then Laura's social and modelling career continued as if nothing had happened.

It was funny, she always thought it would have been a boy. She didn't know why, but that was how she always imagined her child.

She heard a car in the drive. Heinz. She sighed, rose from her chair and made her way out to the entrance hall.

CHAPTER 13

Noon, Sunday, 21 March:
Naturpark Harburger Berge, south of Hamburg

They had made the discoveries almost simultaneously.

Kommissar Hermann had radioed in that two cars – a flash Mercedes sports and an older VW Golf – had been discovered part-concealed in woodland at the southern end of the Naturpark. This guy was cool. Methodical. Having driven the first car to the spot, it would have taken the killer twenty minutes to walk back for the second car. Fabel wanted details, but didn't want to discuss the discovery over the radio, so he called Hermann back on his cell phone.

'I'll get Herr Brauner and his team over there as soon as they're finished here. Make sure the locus stays protected.'

'Of course,' said Hermann, and Fabel could tell that he was slightly offended.

'Sorry,' said Fabel. 'You've made it very clear from your work here that you know how to preserve a scene. Is there anything that leaps out at you there?'

'The Mercedes is the murder scene, as I thought. Let's put it this way, the upholstery is never going to be the same again. There's a briefcase in the back. We may well get an identity from that, but obviously we haven't touched it yet. We've checked out the number – registered owner is a company. Backstube Albertus, located in Bostelbek, in the Heimfeld area of the city. I've got someone checking with them as to who drives it. At the moment we're just saying that it has been found abandoned. The Golf belongs to a Hanna Grünn. It's registered to an address in Buxtehude.'

'Good. I'll come over with Herr Brauner when we're through here.'

'Funny,' said Hermann. 'It's almost as if he was half-hearted about hiding the cars. He could even have burned them out.'

'No . . .' said Fabel. 'He was just buying himself a little extra time. Putting that extra distance between us and him. He wanted us to see where he had killed them. It's just that he wanted us to see it when it suited him.'

It was Holger Brauner who made the other discovery. He led Fabel back to the main car park and to the fringes of the forest. The undergrowth thinned out at one point and both men pushed back branches to reach a narrow pathway, not even wide enough to constitute a firebreak. This, at one time, had been a second way into to the clearing, but so narrow that it had obviously been intended solely for walkers or cyclists, or simply as an access. Fabel cursed as the tan shoes he had paid so much for in London sank into the peaty earth.

'Here . . .' Brauner indicated where he had placed several scene-of-crime tent cards on the ground. 'These are fresh boot prints. Good ones, too. And from the size I would guess definitely male.' He led Fabel further along the track, pointing to another boot print. 'Just keep clear of that, Jan. I haven't got a photograph or a cast of it yet.'

Fabel followed Brauner's lead and struggled to make his way along the grassy edge of the track. Brauner stopped beside a row of tent-card markers. 'And these are tyre tracks – again fresh.'

Fabel squatted down and examined the tracks. 'Motorbike?'

'Yep . . .' Brauner indicated where the sweep of the track curved out of sight, consumed by the tangled darkness of the forest. 'My guess is that if you get one of your guys to follow this path, they'll end up coming out somewhere near the main road. Someone rode their motorcycle all the way up here until they were about 150 metres from the car park. If my interpretation of these tracks and boot marks is right, he killed the engine and pushed the bike the rest of the way.' He pointed back to the original boot prints. 'And those marks indicate that he stood just out of sight of the car park, probably observing it.'

'Our killer?'

'Could be.' Brauner's face broke into its usual good-natured grin. 'Or perhaps simply a nature lover watching the nocturnal wildlife in the car park.'

Fabel returned Brauner's smile, but an alarm bell was sounding somewhere in his mind. He moved back to re-examine the footprints, straddling them to avoid damaging them. The branches he had to push back to gain access to the path now shielded his body. In his mind he rewound a clock, making it night. You waited here, didn't you? It was like you were invisible, part of the forest. You felt safe and hidden here while you watched and waited. You saw them arrive, more than likely separately. You kept a watch on one of them while he or she waited for the other to turn up. You knew them, somehow, or at least their movements. You knew to wait for your second victim to arrive. Then you struck.

Fabel turned to Brauner. 'I hope you get a good impression from this, Holger. This guy was no peeping Tom. He had a purpose here.'

CHAPTER 14

3.20 p.m., Sunday, 21 March:
Hausbruch, South Hamburg

By the time Fabel and Werner arrived, the local SchuPo uniformed police had informed Vera Schiller that a body had been found and the indications were that it was her husband. A search of the man's pockets had produced a wallet and a Personalausweis identity card: Markus Schiller. Holger Brauner and his SpuSi forensics team had examined the two dumped vehicles and confirmed that the male victim had been murdered inside the Mercedes. There was a 'shadow' on the passenger seat where the passenger, the girl, had blocked the man's arterial spray from soaking the leather upholstery. There were traces of blood in the sills of the car's bonnet and Brauner had surmised that the girl had been taken out of the car and that her throat had been cut while she was held down on the bonnet. 'As if it were a butcher's block,' had been how Brauner had described it. The SpuSi forensics team had retrieved the briefcase from the car. It had contained nothing more than a pile of fuel receipts, a receipt for an on-the-spot speeding penalty and some brochures on commercial baking equipment and products.

The Schiller residence was set in huge grounds that backed on to the wooded fringes of the Staatsforst. The drive up to the house led through a dense mass of trees that crowded broodingly on to and over it before opening out on to vast, manicured lawns. Fabel had the feeling of again entering a clearing in woodland. The house itself was a large nineteenth-century villa with a pale-cream painted exterior and large windows.

'There's obviously money in the bun business,' muttered Werner as Fabel parked on the immaculate gravel drive.

Vera Schiller answered the door herself and conducted them through a marble-floored and pillared hall and into a spacious drawing room. At Frau Schiller's invitation, the two policemen sat down on an antique sofa. Fabel's tastes ran more to the contemporary, but he could recognise a valuable antique when he saw one. And it wasn't the only one in the room. Vera Schiller sat opposite them and crossed her legs, resting her hands, palms down, on her lap. She was an attractive, dark-haired woman in her late thirties. Everything about her – her face, her posture, her polite half-smile when inviting them in – communicated an overdone composure.

'First of all, Frau Schiller, I know this must be very distressing for you,' began Fabel. 'Obviously, we will need you to identify the body formally, but there is little doubt it is your husband. I want you to know how sorry we are for your loss.' He shifted awkwardly: this sofa had been uncomfortable for the best part of two centuries.

'Are you?' There was no hostility in Vera Schiller's voice. 'You didn't know Markus. You don't know me.'

'Nonetheless,' said Fabel, 'I am sorry, Frau Schiller. Really.'

Vera Schiller gave a brusque nod. Fabel couldn't tell whether this was a dam she had hastily thrown up to hold back her grief, or whether she really was quite simply a cold fish. He produced a transparent evidence bag from his pocket. Markus Schiller's photograph on his Personalausweis ID card was visible through the polythene. He handed it to her.

'Is this your husband, Frau Schiller?'

She gave it a swift glance and then held Fabel's eyes in a too-steady gaze. 'Yes. That's Markus.'

'Have you any idea why Herr Schiller would be in the Naturpark so late in the evening?' asked Werner.

She gave a bitter laugh. 'I would have thought that was obvious. You found a woman as well, I believe?'

'Yes,' said Fabel. 'A woman called Hanna Grünn, as far as we can ascertain at the moment. Does that name mean anything to you?'

126

For the first time there was something akin to pain in Vera Schiller's eyes. She reined it back in and both her false laugh and her answer dripped acid.

'Fidelity, to my husband, was a concept as abstract and difficult to understand as nuclear physics. It was something that simply lay beyond his capacity to comprehend. There were countless other women, but yes, I recognise the name. You know, Herr Hauptkommissar, what I find really so distasteful about all this isn't that Markus was having a liaison with another woman – God knows I've grown accustomed to that – but that he didn't have the courtesy, or the imagination, or indeed the taste to raise his sights above our own factory floor.'

Fabel exchanged a quick glance with Werner. 'This girl worked for you?'

'Yes. Hanna Grünn has worked for us for about six months. She worked on the production line, under Herr Biedermeyer. He would be able to tell you more about her than I. But I remember her starting. Very pretty in an obvious, provincial sort of way. I recognised her immediately as Markus's kind of meat. But I didn't think he would have fucked the help.'

Fabel held her gaze. The obscenity didn't sit comfortably with Vera Schiller's dignity and composure. Which was, of course, why she had used it.

'I'm sure you understand, Frau Schiller, that I have to ask where you were last night?'

Again a bitter laugh. 'The enraged, cheated wife exacting revenge? No, Herr Fabel, I had no need to resort to violence. I didn't know about Markus and Fräulein Grünn. And if I did I wouldn't have cared. Markus knew there were limits beyond which he could not push me. You see, I own the Backstube Albertus company. It was my father's business. Markus is . . .' She paused and frowned, then shook her head, as if annoyed with her inability to adapt to a new reality. 'Markus *was* merely an employee. I also own this house. I had no need to kill Markus. In one fell swoop I could render him incomeless and homeless. For someone with Markus's expensive tastes, that was the ultimate threat.'

'Your whereabouts last night?' Werner repeated the question.

'I was at a function in Hamburg, a catering industry event, until about one a.m. I can give you full details.'

Fabel took in the room once more. There was real money here. Lots of it. With the right connections, you could buy anything in Hamburg if you had enough money. Including a killer. He rose from the expensive discomfort of the sofa.

'Thanks for your time, Frau Schiller. If you don't mind I would like to visit your business premises and talk to some of the staff. I understand that you will probably close the Backstube Albertus for a few days, but—'

Vera Schiller cut Fabel off. 'We will be open tomorrow as usual. I will be in my office.'

'You're going to work tomorrow?' If Werner was trying to hide his incredulity, he failed miserably.

Frau Schiller stood up. 'You can advise me of the arrangements for a formal identification there.'

As they came out of the drive on to the main road, the crowding trees seemed to close behind them. Fabel tried to imagine Frau Schiller, now alone in the ornate drawing room, the sea-wall defence cracking, allowing her grief and her tears to come flooding through. But somehow he couldn't.

CHAPTER 15

9.00 p.m., Sunday, 21 March:
Pöseldorf, Hamburg

When Fabel opened the door to his apartment, a classical CD was playing and he could hear noises from the galley kitchen. It filled him with an odd mix of feelings. It reassured him, comforted him, that he was returning to something more than an empty space. That someone waited for him. But, at the same time, he couldn't help experiencing something of a sense of intrusion. He was glad that he and Susanne hadn't yet made the decision to move in together, or, at least, he thought he was glad. Perhaps the time would be right soon. But not yet. And he suspected that she felt the same. But somehow deferring the decision worried Fabel: it was very much his role to be decisive in his professional life, but in his personal life he seemed incapable of making decisions – good ones, anyway, which was why he always tended to put them off. And he was only too well aware that his indecisiveness, his vagueness had, at least in part, led to the failure of his marriage to Renate.

He slipped off his Jaeger jacket and unclipped his gun and holster, laying both on the leather sofa. He moved through to the kitchen. Susanne was making an omelette to go with a salad she'd already prepared. Some chilled Pinot Grigo was already frosting two wine glasses.

'I thought you'd be hungry,' she said as he came up behind her and slipped his arms around her waist. She had her long dark hair up and he kissed her exposed neck. The sensual smell of her filled his nostrils and he drank it in. It was the smell of life. Of vigour. It was itself like good wine after a day with the dead.

'I am hungry,' he said. 'But I need to shower first . . .'

'Gabi phoned earlier.' Susanne called through to him as he stepped into the shower. 'Nothing important. Just a chat. She spoke with your mother: she's doing well.'

'Good. I'll call them both tomorrow.' Fabel smiled. He had been worried that his daughter Gabi would be resentful of Susanne. She wasn't: they had hit it off from the start. Susanne had warmed immediately to Gabi's intelligence and sharp wit and Gabi had been impressed by Susanne's beauty, style and 'super-cool job'.

After they finished their meal, Fabel and Susanne sat and chatted about everything and anything but their work. The only reference Fabel made to the day's events was to ask Susanne if she could attend his case conference the following afternoon. They went to bed and made love in a drowsy, lazy way before falling asleep.

He was bolt upright in bed when he awoke. He felt the prickle of sweat on his back.

'You okay?' Susanne sounded alert. He must have woken her. 'Another dream?'

'Yes . . . I don't know . . .' He frowned in the darkness, peering out through the bedroom door and the picture windows, across the glitter of lights reflected on the water of the Aussenalster, as if to catch sight of his fleeing nightmare. 'I think so.'

'This is happening too much, Jan,' she said, resting her hand on his arm. 'These dreams are a sign that you're not coping with . . . well, with the things you have to cope with.'

'I'm fine.' His voice was too cold and hard. He turned to her and softened the tone. 'I'm fine. Honestly. Probably just that cheese omelette of yours . . .' He laughed and lay back down. She was right: the dreams were getting worse. Every case now seemed to invade the landscape of his sleep. 'I can't even remember what it was about,' he lied. Two faceless children, a boy and a girl, had sat in a clearing in the forest, eating a meagre picnic. Vera Schiller's villa loomed through the trees. Nothing had happened in the dream, but there had been an overwhelming feeling of malevolence.

He lay in the dark, thinking; spreading his mind over the city outside. His thoughts roamed over the lonely woodland park to the south. *Hänsel und Gretel*. Children lost in the dark of the forest. Out along the dark Elbe towards the pale sands of the Blankenese Elbstrand. A girl lying by the shore. That was the start. Fabel was meant to get that. These were the overture notes and he had missed their meaning.

His tired mind misfired, jumbling unconnected things together. He thought of Paul Lindemann, the young policeman he'd lost on their last major case and his thoughts turned to Henk Hermann, the uniformed Kommissar who had secured the scene in the Naturpark, and then to Klatt, the KriPo Kommissar from Norderstedt. Two outsiders to the Mordkommission team, one of whom he believed would become a permanent insider. But he did not yet know which one it would be. There was the sound of laughter outside. Somewhere down on the Milchstrasse people were coming out of a restaurant. Other lives.

Fabel closed his eyes. *Hänsel und Gretel*. A fairy tale. He remembered the radio interview he had heard when driving back from Norddeich, but his tired brain locked out the name of the author. He would ask his friend Otto, who owned a bookstore down in the Alsterarkaden.

A fairy tale.

Fabel fell asleep.

CHAPTER 16

10.00 a.m., Monday, 22 March:
Alsterarkaden, Hamburg

The Jensen Buchhandlung was situated in the elegant covered Arcades on the Alster. The brightly lit bookstore exuded Northern European cool, and would have looked just as much at home in Copenhagen, Oslo or Stockholm as it did in Hamburg. The interior styling was simple and contemporary, with beechwood bookshelves and finishings. Everything about it suggested organisation and efficiency, which always made Fabel smile, because he knew the owner, Otto Jensen, to be totally disorganised. Otto had been a close friend of Fabel's since university. He was tall, gangly and eccentric: a moving focus for chaos. But concealed in the tangle of bungling physicality was a supercomputer mind.

The Jensen Buchhandlung was not busy when Fabel arrived, and Otto had his back to the door, stretching his near-two-metre frame to stack books on the shelves from a new stock box. One dropped from his grasp and Fabel lunged forward and caught it.

'I suppose lightning reactions are a prerequisite for a crime fighter. It's most reassuring.' Otto smiled at his friend and they shook hands. They inquired about each other's health, about their respective partners and children, then chatted idly for a few minutes before Fabel explained the purpose of his visit.

'I am after this new book. A novel. A *Krimi*, I suppose. I can't remember the title or the author, but it's based on the idea of one of the Grimm brothers being a murderer . . .'

Otto smiled knowingly. '*Die Märchenstrasse*. Gerhard Weiss.'

Fabel snapped his fingers. 'That's the one!'

'Don't be impressed by my amazing knowledge of fiction – it's being punted big time by the publishers at the moment. And I think you would offend Herr Weiss's literary sensibilities by describing it as a *Krimi*. It's based on an "art imitating life imitating art" premise. There are more than a few members of the literary establishment getting themselves worked up about it.' Otto frowned. 'Why on earth would you want to buy a historical murder thriller? Isn't Hamburg serving you up enough of the real thing?'

'If only it weren't, Otto. Is it any good? This book, I mean.'

'It's provocative, that's for sure. And Weiss knows his stuff about folklore, philology and the work of

135

the Brothers Grimm. But his style is pretentious and overblown. Truth is, it really is just a common-or-garden thriller with literary pretensions. That's my opinion, anyway . . . Come and have a coffee.' Otto led Fabel to the Arts section of the shop. There had been some changes since Fabel's last visit: an aisle had been removed to open up the space. The gallery above now looked on to an area with leather sofas and coffee tables piled with newspapers and books. There was a counter in the corner with an espresso machine.

'It's all the thing, nowadays,' grinned Otto. 'I came into this business because I love literature. Because I want to sell books. Now I serve *caffè lattes* and *macchiatos*.' He indicated a sofa and Fabel sat down while Otto went over to the coffee bar. After a couple of minutes he came back with a book jammed under his arm and carrying two coffees. He put one down in front of Fabel. Otto, unsurprisingly, had spilled some of the coffee and it swirled in the saucer.

'I'd stick to books, Otto, if I were you.' Fabel smiled at his friend. Otto handed him the book, sloshing some of his own coffee into his saucer.

'This is it. *Die Märchenstrasse*. The Fairy Tale Road.'

It was a thick hardback. The book jacket was dark and brooding, with the title set in a Gothic Fraktur typeface. A nineteenth-century copper-plate illustration was set, small, in the centre of the cover. It showed a small girl in a hooded red cape walking through a forest. Red eyes glowed in the darkness behind her. Fabel flipped the book over and looked at the back. There was a photograph of Weiss: the unsmiling face was hard and broad, almost brutish, above the bulk of his neck and shoulders.

'Have you read anything of his before, Otto?'

'Not really . . . I've flicked through a couple. He has had similar stuff published before. He has quite a following. A weird following at that. But he seems to have broken into the mainstream with this.'

'What do you mean, a "weird" following?'

'His previous books were fantasy novels. He called them the "*Wahlwelten Chronik*" – the "Choose-Worlds Chronicles". They were based on the same sort of premise as this new one, but set in a totally fictitious world.'

'Science fiction?'

'Not exactly,' said Otto. 'The world Weiss created was almost the same as this, but the countries had different names, different histories, et cetera. More like a parallel world, I suppose. Anyway, he invited fans to "buy" a place in his books. If they sent him a few thousand Euros, he would write them into the story. The more they paid, the bigger part they played in the storyline.'

'Why would anyone pay for that?'

'It's all to do with Weiss's oddball literary theories.'

Fabel gazed at the face on the back cover. The

eyes were incredibly dark. So dark it was difficult to distinguish the pupils from the irises. 'Explain them to me . . . His theories, I mean.'

Otto made a face that suggested the difficulty of the task. 'God, I don't know, Jan. A mixture of superstition and quantum physics, I guess. Or I suppose, more accurately, superstition dressed up in quantum physics.'

'Otto . . .' Fabel smiled impatiently.

'Okay . . . Think of it this way. Some physicists believe that there is an infinite number of dimensions in the universe, right? And that consequently there is an infinite number of possibilities – and infinite variations on reality?'

'Yes . . . I suppose so . . .'

'Well,' Otto continued, 'the scientific proposition has always been an artistic belief for many writers. They can be a superstitious bunch. I know for a fact that several well-known authors avoid basing characters on people they know, quite simply because they fear that their imaginings for the characters may become reflected in reality. You kill a child in a book, and a child dies in reality, that kind of thing. Or, scarier still, you write a novel about horrific crimes and somewhere, in another dimension, your fiction becomes fact.'

'That's nonsense. So, in another dimension, you and I might simply be fictional characters?'

Otto shrugged. 'I'm only laying out Weiss's premise. Added to the metaphysical mumbo-jumbo, he layers in this proposition that our concept of history tends to be shaped more by literary or, increasingly, screen portrayals of characters rather than by the historical record and historical or archaeological research.'

'So, despite all his denials, Weiss is implying that, simply by writing this fiction about him, Jacob Grimm *is* guilty of these crimes in some other invented dimension. Or that Grimm will be judged guilty by future generations who will choose to believe Weiss's fiction rather than documented fact.'

'Exactly. Anyway, Jan . . .' Otto tapped the book that Fabel held. 'Happy reading. Anything else I can get you?'

'As a matter of fact you can . . . Do you have any fairy tales?'

CHAPTER 17

3.00 p.m., Monday, 22 March:
Polizeipräsidium, Hamburg

The conference room of the Mord-kommission would have had the look of a library reading room had it not been for the scene-of-crime photographs that were taped to the incident board, alongside the blown-up images of the notes left in the hands of all three victims. The cherrywood table was completely covered with books of all sizes. Some had the glossy sheen of the freshly published, while others were handworn and a couple were clearly anti-quarian volumes. Fabel's contribution had been the books he had bought from the Jensen Buchhandlung – three copies of Gerhard Weiss's thriller, a copy of *Grimms' Household and Fairy Tales*, a volume of Hans Christian Andersen and one of Charles Perrault. Anna Wolff had gathered the others from the Hamburg Zentralbibliothek library.

Anna Wolff, Maria Klee and Werner Meyer were already there when Fabel arrived. Kommissar

Klatt, from the Schleswig-Holstein KriPo also sat with them but, although the team chatted animatedly with Klatt, there was something about their body language that set the newcomer apart. Fabel had just sat down at the head of the table when Susanne Eckhardt arrived. She apologised to Fabel for her late arrival with the formality that the two lovers automatically adopted when their professional paths crossed.

'Okay,' Fabel said in a decisive tone. 'Let's get started. We have two murder scenes and three victims. And given that the first victim bore a direct reference to Kommissar Klatt's three-year-old missing-person inquiry, we have to assume, unfortunately, that there is a fourth victim.' He turned to Werner. 'What have we got so far?'

Werner ran through the details they had to date. The first victim had been discovered by a woman from Blankenese out for an early-morning walk along the beach with her dog. In the second case, the police had been tipped off by an anonymous telephone call to the Polizeieinsatzzentrale control room. The call had come from a phone booth at a service station on the B73 Autobahn. Fabel thought back to the motorcycle tyre marks on the track leading out of the Naturpark. But why would this man hide the cars to buy time and then call to tell the police where to find the bodies? Werner also explained that Brauner had got back to them about the two sets of boot prints. The ones that Hermann had pointed out on the

Wanderweg didn't match those found next to the car park. 'The odd thing is,' said Werner, 'that although they were different boots, the size was the same. Huge . . . size 50.'

'Maybe he changed boots, for some reason,' said Anna.

'We focus on the motorcyclist who used the foresters' service path,' said Fabel. 'He was watching and waiting for them to arrive. That's our premeditation.'

'We're still waiting for the autopsy results on the first victim,' continued Werner, 'as well as the forensic reports on the cars we found dumped in the woods. But we do know that it's likely the first victim was strangled, and the double murder obviously involved a weapon and a different form of killing. Our link between the murders is these small notes pressed into the victims' hands.' Werner stood up and read the contents of the notes out loud.

'What we have to ascertain,' said Susanne, 'is whether this latest *reference* – the use of the Hänsel and Gretel story – is just some kind of sick one-off joke, because he abandoned his victims in the woods, or whether he really is making some kind of link to fairy tales.'

'But there's no "fairy tale" link in the first note,' Fabel turned and stared at the blow-ups of the notes, as if concentrating on them would squeeze further meaning from the tiny, obsessively neat handwriting.

'Unless we're simply missing the reference,' said Susanne.

'Let's stick with "Hänsel und Gretel" for the moment,' Fabel continued. 'Let's assume our guy is trying to tell us something. What could it be? Who are "Hänsel und Gretel"?'

'Innocents lost in the wood. Children.' Susanne leaned back in her chair. 'Neither of which fits with what we know about the victims. It's a traditional German folk tale . . . one of the ones collected and recorded by the Brothers Grimm . . . it's also an opera by Humperdinck. Hänsel and Gretel were brother and sister — again something that doesn't fit with the two victims. They epitomise innocence in danger from corruption and evil, over which they ultimately triumph . . .' Susanne made a 'that's it' gesture with her hands.

'I've got it!' Anna Wolff had been flicking through one of the books on the table, she slapped her hand down on the open pages.

'What?' said Fabel. 'The "Hänsel und Gretel" connection?'

'No . . . No . . . sorry, *Chef*, I mean the first girl. I think I may have the "fairy tale" link. A young girl found on a beach, right? Beside water?'

Fabel nodded impatiently.

Anna held up the book so the others could see. On the page opposite the text was a pen-and-ink illustration of a sad-looking girl sitting on a rock by the sea. The illustration echoed the famous small statue that Fabel had himself seen when visiting Copenhagen.

'The Little Mermaid? Hans Christian Andersen?' Fabel's tone sounded unconvinced, although there was a chorus of approval from around the table. He looked at the picture again. It was an icon. The legs folded, mermaid's-tail-like, underneath the body as she sat on the rock. It would be a gift to a serial killer seeking to pose a victim: an instantly recognisable pose. Yet the girl on the beach hadn't sat on or rested against a rock. There hadn't even been a rock anywhere near her. But there was the note. There was the false identity. And there was the statement 'I have been underground.' At last he said, 'I don't know, Anna. It's a possibility. But so much doesn't fit. Can we keep looking?'

Each member of the team took a volume and flicked through it. Fabel selected the Andersen tales and speed read 'The Little Mermaid'. He thought back to the dead girl, her azure gaze. Lying, waiting to be found, by the water's edge. Anna had a copy of *Grimms' Household and Children's Fairy Tales*, while Susanne scanned through *German Legends*. Suddenly, Susanne looked up as if stung.

'You are wrong, Frau Kriminalkommissarin,' she said to Anna. 'Our killer is using the Brothers Grimm as his literary reference, not Andersen, nor Perrault. Our dead girl isn't meant to be The Little Mermaid . . . she's meant to be a Changeling.'

Fabel felt an electric tingle on his skin. 'Go on . . .'

'There's a story here recorded by the Grimms, called "The Changeling" and another called "The Two Underground Women".' The current across Fabel's skin was turned up a notch. 'According to the notes that accompany these tales, there was a whole system of belief about how children – specifically unbaptised children – were abducted by 'the underground people,' who would leave changelings in their stead. But listen to this – these 'underground people' would often use water as their medium of transport, and many of these tales relate to changelings being left on the banks of the Elbe and Saale rivers . . .'

'And Blankenese is on the shore of the Elbe,' said Fabel. 'What's more, we have a direct mention in the note left in the girl's hand of "underground people", as well as the girl being left there with the identity of another missing girl. A Changeling.'

Werner let out a breath. 'My God, that's all we need. A literary psycho-killer. Do you think he intends to stage a killing based on each of the Grimms' fairy tales?'

'We'd better pray that he doesn't,' said Susanne. 'According to the contents page of this version, the Grimms gathered more than two hundred stories.'

CHAPTER 18

5.10 p.m., Monday, 22 March:
Institut für Rechtsmedizin,
Eppendorf, Hamburg

Möller was tall; taller than Fabel, and slim-framed. His hair was a pale butter-yellow flecked with ivory and his features were thin and angular. Fabel always felt Möller was one of those people whose appearance changed according to whatever style of clothes they happened to be wearing when you saw them: Möller had a face that could belong to a North Sea fisherman or to an aristocrat, depending on his outfit. As if aware of this fact, and to maintain an image in keeping with his imperious nature, Möller habitually adopted the style of an English gentleman. When Fabel walked into the pathologist's office, Möller was putting on a green corduroy jacket over his Jermyn Street shirt. When he stepped round from behind his desk, Fabel half expected to see him wearing those green rubber boots that the British royal family seemed to prefer to Gucci.

'What do you want, Fabel?' Möller asked charmlessly. 'I'm going home now. *Feierabend*. Whatever it is it can wait until tomorrow.'

Fabel remained silent and stood in the doorway. Möller sighed, but did not sit down again. 'All right. What is it?'

'You've done the post-mortem on the girl found on Blankenese Elbstrand?'

Möller nodded curtly, flipped open a file on his desk and pulled out a report. 'I was going to give you this tomorrow. Happy reading.' He gave a tired, impatient smile and slapped the report into Fabel's chest as he made his way to the door. Fabel still didn't move from the doorway but attempted a disarming grin.

'Please, Herr Doktor. Just the main points.'

Möller sighed. 'As I've already informed Kriminaloberkommissar Meyer, the cause of death was by asphyxiation. There was evidence of small blood-vessel damage around the nose and mouth, as well as the ligature marks around the neck. It would appear that she was strangled and smothered simultaneously. There were no signs of sexual trauma or any form of sexual activity in the forty-eight hours prior to death. Although she has been sexually active.'

'Sexual abuse?'

'Nothing to suggest anything other than normal sexual activity. There was no evidence of the type of internal scarring indicative of early sexual abuse. The only other fact revealed by the autopsy is that her teeth were in a bad way. Again I explained this to Herr Meyer. She hadn't seen a dentist much, and when she did, it was obviously for emergency treatment when she was in pain. There was extensive caries, gum erosion and a lower left molar had been extracted. There were also two ancient fractures. One on the right wrist and the other in the left hand. They had been left to heal themselves. They would be consistent not only with neglect, but active abuse. The wrist fracture is consistent with it having been severely twisted.'

'Werner told me that she hadn't eaten much in the two days before her death.'

Möller snatched the report back from Fabel and flicked through the pages. 'Certainly not in the previous twenty-four hours, other than some rye bread consumed an hour or two before death.'

For a moment, Fabel was somewhere else: in a dark, frightening place with a young girl fearfully eating her last, insubstantial meal. He knew no detail about this girl's life, but he did know that it had been as unhappy as it was short. Möller handed him back the report, raised his eyebrows and nodded towards the door.

'Oh, sorry, Herr Doktor.' Fabel moved to one side. 'Thanks. Thank you very much.'

Fabel didn't head back to the Mordkommission. Instead he drove home, parking his BMW in the underground space reserved for his apartment. He still couldn't get the girl's blue eyes out of his mind. More than the horror of the second murder scene, it was the almost alive gaze of the girl on the Blankenese shore that haunted him. The Changeling. The unwanted and false child substituted for the loved and true one. Again, he imagined her final hours: the frugal meal that she had consumed, more than likely served to her by her killer; then she had been strangled and smothered. It made Fabel think of the ancient sacrifices that would turn up every so often in the peat bogs of Northern Germany and Denmark: bodies preserved for three millennia or more in the dark, thick, damp soil. Many of them had been garrotted or deliberately drowned. Even those bodies whose accoutrements suggested high rank revealed they had been fed a meagre final, ritual meal of grain gruel. What had this girl been sacrificed to? There was no evidence of a sexual motive, so what was it that she'd had to surrender her life for? Had it been that she had had to die simply because she looked so much like another girl, also most likely dead?

Fabel let himself into his apartment. Susanne was working late at the Institut and wouldn't be over till later. He had brought home the books from Otto's shop and set them down on the coffee table. He poured himself a glass of crisp white wine and slumped on to the leather sofa. Fabel's apartment was in the attic of what had once been a grand and solid villa. It was situated in the trendy Pöseldorf part of the Rotherbaum district of the city. He could step out of the front door and within a minute's walk he would be amongst some of the best restaurants and cafés in Hamburg. Fabel had stretched himself to afford this apartment, sacrificing space for a fantastic view and a great location. He had also bought it at a time when the economy had been shaky and property prices in the city had dropped: he had often reflected bitterly that the German economy and his marriage had slumped at the same time. Fabel knew he could never have afforded a place like this now, even on his Erster Kriminalhauptkommissar's salary. The apartment was a block back from the Milchstrasse, and the floor-to-ceiling picture windows looked over Magdalenen Strasse, the Alsterpark and the vast lake of the Aussenalster. He gazed out of the window at the city and the vastness of the sky. Hamburg lay spread out before him. A dark forest in which a million souls could become lost.

Fabel phoned his mother. She said she was well and complained about the continual fussing, and told him that she was getting worried that Lex was losing business by staying with her instead of getting back to his restaurant on Sylt. Again Fabel felt reassured by his mother's voice on the phone. An ageless voice that he could separate from the whitening hair and the reducing briskness of movement. As soon as he rang off from talking with his mother, he called Gabi. Renate, Fabel's ex-wife, answered the phone. Her tone, as always, lay somewhere between disinterest and hostility. Fabel had never quite understood why Renate was habitually like this with him. It was as if she held him responsible for her having an affair which blew their marriage into irreparable pieces. Gabi's voice, on the other hand was, as usual, full of light. They chatted for a while about Fabel's mother, about Gabi's school work and their forthcoming weekend together.

After a while, Fabel asked: 'Do you remember when I used to read you bedtime stories?'

'Yes, I do, *Papi*. Don't tell me you're going to tuck me up with warm milk and read me *Struwwelpeter* when I come to stay.'

Fabel laughed. 'No . . . No, I won't. Do you remember you would never let me read you any Brothers Grimm stories? Even "Snow White" or "Sleeping Beauty"?'

'I remember, all right. I hated those stories.'

'Why?'

'I don't know, really. They were scary. No . . . creepy. It was like they were supposed to be for children but they were really for grown-ups. It's kind of like clowns, you know? They're supposed to be funny and friendly, but they're not. They're dark. Old dark . . . like those carved wooden faces they wear down in the South for Fasching. You can tell that these things are to do with all kinds of old stuff that people really used to believe at one time. Why do you ask?'

'Oh, nothing. Just something that came up

today.' Fabel steered the conversation back to family matters and arrangements for the weekend. He had gone as far as he ever would in bringing the shadow of his work into his relationship with his daughter. After he had hung up, he made himself some pasta, poured some more wine, and sat down to read, while he ate, the introduction to Gerhard Weiss's book.

Germany is the heart of Europe and the Märchenstrasse is the soul of Germany. The Märchenstrasse is the history of Germany. The Märchenstrasse is Germany.

Our language, our culture, our achievements and our failures, our grace and our wickedness: all these things are to be found on the Fairy Tale Road. It was always so and it always will be so. We are the children lost in the woods with only our innocence to guide us; but we have also been the wolves who prey on the weak. More than anything, we Germans have aspired to greatness: great good and great evil. These are the turns and twists we have always taken and the German folk tale is a tale of purity and corruption, of innocence and guile.

This tale is a tale of a great man. A man who helped us understand ourselves and our language. This tale, for tale is all it is, follows this great man down the Märchenstrasse, along the path he truly took; but it also asks the question: What if he strayed from the path and into the darkness of the forest?

Fabel flicked through the pages. The book was a fictionalised Reisetagebuch – the travelling diary of Jacob Grimm as he toured Germany in search of fairy tales to collect. Grimm was portrayed as a fastidious pedant who applied the same attention to detail to the murders he committed as he did to his work as a philologist and folklorist. Then Fabel came to a chapter that made him put down his wineglass. It was titled *The Changeling*.

The tale of **The Changeling** is a cautionary one; it is also one of our most ancient. It not only articulates that greatest of fears, to lose one's child, but also the horror of having something false, malevolent and pernicious inveigled into the family and home. Moreover, it cautions parents that they shall be punished for any lack of vigilance in their care of their charges. **The Changeling** tale has appeared in countless forms, throughout Germany, the Low Lands, Denmark, Bohemia, Poland and beyond. Even Martin Luther had an unshakeable belief in Changelings and wrote several treatises on how to scald, drown or beat them until the devil came to call them back unto him.

I shirk not from hard work, but this has

been the most challenging tale to re-establish as a living truth. As with each of the tales I have re-enacted, I first busied myself assiduously and enthusiastically with the preparations. For this tale, I needed to find two children: one to play the part of the Changeling while the other had to be a true child that I could steal from its mother.

My brother's and my researches had brought us to the North of Germany and we had found modest lodgings in a village near the Baltic coast. Lately, whilst in the village, I had observed a young woman with a florid complexion and flaxen hair who exemplified the robust, honest and earnest stupidity of the Northern German peasant. This woman bore with her a newborn child which she carried first in one arm, and then in the other. I knew, from the work of other eminent folklorists, and from my own research, that this habit of changing arms was known as carrying the baby 'on the switch'. From the Rhineland and Hessen to Mecklenburg and Lower Saxony, it is a widely held superstition that carrying a baby 'on the switch' greatly increases the chances of its abduction by the Underground People. I guessed that this child was yet be baptised, and less than six weeks old, which is known to be the preference of the abductors. Moreover, neither this peasant woman nor her family had heeded the four precautions to protect a newborn from the Underground People. I have, of course, enumerated these in my volume **Deutsche Mythologie**, namely: place a key next to the infant; never leave women alone in the six weeks after giving birth for they are easily swayed by the devil; allow not the mother to sleep during the first six weeks unless someone has come to keep vigil over the child; whenever the mother leaves the room, an article of the father's clothing, particularly his breeches, should be lain across the child.

The mother having taken none of these precautions, this then would be the 'true' child of the tale and would illustrate most perfectly the abiding truth of the legend and remind the people of this area of the folly of ignoring ancient prohibitions. This child's abduction presented itself as the comparatively easy part of the plan. I had most closely observed the woman's routine and had taken detailed notes. I had established that there was a time, immediately before midday, when the babe was left to sleep in the open air while its mother busied herself with household chores. I knew that this was when I could make the substitution. Once stolen away, I would, of course, have no further need of the 'true' child and would do away with it swiftly. In its place I would leave a changeling child; this would be more difficult to achieve. Changeling children are known to be coarser than those whose place they have usurped. This is in keeping with them being the progeny of the Underground People, a race so inferior to true mankind and so ugly to behold that they conceal themselves underground, in the night or in the darkest shadows of the forest.

I pondered this problem for some days until I heard talk of some gypsy folk who had camped close to the village. I knew that the hostility felt towards these people by the villagers would mean that the gypsies dared not venture into the village itself. If, therefore, my plan did not succeed and the villagers did not look to their ancient belief in the Underground People to account for the abduction and substitution, then they would look no further than the gypsies camped nearby. Indeed, I am uncertain if this would, in fact, be a failure to recreate the tale as I recorded it, for I have, in the course of my researches, often wondered if it was, indeed, gypsies and other itinerants who had inspired tales of the Underground People. The mistrust and hostility we instinctively feel towards the foreign and the strange is something I have always held to be a potential tool for manipulation. In this case, ignorant prejudice furnished me with a protection from suspicion.

I therefore set about a plan to steal away a child, should there be one of a suitable age, from the gypsy encampment . . .

Fabel put down the book, still open at the page, on to the coffee table. He felt as if the temperature of the room had dropped a couple of degrees: a malevolent chill that seemed to spring from the open book before him. Here, described in a fictional account, was a plan to abduct and murder based on the Grimms' recording of *The Changeling* folk tale. The painstaking approach that the fictional Jacob Grimm had taken was reflected in the planning and preparation of this all too real present-day killer. He thought again of the girl on the beach. A too-young life snuffed out to fulfil some twisted fantasy.

He was jolted back to the here and now by the ringing of his phone.

'Hi, *Chef* . . . It's Anna here. I've got an identity for the girl on the beach. And this time I think it's the real one.'

CHAPTER 19

9.45 p.m., Monday, 22 March:
Polizeipräsidium, Hamburg

'Blue Eyes' now had a name: Martha.

After the last debacle, Anna Wolff had done nothing about contacting the parents yet. She had, however, secured from the Bundeskriminalamt a photograph of a girl who had been missing since the previous Tuesday: Martha Schmidt, from Kassel, in Hessen. Fabel stared at the photograph Anna had handed him: it was a blow up of a photo-booth image. There was no doubt. This time the photograph didn't set alarm bells ringing in Fabel's mind; instead it filled him with a profound sadness.

Anna Wolff stood next to Fabel. Her large brown eyes lacked their usual sparkle and she looked pale and drawn. Fabel guessed she must have been working almost non-stop until she had uncovered the girl's identity. When she spoke, her voice dragged with a leaden tiredness. 'She was reported missing on the Tuesday, but was probably taken before then.'

Fabel's expression shaped a question.

'The parents are both drug users,' explained Anna. 'Martha had a habit of disappearing for days on end and then turning up. The Hessen police didn't give this last disappearance immediate priority. Both parents have already been reported twice for neglecting Martha, but I get the feeling that the father is hardly ever there now.'

Fabel drew a deep breath and read through the file notes faxed up from Kassel. The parents were junkies and committed petty theft to support their habit; the mother had been known to resort to prostitution. The German underclass: 'underground people'. And from Kassel: for many years home to the Brothers Grimm. Kassel, a normally unremarkable, quiet city, had recently been in the news because of the 'Rotenburg Cannibal' case that had shocked a Germany that had believed itself unshockable. Armin Meiwes had been convicted of assisting in the suicide of Bernd Brandes, who had volunteered to be eaten. Meiwes had videotaped the whole event: amputating Brandes's penis, sitting down together with him to eat the dismembered organ, then drugging him, stabbing him to death and butchering him into cuts of meat which he froze. Before his arrest, Meiwes had consumed nearly twenty kilos of his victim – if Brandes could be described as a victim. He had been a more than willing volunteer, one of many who had applied to Meiwes to be eaten. They had met through a gay cannibal website.

A gay cannibal website. Sometimes, despite the nature of his work, Fabel found it almost impossible to come to terms with the world that had suddenly formed around him. Every kind of sick desire and appetite seemed to have a place to feed. And now there was a new grim tale to be associated with Kassel.

'You'd better get the parents, or at least the mother, up to make an identification,' said Fabel.

'I've been in touch with Martha's social services caseworker,' said Anna. 'She's going to break the news to her parents, if they care, and then get one of them up for a formal ID.'

'I suppose that's why she didn't emerge until now. I'm guessing that she didn't see much of school.' Fabel looked at the photograph again; at the face he had gazed into on the beach at Blankenese. In the photograph, Martha was smiling but the eyes still looked sad; too old and experienced for her sixteen years. A girl much the same age as his own daughter, yet who looked out on to the world through those bright azure eyes and saw too much. 'Any idea of exactly when and where she disappeared?'

'No. Like I said, sometime between nine p.m. on the Sunday and . . . well, when she was reported on the Tuesday, I suppose. Do you want me to go down there . . . to Kassel, I mean, and start asking around?'

'No.' Fabel rubbed his eyes with the heels of his hands. 'Leave that to the Hessen police, at least for the moment. There's nothing of any worth to be found down there, unless the local boys get a witness to her being taken. But get them to check out anyone Martha had contact with who has a Hamburg connection. My guess is that our killer is from here – from Hamburg or close by – and that he has no direct connection with Martha Schmidt or anyone to do with her. But get as much detail from them on her final movements as possible.' He smiled at his subordinate. 'Go home, Anna, and get some sleep. We'll pick this up in the morning.'

Anna nodded dully and left. Fabel sat on at his desk, took out his sketch pad and scored out the name 'Blue Eyes' and replaced it with 'Martha Schmidt'. On his way out, he pinned the photograph on to the incident board in the conference room.

CHAPTER 20

11.10 a.m., Tuesday, 23 March:
Institut für Rechtsmedizin,
Eppendorf, Hamburg

The father was clearly no longer part of the picture.

Ulrike Schmidt was a small woman who looked as if she were well into her forties but Fabel knew, from the information supplied by the Kassel police, that she was only in her mid-thirties. She had probably been pretty once, but she now wore the hard-faced weariness of the habitual drug user. The blue of her eyes lacked any lustre and the shadows beneath them had a jaundiced tinge. Her hair was lifeless blonde and she had scraped it back from her face, gathering it into a hasty ponytail; the jacket and trousers she wore had probably passed for smart until comparatively recently, but had not passed for fashionable for a decade or more. It was clear to Fabel that she had fished her outfit out from a meagre wardrobe in an attempt to dress appropriately for the occasion.

And the occasion was to identify her dead daughter.

'I came up by train . . .' she said, for the sake of saying something, as they waited for the body to be brought to the viewing room. Fabel smiled bleakly. Anna said nothing.

Before coming to the mortuary in the Institut für Rechtsmedizin, Fabel and Anna had sat with Ulrike Schmidt in the Polizeipräsidium and asked her about her daughter. Fabel remembered how he had prepared himself to delve into every corner of the life of this dead girl, this stranger to him, whom he would know intimately. But he never did get to know the girl on the beach. For a few hours she had been someone else, then she had become nobody again. As they had sat in the Mordkommission's interview room, Anna and Fabel had tried to add dimensions to the name 'Martha Schmidt': to make a dead girl live once more, in their minds. The autopsy had revealed that Martha had been sexually active and they had asked her mother about boyfriends, about who she was friendly with, what she did in her free time – and in the time when she should have been at school. But Ulrike Schmidt's answers had been vague, uncertain; as if she had been describing an acquaintance, someone on the periphery of her awareness, rather than her own flesh and blood: her daughter.

Now they sat in the ante-room of the state mortuary, waiting to be called to identify Martha's body. And all Ulrike Schmidt's conversation revolved around was her journey. 'Then I took the U-Bahn from the Hauptbahnhof,' she said, dully.

When they were called forward and the sheet was folded back from the face of the body on the trolley, Ulrike Schmidt looked down on it without expression. For a moment, Fabel felt a small panic rise in his chest as he wondered if this was going to be another failed identification of the 'Changeling' body. Then Ulrike Schmidt nodded.

'Yes . . . yes, that's my Martha.' No tears. No sobbing. She stared emptily at the face on the trolley and her hand moved towards it, towards the cheek, but checked itself and fell limply to her side.

'Are you sure this is your daughter?' There was an edge to Anna's voice and Fabel fired a warning look in her direction.

'Yes. That's Martha.' Ulrike Schmidt didn't look up from the face of her daughter. 'She was a good girl. A really good girl. She looked after things. After herself.'

'The day she went missing,' said Anna, 'did anything unusual happen? Or did you see anyone unusual hanging about?'

Ulrike Schmidt shook her head. She turned to Anna for a moment, her eyes dull and dead. 'The police already asked me that. I mean the police at home, in Kassel.' She turned back to the dead girl on the trolley. The girl who died because she looked like someone else. 'I told them. About that day . . . that I was having a bad day. I was kind of out of it. Martha went out, I think.'

Anna stared at Ulrike Schmidt's profile. Hard. Schmidt was oblivious to Anna's silent reproach.

'We'll be able to release the body to you soon, Frau Schmidt,' said Fabel. 'I take it that you would like to make arrangements for her to be taken to Kassel for her funeral?'

'What's the point? Dead is dead. She doesn't care. It doesn't matter to her now.' Ulrike Schmidt turned to Fabel. Her eyes were red-rimmed, but not from grief. 'Is there somewhere nice here?'

Fabel nodded.

'Don't you want to be able to visit her?' A sharp, bitter incredulity edged Anna's voice. 'To visit her grave?'

Ulrike Schmidt shook her head. 'I wasn't meant to be a mother. I was a lousy mother when she was alive, I don't see how I'll be a better one now she's dead. She deserved better.'

'Yes,' said Anna. 'I rather think she did.'

'Anna!' Fabel snapped, but Ulrike Schmidt was either ignoring Anna's reproach or thought it fair comment. She stared at Martha's body for a silent moment, then turned to Fabel.

'Is there anything I have to sign?' she asked.

After Ulrike Schmidt left to catch the train home, Fabel and Anna walked out of the Institut für Rechtsmedizin and into the day. A milky sheet of cloud diffused the sun into a soft-edged brightness and Fabel put on his sunglasses. He rested his hands on his hips and looked up, squinting at the sky; he turned to Anna.

'Don't do that again, Kommissarin Wolff. Whatever you think of the likes of Frau Schmidt, you cannot voice your opinions like that. Everyone grieves in a different way.'

Anna snorted. 'She wasn't grieving at all. Just a smack-head waiting for her next fix. She doesn't even care what happens to her daughter's body.'

'It's not our place to judge, Anna. Unfortunately it's all part of being a Mordkommission officer. We don't just deal with death, but the aftermath of death too. Its consequences. And sometimes that means being diplomatic. Biting our tongues. If you can't handle that then you have no place here. Do I make myself clear?'

'Yes, *Chef.*' She rubbed her scalp frustratedly through the short black hair. 'It's just . . . it's just that she's supposed to be a mother, for God's sake. There's supposed to be some kind of . . . I don't know . . . *instinct* at work there. To protect your kids. To *care* about them.'

'It doesn't always work that way.'

'She let this happen to Martha.' Anna's tone was defiant. 'She obviously knocked her about when she was a kid . . . there's the twist fracture to the wrist from when Martha was about five and God knows what else in the meantime. But, worse than that, she let that poor girl fend for herself in a dangerous bloody world. The result is that she was taken by a maniac, spent God knows how long terrified witless and then she's killed. And that cow hasn't the heart to even give her a decent burial, let alone visit her grave.' She shook her head, as if in disbelief. 'When I think of the Ehlers, a family torn to pieces for three long years because they have no body to bury, no grave to grieve over . . . and then that cold-hearted bitch who doesn't give a toss about what we do with her daughter's body.'

'Whatever we think of her, Anna, she's the mother of a murdered child. She didn't kill Martha and we can't even prove that her neglect of her was a contributory factor. And that means we still have to treat her like any other grieving parent. Do I make myself clear?'

'Yes, Herr Hauptkommissar.' Anna paused. 'It said in the Kassel report that the mother was an occasional prostitute. You don't think that she swapped over to pimping for her own daughter? I mean, we know that Martha had sexual part-ners.'

'I doubt it. From what I can see from the report it was just, as you said, an occasional thing to feed a habit when necessary. I doubt that Frau Schmidt would be organised enough for anything else. Anyway, you heard the way she spoke about Martha. It clearly wasn't a close relationship and I get the feeling mother and daughter went their own ways. Did their own thing, as it were.'

'Maybe Martha was the organised one,' said Anna. 'Maybe she was in business for herself.'

'I doubt it. There's no suggestion of that in any of the police or social services reports. She had no habit to support. No. I just think that she was trying to be as normal a teenager as her family background would allow.' Fabel fell silent for a moment, thinking about his own daughter, Gabi, and how much Martha Schmidt had reminded him of her. Three girls of roughly the same age, who looked like each other: Martha Schmidt, Paula Ehlers, and Gabi. Some part deep within him shuddered at the thought. A universe of unlimited possibilities. 'Let's get back to the Präsidium . . . I've got a bakery to visit.'

CHAPTER 21

2.10 p.m., Tuesday, 23 March:
Bostelbek, Heimfeld, South Hamburg

The weather had taken a turn for the worse. The previous week's promise of spring, which had stretched into the bright morning, now faded in the cheerless, blustery sky that crowded down on North Germany. Fabel wasn't sure why – perhaps because he knew it was a long-standing family business and because he always associated bakeries with a traditional craft – but he was surprised to find that the Backstube Albertus was a large industrial unit situated close to the A7 autobahn. 'For ease of distribution . . .' Vera Schiller had explained, as she conducted Fabel and Werner into her office. 'We deliver to Konditoreien, cafés and restaurants throughout northern and central Germany. We have built up excellent relationships with our customers and often have senior staff deliver important items personally. Of course, we have our own delivery department – we have three vans almost continuously on the road.' Fabel could tell that they were being treated to the standard speech that Vera Schiller would make to any visitors to the premises. It was clearly tailored more for potential customers than for murder detectives.

Her office was large, but functional rather than plush: a very different environment from the classical elegance of the Schiller villa. As Frau Schiller took her place and invited Fabel and Werner to sit down, Werner gave his boss a covert nudge with his elbow and cast his gaze towards a second desk, at the far side of the office. No one sat at the desk but it was piled with papers and brochures. A wall planner behind it laid out dates and places. Fabel was a sliver of a second too slow in turning back to face Vera Schiller.

'Yes, Herr Kriminalhauptkommissar,' she said, 'that is Markus's desk. Please feel free to . . .' she considered the word for a moment, '. . . to *examine* anything. I'll also take you down to meet Herr Biedermeyer, our Chief Baker. He can tell you more about the other victim.'

'Thank you, Frau Schiller. We appreciate your cooperation.' Fabel was about to say again that it must all be very distressing for her, but somehow he felt it was redundant. No, not redundant, inappropriate. This wasn't distressing for her: it was inconvenient. He examined her face. There was no hint of anything underlying the superficial calm. There was no suggestion of recently shed tears nor of lack of sleep. And there had been no malice in her reference to Hanna Grünn as 'the other victim'. It was simply an appropriate description. Vera Schiller's coldness was more than a surface frost: it was a thoroughgoing sterility that bound her heart in ice. Fabel had met her twice: once in the home she had shared with her husband and now in the office she had shared with her husband. Yet, less than forty-eight hours after she had found out that her spouse was dead, there was no sense of the 'incompleteness' Anna Wolff had described when talking about visiting a victim's home.

It took a lot to unnerve Fabel, but Vera Schiller was one of the scariest people he had ever encountered.

'Is there anyone you can think of who would have wished your husband harm, Frau Schiller?'

She laughed and the immaculately lipsticked lips drew back from the perfect teeth in something that couldn't be described as a smile. 'Not specifically, Herr Kriminalhauptkommissar. Not anyone to whom I could put a name, but in the abstract, yes. There must be a dozen cuckolded husbands and boyfriends out there who would have wished Markus harm.'

'Did Hanna Grünn have a boyfriend?' asked Werner. Frau Schiller turned to him. The smile that wasn't a smile faded.

'I'm not familiar with the personal lives of my employees, Herr Kriminaloberkommissar Meyer.' She stood up and, as with all her movements, she did so brusquely. 'I'll take you down to the bakery floor. As I explained before, Herr Biedermeyer will be able to furnish you with more specific details about the girl who was killed.'

The main hall of the bakery was divided into what looked like small conveyor-belt systems upon which different products were being assembled or prepared. The air itself seemed doughy, thick with the fragrances of flour and baking. Both walls were lined with huge brushed-steel ovens and the staff were dressed in white coats and protective caps and hairnets. If it hadn't been for the nearly edible air, it could have been a semiconductor factory or some 1960s movie vision of a futuristic mission control. Again the reality jarred with Fabel's image of a traditional German bakery.

Vera Schiller led the way down to the factory floor and took them to a very tall powerfully built man whom she introduced as Franz Biedermeyer, the Chief Baker. She turned on her heel before Fabel had had a chance to thank her. There was a moment of embarrassed silence before Biedermeyer smiled amiably and said, 'Please excuse Frau Schiller. I suspect she is finding this very difficult.'

'She seems to be coping rather well,' said Fabel, trying to keep any hint of sarcasm from his voice.

'It is her manner, Herr Fabel. She is a good employer and treats her staff very well indeed. And I cannot imagine that she is taking her loss anything other than really badly. Herr and Frau

Schiller were a very effective, even formidable partnership. In business, at any rate.'

'And personally?' asked Werner.

Again the Chief Baker smiled amiably, this time shrugging. There was something about the wrinkles around Biedermeyer's eyes that suggested that he smiled a great deal. It reminded Fabel of his own brother, Lex, whose mischievous personality always revealed itself in and around his eyes. 'I really don't know anything of their personal relationship. But they were a good working team. Frau Schiller is an astute businesswoman and knows all about commercial strategy. She has kept this bakery highly profitable during what has been a bad time for German business generally. And Herr Schiller was a very, very good salesman. He had a great way with the customers.'

'I gather he had a great way with women, as well,' added Fabel.

'There were rumours . . . I can't deny that. But, as I said, it's not my place to speculate on such things and your guess is as good as mine as to how much Frau Schiller was aware of and how it affected their marriage – excuse me . . .' As they had approached him, Biedermeyer had been decorating a cake and was holding a small, intricate icing detail between his massive forefinger and thumb, and he now turned to lay it down carefully on the burnished stainless-steel counter. Fabel noticed that, obviously to meet hygiene regulations, Biedermeyer wore white latex gloves which were coated with a fine dusting of flour. His hands looked too big and the fingers too clumsy for Fabel to imagine the Chief Baker carrying out any delicate cake decoration or fancy pastry work.

'And his relationship with Hanna Grünn?' asked Werner. 'Were you aware of that?'

'No. But it doesn't surprise me. I knew that Hanna was – how can I put this – a little *indiscreet* in her choice of boyfriends. Again, there were all kinds of rumours. A lot of them were malicious, of course. But I don't remember anyone suggesting that anything was going on between Hanna and Herr Schiller.'

'Malicious? You said a lot of the rumours were malicious.'

'Hanna was a very attractive young lady. You know how bitchy women can be about things like that. But Hanna didn't do herself any favours. She made it more than clear that she looked down her nose at this job and, particularly, at the other women on the production floor.'

'Did she have any particular enemies here?' Fabel indicated the production floor with a nod of his head.

'Who would hate her enough to murder her?' Biedermeyer laughed and shook his head. 'No one would have given her enough thought. She was disliked, not hated.'

'What did you think of her?' asked Fabel.

Biedermeyer's habitual smile was tinged with sadness. 'I was her supervisor. Her work was never really up to par and I would have to talk to her from time to time. But I felt sorry for her.'

'Why?'

'She was lost. I suppose that's how you would describe it. She hated working here. Being here. I think she was ambitious, but had no way of fulfilling her ambitions.'

'What about other boyfriends?' asked Werner. A young apprentice came past, pushing a two-metre-high trolley rack; each tray was covered with swirls of unbaked dough. The three men moved out of the way before Biedermeyer answered.

'Yes. I think there was one. I don't know anything about him, other than he used to pick her up sometimes on his motorbike. He looked a bad sort.' Biedermeyer paused. 'Is it true that they were found together. Herr Schiller and Fräulein Grünn, I mean?'

Fabel smiled. 'Thank you for your time, Herr Biedermeyer.'

They were out in the car park before Fabel turned to Werner and said what they had both been thinking.

'A motorbike. I think we'd better chase up forensics for a type and make for the tracks we found in the Naturpark.'

CHAPTER 22

6.30 p.m., Tuesday, 23 March:
Hauptbahnhof-Nord U-Bahn station, Hamburg

Ingrid Wallenstein hated taking the U-Bahn these days. The world had changed beyond her understanding and there were so many undesirable people about. Young people. Dangerous people. Mad people. Like the 'S-Bahn Schubser': the maniac who had been pushing people under the S-Bahn trains. The police had been looking for him for months. What kind of person would do a thing like that? And why had things changed so much in the last fifty years? God knew Frau Wallenstein and her generation had lived through enough to drive them into madness, but it hadn't. All that the post-war generations had to deal with was having everything they wanted, when they wanted it. That was why she had little time for young people: they hadn't had to experience everything Frau Wallenstein's generation had had to go through, yet they were discontented. They had become rude, careless, disrespectful. If only they had had to endure what she had endured as a child and as a young woman. The war, and the terror and destruction it had brought. Then, afterwards, the hunger, the want; everyone having to work together to rebuild, repair, to put things right again. Not today: today young people threw everything away. Nothing held any value for them. They appreciated nothing.

Since she had first heard of the 'S-Bahn Schubser', Frau Wallenstein always made sure she either sat down or stood with her back to the platform wall while she waited for a train.

Her knee hurt and she leaned heavily against her walking stick as she scanned the platform and surveyed her fellow travellers. There was only a handful of people on the U-Bahn platform, a couple of whom had those tiny headphones in their ears, with the dangly wires coming from them. Frau Wallenstein hated those things. If you sat next to one of them on the bus or the train and they were listening to that awful music of theirs, it was like having a wasp buzzing ill-temperedly next to you. Why did they do that? What was so terrible about hearing the world around you and, God forbid, actually having a conversation with someone?

She looked further up the platform. There was a youngish woman, sitting on a bench. At least she was dressed in a decent-enough-looking suit. The pain in Frau Wallenstein's knee always got worse if she stood for any period of time, so, silently cursing her arthritic joint, she sat next to the woman, and said: 'Guten Tag.' The young woman smiled back at her. Such a sad smile. Frau Wallenstein noticed that she was perhaps not as clean as she had first thought, and had a pale face with dark shadows beneath her eyes. She began to wonder if she'd made a mistake in sitting next to her.

'Are you all right, dear?' asked Frau Wallenstein. 'You don't look well.'

'I'm fine, thank you,' said the younger woman. 'I've not been well, for a long time, but it's all right now. I'll be fine now.'

'Oh,' said Frau Wallenstein, unsure what to say next and a little regretful that she had started the conversation. The young woman looked so strange. Maybe it was drugs. Frau Wallenstein was an avid viewer of *Adelheid und ihre Mörder* and *Grossstadtrevier*. They always showed people who used drugs as looking like that. But maybe the poor woman had simply been ill.

'I've been to see my little girl.' The younger woman's smile was faltering, as if it struggled to cling to the lips. 'I've been to see my little girl today.'

'Oh, that's lovely. How old is she?'

'She's sixteen, now. Yes, sixteen.' The younger woman searched her pockets and Frau Wallenstein noticed that the blouse beneath the jacket was faded and worn, and that she didn't seem to have a handbag of any kind. The woman produced a creased, dog-eared photograph. She held it out to

Frau Wallenstein: it showed a small, unremarkable toddler with the same kind of lustreless blonde hair as its mother.

'Yes,' said the pale woman. 'My little Martha. My little baby. She was always such an energetic little thing. A scamp. That's what I used to call her when she was a toddler: my little scamp . . .'

Frau Wallenstein was now decidedly uneasy, but she was worried about the young woman. She looked so forlorn. Frau Wallenstein was relieved to hear the rumble of the U-Bahn train approaching. The young woman stood up and looked down the tunnel towards the sound of the arriving train. She seemed suddenly alert. Frau Wallenstein stood up too, but more slowly, leaning heavily on her stick.

'So where is your little girl now?' she asked, more to fill the final few moments of their acquaintance until the train arrived than anything else. The young woman turned to her.

'That's where I'm going now . . . to be with my little Martha. I'm going to be a good mother now . . .' The young woman's face was animated; suddenly happy. The U-Bahn train emerged from the tunnel, still travelling fast. The younger woman smiled at Frau Wallenstein. 'Goodbye, it was so nice talking to you.'

'Goodbye dear,' said Frau Wallenstein and was about to say something else, but the younger woman had stepped forward to the edge of the platform. And she didn't stop. Frau Wallenstein stared at the space on the platform where the woman should have been standing, but she was gone.

There was a sickening, reverberating thud as the train hit the body. Then the screams of others on the platform echoed in the U-Bahn station.

Frau Wallenstein stood still, leaning on her walking stick to ease her aching arthritic knee and stared at where a young woman with whom she had been talking just a minute before had been standing.

She had thrown herself in front of the train. Why on earth had she done that? What kind of world had this become?

CHAPTER 23

1.10 p.m., Wednesday, 24 March:
Buxtehude, Lower Saxony

It took just over half an hour for Fabel and Werner to drive out to Buxtehude. The sky had brightened and now bathed the small town in a stark light, but an angry wind still snapped and tugged at Fabel's raincoat as he and Werner made their way from the car to a small restaurant on Westfleth, in Buxtehude's Altstadt. Buxtehude looked as if it were a small Dutch town that had, somehow, been shunted east until it had almost collided with Hamburg. The River Este split into the Ostviver and Westviver as it flowed through the town's Altstadt, where it was channelled into canals and spanned by a half a dozen Dutch-style bridges. Even the building the restaurant was in seemed to have shrugged up its shoulders to squeeze in between its neighbours, and Fabel guessed that it had looked out over the canals and bridges for at least two centuries.

As they had driven into the town, something else about Buxtehude had resonated with Fabel:

181

even the street names Gebrüder-Grimm-Weg, Rotkäppchenweg and Dornröschenweg – Brothers Grimm Way, Red Riding Hood Way and Sleeping Beauty Way – seemed to conspire to remind Fabel of the dark tones that lurked in the shadows of this investigation. Every time Fabel heard mention of the Brothers Grimm, he envisaged Jacob Grimm as the fictionalised character in Weiss's book: the respected and influential historical figure was being displaced by Weiss's pedantic monster. Weiss's theories seemed to be working.

They sat by the window and looked out over the Fleth Haven canal, edged by trees and white fences, and across to the Ostfleth. A small, nineteenth-century river-sail freighter was moored on display and its multicoloured pennants flapped and snapped restlessly in the stiff breeze. Fabel glanced at the menu and ordered a tuna salad and a mineral water; Werner, on the other hand, studied the entire menu before asking for the Schweineschnitzel and a pot of coffee. Fabel smiled as he thought of how, in that small act of thoroughness, Werner had so clearly illustrated the difference between them. As policemen. As people. As friends.

'I've been reading this book,' Fabel spoke to Werner but kept his gaze focused out of the window, watching the wind tease the old sailboat with memories of its Ewer fleet days, carrying tea, flour, wood along North German waterways. 'By a guy called Gerhard Weiss. It's called the

Märchenstrasse. It's all about Jacob Grimm – well, it's not actually – but it's all about murders being based on Grimm Fairy Tales.'

'Shit. There's a connection?'

Fabel turned from the window. 'I don't know. It's a bit too close for comfort, though, isn't it?'

'I would say so.' Werner put his coffee cup down and frowned. 'Why didn't you mention this earlier?'

'I only started reading it last night. And I only found out about the book by pure chance. It was away on the edge of this whole thing, but now that I've started reading it . . .'

Werner's face suggested Fabel had dropped an easy ball. 'It needs to be looked into, if you ask me. For all we know, our killer may be working his way through this book instead of the Grimm Fairy Tales, *Deutsche Sagen* and all the other stuff the Grimms put together.'

'A serial killer using a study guide?' Fabel's laugh had a bitter edge. 'I suppose it's possible.'

'Jan, you know we're going to have to check out this author guy . . .'

'Weiss.' Fabel filled the gap. He turned and looked back towards the boat. Boats like these had plied their trade on the rivers and canals since before Jacob and Wilhelm Grimm travelled Germany collecting tales, legends and myths. And before them, other boats had met here and bartered goods when those tales, legends and myths had been given voice for the first time. An ancient land. An ancient land and Europe's heart, was how Fabel's father had explained Germany to him as a child. A place where things were felt more acutely, experienced more intensely, than anywhere else. 'I will,' said Fabel eventually.

The contrast with the Schiller villa was as stark as it could be. The Grünn family lived on the outskirts of Buxtehude, in a rented apartment in a block of six. The block, the grounds around it and the Grünns' apartment itself were clean and well-kept. But when Fabel and Werner joined Herr and Frau Grünn and Hanna's eighteen-year-old sister Lena in the living room, it was as if the apartment's capacity had been exceeded.

It wasn't just the apartment that contrasted with the circumstances of Fabel's last interview: unlike with Vera Schiller, the sense of loss here was raw and immediate. Fabel couldn't help making another comparison: with the Ehlers, who had thought they had found their missing child, dead, only to find they had been the victims of a hoax of intolerable cruelty. Unlike the Ehlers, the Grünn family could at least experience the release of intense grief. They would have a body to bury.

Erik Grünn was a large, stocky man with a shock of ash-blond hair that had not been thinned by his fifty-two years. His wife Anja and his daughter both showed hints of Hanna Grünn's beauty, but in lesser proportions. All three answered the detectives' questions with a leaden politeness. It was clear that the Grünns were eager to help, but it was also clear that the interview was not going to yield much. Hanna hadn't told them a great deal about her life in Hamburg, other than that she'd been hopeful of getting a modelling contract soon. In the meantime, she had told them, she was getting on well at the Backstube Albertus and was expecting promotion soon. This, of course, Fabel knew to be false from what he had been told by Biedermeyer, Hanna's immediate boss at the bakery. It became obvious to Fabel that Hanna had kept in touch with her family, but that the contact had been limited, and she had kept a great deal of what was going on in her life to herself. Fabel had felt awkward, almost guilty, as he had explained the circumstances of Hanna's death: that she had been having an affair with her boss and that he had been the other victim. He had gauged their reactions: Frau Grünn's shock was genuine, as was the dark shame that clouded Herr Grünn's expression. Lena simply stared at the floor.

'What about other boyfriends? Was there anyone special?' As soon as Fabel asked the question, he sensed tension between the three.

'No one special.' Herr Grünn's answer was a little too quick in coming. 'Hanna had her pick. She wasn't into getting serious with anyone.'

'And what about Herr Schiller? Did Hanna ever mention her relationship with him?'

It was Frau Grünn who answered. 'Herr Fabel, I want you to know that we did not bring our daughter up to . . . to get *involved* with married men.'

'So Hanna wouldn't have discussed it with you.'

'She wouldn't have dared,' said Herr Grünn. Fabel could tell that, even in her death, Hanna had incurred her father's dark wrath. He wondered just how dark that wrath had been when Hanna was a child, and how much it had to do with her minimising contact with her family.

As they were leaving, Fabel and Werner expressed their condolences for a second time. Lena said to her parents that she would see the policemen out. Instead of saying goodbye at the door, Lena led them in silence down the communal stairs of the apartment building. She stopped in the entrance hallway and when she spoke her voice was low, almost conspiratorial.

'Mutti and Papi don't know, but Hanna had been with someone. Not her boss . . . someone before that.'

'Did he have a motorcycle?' Fabel asked. Lena looked slightly taken aback.

'Yes . . . yes, he did, as a matter of fact. You know about him?'

'What is his name, Lena?'

'Olsen. Peter Olsen. He lives in Wilhelmsburg. He's a motorcycle mechanic. I think he has his own business.' Lena's pale blue eyes clouded. 'Hanna liked her men to have money to spend on her. But I got the impression that Peter was a temporary thing. Money was Hanna's thing. Oily hands weren't.'

'Did you ever meet him?'

Lena shook her head. 'But she told me about him on the phone. Friday nights are when Mutti and Papi go out. She would phone then and tell me all kinds of things.'

'Did she mention Markus Schiller at all?' asked Werner. 'Or his wife, Vera Schiller?'

There was a sound in the stairwell, like a door opening, and Lena cast an anxious look upwards. 'No. No, I can't say she did. Not directly. Hanna told me she had found someone new – but she wouldn't tell me any more than that. It never occurred to me it might be her boss. But I did know she was worried about Peter finding out. I'm sorry, I've told you everything I know. I just thought you ought to know about Peter.'

'Thank you, Lena.' Fabel smiled at her. She was a pretty, bright eighteen-year-old who would now go through the rest of her life carrying the scars of this experience within her. Deep, unseen, but always there. 'You really have been very helpful.'

Lena was about to head back towards the stair when she checked herself. 'There is one other thing, Herr Hauptkommissar. I think Peter was violent. I think that's why she was worried about him finding out.'

CHAPTER 24

10.10 a.m., Thursday, 25 March:
Wilhelmsburg, Hamburg

Tracking down Olsen had not been difficult. He didn't have much of a record, but
what he did have suggested someone who
was quick to resolve problems with his fists. He
had three recorded convictions for assault, as well
as having been cautioned on a trading offence: he
had sold on parts that came from a stolen motorcycle.

Wilhelmsburg is Hamburg's biggest Stadtteil –
its largest city division. It is effectively an island in
the Elbe, Europe's largest river island, and it bris-
tles with bridges, including the Köhlbrandbrücke,
which connect it to the main city to the north and
Harburg to the south. Wilhelmsburg has a strange,
undecided look to it, a combination of the rural
and the heavy industrial: sheep graze in fields next
to hulking industrial sheds. Wilhelmsburg also has
a rough reputation often jokingly referred to as
Hamburg's Bronx, and more than a third of its
population is immigrant in origin.

Peter Olsen sold and repaired motorcycles from a battered industrial unit down on the riverside in the shadow of the oil refinery. Fabel decided to take both Werner and Anna with him when he went to question Olsen, and asked for a uniformed Schutzpolizei unit to join them. They hadn't enough evidence to arrest him, but Fabel had managed to get a warrant from the Staatsanwaltschaft state prosecutor's office to seize his motorcycle for forensic examination.

Fabel pulled up at the overgrown kerb next to the two-metre-high mesh fence that ringed Olsen's workshop. As they waited for the SchuPo unit to arrive, Fabel surveyed the workshop and yard. The skeletons of four or five motorcycles lay tangled and rusting and a vast Rottweiler dog lay on its side in the yard, occasionally raising its massive head to cast an indolent glance around its domain. Fabel couldn't see if the dog was tethered or not.

'Werner, get on to the Wilhelmsburg Polizeirevier,' Fabel said, still scanning Olsen's premises. 'See if they can provide a dog handler. I don't like the look of Olsen's pet.' A green and white marked police van pulled up behind them. It was as if Olsen's guard dog was trained to respond to police vehicles, because as soon as the van arrived, the dog leapt to its feet and started to bellow deep, loud barks in its direction. A large man, dressed in overalls, emerged from the workshop, wiping his hands on a cloth. He was massively built, with huge shoulders into which the neckless head seemed to have been rammed: he was the human equivalent of the Rottweiler that guarded his yard. The man stared hard at the dog and muttered something, then looked across towards the police vehicles before turning and going back into the workshop.

'Forget the dog handler, Werner,' said Fabel. 'We'd better go and chat to our chum now.'

As they approached the gate it became clear that the dog wasn't tethered. It bounded towards the approaching group of policemen with a speed and agility that belied its bulk. Fabel noted with relief that the gate was chained closed and padlocked. The Rottweiler snarled and barked viciously, the white teeth flashing. Olsen appeared again at the door of the workshop.

'What do you want?' His voice was barely audible at such a distance and over the continuing barking of the Rottweiler.

'We have a warrant, Herr Olsen,' said Fabel, holding up the document so that Olsen could see. 'And we'd like to ask you a few questions.' The dog was now leaping up at the gate, making it rattle and strain against the chain and padlock. 'Would you please call off your dog, Herr Olsen? We need to ask you some questions.'

Olsen made a dismissive gesture and made to turn back into the doorway. Fabel nodded to Werner, who drew his pistol, snapped back its carriage and took aim at the Rottweiler's head.

Olsen called out 'Adolf!' sharply and the dog

obediently returned to where it had been lying, but remained on its feet, alert.

Anna cast a glance at Fabel. '*Adolf?*'

Fabel nodded to Werner, who responded by reholstering his gun. Olsen came up to the gate with a bunch of keys and unlocked the padlock. He swung open the gate and stood, sullenly, to one side.

'Would you tether your dog, please, Herr Olsen?' Fabel handed him a copy of the warrant. 'And could we see your motorcycle, please? Your own machine. The index number is on the warrant.'

Olsen jerked his head in the direction of the workshop. 'It's over here. Forget about the dog. He won't hurt anyone – unless I tell him to, that is.'

They made their way across to the building. Adolf watched them from his station, where Olsen had secured with a sturdy chain. The dog's posture was tense, and it turned its gaze from the police officers to Olsen and back again, as if waiting for the order to attack.

The interior of the workshop was surprisingly tidy and bright. Rammstein or something similar roared coarsely from a CD player. Olsen turned the volume down but not off, as if to indicate that this was only a temporary interruption to his day. Fabel had expected the walls to be covered with the usual soft-core or even hard-core posters; instead the images were either aesthetic shots of motorcycles or technical illustrations. There was a row of motorbikes at the far end, a couple of which were clearly classics. The workshop had a concrete floor that Olsen obviously swept regularly and there was shelving along one wall on which parts were arranged in red plastic trays and boxes, each of which was neatly tagged. Fabel took a long look at Olsen. He was a big man in his late twenties, and would almost have been handsome had his features not been just that little bit too big and coarse. Added to that, he had bad, mottled skin. Fabel found the methodical ordering and labelling of parts at odds with Olsen's brutish appearance. He leaned closer to the parts store and peered at the labels.

'You looking for something special?' Olsen's voice was flat. He had clearly decided to be co-operative, but indifferent. 'I thought you wanted to see my motorcycle?'

'Yes . . .' Fabel moved away from the stores rack. The writing on the labels was small and neat, but Fabel couldn't have said whether it was the same as the tiny handwriting on the notes left with the bodies. 'Yes, please.'

A large American motorcycle sat in the centre of the workshop, supported on a stand. Several parts had been removed from the engine and laid out on the floor. Again, Fabel sensed order and care in the way they had been placed on the concrete. Olsen had obviously been working on this bike when they'd arrived.

'No, not that one. Over here.' Olsen indicated

192

a silver and grey BMW motorcycle. Fabel knew nothing about motorbikes but noted that the model was an R1100S. He had to admit there was a beauty to it: a sleek, elegant menace that made it look fast even when standing dormant – in an odd way it reminded Fabel of Olsen's guard dog: full of pent-up power, even violence, aching to be released. He nodded to the two uniformed officers who pushed the bike from its space and out towards the waiting van.

'What do you want it for?' asked Olsen. Fabel ignored the question.

'You know about Hanna Grünn? I take it you've heard?'

Olsen nodded. 'Yeah, I heard.' He feigned as much disinterest as he could muster.

'You don't seem particularly upset, Herr Olsen,' Anna Wolff said. 'I mean, I thought you were her boyfriend.'

Olsen spurted a laugh and did nothing to keep the raw bitterness from it. 'Boyfriend? Not me. I was just a mug. One of Hanna's many mugs. She dumped me months ago.'

'Not according to the people who worked with her. They say you picked her up there on your motorcycle. Until quite recently.'

'Maybe I did. She was the user. I was the used. What can I say?'

Fabel could see that Olsen clearly visited a gym regularly: there was great power in the shoulders and arms that bulged against the fabric of his overalls. It was not hard to imagine Olsen over-powering the smaller, slighter Schiller and killing him with two strokes of a sharp knife.

'Where were you, Herr Olsen,' asked Anna, 'on Friday evening? The nineteenth – right up until Saturday morning?'

Olsen shrugged. You're overdoing the disinterested thing, thought Fabel. You've got something to hide. 'I went out for a drink. In Wilhelmsburg. Then I went home about midnight.'

'Where did you go?'

'Der Pelikan. It's a new bar in the Stadtmitte. I thought I'd go to check it out.'

'Did anyone see you?' asked Anna. 'Anyone who could confirm that you were there?'

Olsen made a face that suggested Anna's question was stupid. 'There were hundreds of people. Like I said, it's a new place and a lot of people obviously had the same idea as me, but I didn't see anyone I know.'

Fabel made an almost apologetic gesture. 'Then I'm afraid we're going to have to ask you to come with us, Herr Olsen. You're not giving us enough information to eliminate you from our inquiry.'

Olsen gave a resigned sigh. 'Fair enough. But I can't help it if I haven't got an alibi. If I was guilty of something I would have made an effort to have a convincing cover story. Will this take long? I've got repairs I need to get out.'

'We'll keep you only for as long as it takes to get to the truth. Please, Herr Olsen.'

'Can I lock up first?'

'Of course.'

There was a rear door at the far side of the workshop. Olsen went over to it and turned the key in the lock. He then made his way out, followed by the three detectives. The dog was now asleep in the yard.

'If I'm going to be away overnight I'll have to arrange for the dog to be fed.' He stopped suddenly and looked back at the workshop. 'Shit. The alarm. I can't leave the bikes in there without the alarm on. Can I go back and set it?'

Fabel nodded. 'Werner, go with Herr Olsen, please.'

When they were out of earshot, Anna turned to Fabel. 'Do you get the feeling we're backing a loser here?'

'I know what you mean. I get the feeling that the only thing Olsen is hiding is how upset he is about Hanna's death . . .'

It was then that they heard a sudden urgent, throaty roar from inside the workshop. Anna and Fabel exchanged a look and started to run towards the building. The guard dog, startled from its sleep by the noise and its predator's instinct stimulated by the two running police officers, started to thrash around rabidly, its vicious jaws snapping at the empty air. Fabel arced his run, hoping he had correctly estimated the limit of the Rottweiler's restraining chain. They had covered about half the distance to the workshop when

Olsen swept round its side on a huge red beast of a motorcycle. Both Fabel and Anna froze for a moment as the heavily muscled racing bike loomed towards them. Olsen's head was encased in a red motorcycle helmet and the visor was down over the eyes, but Fabel recognised the oil-stained overalls. Olsen steered the bike like a weapon. The front wheel lifted slightly as he throttled the engine into an angry whine.

Adrenalin surged through Fabel's body, slowing time. The bike had been travelling fast, but now it seemed to lunge forward with impossible acceleration, as if Fabel had focused on it with a fast zoom lens. Fabel and Anna threw themselves in opposite directions as the bike flashed between them. Fabel rolled over on the ground a couple of times before coming to rest. He had just raised himself on to one knee when something massive and dark collided with him. For a sliver of a second, Fabel thought Olsen had come back with the bike to finish them off, until he turned to see the massive jaws of the Rottweiler lunge towards him. Fabel jerked his head back as the dog snapped its teeth shut. He felt cold mucus and saliva on his cheek, but knew that the dog had missed. He rolled again, this time in the opposite direction, and felt a sharp pain as something clamped down hard and tore at his shoulder. Fabel kept rolling in a continuous movement and heard the dog's vicious snarling turn to furious, frustrated barking as it reached the limit of its chain.

He pulled himself to his feet. Anna Wolff was also standing and looked over to Fabel to check that he was okay. Her poise was almost that of someone ready to start a race and Fabel nodded to her. She sprinted towards Fabel's car and the green and white police van. The two uniformed officers stood as if stunned, each at either end of the motorcycle they had been loading into the back of the van. Anna Wolff's run switched trajectory from Fabel's car to the motorbike.

'Is the key in it?' she screamed at the two still-motionless SchuPos. Before they could answer she was over at the bike and shoved aside the SchuPo at its rear. Anna rolled the bike back from the tailgate of the van, started the engine and fired off in the direction Olsen had taken.

Fabel clutched his shoulder. The fabric of his Jaeger jacket had been ripped and the padding fluffed where the Rottweiler's teeth had torn at it. His shoulder felt bruised, but the fabric of his polo-neck was intact and there was no trace of blood. He cast a resentful eye at the dog, which responded by straining at its chain, raising itself up and clawing the air impotently with its forelegs.

'Over here!' Fabel called to the two uniformed officers as he ran to the open door of the work-shop. Werner was on the floor. He had pulled himself up into a half-sitting position and was using an already encrimsoned handkerchief in an unsuccessful attempt to staunch the flow of blood from the right side of his head. Fabel dropped down next to him and eased Werner's hand and the blood-soaked handkerchief back from the wound. The gash was ugly, deep and raw, and the flesh of Werner's bristle-cropped scalp was already distended by swelling. Fabel took his own unused handkerchief out and replaced Werner's with it, pushing the injured man's hand back to the wound. Then he placed a supporting arm around Werner's shoulders.

'Are you okay?'

Werner's gaze was glassy and unfocused, but he managed a small nod that did nothing to reassure Fabel. The two uniformed officers were now in the workshop. Fabel jerked his head in the general direction of the workshop shelves.

'You. See if you can find a first-aid box over there.' He looked over to the other officer. 'You. Radio for an ambulance.' Fabel searched the workshop floor. The wrench was lying a metre or so away from Werner. It had a heavy, clumpy head and the adjusting barrel and jaws were coated in Werner's blood. Fabel could see that the door at the far end of the workshop was lying open. The bastard, thought Fabel. Olsen was a cool one, all right. He had casually unlocked the door in front of them all, while pretending to secure the premises. He had calculated his performance exactly, guessing that his impatient and irritated cooperation would mean that only one *Bulle* would come back with him to 'set the alarm'. Then he had hit Werner with the wrench and skipped out through the back door, where the red motorcycle must have been waiting. Fabel was sure he had not seen the red bike among the others in the workshop.

Werner groaned and moved as if trying to stand up. Fabel held him firm. 'You stay where you are, Werner, until the ambulance gets here.' He looked up at the uniformed officer who nodded.

'It's on its way, Herr Kriminalhauptkommissar.'

'I wouldn't like to be Olsen when you catch up with him, *Chef*,' Werner said. Fabel was relieved to see that Werner's eyes were less cloudy, but they were still far from alert.

'You bet,' said Fabel. 'No one knocks a member of my team about.'

'I don't mean that.' Werner smiled weakly and nodded towards Fabel's ragged shoulder. 'Isn't that one of your favourite jackets?'

The last corner had been too fast. Anna was wearing her usual leather jacket, but her legs were protected only by the denim fabric of her jeans, and her knee had all but grazed the asphalt on the last turn. She knew that if Olsen knew as much about riding motorbikes as he did about repairing them, which was likely, then she would have to go full throttle even to catch sight of him. Anna had no helmet and didn't even have her sunglasses with her, so she had to narrow her eyes against the blast of the wind as she accelerated along the straight. She crouched down behind the racing cowl to reduce her profile and to get as much protection from the wind as possible. The road ran alongside the refinery fence and was free of traffic so she opened the throttle full. She had burst out on to Hohe-Schaar-Strasse, causing a Merc to brake and swerve. She just caught a flash of red in the far distance as Olsen thundered across the bridge over the Reiherstieg and she set off in pursuit. The BMW roared beneath her and she measured out the distance to the next bend. Anna and her brother Julius had both had motorbikes and had often gone off on weekends together: to France, down to Bavaria and even once across to England. But then, as both their careers had become more demanding, the trips had become fewer and briefer. And when Julius had got married, they stopped completely. Anna had kept her bike until a year ago, when she had traded it in for a car. Now the only reminder of those days was the oversized leather jacket she still wore almost every day to work.

Anna slowed, easing on the brakes to get her speed down before the sharp left at the bottom of the stretch. She leaned into the bend, straightened out and let the g-force tug at her again as she accelerated. It was another long, straight expanse of road, and she saw the red smudge of Olsen's motorcycle up ahead. She opened the throttle flat out and the BMW gave another surge. Anna's mouth was dry and she knew that she was afraid. And she thrilled at the thought. She didn't look at the gauge: she knew she was pushing the bike to near its 200 kilometres per hour limit and she didn't want to know how near. She was closing the gap on Olsen: he obviously hadn't checked in his rear-view mirror and was taking no risks. He would have expected them to give chase by car, and they would be no match for him in speed or manoeuvrability. The gap closed. Don't check, she thought, don't check yet, you fuck. There it was. An almost imperceptible movement of his red helmeted head and Olsen's bike surged forward. He couldn't pull away from Anna's flat-out BMW, but he could maintain the gap until one of them made a mistake. It was like playing chicken, but while travelling in the same direction.

The next bend came and Olsen took it better and faster than Anna, opening up the gap again slightly. The industrial landscape that had surrounded them evaporated and they were now surrounded by mucky-looking fields. The road had a number of twists in it and Anna found herself taking many of them on the left, thankful that nothing was coming in the opposite direction.

Another sharp bend – this time Olsen misjudged it and only just made it, having to slow down to regain his line on the road. Anna closed the gap between them to twenty metres. Her universe had imploded until all that remained of it was the ribbon of road before her and the bike beneath her to which her body now felt indissolubly fused. It was as if her central nervous system was connected to the BMW's electronics and every thought, every impulse, relayed itself automatically to the bike. Her focus was locked on Olsen's red motorcycle ahead. Her concentration was total, trying to anticipate his next move.

This total concentration meant that she could not move a hand from the bike's steering column. She couldn't reach for her gun; she couldn't phone in her position. She suddenly realised that she had also lost her bearings: she had been so focused on Olsen and the road immediately in front of her that she no longer knew exactly where they were. Her knowledge of Wilhelmsburg wasn't great at the best of times, but the excitement and challenge of pursuit had made her oblivious to passing landmarks. The flat countryside around her and the direction they had taken meant that they were somewhere in Moorwerder: the odd rural tail of Wilhelmsburg that had somehow remained invisible to developers.

Another bend and another straight stretched ahead of them. Olsen's bike surged as he accelerated to its maximum speed again. Anna felt her chest tighten when she realised that the open road was about to give way to a built-up area. A sign indicating that they were approaching Stillhorn flashed by and Anna realised that Olsen had looped them back round and he was heading for the A1 Autobahn. If he pushed things too far here, she would have to ease up and let him go, rather than put civilian lives at risk. But not yet.

The traffic started to thicken and Olsen and

Anna weaved between cars and trucks, many of which had to brake hard with a blast of angry horns. The town began to take a more solid form as they thrust in from the outskirts towards the centre. Anna's heart hammered in her chest. She became aware of a police siren somewhere behind her: she didn't know whether it was back-up or simply the Stillhorn police responding to two motorcycles racing through the place. Whichever it was, she was glad to have some other police around for when she finally cornered Olsen. Up ahead, she saw him brake suddenly and turn, the bike almost sliding out from under him as he disappeared up a side street.

Anna missed the turn and had to loop round in the main street, incurring even more furious horn blasts from other drivers. As she entered the side street, she saw Olsen exit at the far end and once more she opened the throttle out full. The roar of the BMW bike reverberated in the narrow street and a couple of pedestrians had to flatten themselves against the buildings as she thundered past. This was getting too dangerous: she was going to lose Olsen unless she got him before he got further into town.

Anna had just about made it to the end of the street when a green and white patrol car, its lights flashing, turned into the street from the far end. It was clearly trying to block her exit and she gestured wildly for it to get out of the way. Instead the police car screeched to a halt and the doors flew open, a policeman rushing out on either side, their pistols drawn and aimed at Anna.

She braked hard and turned the bike broadside-on to the car. It slid from under her and she smashed into the asphalt, feeling her thigh burn as the denim was ripped from her leg. Anna rolled several times before she came to rest against a parked car. The bike slid, showering sparks as its metal ground against the road surface, until it slammed into the front of the police car.

A second patrol car pulled up behind Anna and the stunned SchuPos walked over to her, holstering their weapons as, still lying on the road and with one hand nursing her skinned thigh, she held up her bronze oval Kriminalpolizei shield. They helped her to her feet and one of them started to say something about not knowing she was a police officer in pursuit of a suspect.

Anna stared hard down the empty street to where Olsen had disappeared, then at the BMW motorbike jammed under the front of the police car. In a quiet, restrained voice, she asked if the two uniformed policemen could radio the direction her suspect had taken and see if they could get a helicopter to search for Olsen. Then, taking a deep breath, she screamed, harsh and shrill at the four SchuPos:

'Fucking idiots!'

CHAPTER 25

4.30 p.m., Thursday, 25 March:
Stadtkrankenhaus hospital,
Wilhelmsburg, Hamburg

Maria Klee stood by the window. She was wearing a dark grey trouser suit with a black linen blouse underneath. Her blonde hair was swept back from her face and the grey eyes glittered bright and cold in the harsh hospital lighting. Maria always looked a little too elegant, in looks and build as well as in dress, to be a Kriminaloberkommissarin. Here, in this hospital room with her weary and injured colleagues, the contrast was even starker.

'Well . . .' she said, smiling and tapping her perfect teeth with the end of her pen, 'all in all, I think we could say that went well. Next time you need to interview someone, I think I'd better come along.'

Fabel laughed mirthlessly. He was slumped in the chair next to Werner's bed. He was still wearing the Jaeger jacket with the ripped shoulder. Werner was raised into a half-lying, half-sitting position.

The side of his face had puffed up grotesquely and was beginning to discolour. X-rays and scans hadn't revealed a fracture or any swelling of his brain, but the doctors had been concerned that the bruising had perhaps obscured a hairline fracture. Werner lay in a no man's land between consciousness and sleep: he had been given something to kill the pain and it had had an even more sedative effect than Olsen's wrench. Anna, wearing a hospital gown and with a massive pad taped to her thigh, sat in a wheelchair on the other side of Werner's bed.

'That's an end to my swimwear-modelling career,' she had said as they had wheeled her in. Her high-speed chase and its spectacular climax had smeared her trademark mascara and lipstick, and one of the nurses had given her some cosmetics wipes: her face was now clear of cosmetics and her skin shone almost translucent. Fabel had never seen Anna without her make-up and was amazed at how much younger than her twenty-seven years she looked. And how pretty she was. It was a look that didn't fit with the aggression with which she pursued her duties. An aggression that Fabel often needed to keep in check.

Fabel pulled himself wearily from the chair and joined Maria at the window, facing Anna and Werner. It was clear that he had something to say, and as Werner was in the room in body only rather than in spirit, it was to Anna specifically, and to Maria.

'I don't need to tell you that this is not good.' His tone suggested that he was about to say something that would not go down too well. 'Basically, it's down to you and me, Maria. Werner will be off for at least a month. Anna, you're not going to be fit for duty for a week or so.'

'I'm fine, *Chef*. I'll be back—'

Fabel stopped her by raising his hand. 'You're no use to me, Kommissarin Wolff, if you're not fully mobile. It'll be a week at the very least before you're fit for duty. The doctors have said that, although you don't feel it now, you are going to hurt like hell when all the muscles you've torn start to heal. Added to that, you're lucky you don't need a skin graft on your leg.'

'All I was doing was trying to stop Olsen getting away.'

'I haven't condemned your actions, Anna.' Fabel smiled. 'Although Herr Brauner wasn't too appreciative of the fact that you rammed a piece of forensic evidence under a car. The fact is, I can't operate with just Maria working the case with me.'

Anna's expression darkened. She knew where this was going. 'There are other teams in the Mordkommission we can draw people from.'

'Anna, I know you were close to Paul.' Paul Lindemann had been Anna's partner: Paul and Anna had, in many ways, been opposites, but they had worked together as a close and highly effective partnership. 'But I need to get the permanent team up to full strength. I'm going to recruit a new member.'

Anna's expression didn't lighten. 'And this will be a new partner for me?'

'Yes.'

Maria raised her eyebrows. She and Anna both knew that Fabel was highly selective in his recruitment to the team. They had themselves been hand-picked by him. Someone had clearly impressed Fabel. 'You're going to ask Kommissar Klatt to join? The guy from Norderstedt police?'

Fabel smiled as enigmatically as his exhaustion and aching shoulder would allow. 'You'll have to wait and see.'

CHAPTER 26

6.00 p.m., Thursday, 25 March:
Wilhelmsburg, Hamburg

If there is one sure way to motivate the police to find you, it is to seriously assault a police officer. Within fifteen minutes of Olsen coshing Werner, a warrant was in place and a Mobiles Einsatz Kommando had Olsen's apartment, in the area of Wilhelmsburg close to the old *Honigfabrik* honey factory, under close surveillance. There had been no sign of life: either Olsen had headed straight back to his apartment and had holed up there, which was unlikely and would have been monumentally stupid, or he knew to stay as far away from home as possible.

The sky hung heavy and grey over the city as Maria and Fabel pulled up directly outside Olsen's apartment block. Fabel had changed his jacket and had taken a couple of codeine to kill the ache in his shoulder as well as the throbbing that had started in his head. As he got out of the BMW, he signalled to a large unmarked van parked halfway down the street. Five heavy-set men in

209

jeans and sweatshirts jumped from the vehicle and moved swiftly up the street. Over their civilian clothes they wore body armour emblazoned with the word 'POLIZEI' and they wore balaclavas and assault helmets. Two of the men carried a short, stocky door-ram between them. Three more, similarly garbed, came running up from a car parked fifty metres or so in the other direction. The MEK commander stopped as he came alongside Fabel, who nodded and said:

'Second floor – 2b. Do your thing . . .'

From the street, Fabel and Maria heard the loud thud as the MEK men burst Olsen's door in with the ram. There was some shouting, then silence. A couple of minutes later the MEK commander emerged from the apartment-block entrance door, carrying his helmet and balaclava in one hand, his SIG-Sauer automatic in his other. He smiled emptily.

'No one home,' he said.

'Thanks, Herr Oberkommissar.' Fabel turned to Maria. 'Shall we?'

The apartment door was still on its hinges, but the frame around the lock was shattered into long, sharp splinters. Fabel and Maria pulled on white latex gloves before entering. It was a reasonably large apartment: a spacious living room, three bedrooms, large dining kitchen and bathroom. The furniture was old and heavy, but Fabel noticed how tidy and clean the apartment was. The TV in the living room was elderly, but Olsen had pushed the boat out on his stereo equipment. A huge Bang & Olufsen system dominated one wall. The size and wattage of the speakers seemed to be out of proportion with the room, but somehow Fabel couldn't imagine any of the neighbours complaining to Olsen about the noise. There was a CD rack fixed to the wall next to the stereo, and Fabel noticed that Olsen had labelled his CD collection with the same systematic care as he had the spares store at the garage. He took a closer look at Olsen's music collection: Rammstein, Die toten Hosen, Marilyn Manson. Not the kind of stuff you played softly in the background for dinner guests.

Holger Brauner, the SpuSi forensic team leader, knocked on the shattered door frame behind Fabel.

'Private party? Or can anyone come in?' He nodded to the CD Fabel had in his hand. 'Rammstein? I wouldn't have thought it was your kind of thing.'

Fabel laughed and replaced the CD in the rack. 'I was just seeing if he had any James Last. Can't beat a bit of *Hansi* after a tough day.'

'And you've had quite a day, from what I've heard . . . Is it true you're applying for a transfer to the dog handling unit?'

Fabel grinned sarcastically.

'And, by the way, Herr Kriminalhauptkommissar, could you have a word with Frau Wolff? I don't think she's quite grasped the concept of protecting the integrity of a forensic exhibit.'

'Sorry about the motorcycle, Holger. Did you get a match?'

'Sure did. The print we took at the scene came from a 120/70-ZR17 motorcycle tyre. They're the standard front tyre on the BMW R1000 S motorcycle. The wear patterns on Olsen's bike match the impression we took exactly. So he's your guy. Or, at least, it was his motorcycle in the Naturpark. All we need is to find the boots he was wearing. I'll have a look around here.'

'He's probably wearing them,' said Fabel, trying to remember Olsen's footwear from earlier in the day.

Maria had been searching the bathroom. She came through, carrying some pharmaceutical-looking bottles. 'Herr Brauner, do you have any idea what these are for?'

Brauner examined the bottles. 'Isotretinon and benzoyl peroxide . . . Does your guy have bad skin, by any chance?'

'Yes, he does,' said Fabel.

'These are acne treatments . . .' Brauner's voice trailed off, and he stared at the bottles as if a thought was struggling to come to the surface and he had to concentrate to help it rise. 'Those boot-prints were huge. Size fifty. Was your guy really tall? And heavily muscled?'

Maria and Fabel exchanged a look. 'Yes. Really big.'

'This may seem a strange question, but was there anything else, well, *odd* about his appearance? Was he pigeon-chested, or did he have a cast in one eye?'

'Are you being funny? Or do you think you know him?' Fabel laughed.

Brauner was still looking at the acne treatment and shook his head in annoyance. 'Did you notice anything like that?'

'No,' said Fabel. 'He didn't have a cast in his eye or a pigeon-chest. Nor was he a hunchback with two heads.'

'No . . .' Fabel's sarcasm didn't reach Brauner, who spoke more to himself than to Fabel. 'It doesn't necessarily follow.'

'Holger?' Fabel said impatiently. Brauner looked up from the medication.

'Sorry. I think your guy might be one in a thousand. Literally. His record is for violence exclusively, isn't it? Cases of him losing his temper rather than premeditated criminal acts?'

'From what I can see, yes,' said Fabel. 'Other than one conviction for selling on stolen goods. What have you got, Holger?'

'Maybe nothing, but Olsen has an explosive temper, is unusually tall and powerfully built and suffers from acne at an age when most of us have long put it behind us. I suspect we could be dealing with Karotype XYY.'

'Supermale Syndrome?' Fabel thought for a moment. 'Yes. Yes, it would fit. Now that you mention it, it really would fit. I didn't know about the acne thing, though.' Fabel had come across an 'XYY' male before.

Karotype XYY Syndrome is caused when,

instead of the normal male chromosome type '46XY', a male is born with an extra male chromosome and the chromosome type '47XYY'. These 'supermales' are characterised by excessive height, heavier male features, slower emotional and social maturity, and a system surging with testosterone. This often led to hair-trigger, violent tempers. Medical opinion was divided on exactly what effect XYY had, if any, on violent behaviour or criminal tendencies, but the XYY male Fabel had encountered had, like Olsen, been huge and unpredictably violent. Controversial research had revealed a disproportionate ratio of XYY males in the prison population: many XYYs, however, led productive and highly successful lives, channelling their aggression into dynamic careers. Fabel looked again at the CD.

'I don't know, Holger. It would fit with the aggressive rock, but his behaviour at his workshop was very cool – the way he lured Werner back into the workshop, for instance. He had his escape strategy all worked out.'

'He was probably boiling under the surface, but had worked out that he needed to keep a lid on it until he had a chance to get away. It would fit with the excessive force. He didn't need to hit Kriminaloberkommissar Meyer so hard. Classic lack of control when his temper explodes.'

'Wouldn't it be on his record?' asked Maria.

'Perhaps,' answered Brauner. 'If he submitted to Karotype testing at the time of his arrest. And if, indeed, he is Karotype XYY at all. He might just be a big bad-tempered bugger.'

They split up and set about their independent searches of Olsen's home, like visitors to a gallery or museum exhibit, scanning the whole, then stopping to examine closer where some detail took their interest. There was nothing here to suggest the supercharged psychotic ego of a serial killer; but Fabel's senses continually jarred against the contradiction in Olsen's personality. Everything was neat and ordered. Fabel went through to one of the two bedrooms. This was obviously Olsen's. The posters on the wall would have been more at home in the bedroom of an adolescent than in the apartment of a man pushing thirty. Some personal items – a chunky but cheap watch, a comb and brush, some toiletries and a couple of bottles of aftershave – sat, ordered, on his dresser. Fabel swung open the heavy doors of a stout wall cupboard. The clothes and footwear inside were huge, and Fabel felt as if he were skulking around the chamber of some sleeping giant. As well as being outsize, Olsen's wardrobe was functional and efficient: one formal suit with one pair of dress shoes; a half-dozen T-shirts, emblazoned with hate-rock band names and logos, yet folded and stored as if his mother had been round that very morning; two pairs of jeans, one black, one blue denim; two pairs of trainers; two pairs of boots. Boots.

'Holger . . .' Fabel called over his shoulder to the

other room, snapping on a pair of latex forensic gloves. He picked up one pair of boots and examined the soles. The tread pattern was shallow. The second pair was much more robust-looking. Each boot had ten pairs of lace eyes and two heavy strap-and-buckle fasteners. They were clearly motorcycle boots. He was turning the boots over to look at the soles when Brauner came in. The forensics chief held out a glossy print-out copy of the bootprint found in the Naturpark. Even Fabel could tell at first glance that they were a match.

Brauner held open a clear plastic evidence bag as Fabel lifted each boot in turn between his latex-sheathed forefinger and thumb and dropped it in.

'All we've got to do now,' said Fabel, 'is find our Cinderella . . .'

CHAPTER 27

9.00 p.m., Friday, 26 March:
Pöseldorf, Hamburg

It was yet another relationship ritual: where the friends of the individual became the friends of the couple. This meal together had been Fabel's idea, and when he saw Otto, his oldest friend, sitting chatting with Susanne, the newest element in Fabel's life, he felt surprisingly content. The usual initial awkwardness of greetings and introductions had evaporated almost instantly under Susanne's natural Southern warmth and it was clear from the start that Otto and Else liked her. Approved of her. He wasn't sure why, but that approval was very important to Fabel. Perhaps it was because Otto and Else had been there throughout Fabel's marriage to Renate and they had sat around a restaurant table, just like this, so many times before.

He looked across at Susanne and smiled. Her raven hair was tied up, revealing her neck and shoulders. Susanne's beauty was striking and natural and the subtlest application of make-up highlighted her stunning eyes under the high-arched eyebrows. She smiled back, knowingly. Fabel had reserved a table in an Italian restaurant down on Milchstrasse, only two minutes' walk from his apartment. The disadvantage about his flat was that it didn't lend itself to hosting dinner parties and Fabel had become a regular in this restaurant whenever he had guests. They were chatting idly about this and that, when Otto brought up the subject of the books that Fabel had bought.

'How are you getting on with Weiss's novel?' he asked.

'Fine . . . well, okay. I see what you mean about his overblown style. But it's amazing how you get sucked into the world he describes. And how you start to associate Jacob Grimm with the fictional character rather than the historical personage. Which is what Weiss's theory is all about, I suppose.' Fabel paused for a moment. 'I've been going through the works of the Brothers Grimm, too. I knew that they had collected a lot of folk tales, but I had no idea just how many. As well as all those myths and legends.'

Otto nodded his huge domed head. 'They were very dedicated and talented individuals. And a powerful team. Their work on the German language, on linguistics generally, was, as you know, ground-breaking. And it is still influential. They defined the mechanics of language, of how languages evolved and how they borrow from one another. The irony is that they are remembered as the authors of tales they didn't actually write. Well, actually, they did do a bit of editing and rewriting on the later versions – to make them more palatable.'

'Mmm, I know . . .' Susanne took a sip of wine, then put her glass down. 'As a psychologist, I find fairy tales fascinating. There's so much deep stuff in them. Sexual, a lot of it.'

'Exactly.' Otto beamed at Susanne. 'The Grimm brothers weren't writers, they were recorders – linguists and philologists who travelled remote parts of Hessen and elsewhere in northern and central Germany, collecting old folk tales and fables. To start with they didn't rewrite or embellish the traditional tales they compiled. But most of the stories they collected were not as cosy as they appeared in later editions – or as nauseatingly saccharine as their retelling by Disney and others. When their collections turned out to be best-sellers, particularly when they compiled children's tales, they found themselves removing or sanitising some of the darker and sexual elements.'

'That's why we all remain that little bit afraid of fairy tales,' said Susanne. 'We're told them as bedtime stories when we're children but they're really warnings and instructions on how to avoid all types of danger and evil. But they're also about the dangers within the known and trusted. The home. The threat from the known and familiar is as much part of these fables as the fear of the unknown. And it's funny how one of the most common motifs in these tales is the wicked stepmother.'

'Weiss claims that these folk tales are the fundamental truths behind our fears and prejudices. Like Susanne said, our psychology.' Fabel paused to take a forkful of tagliatelle. 'He claims that, whenever we sit down to read a novel or watch a movie, especially if they're about things that threaten us, then it's really just a retelling of these tales.'

Otto nodded vigorously and pointed to Fabel with his fork. 'Yes, well . . . he really does have a point. What is it they say, there are only four basic stories you can tell – or is it six?' He shrugged.

'Anyway,' said Fabel. 'This is, in an odd sort of way, all related to a case I'm working on. And that means it's shop talk, which is strictly forbidden.'

'Okay,' said Otto with a mischievous grin, 'but my last word is that I can understand why Jan has an interest in fairy tales . . .'

Susanne raised a questioning eyebrow.

'Beauty . . .' Otto raised his glass to Susanne, then to Fabel '. . . and the Beast.'

CHAPTER 28

11.20 p.m., Sunday, 28 March:
Blankenese, Hamburg

The pool room was dark and silent, the still water mute in the night.

Laura stripped in the changing cabana and stood naked before the glass. Her skin was still flawless, her hair retained its lustrous gold and the lines of her body remained sleek and smooth. She had sacrificed so much to maintain this body, this face. She gazed at this ideal of feminine perfection that so many photographers and designers had paid so much for. She laid her palm upon her belly. It was flat. Tight. It had never been required to bulge and stretch. She looked down at her own perfection and was filled with disgust and self-loathing.

Laura walked naked into the pool room. She left the main lights off and let the darkness and quiet cloak her. Laura breathed in deeply and looked out across the glossy obsidian of the pool to the vast window that framed the nightscape of a heavy sky. She could swim into that sky, her mind free and clear. She turned on only the underwater lights. A pale blue luminescence bloomed along the edges of the pool. Laura stepped into the shallow end, letting the cool, almost cold water make her skin go tingle-tight, raising goosebumps and pinching her nipples to hard points. She started to walk towards the deeper part of the pool, the water rippling a pale electric blue around her.

It was then that she saw it.

A shape. More like a large, dark shadow in the pale blue gloom of the pool. There was something lying at the bottom. There was something lying at the bottom of the pool and it just didn't make sense. Laura moved forward towards it, frowning. She tried to think of what on earth could have found its way there and who could have left it. She drew closer and still could not make out what the motionless object was. She was about two metres from it when the shape unfolded and thrust up and out of the water in a single motion. It loomed massive in the dim blue light, surging up and towering above her and closing the gap between it and her in a second. Time slowed. Her brain tried to make sense of what was happening. A man shape? No. Surely too big. Too fast. His body was dark. Dark with words. He – it – was covered in words. Thousands of words in the old Germanic lettering. Spanning the vast chest; spiralling and coiling around the arms. It didn't make sense. A story in the shape of a giant man was surging towards her. It was upon her now. A hand gripped her throat while the other pushed her head down and into the blue-lit water. Yes. A man. A man – but a huge, dark hulk of a man, covered in words in old-fashioned writing. His grip was unshakeable but not crushing, as if he knew how to apply just enough pressure to control without damaging. The hands were vast and immeasurably powerful. Her head was under water. Now the fear came. She tried to scream and her nose and mouth filled with the faintly chlorinated water and the fear became the blinding panic of her survival instinct. She thrashed wildly, clawing at the arms and body of her attacker, but it was as if he were made of stone. She gasped and with each gasp her slim frame became even more inundated. As the water filled her lungs the contortions, and the fear, faded. Her limbs ceased to flail. The serenity and the beauty of her face was restored.

The most profound joy filled Laura von Klosterstadt's dying mind. This was right. This was what had to be. Punishment and forgiveness. Her mother had always been right: Laura was bad. Worthless. Unfit to be a mother. Unfit to be a bride. But now she was absolved. Laura's joy in death came from her awareness of two facts. Now she would never age. Now she would be with her child.

CHAPTER 29

8.40 a.m., Monday, 29 March:
Stadtpark, Winterhude, Hamburg

Fabel gazed up at the building which thrust upwards from the trees that flanked it and loomed over the vast open area of grass that lay before it. The impossibly high arches of the red-bricked frontage seemed stretched, as if the whole structure was being pulled skywards by some unseen hand. The clouds scudded past the huge domed roof. Fabel had always been fascinated by this building: if you didn't know what it had been originally built as, and if it didn't have its current function emblazoned across it, above the high arches, in metre-high letters, then you could spend hours guessing its primary purpose. Fabel always felt it looked like a high temple of some ancient lost religion: part Egyptian, part Greek, part alien.

The Planetarium had, originally, been constructed as nothing more than a water tower. But, at the time when it had been built, there had been the surging confidence of a recently united

Germany and the dawn of a new century, combined with the then near-religious zeal of civic engineering. Now, a century on, the building remained, having watched over the failure of the last century and having seen Germany disunite and reunite. The monumental water tower was now the Planetarium and Winterhude's most famous landmark.

Fabel surveyed the vast area of park that lay in front of the Planetarium. Two hundred metres away, a temporary fence of metal poles linked with police tape fanned out: on one side a line of policemen, on the other a growing crowd.

'It looks like the word's already got out who our victim is.' Maria Klee joined Fabel on the steps. 'There's no doubt we'll have press and TV here before long.'

Fabel moved down to the grassed area. A large white forensic tent had been assembled to protect the locus, and Fabel and Maria slipped on the protective overshoes the SpuSi forensic technician handed them before opening the flap and stepping inside. Holger Brauner was bent over the body and stood up as they entered. A young woman lay naked on the grass, her legs together and her hands folded over her breast. Her hair was a striking gold and had been brushed out and fanned around her head like a sunburst. Fabel noticed that a small section of the radiating hair had been deliberately cut away, leaving a gap. Even in death, the beauty of the woman's face and perfectly formed body was extraordinary. Her eyes were closed, a red rose lay between her folded hands and her breast and she looked for all the world as if she were asleep. Fabel looked down at her, at the perfect structure of bone and flesh: an architecture that would soon collapse and crumble into dust. But, for now, the pallor of death on her face seemed only to give her skin a porcelain flawlessness.

'I take it you need no introduction,' said Holger Brauner, squatting down again by the body.

Fabel gave a small, bitter laugh. He had struggled to establish the identity of the first victim; there would be no such struggle with this one. Almost anyone in Hamburg could recognise her. As soon as he had seen her face, Fabel knew that he was looking at Laura von Klosterstadt, the 'supermodel' who could be seen on billboards and magazines all over Germany. As the 'von' suggested, Fabel knew that Laura came from an aristocratic family. But the prominence of the von Klosterstadts did not come from the family's tired nobility but from its very contemporary commercial and political clout. This, Fabel knew, was going to get messy. Already there was a media storm brewing outside this scene-of-crime tent and Fabel's radar could even now sense top brass heading full speed towards him.

'God,' he said at last, 'I hate celebrity murders.'

'How about a celebrity murdered by a serial killer you're tracking?' Brauner handed Fabel a clear evidence bag. It contained a tiny slip of yellow paper.

'Oh God, no,' said Fabel. 'Tell me it isn't.'

''Fraid so.' Brauner rose to his feet. 'It was protruding slightly from her hands. That's why I suggested to the first team out here that they should call you in. This is your guy again, Jan.'

Fabel examined the paper through the plastic. Same paper. Same tiny, obsessively neat writing in red ink. This time it had only one word on it: Dornröschen.

'Briar Rose?' Maria had moved in closer to examine the note.

'A tale by the Brothers Grimm. Better known these days as *Sleeping Beauty*, because of its Hollywood make-over.'

'Look at this . . .' Brauner indicated the dead woman's hand, where she held the rose. A thorn had been pushed deep into the fleshy part of the thumb. 'No blood. This was done deliberately, post-mortem.'

'It was how Briar Rose, or Sleeping Beauty, was put to sleep. She pricked her thumb.'

'I thought it was supposed to be on a spindle, not a rose,' said Maria.

Fabel stood up again. Laura von Klosterstadt lay still, although Fabel half expected her to give a contented sleepy sigh and roll on to her side. 'He's mixing metaphors – or condensing story elements, however you want to put it. Sleeping Beauty did prick her thumb on a spindle, on her fifteenth birthday, but as she slept she and her castle became surrounded by briar roses – a beautiful but impenetrable defence. I suppose the Planetarium is meant to represent the castle.' He turned back to Brauner. 'Can you hazard a guess at a cause of death?'

'Not at this stage. There's very little to indicate violence, other than some slight bruising on the neck, but it's not enough to suggest strangulation. Möller will be able to tell you when he does the post-mortem.'

Fabel pointed vaguely at the fan of golden hair. 'What do you make of this with the hair? Cutting a section out of it. I can't see any connection to the Sleeping Beauty story.'

'Your guess is as good as mine,' said Brauner. 'Maybe a trophy. She certainly has beautiful hair, maybe it's something he sees as characterising her.'

'No . . . no, I don't think so. Why start taking trophies now? He took nothing from the other three bodies.'

'Nothing that we know about,' said Brauner. 'But maybe this thing with the hair is something else. Some kind of message.'

The sky had brightened slightly as Fabel and Maria stepped out of the tent and the red brickwork of the Planetarium looked rain-washed and sharp in the cold light.

'This bastard's getting cocky, Maria. There's a message here all right.' Fabel waved his hand in the direction of a wall of trees, but his gesture suggested that he was looking beyond them. 'You can just about see this spot from the Polizeipräsidium. We're exactly due south of it. In fact, the top of the Planetarium is clearly visible from the upper floors of the Präsidium. He's flaunting himself in front of us – literally.'

Maria folded her arms across her body, tilting her head slightly. 'Well, our prime suspect to date is Olsen, and we got very close to him. Maybe there's a message in his choice of location. We got close to him, so he's getting close to us. As you say, practically in view of police headquarters.'

'Could be. Or it could be the choice of location has something to do with its history.'

'The Stadtpark's history?'

Fabel shook his head. 'Not specifically. But this place, Winterhude. This is ancient ground, Maria. This goes way back to before Hamburg grew around it. There was a Stone Age settlement here. I suspect any deeper meaning is secondary to him doing this so close to the Präsidium, but there's maybe something in the history of the place.' When Fabel had been at university he had spent much of his summers here, in the Stadtpark, with a pile of books at his side. No one knew for sure where the name 'Winterhude' had come from, but 'Hude' was an old Plattdeutsch word that meant 'protected place'. He had always found a strange comfort in being on ground that had been continuously occupied for six thousand years. It was as if it connected him to the history he was studying.

'Or,' said Maria, 'it could simply be that it fitted with the kind of location he needed to play out his fantasy.'

Fabel was about to answer Maria when he saw a large Mercedes 4x4 drive over the grass and stop beside the police cordon. Two men got out. Fabel recognised them instantly.

'Shit . . .' Fabel got no satisfaction to see how accurate his 'top brass' radar had been. 'That's all we need.'

The two men from the 4x4 made their way across to Fabel and Maria. The first man was in his mid-fifties. The hair, cropped close to the scalp, was almost all white, as was the beard, except for the odd hints of a butter-blond past. He was dressed in a pale grey suit which, as always, he managed to wear as if it were a SchuPo uniform.

'Good morning, Herr Kriminaldirektor,' Fabel said to his boss, Horst van Heiden. The second man was shorter and plumper, with a scrubbed, pink complexion; Fabel, recognising the Interior Minister of the Hamburg senate, gave a brief nod. 'Herr Innensenator Ganz . . .'

'Good morning, Kriminalhauptkommissar Fabel.' Van Heiden indicated the tent with a nod of his head. 'Is it true?'

'Is what true, Herr Kriminaldirektor?' Fabel knew exactly what van Heiden was asking, but he was damned if he was going to willingly divulge case information in front of Ganz. Fabel had had dealings with Ganz before: he was a career politician and, as the minister responsible for crime and security within Hamburg, he seemed to hold the police personally responsible for any high-profile case that raised public fears or caused the city-state government embarrassment.

Van Heiden's face, never genial at the best of times, clouded. 'Is it true, Herr Kriminalhauptkommissar, that the body discovered this morning is that of Laura von Klosterstadt, the society model?'

'There has been no positive identification made as yet, Herr Kriminaldirektor.' Fabel looked at Ganz pointedly. 'And I certainly do not want anything being announced publicly before we do.'

Ganz's already florid complexion turned a deeper red. 'I am here as much in a personal capacity as a professional one, Herr Fabel. I am a family friend of long standing. In fact, I attended Laura's birthday party only this Saturday. I have known Peter von Klosterstadt for many years. If this is, indeed, his daughter, I would like to break the news to the family personally.' He thought for a moment. There was something akin to unease in his expression. 'I could positively identify the body, if you wish.'

'I'm sorry, Herr Innensenator, this is still a protected crime scene. I'm sure you understand. Anyway, your presence in there may be seen as . . . well, inappropriate.'

'Fabel . . .' Van Heiden's tone was more beseeching than threatening.

Fabel sighed. 'Yes, the body would appear to be that of Laura von Klosterstadt. We have no exact time or cause of death, but it's certainly foul play.' He paused. 'In fact, we are practically certain that she has fallen victim to a serial killer who has taken at least three lives, perhaps four, previously.'

Van Heiden's expression darkened even further. Ganz shook his head disbelievingly. 'How could this happen? How could this happen to Laura?'

'I'm not sure I understand your point, Herr Ganz. Do you mean how could this happen to someone with such a public profile? Rather than to some anonymous shopgirl?'

'That is quite enough!' Fabel had succeeded in igniting van Heiden's notoriously short fuse. Ganz held up a hand and stopped the Kriminaldirektor.

'It's okay, Horst.' There was no animosity in the plump, florid face. 'It's not that, Herr Fabel. It's not that at all. I am – I was – Laura's godfather. I've known her since she was a little girl.'

'I'm sorry, Herr Ganz. I was out of line. You say you saw her on Saturday?'

'Yes. Her birthday party. Her thirty-first. In her villa at Blankenese.'

'Were there many people there?'

'Oh yes. I'd say over a hundred guests. Maybe a hundred and fifty.'

'Did anything particular happen? Any incidents?'

Ganz gave a small laugh. 'It was a society

event, Herr Fabel. Such gatherings are carefully engineered and arranged. Everyone there has an agenda, from being seen with the right people to doing deals. So no, there weren't any *incidents*.'

'Did she have a partner? A boyfriend?'

'No. No boyfriend. No partner. Or rather, none of any significance that I can remember. Despite all her beauty and her wealth, poor Laura was a very lonely person. I would say the person closest to her was Heinz. Heinz Schnauber. Her agent.'

'Were they involved?'

Ganz laughed briefly. 'No. Nothing like that. Heinz is a member of the *Schwul ist Cool* brigade.'

'Gay?'

'Very. But a devoted friend to Laura. He's going to be devastated to hear about this.'

Down by the police cordon, a television crew had arrived and Fabel could see that several press photographers had focused long zoom lenses on them, like snipers waiting for the clearest shot. 'I think we're beginning to attract a little too much attention. Herr Ganz, I would like to talk to you some more about Fräulein von Klosterstadt, but somewhere less public. In the meantime, I'd appreciate it if you would speak to the family. And if I may make a suggestion, Herr Kriminaldirektor, I think, it would be a very good idea if you were present.'

Van Heiden nodded. Fabel watched the two men make their way back to the Mercedes 4x4. He noticed that the usually press-friendly Ganz waved away the reporters with the same irritated conviction as did van Heiden. The last occasion Fabel and Ganz had crossed paths, the friction had been considerable. Last time, the serial murderer that Fabel had been hunting had been seen by Ganz as a generator of embarrassing headlines; this time, death had come too close to home for Ganz to worry about bad press.

Fabel looked up at the vast edifice of the Planetarium's tower. There was a message here. And he wasn't getting it.

CHAPTER 30

10.10 a.m., Monday, 29 March:
Polizeipräsidium, Hamburg

Fabel looked around the conference table and was very aware of Werner's and Anna's absence. Only Maria and himself remained of the core team and he had seconded two Kommissars, Petra Maas and Hans Rödger, from Kriminalhauptkommissarin Ute Walraf's sexual-crime Sonder Kommission, which was based on the same floor of the Präsidium. Fabel knew both detectives well, and valued their support, but they weren't his regular Mordkommission team and he felt exposed. Olsen, if it was Olsen who was committing these murders, was getting bolder and more prolific, despite having come close to capture. Fabel and his team would have to move as fast and as efficiently as possible to prevent him killing again.

Also seated around the table were Susanne and Klatt, the Norderstedt Kommissar. Fabel had just asked Maria to start briefing the team on the latest killing when there was a knock at the conference room door and a tall, sandy-haired, uniformed SchuPo officer hovered awkwardly on the threshold.

'Ah . . . Kommissar Hermann.' Fabel indicated a free seat with a sweep of his hand. 'Thanks for coming along. I thought you'd like to sit in on this briefing.'

Hermann beamed as he sat down at the table, placing his green and white peaked cap on the table before taking out a notebook and laying it on the cherrywood surface.

'Kommissar Hermann,' explained Fabel to the others, 'was the officer who identified the double murder in Naturpark Harburger Berge as a possible serial killing, and who did so well in preserving the locus for forensics.'

Hermann nodded his thanks. Fabel asked Maria to continue. She summarised what they knew, and didn't know, to date about the latest killing, as well as going over the previous three murders.

When Maria had finished, Fabel took over. 'What we have is a violent and unpredictable suspect on the loose. Peter Olsen. Twenty-nine. He has a record for violence and was involved with Hanna Grünn, whom we found along with Markus Schiller in the Naturpark Harburger Berge. So there is a link and a possible motive. But we still have to establish what connection, if any, he had with the other victims. We also believe that he may be what is known as Karotype XYY . . . a genetic disorder that may predispose him to violent rage. Frau Doktor Eckhardt?'

'We are all born with a chromosome mix,' Susanne explained. 'Men are XY, women are XX. Sometimes, however, there are variations on this mix. This can lead to Down's Syndrome, Turner Syndrome or intersex conditions such as hermaphroditism, or we can end up with an extra male or female chromosome. In men, this is called XYY or 'supermale' syndrome. Such men can be extremely tall, exceptionally muscular, and are often highly aggressive with difficult-to-control tempers. Sometimes they develop severe acne and have skeleto-muscular problems. Current research suggests that they are within the normal IQ range, if slightly below the average. They can, however, have educational problems because they are developmentally immature. Kriminalhauptkommissar Fabel has described Olsen as having an almost adolescent taste in music and decor.' Susanne paused and leaned back in her chair. 'For the sake of clinical balance, I have to point out that there's a lot of discussion about just how much XYY contributes to criminality. The debate all started with a spree killer in the United States – Chicago, I think – called Richard Speck. He killed eight nurses in the 1960s and then appealed for leniency on account of his XYY genotype. It came out later that he'd been misdiagnosed and it threw the whole XYY argument into discredit for a while. And there are many XYY men who control their condition well. I knew a highly respected psychologist who was XYY. He had strategies for dealing with the difficulties it presented, particularly with his temper.'

'And,' added Fabel, 'we can't be certain that Olsen is XYY. As far as we know, he has never submitted to Karotype testing. But it should be pointed out that we know from experience that he can be extremely violent and has no qualms about injuring police officers. And, if he is our guy, he is capable of slashing a throat with a single blow.'

Fabel noticed that Susanne had removed her glasses and was turning them thoughtfully in her hands. 'Frau Doktor?'

'Sorry. I was just thinking that that is the thing which doesn't fit with me. If Olsen is XYY, then he's a rager. The typical XYY in prison is there for wife-beating or other loss-of-control assaults. When he hit Kriminaloberkommissar Meyer, he struck him with unnecessary, excessive violence. My belief is that if he were the killer, then we would see the excess of a psychotic fury . . . repeated stabbing, including post-mortem wounds where he would continue to attack his victim even after he knew he or she was dead. A single throat-slash doesn't seem to fit.'

'But it doesn't exclude him?'

'No. Probably not.'

Fabel flipped open the file in front of him. It wasn't just Susanne's reservations that were ringing an alarm bell somewhere deep in his mind. Olsen murdering Hanna Grünn and Markus Schiller would have been a crime of passion – of jealous rage. And that didn't fit with the bizarre staging of the bodies. Then there was the girl found on Blankenese beach, and this latest murder. All had notes written by what seemed – at first sight – to be the same hand.

It was as if Maria had been reading Fabel's mind. 'I'm not convinced about Olsen. I would have thought that he would be trying to keep a low profile at the moment, considering half of the Polizei Hamburg is out looking for him.'

'I don't know, Maria. He's our prime suspect so far, but I can't seem to get to grips with Olsen as a person. Or perhaps the problem is that I have. I keep on expecting to discover that there's more to Olsen than meets the eye. Perhaps there isn't. Maybe there's *less* to him than meets the eye. We've placed him at the Naturpark murders, that's for sure. He was lurking, waiting for them. We have his boot print and a match for his motorcycle tyre tread. He must be the killer there. It's the other two murders I can't fit him with. Nor the whole Grimm Brothers theme.' He turned to Susanne. 'Why would Olsen commit two murders with a motive, but also two without?'

'There's no such thing as a motiveless killing. Even the most random acts of violence are inspired by some desire or need. It could be that in Olsen's mind there is no connection with the other two killings, other than the fact that he is on some kind of Grimm Brothers-inspired crusade, and he included Grünn and Schiller because it suited him to combine objectives. Or mix business with pleasure, as it were.'

'"*To kill two birds with one stone*",' Fabel said, in English. The others stared blankly at him. 'Never mind.' He looked down at the file. At Olsen's almost handsome face. 'Maybe these other victims aren't the random choices we first thought. Maybe Olsen is picking them for who they are or what they represent. This latest victim was a model famed for her beauty, and she was posed as Sleeping Beauty. The first girl was from a family at the lowest social level – the underground people who were supposed to leave their children in the place of those they abducted. A question that remains is: did Olsen abduct the original girl, Paula Ehlers, three years ago?'

Klatt, the Norderstedt officer, answered. 'I'm convinced he must have. The similarity in appearance between the two girls is unnerving. I'm positive that whoever abducted and killed Martha Schmidt abducted Paula Ehlers.'

Fabel nodded. It was clear even to him, despite the fact that he had never seen either girl in life, that they were far too close in appearance for it to be a coincidence. 'What about the other victims – Hänsel and Gretel? If Olsen chose to combine his sexual jealousy with his "killing theme", then there must have been a conflict. He knew, only

240

too well, that his chosen victims were not brother and sister.'

'He probably doesn't feel he has to be too "literal" . . .' It was Petra Maas, the Kommissarin whom Fabel had drafted into the team, who answered. She was a tall, thin woman in her late thirties with mid-brown hair that framed an intelligent face. 'For example, this latest victim fitted with Sleeping Beauty or Briar Rose because of her famed beauty, but she was twice the age of the character in the fairy tale. There's flexibility in most psychotic agendas. We see the same kind of thing in the Sexual Crime SoKo. Serial rapists and serial killers have similar psychoses. If Olsen is your "Fairy Tale" killer, then he probably sees his victims' suitability in general, rather than specific, terms.'

'Or maybe he sees something specific in the two Naturpark victims that we don't,' Susanne proposed.

Fabel paused, staring down at the table's surface but seeing again the Schillers' opulent villa, their functional office, Vera Schiller's coldness. 'Okay, so Hanna Grünn was an employee in Markus Schiller's business. Or, more correctly, in the business run by Markus Schiller for his wife, Vera. She was the real power behind the concern, having inherited it from her father. Is there anything we're missing here?'

'Maybe the killer cast Vera Schiller, allegorically, as the wicked stepmother, with Hanna and

Markus as the Babes in the Wood?' suggested Hans Rödger, the other officer from the Sexual Crimes SoKo.

'It's not very convincing,' said Henk Hermann, the SchuPo Kommissar. 'But, if it is true, then the killer knew at least something about the victims' backgrounds. Which brings us back to Olsen.'

'The question is, what knowledge did the killer have of the other victims?' said Fabel. 'What was his connection with them?'

Susanne swivelled her chair to face Fabel fully. 'That he has knowledge of their backgrounds doesn't mean that he had any kind of significant contact with them. If we take Olsen out of the picture for a moment, the killer may have just been waiting for a courting couple – any courting couple – to use that spot for a tryst and then kill them, much as Son of Sam did in the US.'

Fabel stared out of the window towards Winterhuder Stadtpark and the city beyond. 'The main thing that concerns me is that he is getting bolder.'

'But that means he might also be getting sloppier.' The voice came from the doorway. A young, pretty woman, with short black hair and too-red lipstick and wearing a rather battered-looking leather jacket, made her way over to the table. She moved with an exaggerated ease, but Fabel noticed her wince slightly as she sat down.

'You should be recuperating,' he said.

'I'm fine, *Chef . . .*' said Anna Wolff, and, in response to Fabel's raised eyebrow, '. . . and fit enough to return to duty.'

Fabel called Anna and Maria into his office after the meeting was over. Fabel was less than convinced Anna was fit for anything other than the lightest duties, but he had to admit to himself that he was glad to see her back. The team he had built was greater than the sum of its parts: each officer had his or her own special abilities and individual strengths that were amplified in combination. When one member was down, it weakened the team generally, not just numerically. Fabel knew that, like Anna, Werner would probably be back on duty before it was medically advisable; but Werner's injury was more serious and any return would still be some time away.

He looked across at the two very different female members of his team. Anna sat stiffly in the chair, still trying to hide the discomfort that her severely grazed thigh was causing her. Next to Anna, Maria sat, as ever, in calm, colour-coordinated composure. Yet, less than a year before, an injury sustained in the course of an investigation had thrown Maria's life into the balance. One recovered officer, one recovering and one in hospital. Fabel didn't like it. At all. The investigative process seemed to be becoming an ever more dangerous enterprise. He knew he needed to strengthen his team.

'Anna, I need you to be partnered up with someone again. You too, Maria, at least until Werner gets out of hospital. As you can see, I've seconded Petra Maas and Hans Rödger from the Sexual Crimes SoKo. They're good people. I'm inclined to ask for their secondment to be extended at least until the end of this inquiry. But we need a new permanent member of the team. I've been putting this off because, well, I think we all needed time to come to terms with Paul's death, but it's mainly been that I haven't found anyone whom I think has what it takes to fit in with the team. Until now.'

'Klatt?' asked Anna.

Fabel didn't answer but stood up and made his way over to the office door, opened it and called across to the main section of the Mordkommission.

'Could you come in now, please?'

A tall, uniformed officer stepped into the office. Maria stood up and smiled. Anna remained seated, her expression one of sullen resignation.

'Herr Kommissar Hermann . . .' said Fabel. 'You've already met Kriminaloberkommissarin Klee. And this is Kriminalkommissarin Wolff, with whom you'll be working . . .'

CHAPTER 31

9.40 a.m., Tuesday, 30 March:
Blankenese, Hamburg

Fabel had arranged to meet Maria at Laura von Klosterstadt's villa in Blankenese. It was, predictably, an enormous property. Its construction was later than that of its neighbours and its design was definitely Jugendstil-influenced. In many ways, it reminded Fabel of these opulent Art Deco Californian mansions that seemed to dominate Hollywood *films noirs* of the 1930s and 1940s. Fabel felt as though he should be pulling up in an Oldsmobile and tugging up the collar of a trench coat as he parked in the drive outside.

The interior of the house was full of open spaces and clean lines. Fabel and Maria entered a vast reception hall. It was double height and facing them was a tall, elegant, arched, feature window that stretched the hall's full elevation. The window was filled with stained glass in a Modernist design and provided the only colour in the otherwise ice-white hall. 'The only thing about minimalism is that you can have too much of it . . .' Fabel gave a small laugh which died under Maria's uncomprehending stare.

Fabel was surprised to see Hugo Ganz, the Innensenator, waiting for them in the hall. His complexion was even more florid than usual. Next to him was a lean young man who could only have been twenty-seven or twenty-eight, but who wore an overly conservative suit, as if to lend himself the authority that his age denied him. He had the same fine features and pale blond hair as the dead woman, but they did not look quite right on a man.

'Herr Kriminalhauptkommissar Fabel, this is Hubert von Klosterstadt.' Ganz made the introduction. 'Laura's brother.'

'I'm very sorry for your loss, Herr von Klosterstadt,' said Fabel, shaking hands with him. Von Klosterstadt's hand was cool and his grip perfunctory. He nodded a curt acknowledgement of Fabel's condolences. The pale blue eyes were clear and frank. Either he had bound up his grief in a glacial coolness, or there were genuine limits to how much his sister's death was affecting him.

'Are you any further forward in your investigation, Herr Kriminalhauptkommissar?'

Ganz spoke before Fabel had a chance to answer. 'The prime suspect has taken flight, Hubert. A psychotic called Olsen. But it is only a matter of time before Kriminalhauptkommissar Fabel and his team track him down and arrest him.'

Fabel was silent for a moment. It was clear that Kriminaldirektor van Heiden was keeping Ganz fully informed of every detail of the investigation and, in turn, the Innensenator was passing on the information as he saw fit, to whomever he saw fit. Fabel decided there and then to limit his reporting of progress to van Heiden.

'We're keeping a number of lines of inquiry open.' Fabel gave Ganz a meaningful look. 'Do you live here, Herr von Klosterstadt?'

'No. God no. The "Ice Palace"? This was Laura's place for solitude. I have an apartment on the Alster. I'm just here to help in any way I can.'

'What about your parents – have they been informed?'

'They're on their way back from New York,' said Hubert. 'They were there for a charity event . . . for German victims of September the eleventh.'

'We got the New York police to notify them,' explained Maria.

Fabel nodded. 'If you don't mind, I'd like to have a look around.'

Hubert smiled a chilly, polite smile and indicated one of the rooms off the hall. 'I will be in the office with Herr Ganz. I have some of Laura's papers to sort out.'

'If you don't mind, Herr von Klosterstadt,' Maria said, 'we'd like you not to disturb anything for the moment. We need to check everything first.'

'Of course.' The temperature of Hubert's smile dropped a few degrees further. Ganz rested an avuncular hand on Hubert's elbow.

'We'll wait at my house, Hubert.'

Fabel and Maria made their way through the villa, moving from room to room like a couple of prospective homebuyers. Laura von Klosterstadt clearly had excellent taste in furniture and furnishings. A restrained taste. Too restrained. It was as if she had deliberately sought to combine opulence with Spartanism. One room in particular bothered Fabel: a large, airy room that was flooded with light from a south-facing window. It was the type of room most people would make into a main living space; but the only furniture was a sideboard cabinet on which sat a CD system along one wall and a single high-back armchair that sat, throne-like, in the centre of the room facing the window. Despite its emptiness, Fabel could tell that this was a room that was used. There was a sense of desolation, of loneliness, about the room and Fabel knew that Laura von Klosterstadt had been a very troubled person. He made his way over to the cabinet and slid open a door. There was a handful of CDs inside, all contemporary classical music. Fabel was surprised to discover that Laura von Klosterstadt's musical taste and his own coincided to a certain extent. The CDs were by modern Scandinavian or Baltic composers: there were pieces by Arvo Pärt and Georg Pelecis, as well as Peteris Vasks's *Musica Dolorosa*. Fabel checked the CD-player. There was a disc inside: the Finnish composer Einojuhani Rautavaara's *Cantus Arcticus, Opus 61*.

Fabel pressed the play button and sat in the single chair. A flute imitated the rise and fall of a bird. Then the *Cantus* began, not with human voices but those of Arctic sea birds. The birdsong swelled, the dissonant cries of terns and gulls combining, and the flute and brass gave way to broad, slow orchestral sweeps and ripples of a harp. Fabel had heard this piece before, in fact he had the same CD, and, as always, he was transported to a vast white Arctic icescape: an imagined vista that was as barren as it was beautiful. The Ice Palace. Fabel remembered the phrase that Hubert, Laura's brother, had used to describe this house; to describe his sister's frigid isolation here.

He listened to the music for a moment before switching the CD off. He and Maria then continued to make their way through the house: a quiet yet remorseless invasion of the most private spaces in another person's life. They rifled through Laura's books, through her bedside cabinets and, in the dressing room that fed off the bedroom, through her cosmetics in the huge 1930s dressing table with its illuminated mirror.

Fabel and Maria worked through to the back of the house. Double panel doors opened up on a long pool room. The pool ran close to the wall on one side and on the other there was a changing cabana and a sauna. The windows at the far end of the pool filled the wall. All Fabel could see was sky. It was like looking at a moving painting of clouds.

'Wow . . .' Fabel heard Maria say at his side. 'This must have cost a fortune.'

Fabel imagined himself swimming in the pool,

towards the sky. Like the sparsely decorated room downstairs, Laura von Klosterstadt had left something of herself in here. This was another place for solitary contemplation. For some reason, the idea of a pool party in this space seemed ludicrous. He walked the length of the pool to the window end. Standing at the window, Fabel could see the terraces of Blankenese bank steeply away below him until the land flattened out on to the Elbe's shore and beyond to the flat, green patchwork of the Altes Land. Laura had placed herself above everyone else. Out of reach.

The urgent ring of Fabel's cell phone, amplified and echoing in the tiled pool room, gave both police officers a start.

'Hello, *Chef*. Are you still at the von Klosterstadt house?' Anna asked.

'Yes. Maria and I are both here. Why?'

'Is there, by any chance, a swimming pool there?'

Fabel looked around himself, confused, as if to confirm that he was where he thought he was. 'As a matter of fact we're standing by the pool at the moment.'

'I'd preserve the locus, if I were you, *Chef*. I'll get Herr Brauner and his team over right away.'

Fabel looked into the silky water. He knew the answer before he asked the question. 'What have you found out, Anna?'

'Herr Doktor Möller has just confirmed Laura von Klosterstadt's cause of death. Drowning. The water in her lungs and airway was chlorinated.'

CHAPTER 32

2.40 p.m., Tuesday, 30 March:
Bergedorf, Hamburg

Fabel misjudged the house numbers and parked too far down Ernst-Mantius-Strasse. During the course of his short walk, he passed three imposing villas, each presenting its own subtly different expression of wealth. Here he was in Bergedorf, at the other side of the city from Blankenese, yet he was again being presented with substantial reminders that Hamburg is Germany's richest city – and of the limits of his own salary.

Although part of Hamburg, Bergedorf had its own identity and was known as the 'city within a city'. And this was the Bergedorfer Villenviertel – the villa quarter – where each of the properties that Fabel strolled past was worth several million Euros. Fabel checked the number of each villa he passed until he had the one he sought. Like its neighbours, it was three storeys high. The walls were limewashed with a discreet blue-grey against which the white decorative plasterwork stood out clean and fresh. One of the lower-level rooms jutted out into the garden, and its roof formed a balcony for the room above. Blue and white canopies optimistically shaded the windows from a sun that had yet to make its presence sufficiently felt.

When Fabel rang the doorbell, it was answered by a massive man with coal-black eyes. His thick dark hair was heavily flecked with white and swept back from a broad forehead that loomed above heavy brow ridges. The wide, heavy jaw jutted a little too much underneath the fleshy mouth. If it hadn't been for the fire of a dark intelligence that burned in the eyes, the look would have been almost Neanderthal.

'Kriminalhauptkommissar Fabel?' The man in the doorway smiled.

Fabel smiled back. 'Thanks for seeing me, Herr Weiss . . .'

Gerhard Weiss stepped back, pulling the door wider and indicating that Fabel should enter. Fabel had seen Weiss's photograph on the cover of *Die Märchenstrasse*: it had been a good likeness, but it had not indicated the author's great height. His stature was easily the equal of Olsen's: Fabel estimated that Weiss was at least two metres five. Fabel was relieved to be out of Weiss's shadow when the author led him to a study off the entrance hall and, having asked Fabel to sit, took his own place behind his desk.

The study was vast; Fabel guessed it was the

main room at floor level and it was clearly the one which supported the balcony above. Everything was rich, dark wood of varying tones: the enormous desk looked as if it had consumed half a rainforest of mahogany and all but one of the walls were lined, floor to ceiling, with fully stocked walnut bookshelves. Only the floor was of a lighter wood, probably red oak, Fabel guessed. The ceiling downlighters were switched on, as was Weiss's desk light, casting pools of brightness on the various wooden surfaces. This extra illumination was needed, even now in the afternoon: it was as if the dark, polished wood in the study sucked up the daylight from the French windows that opened out on to the garden and the street beyond. The surface of Weiss's desk was uncluttered. An early edition of the Grimms' *Fairy Tales* sat to one side and Weiss's laptop sat in the centre. The desk was dominated, however, by a striking sculpture. Again it was made out of wood, but a black, black wood, like ebony. Weiss caught Fabel's glance.

'Extraordinary, isn't it?'

'Yes . . . yes, it is.' Fabel stared at the sculpture. It was a stylised wolf: the body was stretched and slightly twisted and the heavy head snapped round, the jaws snarling. It looked as if the wolf, having heard something behind it, had suddenly turned and was caught here in the taut, sinuous, transitional moment between surprise and attack. It was a magnificently executed piece and Fabel could not decide whether it was beautiful or hideous.

'A very talented, very remarkable man created this for me,' explained Weiss. 'A uniquely talented artist. And a lycanthrope.'

Fabel laughed. 'A werewolf? There's no such thing.'

'Indeed there is, Herr Kriminalhauptkommissar. Lycanthropy exists – not as a supernatural occurrence of transformation from man to beast, but as a recognised psychiatric condition. People who *believe* they turn into wolves.' Weiss tilted his huge head and contemplated the sculpture. 'The sculptor was a close friend of mine. He was otherwise perfectly sane, except when there was a full moon. Then he would have a seizure – a fit – in which he would twist and thrash, tearing at his clothes, then fall asleep. That was all that happened. It was observed by others, including myself. Nothing more than a fit caused by the subtle changes of pressure in brain fluid caused by a full moon. But what we saw was not what he experienced. So I asked him to capture the moment, as it were.' Weiss's eyes cast a dark searchlight over the sculpture. 'And this is what he crafted.'

'I see.' Fabel examined the artwork again. He had decided: it was hideous. 'What happened to him? Was he successfully treated?'

'Unfortunately not. He spent more and more time in institutions. Ultimately he could take no more of it and hanged himself.'

'I'm sorry.'

Weiss's vast shoulders moved dismissively in something too small to be called a shrug. 'You have an interesting name, Herr Kriminalhauptkommissar. Fabel. Quite appropriate to my line of work – fables, as it were.'

'I believe it's Danish in origin. It's more common in Hamburg than in any other German city, although I'm Frisian originally.'

'Fascinating. What can I do for you, Herr Fabel?' Weiss stressed Fabel's name, as if still playing with it.

Fabel explained to Weiss about the murders he was investigating, and how they clearly had a 'Grimm Fairy Tale' theme. And that, perhaps, they were inspired by Weiss's novel, *Die Märchenstrasse*. There was a moment's pause when he had finished, and in that moment, Fabel suspected there was the merest hint of satisfaction in Weiss's expression.

'It is also clear that we are dealing with a serial offender,' Fabel concluded.

'Or offenders . . .' said Weiss. 'Has it never crossed your mind that you are perhaps dealing with two people? If these killings are united by a Grimm-related theme, then it's worth remembering that there were, after all, two Brothers Grimm.'

'Obviously, we hadn't ruled that out.' The truth was that Fabel had not fully considered that it might be a team. It certainly wasn't unknown for

255

two killers to work together, as he knew only too well from a recent investigation where there had been. It could also explain why Olsen had a motive for the Naturpark murders but not for the others. Fabel changed tack.

'Have you had any, well, *odd* correspondence recently, Herr Weiss? It could be that our killer – or killers – has sought to make contact with you.'

Weiss laughed. 'Odd correspondence?' He stood up, looming high in the room, and went across to a wooden escritoire that sat against the only wall free of bookshelves. Above the escritoire the wall was covered with framed, old-fashioned illustrations. Weiss picked up a fat file, carried it over and thumped it on to the desk before sitting back down. 'That's only the last three or four months. If you were to find anything in that that wasn't "odd", I'd be very much surprised.' He made a 'help yourself' gesture.

Fabel flicked open the folder. There were dozens of letters, some with photographs, some with cuttings that the sender thought would be helpful to Weiss. Most seemed to relate to Weiss's *Wahlwelten* fantasy novels: people with sad, empty lives sought the solace of living out an alternate, literary existence by having Weiss incorporate them into one of his stories. There was a sexually very explicit letter from a woman asking Weiss to be her 'big, bad wolf'. It was accompanied by a photograph of the correspondent, naked except for a red hood and cape. She was an overweight woman of about fifty, whose body had obviously submitted some time ago to an unequal battle with gravity.

'And that pile is tiny compared with what comes in electronically to my personal and my publisher's websites,' explained Weiss.

'Do you reply to these?'

'Not now, no. I used to. Or at least to those that were reasonably sane or decent. But now I just don't have the time. That's why I started to charge set fees to include people as characters in my *Wahlwelten* novels.'

Fabel gave a small laugh. 'So how much would you charge me to have a part in one of your novels?'

'Herr Fabel, one of the main lessons of the fairy tale is to be very careful what you wish for. I might include you in one of my works just because I find you an interesting character, with an unusual name. Unlike the people who pay for inclusion, you have met me. I have an *idea* of you. And once you are in one of my stories, I have total control over you. I and I alone decide your fate. Whether you live or die.' Weiss paused and the black eyes sparkled beneath the heavy bridge of his brow. The werewolf sculpture remained frozen in its snarl. A car passed by on the street outside. 'But normally I charge five thousand Euros for a half-page mention.' Weiss smiled.

Fabel shook his head. 'The price of fame.' He tapped the file on the desk. 'May I take these away with me?'

Weiss shrugged. 'If you think they'll help.'

'Thanks. I'm reading *Die Märchenstrasse* at the moment, by the way.'

'Are you enjoying it?'

'I'm finding it interesting, let's put it that way,' said Fabel. 'I'm too focused on any possible connection to these murders to assess its literary merits. And I do think it's possible that there is a connection.'

Weiss leaned back in his chair and locked his fingers together, stretching the two index fingers against each other and tapping his chin. It was an overdone gesture of thoughtfulness. 'It would sadden me greatly if that were so, Herr Kriminalhauptkommissar. But the main theme of all my work is that art imitates life and life imitates art. I cannot *inspire* someone to commit murder through my writing. They're already killers or potential killers. They may seek to imitate a method or a setting . . . or even a theme, but they would murder anyway, whether they read my books or not. Ultimately, I do not inspire them. They inspire me. Just as they have always inspired writers.' Weiss allowed his fingers to rest gently on the leather-bound volume of fairy tales that sat on his desk.

'Like the Grimm Brothers?'

Weiss smiled and again something sparkled darkly in his eyes. 'The Grimm Brothers were academics. They sought absolute knowledge – the origins of our language and our culture. Like all men of science of their time, a time when science was emerging as the new religion of Western Europe, they sought to lay our past under a microscope and dissect it. But there is no absolute truth. There is no definitive past. It's a tense, not a place. What the Grimm Brothers discovered was the same world that they themselves lived in; the same world we inhabit now. What the Grimms discovered was that it's just the frames of reference that differed.'

'What do you mean?'

Weiss rose again from his leather chair and beckoned for Fabel to follow him across to the wall covered with pictures. They were all illustrations from nineteenth- and early twentieth-century books.

'The fairy story has inspired more than literary interpretation,' explained Weiss. 'Some of the finest artists lent their talents to illustrating the tales. This is my collection – Gustave Doré, Hermann Vogel, Edmund Dulac, Arthur Rackham, Fernande Biegler, George Cruickshank, Eugen Neureuther – each with a subtly different interpretation.' Weiss drew Fabel's attention to one illustration in particular: a woman was stepping into a stone-flagged room; a key tumbled from her grasp in horror as she did so. A tree-stump chopping block and an axe sat in the foreground of the picture: both were covered in blood, as was the stone floor around it. The dead bodies of several women, all in nightgowns, were hung around the walls, as if from meat hooks.

'I am guessing,' said Weiss, 'that this type of scene, perhaps not to such excess, is not unfamiliar to you, Herr Fabel. It is a murder scene. This poor woman here –' he tapped on the glass that protected the illustration '– has clearly stumbled upon the lair of a serial killer.'

Fabel found himself fixed to the image. It was in the familiar style of a nineteenth-century illustration, but it struck too many resonances with Fabel. 'Where is this illustration from?'

'It's the work of Hermann Vogel. Late 1880s. It is, Herr Fabel, an illustration for Charles Perrault's *La Barbe bleue – Bluebeard.* A French tale of a monstrous nobleman who punishes the curiosity of women by killing and mutilating them in a locked room in his castle. It is a story. A fable. But that does not stop it being a universal truth. When Perrault wrote his version down, the memories of real atrocities committed by noblemen were still very much alive in the French psyche. Gilles de Rais, Marshal of France and comrade-in-arms of Joan of Arc, for example, who sodomised and murdered hundreds of boys to feed his perverted, and unchecked, lusts. Or Cunmar the Accursed, who ruled Brittany in the sixth century. Cunmar – or Conomor, if you prefer – is perhaps the closest historical reference for Bluebeard. He decapitated each of his wives, finally cutting off the head of the beautiful, pious and heavily pregnant Triphine. Incidentally, the tale exists throughout Europe: the Grimm brothers recorded it as "Fitcher's

Bird", the Italians call it "Silvernose" and the English Bluebeard is called "Mr Fox". All of them relate to feminine curiosity leading to the discovery of a hidden, bloody chamber. A murder room.'

Weiss paused, as if appreciating the illustration anew. 'Hermann Vogel, the artist of this piece, was German. Even although he was illustrating a French fable, he couldn't help introducing something of his own cultural background . . . the chopping block and the axe is borrowed from the Grimms' "Fitcher's Bird" tale. The fact is that this tale is told across Europe and the details are always broadly the same. There must have been real events, whether they were the deeds of Cunmar the Accursed or not, to inspire them. My point is this: these cautionary tales for children, these ancient fables and legends – they all prove that the serial rapist or killer or child-abductor is not a modern phenomenon. The big, bad wolf has nothing to do with wolves.' Weiss laughed. 'Funnily enough, the curse that earned Cunmar the epithet "Accursed" was supposed to have been that he was turned into a werewolf for his sins . . . Eventually all history blurs into myth and legend.'

Weiss took a novel from the bookshelf before him. Unlike the others, it was new: a modern hard-back in a glossy dust jacket. Fabel could see that it was written by another author. He did not recognise the name, but it was English or American rather than German. Weiss dropped it on top of his correspondence file. 'Today we continuously reinvent these tales. The same stories, new characters. This is a best-seller – a story about the hunt for a serial killer who ritually dismembers his victims. These are our fairy tales today. These are our fables, our Märchen. Instead of elves and kobolds and hungry wolves lurking in the dark corners of the woods, we have cannibals and dissectors and abductors lurking in the dark corners of our cities. It is in our nature to guise our evil as something extraordinary or something different: books and films about aliens, sharks, vampires, ghosts, witches. The fact of the matter is that there is one beast that is more dangerous, more predatory, than any other in the history of nature. Us. The human being is not only the planet's top predator, it is the only creature that kills for the sheer pleasure of it, for sexual satisfaction or as organised groups to satisfy abstract concepts of religious, political or social dogma. There is nothing more deadly or menacing than the ordinary man or woman in the street. But that is something, of course, you know only too well through your work. All the rest. All the horror stories and the fables and the belief in greater malevolence – it's all a veil drawn over the mirror we have to look in every day.'

Weiss sat down again and indicated that Fabel should do the same. 'The thing we need fear most is our neighbour, our parent, the woman or man next to us on the U-Bahn . . . ourselves. And the most difficult thing we can do is to face up to the monstrous banality of that fact.' Weiss turned the heavy sculpture on his desk slightly so that the snarling jaws faced Fabel. 'This is what lies within us, Herr Kriminalhauptkommissar. We are the big, bad wolves.'

Fabel sat and stared at the sculpture, drawn to its hideous beauty. He knew that what Weiss was saying was right. He did, as Weiss had said, see the evidence of it in his work. The monstrous creativity of which the human mind was capable when it came to tormenting others. To killing others.

'So you're saying that the serial killer isn't a modern phenomenon – it's just that we didn't have that name for them?'

'Exactly. We are all born arrogant, Herr Fabel. We each believe we reinvent the world anew when we are born into it. The sad truth is that we are merely variations on a theme . . . or at least on a common experience. The good and the evil there is in the world came into it with the very first man. It evolved with us. That is why we have these ancient folk tales and myths. The Grimm Brothers recorded, they didn't create. None of their fairy tales were their invention, but ancient folk tales they gathered as part of their linguistic research. The existence of these tales and the warning implicit in each one to 'never wander far from home' and to 'beware of strangers' proves that the serial killer is no mere side effect of modern life, he has been with us throughout our history. And they must have been inspired by real events. The true origins of these fairy tales must lie in actual abductions and murders. Just as the truth of lycanthropy, the myth of the werewolf, lies in the inability of previous generations to recognise, define or understand psychopathy. The fact is, Herr Fabel, everyone accepts that we frequently make fiction out of fact. What I assert is that we also make fact out of fiction.'

Fabel watched Weiss as he spoke. He tried to work out what kindled the dark fire, the passion, in his eyes. 'So, when you write about Jacob Grimm being a child-murderer, do you believe that your act of fictive creation translates into some kind of truth?'

'What is the truth?' Weiss's knowing smile had a patronising edge to it, as if Fabel could not possibly possess the intellectual resources to deal with the question.

'The truth,' replied Fabel, 'is an absolute, incontrovertible fact. I deal with the truth, absolute truth, every day. I understand what you're trying to say – that sometimes truth is abstract or subjective. Jacob Grimm was not a murderer. The person I am seeking is a murderer: that is an incontrovertible fact. The truth. What I need to establish is how far, if at all, your book has inspired them.'

Weiss made a submissive gesture with his hands. Big, powerful hands. 'Ask your questions, Herr Kriminalhauptkommissar . . .'

The interview lasted a further twenty minutes.

Weiss's knowledge of myth and fable was ency-clopaedic and Fabel found himself taking notes as the author spoke. But there was something about Weiss that Fabel did not like. There was a menace about him, not just in his size – he didn't convey the same sense of pent-up violence that Olsen had – it was something in the coal-black eyes. Something almost inhuman.

Finally, Fabel asked: 'But these are all, when it comes down to it, just fairy tales. You can't believe that they were inspired by real events?'

'Weren't they?' said Weiss. 'Take the Russian tale of Baba Yaga's hut, where all the furniture is made out of bones. You've heard of Ed Gien, of course – the American serial killer who inspired the book and film *Psycho* as well as *The Silence of the Lambs*. When the police raided his farmhouse they found chairs and stools made out of human bones, as well as an almost complete body-suit made from the skins of dead women. Like I say, no one is unique. There will have been countless Ed Giens before. It is entirely likely that some early Russian version inspired the fable of Baba Yaga. And please bear in mind, Herr Fabel, that many of these fairy tales have been sanitised. Take your "Sleeping Beauty" victim. The original "Sleeping Beauty" tale didn't have her awoken with a chaste kiss – it was a tale of rape, incest and cannibalism.'

When Fabel was back out on Ernst-Mantius-Strasse, Weiss's correspondence file under his arm, he felt the need to pull a deep, cleansing breath into his body. He couldn't work out why, but he had the feeling of having escaped a lair; that Weiss's study, with its burnished, dark wood, had been closing in on him. The sun had broken through and bathed the pristine villas with a warm light. Fabel gazed at each as he walked back to his car; how many hidden rooms, how many dark secrets, lay behind the elegant façades? He flipped open his cell phone.

'Maria? It's Fabel. I want you to get me a full background on Gerhard Weiss. Everything you can find . . .'

CHAPTER 33

8.00 p.m., Tuesday, 30 March:
Krankenhaus Mariahilf, Heimfeld, Hamburg

'I'm sorry, *Mutti*, I can't stay as long tonight. I've got so many preparations to make. I'm a busy, busy boy these days, let me tell you.' He nudged his chair even closer to the bed, glancing around conspiratorially, before whispering into her ear. 'I did another one. I made another story come to life. She was so sad, this one. I saw it in her beautiful, beautiful face when she let me into that great big empty villa of hers. A princess in an ivory tower. I did her a great favour, *Mutti*. I really didn't want this one to suffer. And now, of course, I have to prepare for you coming home. I've been busy with that, too.'

He paused and stroked the old woman's hair. 'But you will suffer terribly. I guarantee that.' There were sounds outside the room: clog-soled footsteps as a duty nurse headed down the hall. He sat back in his chair and listened to them fade. 'It's a wondrous thing that I do, mother. I return them to being children again. In those precious moments

I share with them – before they die, I mean – everything that they have become is lost . . . years of adult life wiped away, and they are once more small, frightened children. Lost little souls terrified by how little they understand what is happening to them.' He fell quiet for a moment and the room was silent other than the distant sound of a laughter-punctuated conversation that was taking place a little down the hall, and in another universe. After a while he continued. 'The police came to see me, *Mutti*. They're very, very stupid people, you know. They think they have all the answers and they have nothing. They have no idea of who they're dealing with at all. What they are dealing with. They'll never catch me.' He gave a small laugh. 'At least they won't catch me until you and I have our fun together. What frightens you more, mother, the fact that you're going to die, or the fact that you won't die quickly enough? Does the pain frighten you? The *idea* of it? It will be great. That I can tell you: your pain will be very great indeed. And it's nearly time, *Mutti* . . . nearly time . . .'

CHAPTER 34

2.45 a.m., Sunday, 11 April:
Pöseldorf, Hamburg

Fabel lay, listening to Susanne's even, deep breathing. More and more he found her presence comforting: the dreams did not seem to come so often when she was beside him. It was as if her being there consoled him into a deeper, better sleep. But tonight his mind raced. There was so much to do. This case was growing, spreading, like a dark malignancy and was squeezing into the few spaces that Fabel had left for a private life. So many things on his mental 'to do' list remained unchecked. His mother was ageing. His daughter was growing up. Neither was getting the time they deserved; the time Fabel wanted to give them. His relationship with Susanne was good, but it wasn't taking the definite form that it should by this stage and he knew he wasn't giving it the attention it needed. He was surprised by the sharp pang of panic in his chest at the thought of maybe losing her.

Fabel had phoned his mother several times over the last few days, but he needed to find the time to get back out to Norddeich to see her. Lex had been forced to succumb to the commercial pressures of his business and return to Sylt to run his restaurant. His mother had insisted that she was more than capable of taking care of herself, but Fabel wanted to see her to make sure for himself.

He got up and sat for a moment on the edge of his bed. It seemed that everywhere he turned there was so much that clamoured for his attention. At least he had filled the gap in his team; but even that was causing problems. Anna was showing Henk Hermann the ropes, but Fabel's unorthodox recruitment strategies had already ruffled the feathers of the bureaucrats within the Polizei Hamburg. Technically it should have been easy for Fabel to pluck Hermann from the ranks of the uniformed SchuPo branch – as a Polizeikommissar, Hermann had already undergone the required training at the Landespolizeihochschule, next to the Präsidium. But Hamburg's uniform branch was always short of officers, and Fabel knew he would have a battle to transfer Hermann permanently to the Kriminalpolizei. In the meantime, Fabel had basically 'seconded' Hermann to the Mordkommission until this case was over, at which time Hermann could go through the appropriate course. A new team finding its way together was always a tense time and Fabel was also worried about how Anna Wolff would respond to having a new partner. She was very much the loose cannon in the team: it was an impulsiveness so clearly exhibited by her high-speed motorcycle pursuit of Olsen. It was also something that Fabel did not entirely discourage: Anna's intuitive and impulsive approach to her work often gave her a perspective on a case that the others missed. But she needed a counterbalance and, until his death, Paul Lindemann had provided that. Even in that partnership there had, to begin with, been a friction between them. Fabel hoped that, now Anna was more experienced, more mature, the transition would be easier with Henk Hermann. But, from her sullen response to the news of Hermann's recruitment, Fabel knew that he was going to have to have a serious talk to her. No one was bigger than the team.

So much of this case seemed out of Fabel's control. Olsen seemed to have vanished from the face of the earth: he had evaded arrest for over a week now. The first three killings had sparked the usual media interest, particularly the double murder in the Naturpark. But everything had changed with Laura von Klosterstadt's murder. As a living person, Laura possessed the elements of high social status, celebrity and beauty. As a murder victim, these elements had combined like fissile material and Laura exploded into the number one Hamburg media story. Then, inevitably, the watertight security that Fabel had attempted to wrap around the case had been compromised. He suspected that his fears about van Heiden passing on so much information to

Ganz had been justified. Not that Ganz would have wanted to fan the flames of publicity, but he was proving injudicious in his choice of confidants. The truth was that the leak could have come from any one of a hundred possible sources. Whatever the source, a few days earlier Fabel had switched on the television news to see it announced that the Polizei Hamburg were hunting the 'Märchenmörder', the 'Fairy Tale Murderer'. The next day he had seen Gerhard Weiss being interviewed on NDR's *Hamburger Journal*. Sales of Weiss's book had apparently skyrocketed overnight and now he was announcing to the public that the Polizei Hamburg had already sought his advice on these latest murders.

Fabel rose and stepped out of the bedroom and into the lounge. The picture windows of his apartment framed the glittering nightscape of the Aussenalster lake and the lights of Uhlenhorst and Hohenfelde beyond. Even at this hour, he could trace the lights of a small boat as it made its way across the Alster. He always drew calm from this view. He thought of Laura von Klosterstadt, swimming towards her view. But where Fabel loved his outlook for the sense of connection it gave him with the city around him, Laura had spent a fortune on an architecture of remoteness, creating a panorama of sky and disconnecting herself from the landscape; detaching herself from people. What was it that made such a beautiful, intelligent young woman sequester herself?

Fabel could see Laura, swimming towards the sky, the night sky framed in those huge windows. But he could see only her. Alone. Everything about her home suggested isolation; a retreat from a life before cameras and the public eye. A lonely, beautiful woman making quiet, small waves in the silky water as she swam towards infinity. No one else. But there had to have been someone else there, in the water with her. The autopsy had revealed that she had been drowned in that pool, and the immediate pre-mortem bruising on her neck suggested that she had been held down. Möller, the pathologist, had suggested that it was a single hand, that the bruises corresponded to an extended thumb on one side, the grip of the fingers on the other. But, Möller had said, the span of the hand had been huge.

Big hands. Like Olsen's. But like Gerhard Weiss's too.

Who was it, Laura? Who was in the pool with you? Why would you choose to share the isolation you so carefully built for yourself? Fabel stared out over the view before him and posed questions in his head to a dead woman; her family had been unable to answer them. Fabel had visited Laura's parents on their vast estate out in the Altes Land. It had been an unsettling experience. Hubert, Laura's brother, had been there and had introduced Fabel to his parents. Peter von Klosterstadt and his wife Margarethe had been the epitome of aristocratic coolness. Peter, however, looked frayed around the edges, the combination of jet lag and grief showing in his eyes and the dullness of his reactions. Margarethe von Klosterstadt, however, had been chillingly composed. Her lack of emotion had reminded Fabel of his first impressions of Hubert. Laura had clearly inherited her beauty from her mother, but in Margarethe's case it was a harsh, uncompromising and cruel beauty. She would have been in her early fifties, but her figure and the firmness of her skin would have been the envy of a woman half her age. Fabel had had the feeling that she regarded him and Maria with a practised haughtiness, until he had realised that, even in repose, her features wore the same expression like a mask. Fabel had disliked her from the moment he saw her. He had also been disturbed by how powerfully sexually attractive he found her. The meeting had yielded little of any value, other than to point Fabel in the direction of Heinz Schnauber, Laura's agent, who had probably been her closest confidant and who was totally distraught by Laura's death. Predictably, as Margarethe von Klosterstadt had described it.

Fabel became aware of Susanne's presence behind him. She slipped her arms around his waist and rested her chin on his shoulder as she shared his view out over the Alster and he felt the warmth of her body against his back.

'I'm sorry,' he said in a three a.m. voice. 'I didn't mean to wake you.'

'It's okay. What's the matter? Another bad dream?'

He turned his head and kissed her. 'No. Just things on my mind.'

'What?'

Fabel turned around, took her in his arms, and kissed her for a long time on the lips. Then he said:

'I'd like you to come to Norddeich with me. I'd like you to meet my mother.'

CHAPTER 35

10.30 a.m., Wednesday, 14 April:
Norderstedt, Hamburg

Henk Hermann had made an effort to keep something resembling a conversation going, but, after so many monosyllabic responses, he had given up and watched the urban landscape slide by as Anna drove them up to Norderstedt. When they parked outside the Ehlerses' family home, Anna turned to Hermann and put together her first full sentence since leaving the Präsidium.

'This is my interview, okay? You're here to watch and learn, is that clear?'

Hermann sighed and nodded. 'Does Herr Klatt know we're here? The guy from KriPo Norderstedt?' Anna didn't answer and was out of the car and halfway up the path to the front door before Hermann had got his seat belt off.

Anna Wolff had called Frau Ehlers before making the trip up. She didn't want them to think they'd found Paula's body or that there had been any other significant development in the case. It was just that Anna wanted to go over a few details with them again. What Anna had not disclosed was that the central puzzle she was trying to solve was why it was Paula's name that had been placed in the 'changeling' victim's hand. Most of all, she felt an overwhelming impulse to be the one to find Paula. To bring her home to her family, even if it meant bringing home a corpse.

Anna was surprised to find that Herr Ehlers was also at home. A pale blue boiler suit, dulled by a film of very fine brick-dust or something similar, hung baggily on his tall, lean frame. He brought out a kitchen chair and sat on that, rather than stain the upholstery in the living room. Anna guessed that Frau Ehlers had phoned him at his work and he had come straight over. Again there was an intensity in the postures of both Ehlers which Anna found upsetting and annoying: she had made it very clear that they had no news. Anna introduced Henk Hermann. Before Frau Ehlers sat down, she went into the kitchen and re-emerged carrying a tray with a coffee pot, cups and some biscuits.

Anna got straight to the point. And the point was Heinrich Fendrich, Paula's former German teacher.

'We've been over this so many times before.' Frau Ehlers's face looked tired and drawn, as if from three years of insufficient sleep. 'We cannot believe that Herr Fendrich had anything whatsoever to do with Paula's disappearance.'

'How can you be so sure?' Henk Hermann spoke from the corner, where he sat resting a coffee cup on one knee. Anna fired a look in his direction, which he seemed not to have noticed. 'I mean, is there something in particular that makes you so certain?'

Herr Ehlers shrugged. 'Afterwards . . . I mean, after Paula went missing, he was very helpful and supportive. He was genuinely very, very worried about Paula. In a way that he couldn't have faked. Even when the police kept questioning him all the time, we knew they were looking in the wrong place.'

Anna nodded thoughtfully. 'Listen, I know this is an uncomfortable question to answer, but did you ever suspect that Herr Fendrich's interest in Paula was, well, inappropriate?'

Herr and Frau Ehlers exchanged a look that Anna couldn't read. Then Herr Ehlers shook his ash-blond head. 'No. No, we didn't.'

'Herr Fendrich seemed to be the only teacher Paula had time for, unfortunately,' said Frau Ehlers. 'He came to see us . . . it must have been about six months before Paula went missing. I thought it was strange, a teacher coming to the house and all, but he was very . . . I don't know what you'd call it . . . very *definite* that Paula was very bright, especially in German, and that we should come up to the school for a meeting with the principal. But none of Paula's other teachers seemed to think she was anything special and we didn't want her to set her sights too high only to be disappointed later.'

Anna and Hermann sat in her VW outside the Ehlerses' house. Anna gripped the steering wheel and sat unmoving, her gaze focused on the windscreen.

'Do I sense we just hit some kind of dead end?' Hermann asked.

Anna gazed at him blankly for a moment before turning the key in the ignition decisively. 'Not yet. I've a detour to make first . . .'

Given Fendrich's sensitivity to further police investigation, Anna again decided to phone ahead, this time from her cell phone as she drove south from Norderstedt. She had rung the school he was now teaching in, but didn't disclose that she was calling on behalf of the Polizei Hamburg. Fendrich was less than happy when he came to the phone but agreed to meet them at the café in the Rahlstedt Bahnhofsvorplatz.

They parked in a Parkplatz a block away from the café, and walked through alternating shade and bright sunlight as the patchy clouds intermittently shuttered the sun. Fendrich was already there when they arrived, contemplatively stirring a cappuccino. When they entered Fendrich looked up and eyed Hermann with a disinterested suspicion. Anna introduced her new partner and they sat down at the round table.

'What is it you want from me, Kommissarin Wolff?' Fendrich's tone was of weary protest.

Anna slid her sunglasses on to the top of her head. 'I want to find Paula, Herr Fendrich. Paula is either alive and has been subjected to God knows what torment for the past three years, or, and we both know this is more likely, she's lying dead somewhere. Hidden from the world and from her family who just want to grieve for her. I don't know what the basis of your relationship with her was, but I do believe that, at the bottom of it, you truly cared about Paula. I just need to find her. And what I want from you, Herr Fendrich, is anything you can give me that may point me in the right direction.'

Fendrich stirred his cappuccino once more, gazing down at the froth. When he looked up, he said: 'Are you familiar with the playwright George Bernard Shaw?'

Anna shrugged. 'That would be more my boss's thing. Kriminalhauptkommissar Fabel is into all things English.'

'Shaw was Irish, actually. He once said "Those who can, do; those who cannot, teach." It basic-ally condemned all teachers as failures. But it also denied that one can "do" teaching. I didn't drift into this profession, Frau Wolff. I was called to it. I love it. Every day I face class after class of young minds. Minds yet to be fully formed and developed.' He leaned back and gave a bitter laugh. His hand still rested on his spoon and his attention was back on the surface of his coffee. 'Of course, there is so much – well, pollution, I suppose you'd call it. Cultural pollution . . . from television, the Internet and all of the throwaway technologies that are heaped on young people today. But every now and again one comes across a fresh, clear mind that is just waiting for its horizons to expand, to explode.' Fendrich's eyes were no longer lifeless. 'Do you have any idea what it is like to be under police investigation for a crime like this? No. No you don't. Nor can you have any idea what it is like to be in that position when you're a teacher. Someone whom parents trust with those who are most precious to them. Your colleague, Herr Klatt, nearly destroyed my career. Nearly destroyed me. Pupils would avoid being alone with me. Parents and even my colleagues would regard me with undisguised hostility.' He paused, as if he been running and then could not work out where it was he was going. He looked at both police officers. 'I am no paedophile. I have no sexual interest in young girls or young boys. No *physical* interest. It is their minds that I care about. And Paula's mind was a diamond. A crystalline clear, fearsomely sharp and penetrating intellect in the rough. It needed refining and polishing, but it was outstanding.'

'If that is so,' said Anna, 'then I don't understand why you seem to be the only one to have seen that. No other teacher saw Paula as anything other than an average, if that, student. Even her parents seemed to think you were barking up the wrong tree.'

'You're right. No one else saw it. And that was because they weren't looking. Paula was often seen as lazy and dreamy, rather than slow. Exactly what happens when a gifted child is trapped in an educational environment – or a domestic environment, for that matter – that isn't intellectually challenging enough. The other thing is that Paula's giftedness was manifesting itself in my subject – she had a natural ear and talent for the German language. And when she wrote . . . when she wrote it was like singing. Anyway, as well as those who didn't see it there were those who didn't want to see it.'

'Her parents?' said Henk Hermann.

'Exactly. Paula wrote a story as an assignment for me. It was, well, almost a fairy tale. She danced through our language. There, in that small piece of writing in a childish hand, I saw someone who made me feel like a pedestrian. I took it with me when I met her parents and got them to read it. Nothing. It meant nothing to them. Her father asked me what good were stories when it came to her getting a job.' Fendrich suddenly looked as if all the energy that had briefly fired within him had ebbed away. 'But Paula's dead now. Like you say, you know it, I know it.'

'Why do you know it? What makes you so certain that, if she was as intellectually stifled as you say, she didn't just run away?' asked Hermann.

'Because she didn't write to me. Or to anyone

else. If she had run away from home, I am absolutely certain that she would have left a letter, a note . . . something written. As I said, it was as if the written word had been created for Paula. She would not have taken such a major step without putting something down on paper to mark it. She would have written to me.'

The three left the café simultaneously. Hermann and Anna both shook Fendrich's hand and started back towards the Parkplatz. Fendrich had walked to the café and the school lay in the opposite direction, yet he seemed to hesitate at the café doorway. Anna and Hermann had only gone a few metres when they heard Fendrich call out 'Kriminal-kommissarin Wolff!'

There was something about Fendrich's body language, as if he lingered on the threshold of something other than the café, that told Anna she needed to handle this alone. She handed Hermann her car keys.

'Do you mind?'

Hermann shrugged and headed off towards the car. Fendrich met Anna halfway.

'Kommissarin Wolff. Can I tell you something? Something off the record?'

'I'm sorry. I don't know if I can promise—'

Fendrich cut her off, as if he didn't want an excuse for not confiding whatever it was he had to confide. 'There was something. Something I didn't tell the police at the time because . . . well, I suppose because it would have looked bad.'

Anna tried to keep the impatience out of her expression, but failed.

'There was nothing in my relationship with Paula that was inappropriate, I swear to you. But shortly before Paula disappeared I gave her a gift. A book. I didn't say anything at the time because I knew that detective, Klatt, would twist its meaning.'

'What was it?' asked Anna. 'Which book did you give Paula as a gift?'

'I wanted her to understand the foundations of the German literary tradition. I gave her a copy of *Children's and Household Tales*. By the Brothers Grimm.'

CHAPTER 36

3.30 p.m., Wednesday, 14 April:
Winterhude, Hamburg

The sky was now more blue and Hamburg
seemed bathed in a less sterile brightness,
although the sun intermittently veiled
itself in scattered patches of milky cloud.

In a media city like Hamburg, Fabel always had
to be careful about discussing cases in public, but
there were two places that he liked to use as un-
official venues for team meetings. There was the
Schnell-Imbiss snack stand down on the Hafen,
run by an ex-cop and fellow Frisian friend of
Fabel's. And there was the café that sat across
from the Winterhuder Fährhaus. Tucked in behind
the bridge, the café had an outdoor area for sitting
that stretched along the side of the Alsterstreek
waterway and looked across to the spire of St
Johannis. On the other side of the white-painted
iron fence, two swans nosed the water disinter-
estedly where a previous café customer had tossed
broken-up crusts into it. The outdoor decor
comprised white polypropylene tables and chairs

shaded by parasols advertising cigarettes, but the café was both handy for the Präsidium and far enough away from it to offer a change of scene.

There were six of them in total, and Fabel pulled two chairs over from a vacant table so that everyone could sit together. Anna and Maria were used to Fabel's alfresco briefings, while the two Sex-Crime SoKo members, Petra Maas and Hans Rödger, seemed nonplussed by the surroundings. But the expression on Henk Hermann's face suggested that he felt he had just been admitted into a highly exclusive and rather secretive club.

The waiter came and took their orders for coffee. He greeted Fabel by name and chatted briefly about the weather. He had, of course, no idea that this group were members of the Mordkommission, and probably dismissed the murder squad detectives as a bunch of executives taking a break from a seminar. Fabel waited until the waiter withdrew before addressing his team.

'We're not getting this right. I know you're all putting all your energies into this inquiry, but we seem to be generating more heat than light. We have three possible suspects: Fendrich, the teacher; the author, Weiss, who is a long shot; and then there's our prime suspect, Olsen. But when you take them individually, none seems to fit entirely.'

Fabel paused as the waiter brought the coffees over to the table.

'What we may be overlooking,' continued Fabel,

'is that we may be dealing with two killers working in tandem. That would make sense of Henk's theory about the second set of footprints at the Naturpark murder scene. Maybe we were wrong to dismiss those as unrelated.'

'Or it could be that we've got a principal killer and a copycat?' said Hermann, tentatively.

Fabel shook his head. 'As well as the "theme" of the murders being absolutely consistent, we have a direct forensic link between all murders. The small pieces of yellow paper found at each scene are not only identical, they seem to have been cut from a single piece of paper. And the handwriting is a match, too. Two killers working in tandem would perhaps explain Olsen being the murderer in the Naturpark and someone else doing the other two, but only one hand writing the notes.'

'But . . . ?' Maria Klee gave a small, knowing smile.

'But . . . I just don't see this as a team. We've been there before in a previous case and this just doesn't feel the same. This is a single hand. So let's take Olsen first – what have we got?'

'He seems solid for the Naturpark killings,' said Maria. 'He has a motive for killing Grünn and Schiller – sexual jealousy. But, as you say, how does this square with the other, apparently random, murders?'

Fabel took a sip of his espresso. 'It just doesn't fit with the picture we're building of Olsen. He's all rage. Our guy sees poetry in his violence. Olsen stays at the top of the list, but to know more we're going to have to nail him. In the meantime: what about Fendrich, Anna?'

'He's not our guy. I'm sure of it. If he had sexual motives, which he denies, I don't believe he did anything about them. I've checked and rechecked his background. No record. No previous suspicions or concerns about his conduct as a teacher. He appears not to have had any kind of steady relationship for the last three years, when he split up with his long-term girlfriend, Rona Dorff. I spoke to Rona. She's a music teacher at another school. According to her their relationship was a very lukewarm one at the best of times and they broke up after Paula disappeared.'

'Is there a connection?' asked Fabel.

'Well, yes, there is. But it would tend to exculpate rather than incriminate Fendrich. Rona said that Fendrich became obsessed with helping the Ehlerses to find Paula. Then, when Klatt from the Norderstedt police got on Fendrich's back, he got angry and depressed.'

'Violent?'

'No. Distant. As Rona put it, their relationship faded away rather than broke up.'

'It could be that Fendrich's behaviour after Paula's disappearance was a cover,' Henk Hermann said. There was an eagerness in his voice. 'Lots of murderers disguise their post-commission feelings of guilt and fear of detection as grief or concern.'

Fabel had seen it himself many times before. And on more than one occasion he'd been convinced by the crocodile tears of a cold-blooded killer.

'And then there's the "Grimm" analogy that the killer is using.' Hermann seemed to have been encouraged by his new boss's appreciation of his previous point. 'We know that the Paula lookalike found on the beach, Martha Schmidt, was from a so-called underclass, and the killer stretched this to be analogous with the "underground people". It could be that Fendrich saw her as being trapped in the stifling confines of her parent's low expectations of her. Could he have felt that, by killing her, he was "liberating" her?'

Fabel looked at Hermann and smiled. 'You've been reading Weiss's book too, haven't you?' Hermann's face reddened slightly beneath the freckles, as if he'd been caught cheating on a term paper.

'Yes, Herr Erster Kriminalhauptkommissar. I thought it would be good background.'

'It is. And call me *Chef*, it saves time. What do you think, Anna?'

'It could be, I suppose. Although he's been very supportive of the Ehlers family, he couldn't disguise his contempt for their low expectations and aspirations. But Fendrich is only connected to the Paula Ehlers disappearance, which, technically, is still not part of this murder investigation. He doesn't have an alibi for the others, but, as I said, he lives alone in that big house he used to share with his mother. If he had

289

alibis for the others, then I would be suspicious. Anyway, my gut instinct is that he's not our man. Although the thing with the gift of the Grimm fairy tales bothers me. Even if he freely volunteered the information.'

'Okay, but we keep Fendrich on the suspect board. That leaves us with Weiss, the author . . .'

'Well, *Chef*,' said Maria, 'he's very much your baby. Why include him as a suspect?'

'Well, first and foremost, there are disturbing parallels between these killings and Weiss's *Märchenstrasse* novel. Both are "Grimm" themed, both involve a serial killer bringing fairy tales to life. Weiss is reaping media attention and increased book sales because of this very connection.'

Anna gave a small laugh. 'You can't be suggesting that these killings are some kind of twisted launch event for his book.'

'Not specifically. But maybe Weiss is capable of living out his theories. He is certainly a self-important, arrogant prick. But more than that, he is a disturbing person to be around. And he's big. Really big and powerful. And the autopsy on Laura von Klosterstadt suggested she was restrained by someone with a huge hand span.'

'That could be Olsen,' said Anna. 'Or, for that matter, Fendrich.'

Fabel turned to Maria. 'What did you get on Weiss, Maria?'

'No criminal convictions. He's forty-seven, married twice, divorced twice, no children. He was born in Kiel, Schleswig-Holstein. His mother was foreign. Italian, of aristocratic origins, and his father owned a shipping-related company in Kiel. He was educated in an expensive private Internat here in Hamburg as well as in England and Italy. University Hamburg . . . first novel published shortly after graduation, without much success . . . his first *Wahlwelten* novel came out in 1981 and was a massive success. That's about it. Oh, there was a brother. A younger brother. But he died about ten years ago.'

Fabel looked stung. 'A brother? Died? Died how?'

'Suicide, apparently. Some kind of mental illness.'

'Tell me, Maria, he wouldn't have been a sculptor, by any chance?'

Maria looked surprised. 'As a matter of fact he was. How do you know?'

'I think I may have seen some of his work,' said Fabel, and the snarling face of a wolf, carved out of ebony, flashed into his mind. He looked down at the water next to them. The swans had turned their back on the sodden bread in the water and were heading lazily towards the bridge. He turned to his team. 'Kommissar Hermann is right. I think we should all consider Weiss's book *Die Märchenstrasse* required reading. I'll make sure you each get a copy by the end of today. And I want you to make sure you read it.'

Fabel had asked Anna to wait behind, saying that he would run her back to the Präsidium. Henk

Hermann had loitered indecisively until Fabel had instructed him to go back with Maria. They sat alone at the table. Fabel ordered another coffee and raised a questioning eyebrow: Anna shook her head.

'Listen, Anna,' Fabel said, after the waiter had gone. 'You are an exceptional police officer. In my opinion a real asset to the team. But there are, well, issues we need to address . . .'

'Such as?'

He turned his face to her. 'Such as your aggressiveness. And you need to work more as a team member, not an individual.'

Anna's expression hardened. 'I thought that was why you recruited each of us – because of our individuality. Because we were different.'

'I did, Anna. But your individual talents are only of use to me in combination with those of the other team members.'

'I think I know where this is going . . . Henk Hermann?'

'He's bright, Anna. And he's keen. He's a good policeman and I think that you two will work well together. But only if you let him in and give him the chance.'

Anna didn't answer for a moment. Then she held Fabel in her usual defiant gaze. 'Is it just me, or is it a hell of a coincidence that he looks so like Paul Lindemann? I was beginning to wonder if we had our own "changeling".'

Anna's joke annoyed Fabel and he didn't answer right away. They walked back to Fabel's BMW.

He clicked off the alarm and lock with his remote and leaned an elbow on the roof, looking across at Anna. 'I don't recruit officers on sentimental grounds, Kommissarin Wolff.' Fabel paused then gave a small laugh: he knew what she meant. Hermann had the same lean, lanky, sandy-haired look as Paul Lindemann, the officer they had lost. 'He does a bit, doesn't he? But he's not Paul. And I recruited him because of his own merits and potential. I need you to work with him. It's as much up to you as it is up to me to develop that potential – to bring the best out of him. And before you say it, I'm not asking you to nursemaid him. It's just that he has a steep learning curve to deal with and I want you to help, not hinder him. And, I have to say, I think you could learn a few things from him along the way.'

They drove back towards Winterhude and the Polizeipräsidium. The cloud-blanched sun darkened and lightened, as if unsure what to do with the day. Anna remained quiet for most of the journey, then, out of the blue, she said: 'Okay, *Chef*. I'll do a little bridge-building with Hermann. I know I can be an asshole sometimes, but that whole thing last year, with Paul – and with Maria getting hurt – it got to me. Paul was so bloody straight, so by-the-book and precise in everything he did. It used to get on my nerves. But he was a good person: a genuine guy and you always knew where you were with him.' She paused. Fabel didn't look across at her because he knew that tough little

Anna wouldn't want him to see her upset. 'He was looking after me . . .' Her voice was tight. 'That's what keeps me awake at night. That he died trying to get me out of trouble. I survived and he didn't.'

'Anna . . .' Fabel began, but she cut him off, forcing a normal tone into her voice.

'I'll suggest to Henk Hermann that we get together for a chat. A drink or something. Get to know each other. Okay?'

'Okay, Anna.'

They parked at the Präsidium and Anna rested her hand on the car door but made no movement to get out. She turned her frank gaze on Fabel.

'Why not Klatt?' she asked bluntly and when Fabel looked confused for a moment she added: 'I was convinced you were going to ask Klatt to join the team. I probably think the idea had crossed his mind too. Why did you decide on Henk Hermann instead?'

Fabel smiled. 'Klatt is a good policeman, but he hasn't got what it takes to be a Mordkommission officer. He got too focused on Fendrich. I don't know, maybe Fendrich is our guy, but Klatt was too closed off to alternatives. If the killer isn't Fendrich, then maybe, in those early days of the inquiry, maybe even in those vital early hours, Klatt didn't register something on the edge of his vision that could have closed the gap between him and Paula's abductor.'

'God, *Chef*, that's a bit harsh. There wasn't that much to go on. Klatt focused on Fendrich more because there wasn't anything or anyone else to focus on.'

'That he saw . . . but anyway, like I said, he's a good policeman. But you asked me why I picked Henk Hermann and not Robert Klatt. It was more to do with what's right with Hermann than what's wrong with Klatt. Henk Hermann was the first officer to deal with the scene in the Naturpark. He stood there staring at two victims in a tiny forest clearing with their throats cut and the first thing he did was to move his focus out from that spot. Fast. He did the opposite of Klatt. He widened his scope and worked in two directions at the same time: he worked back from the scene of discovery to the moment of death, and he worked forward to a radius in which the cars would probably have been dumped. And all of that started with his instant recognition of a posed scene.' Fabel paused for a moment, leaning forward and resting his forearms on the steering wheel. 'We're all runners in a race, Anna. Every one of us in the Mordkommission. And it all begins as soon as someone fires the starting gun by leaving another human being dead. Henk Hermann is faster off the blocks. It's as simple and as complicated as that. And I need you to work with him as well as you can.'

Anna looked at Fabel intently for a moment, as if considering his words; then she nodded.

'Okay, *Chef.*'

CHAPTER 37

9.30 p.m., Wednesday, 14 April:
St Pauli, Hamburg

Max was an artist.

He cared very, very much about his art. He had studied it, properly, investigating its origins, its history, its development. Max was very aware that he was privileged to work in the very finest medium: the most noble and the most ancient. He worked on the same canvas that artists had worked on for millennia, throughout the human experience: probably even before they had started to create cave paintings. Yes, it was a great and noble and fine art. And that was why Max was so pissed off that, while he worked, he had a major boner. He did everything he could to take his mind off the erection that strained against the leather of his trousers. He even tried to concentrate on the detail of his work, but it was, after all, the simplest of designs, a heart wreathed in flowers, and he could have done it in his sleep. He wouldn't even have agreed to tattoo it on to the shaved *mons pubis* of the hooker at this time in the evening had he not received a phone call from one of his best-ever customers, who had asked if he could come in to see Max at ten. He was going to be hanging around anyway, so when the hooker turned up at the door he reckoned he might as well be earning.

'Ouwwww . . . that hurts . . .' The pretty young prostitute squirmed and Max had to hastily remove the tattooing needle. As he did so her pudenda writhed close to Max's face and he felt himself stiffen a little more.

'I won't be long . . .' he said impatiently. 'But you've got to stay still, or I'll make a mistake.'

The girl giggled. 'This is going to look so classy!' she said, and then winced as Max reapplied the tattooing needle. 'The other girls get, like, taste-less things done, but they told me you was really good. A real artist, kinda.'

'I'm honoured,' Max said, unconvincingly. 'Just let me get this finished.' He wiped the ink and the blood from the tattoo, his thumb grazing her labia. The girl giggled again.

'You know, honey. We could come to an arrangement about payment. I give great head, you know . . .'

Max looked up at her face. She couldn't have been much more than nineteen. 'No, thanks,' he said, turning back to his work. 'If you don't mind I'll just stick with the cash.'

'Okay,' she said. 'You don't know what you're missin'.'

Max took a long, deep breath after the girl left, and tried to put the image of her pussy from his mind. His customer would be here soon and Max felt a thrill of anticipation: this guy was a connoisseur. Max considered the work he had done on him to have been his masterpiece. But the customer had refused when Max had asked to take a photograph of it. And Max hadn't argued. This guy was huge. Massive. And you wouldn't want to argue with him. But his size was a bonus for Max. It meant more skin surface. And that, in turn, meant that this guy had provided the biggest canvas Max had ever worked on.

It had taken weeks, months to complete the work. The pain his customer would have endured must have been incredible – to have so much skin surface raw and inflamed. Yet he would come back, one day each week, insisting that Max close his shop and work on him alone, hour after hour. And this customer had a real appreciation of what Max was all about. It had involved research. Study. Preparation. While he worked, Max would talk to his customer about the nobility of his art, about how he had been a pale, small, sickly child with a talent for art; about how no one had paid much attention to him. Max had explained to his customer how, at twelve, he had set about, with a needle and some Indian ink, to create his first tattoo. On himself. He had explained how he had first read up on *Moko*, the tattoo craft of the Maoris of New Zealand. The Maoris would lie, trance-like, for hours, while the tribal tattooist, the *Tohunga*, who enjoyed the same status as a medicine man, would tap-tap away with his needle and tiny wooden mallet. The *Tohungas* were, for Max, at the apex of the tattooist's art: they were as much sculptors as painters, not just pigmenting skin but reshaping it, making their art three-dimensional by actually crafting folds and ridges into the skin. And each *Moko* was unique, specially conceived and singularly crafted for its wearer.

At ten p.m. sharp the studio buzzer went. Max unlocked and swung open the door to reveal the dark, towering shape of a huge man. He filled the doorway, looming above Max before slipping silently past him and into the studio.

'It's really good to see you again,' said Max. 'It was an honour to work on you . . . What can I do for you tonight?'

CHAPTER 38

9.30 p.m., Wednesday, 14 April: Der Kiez, Hamburg

H enk Hermann had eagerly accepted Anna's invitation to go out for a drink after work, but there had been an element of suspicion in his eyes.

'Don't worry,' Anna had said. 'I won't rape you. But leave your car at the Präsidium.'

Henk Hermann had looked even more uneasy when Anna had arranged for a taxi to take them into the Kiez, dropping them at the Weisse Maus pub. It was usually thronging with customers, but at this time on a mid-week evening they had no trouble finding a table. Anna ordered a rye-and-dry and looked across at Henk.

'Beer?'

Henk held up his hands. 'I better stick with—'

'A rye-and-dry and a beer, then,' she said to the waiter.

Hermann laughed. He looked at the petite, pretty girl across the table from him: she could have been almost anything other than a policewoman. She had large dark eyes that were accented by the slightly overdone eyeshadow. Her full, heart-shaped lips were lipsticked fire-truck red. Her black hair was short and gelled almost spiky. The look, combined with her customary punk-chic ensemble of T-shirt, jeans and oversized leather jacket seemed to have been engineered to make her look tough. It failed: the elements simply combined and conspired to accentuate her girlish femininity. But, Henk had heard, she was tough. Really tough.

Anna made half-hearted small talk while they waited for their drinks: she asked Henk what he thought of the Mordkommission, how different it was to his SchuPo duties, and other uninspired, idle questions. Their drinks arrived.

'You don't have to do this, you know.' Henk took a sip of his beer.

'What do you mean?' Anna arched her dark eyebrows and when she did her face took on a schoolgirl innocence.

'I know you resent me . . . well, no, not resent, that's too strong . . . I know that you don't totally approve of Herr Fabel taking me on to the team.'

'Crap,' said Anna. She slipped off her leather jacket and placed it on the back of her chair. As she did so, her neck chain slipped out from under her T-shirt. She sat back in the chair, slipping the chain back under her shirt. 'He's the boss. He knows what he's doing. If he says you're up to the job, that's good enough for me.'

'But you're not happy about it.'

Anna sighed. She took a large sip of her bourbon and ginger ale. 'I'm sorry, Henk. I know that I haven't exactly rolled out the red carpet for you. It's just . . . Well, it's just that I had a tough time coming to terms with Paul's death. I take it Fabel told you all about that?'

Henk nodded.

'Well, I know we need someone to take his place. But not take his place, if you know what I mean.'

'I do. I really do,' said Henk. 'But, to be honest, it's not my problem. It's a history I'm not part of. You have to accept that I have come into the team to do the best I can. I didn't know Paul Lindemann and I wasn't part of that investigation.'

Anna took another sip of her drink and wrinkled her nose as it went down. 'No. You're wrong. You *are* part of that history. If you're part of the team, you're part of what has happened to the team. And that night out there in the Altes Land, we all changed. Me, Maria – God knows, Maria changed out there – even Werner and Fabel. And we lost one of ours. We're still all dealing with that.'

'Okay.' Henk leaned forward, resting his elbows on the table. 'Tell me about it.'

CHAPTER 39

9.30 p.m., Wednesday, 14 April:
Eppendorf, Hamburg

Fabel didn't have to search for Heinz Schnauber's apartment. He knew Eppendorf very well: the Institut für Rechtsmedizin was located at the Universitätklinikum Hamburg-Eppendorf, and Schnauber's apartment was in one of the elegant nineteenth-century Wohnhäuser on the classy Eppendorfer Landstrasse.

Schnauber had been expecting him, but Fabel still held up his oval KriPo shield and ID when Schnauber came to the door. He was in his mid-fifties, not too tall, and slim without being slight. He showed Fabel into an elegant drawing room. The furnishings were in keeping with the period of the building, but were infinitely more comfortable than those in Vera Schiller's Hausbruch mansion. Fabel never knew how to respond to gay men. He liked to think of himself as a sophisticated, modern and rational man, and he certainly had nothing against gays, but his Lutheran Frisian upbringing made him uncertain and awkward in their company.

He became intensely annoyed with his own provincialism, especially when he noted that he had felt mild surprise that Schnauber was perfectly masculine in manner and speech. One thing that Fabel did notice was the intense pain in Schnauber's eyes when he spoke about Laura von Klosterstadt. Whether Schnauber was gay or not, he clearly loved Laura. An almost paternal love.

'She was my princess,' Schnauber explained. 'That was my name for her: "my little broken princess." I can honestly say that she was the nearest thing to a daughter to me.'

'Why "broken"?'

Schnauber smiled bitterly. 'I'm sure you come across all kinds of dysfunctional families, Herr Kriminalhauptkommissar. In your line of work, I mean. Junkie parents, criminal kids, abuse, that kind of thing. But there are families that are adept at keeping their dysfunctionality under wraps. Their skeletons well and truly locked up in the cupboards. Well, when you have as much money and influence as the von Klosterstadts, you can afford a lot of cupboards.'

Schnauber sat on the sofa and invited Fabel to sit by indicating a large high-backed leather armchair.

'I wanted to ask you about the party,' said Fabel. 'Fräulein von Klosterstadt's birthday party, I mean. Did anything out of the ordinary happen? Or were there any gatecrashers?'

Schnauber laughed. 'There are no gatecrashers at

any of my functions, Herr Fabel,' He emphasised the *no*. 'And no, as far as I'm aware, nothing unusual or unpleasant happened. There was the predictable ice between Laura and her mother. And Hubert, as usual, was being a supercilious little shit. But other than that, the party went like a dream. We had a bunch of Americans over, an exclusive yachting-wear company from New England. They were interested in signing Laura up as their "face" – the *Amis* love her aristocratic European looks.' The sadness in Schnauber's expression deepened. 'Poor Laura, every birthday party she had as a child was engineered to fit with her mother's social agenda. Then, as an adult, they were excuses to promote her to potential clients. I felt rotten about that. But it was my job, as her agent, to promote her as widely and effectively as I could.' His eyes locked with Fabel's. There was an earnestness in the look, as if it were important to him that Fabel believed him. 'I did everything I could to make those parties more than dressed-up promos, you know. I used to buy her little surprise presents for her birthday, get her a special cake, that kind of thing. I really did try to make the parties fun for her.'

'I know. Herr Schnauber. I understand.' Fabel smiled. He allowed Schnauber a moment with his thoughts before asking his next question. 'You said the von Klosterstadts had lots of skeletons in the cupboard. What kind of skeletons? Was there something going on in Laura's family?'

Schnauber walked over to the drinks cabinet and poured himself a single malt with what Fabel considered to be a heavy hand. He tilted the bottle in Fabel's direction.

'No, thanks . . . Not when I'm on duty.'

Schnauber sat down again. He slugged down a considerable portion of the over-large Scotch. 'You met the parents? And Hubert?'

'Yes,' said Fabel. 'I did.'

'The father's a prick. He's as impoverished in brains as he's rich in cash. And he's indiscreet. He has been screwing his way through the secretarial workforce of Hamburg for the last fifteen years. Mind you, I can understand that when you look at Margarethe, his wife.'

Fabel looked confused. 'I would have said she was a very attractive woman. Clearly a beauty in her time, just as Laura was in hers.'

Schnauber gave a knowing smile. 'There are times – most of the time, actually – when I am so damned grateful I'm gay. For a start it makes me immune to Margarethe's witchcraft. But I can see she's bewitched you already, Herr Fabel. Don't for a minute think that all that sexual chemistry Margarethe exudes makes her a satisfying fuck. You can't fuck her if you've got no balls and, all her life, Margarethe has specialised in emasculating men. That's why I think Laura's father dips his wick anywhere he gets a chance. Just to prove it's still there.' He took another gulp and emptied his glass. 'But that's not why I hate Margarethe von Klosterstadt. The reason I despise her is for the way she treated Laura. It was like she locked her up and starved her – starved her of love, of affection, of the thousand little things that bind mother and daughter.'

Fabel nodded pensively. None of this was of direct use to the investigation, but the whisky and his grief had loosened Schnauber's rage at an unfair death which obviously had ended an unfair and unhappy life. Now the empty room and the empty view from the pool room started to make sense. Schnauber got up, went over to the cabinet once more and poured himself another drink. He paused for a moment, bottle suspended in one hand, glass in the other, and looked out of his window, along the Eppendorfer Landstrasse.

'Sometimes I hate this city. Sometimes I hate being a North bloody German, with all of our tight-assed hang-ups and guilt trips. Guilt is a terrible, terrible thing, don't you think?'

'I suppose so,' Fabel said. Schnauber wore a look that Fabel had seen so many times before in his career: that fidgety indecisiveness of someone loitering on the threshold of disclosing a confidence. Fabel let the silence lie, allowing Schnauber the time to decide to commit himself.

Schnauber turned from the window to face Fabel. 'You'll see it all the time, I suppose. As a policeman, I mean. I bet there are people out there who commit the most terrible crimes – murder, rape, child abuse – and who yet will have no sense of guilt.'

'Unfortunately, yes, there are.'

'That's what pisses me off: that without a sense

of guilt there is no punishment. Like some of these old Nazi bastards who refuse to see the wrong in what they did, while the next generation is crippled by guilt for something that happened before they were born. But then there's the other side of the coin.' Schnauber sat down on the couch again. 'Those who do things that most of us would consider venial sins – trivial, even – yet who are haunted by guilt for the rest of their lives.'

Fabel leaned forward in his chair. 'Was Laura haunted?'

'By one of the many skeletons in the von Klosterstadt cupboards, yes. An abortion. Years ago. She was little more than a child herself. No one knows. It was clamped down on with a security that would make the Federal Chancellery look like open house. Margarethe arranged everything and made sure that it remained a secret. But Laura told me. It took her years before she did, and she broke her little heart when she did.'

'Who was the father of the child?'

'No one. That was his sin, to be a no one. So Margarethe made sure he disappeared from the scene. That, more than anything, is why I called her my "broken princess". An hour-long medical procedure and a lifelong guilt.' Schnauber took another swig. His eyes reddened as if stung, but not by the malt. 'Do you know what makes me more sad than anything else, Herr Kriminalhauptkommissar? That, when this monster murdered Laura, she probably felt she deserved it.'

CHAPTER 40

10.00 p.m., Wednesday, 14 April:
Der Kiez, St Pauli, Hamburg

Henk Hermann sat back in the chair. He had listened to Anna's description of the operation in which Paul Lindemann had been killed, in which Maria had been stabbed, in which Anna herself had come close to losing her life.

'Christ, that must have been tough. I see what you mean. I knew about it, obviously. But not all the details. I see what you mean about it shaking the team up. Affecting how you operate, I mean.'

'I know it has really got to Fabel. Did you see the look on his face after Werner got clobbered by Olsen? He hasn't let us go into any kind of hazardous situation ahead of an MEK unit. I suppose he needs . . . I suppose *we* need to get our confidence back a bit.'

There was an awkward silence. It was as if something had occurred to Henk but he had then thought better of it.

'What is it?' asked Anna. 'Go on. What is it you want to ask?'

'It's a personal thing. I hope you don't mind?'

Anna made an intrigued face. 'Okay . . .'

'It's just that I saw your necklace. The chain you wear.'

The smile faded from Anna's lips but her expression remained relaxed. She fished out the Star of David from her T-shirt. 'What . . . this? Does it bother you?'

'No . . . God, no . . .' Henk suddenly looked flustered. 'It's just that I was curious. I heard you spent time in Israel. In the army. And you came back.'

'Is that so surprising? I'm German. Hamburg is my home town. It's where I belong.' She leaned forward and whispered conspiratorially. 'Don't tell anyone . . . but there are five thousand of us in Hamburg.'

Henk looked uncomfortable. 'I'm sorry. I shouldn't have asked.'

'Why not ask? Do you find it strange that I choose to live here?'

'Well. With such a terrible history. I mean, I wouldn't blame you for not wanting to live in Germany.'

'Like I said, I'm a German first and foremost. Then I'm Jewish.' Anna paused. 'Do you know that, right up until the Nazis took power, Hamburg was one of the least anti-Semitic cities in Europe? All over Europe Jews were restricted in what they could do for a living; their voting rights were limited too. But not in the Hanseatic City of

Hamburg. That's why, right up until the Nazis, Hamburg had the biggest Jewish community in Germany: we made up five per cent of the population. Even during the "dark chapter" my grandparents were hidden by friends in Hamburg. That took a lot of courage. More courage, if I'm honest, than I think I would have had. Anyway, today it's a city in which I can feel comfortable. At home. I'm not a desert flower, Henk. I need to be rained on regularly.'

'I don't know if I could be so forgiving . . .'

'It's not about forgiveness, Henk. It's about vigilance. I wasn't part of what happened under the Nazis. Nor were you. Nor was anyone our age. But I'll never forget that it did happen.' She paused, turning her glass idly in her hands. Then she gave a small laugh. 'Anyway, I'm not that forgiving. I dare say you've heard that I've run into the odd bit of . . . *controversy*, I suppose you'd call it.'

'I heard,' Henk laughed. 'Something about a Rechtsradikale skinhead and some bruised testicles?'

'When I see some of these sad wankers with their skinheads and green bomber jackets, I tend to get a little heated, shall we say. Like I said, I stay vigilant. In the meantime, my brother Julius is a major figure in the Hamburg Jewish community. He's a civic lawyer and a leading member of the German-Jewish Society. And he works part-time at the Talmud-Tora-Realschule in the

Grindelviertel. Julius believes in building cultural bridges. I believe in watching my back.'

'It sounds like you think your brother's approach is wrong.'

'We don't need cultural bridges. My culture is German. My parents, my grandparents and their parents . . . their culture was German. We're not different. If I think of myself as different – if you treat me as different – then Hitler won. I have an extra part to my heritage, that's all. I'm proud of that heritage. I'm proud to be Jewish. But everything that defines me is here . . . is German.'

Henk ordered more drinks and they sat and let their talk wander freely. Anna found out that Henk had two sisters and one brother, that he had been born in Cuxhaven, but that when he was still a child his family had moved to Marmstorf, where his father had been a butcher.

'The Metzgerei Hermann . . . the best butcher in south Hamburg,' Henk said. He had tried to affect a mock-proud tone, but Anna smiled as Henk's genuine pride got in the way. 'Like most of the fringes of Hamburg, Marmstorf feels more like a village than a Stadtteil. I don't know if you know it . . . the centre is full of old Fachwerk half-timbered houses, that kind of thing.' Henk suddenly looked sad. 'I still feel bad that I didn't take over my father's butcher's business. My other brother is at the Universität Hamburg. Training to become a doctor. My sisters have no interest in it either: one's an accountant and the other lives with her husband and kids outside Köln. My father is still running the business, but he's too old now. I guess he just keeps hoping that I'll give up the police and take it on.'

'I take it there's no chance of that.'

'None, I'm afraid. I wanted to be a policeman since I was a kid. It was just one of these things you know about yourself.' He paused. 'So. What do you think? Do I pass?'

'What do you mean?'

'Well, this is what this is all about, isn't it? To see if you can work with me?'

Anna grinned. 'You'll do . . . But actually that wasn't the intention. It's just that we'll be working together and I know that I haven't been, well, very welcoming. I'm sorry. But I think you can understand that things are still a little bit raw. After Paul, I mean. Anyway . . .' She raised her glass. 'Welcome to the Mordkommission . . .'

CHAPTER 41

10.15 p.m., Wednesday, 14 April:
St Pauli, Hamburg

The last time he had worked on him, about a year before, Max had become accustomed to his customer's long silences. Max had taken them as a sign of his interest, fascination even, in what Max had to say about his craft.

But tonight the huge man had not spoken since he had come in through the door and now he simply stood, wordlessly, in the middle of Max's studio. Dominating it. Filling it. And all that could be heard was the huge man's breathing. Slow. Heavy. Deliberate.

'Is there something wrong? Are you okay?' Max asked.

Another silence seemed to stretch for ever until, at last, the huge man spoke. 'When you worked on me the last time I asked you to keep no record of it. Or tell anyone about it. I paid you extra for that. Did you do as I asked?'

'Yes, I did. I did . . . and if anyone has told you different it's a lie!' protested Max. He wished that

314

the big guy would sit down. Standing this close to him, in the tight confines of the studio, Max was getting a painful neck looking up at him. The big man held up a hand. He removed his coat and the shirt underneath, exposing to Max his own handiwork. His vast, muscled torso was covered with words, with sentences, with entire stories, all tattooed into his flesh in black, old-Gothic script. The slightest movement, a twitch of a muscle, and the words writhed, as if themselves alive.

'Is that the truth? No one knows about the work you did on me?'

'No one. I swear. It's kinda like a doctor-patient thing . . . you say you want it kept quiet, then I keep it quiet. I wish I *could* talk about it, though. It's the best fuckin' work I ever did. And I'm not just saying that because you're the customer.'

The big man fell silent again. This time his silence was unbroken except by the sound of his breathing that again filled the tiny studio. Deep-sounding, resonant breaths from that cavernous barrel of a chest. His breathing came faster.

'Are you sure you're okay?' asked Max, his voice now high with something that lay between unease and outright fear.

Again no answer. The big man reached down to his coat and took something from one of the pockets. It was a child's tiny rubber mask. A wolf mask. He pulled it across his big face and the lupine features stretched and distorted.

'What's with the comedy mask?' Max asked, but

his mouth was dry and his voice sounded strange. He was aware of his heart hammering in his chest. 'Look. I'm really busy. I stayed open just for you. Now, if you want something . . .' He did his best to squeeze some authority into his stretched, frightened tone.

'Clever Hans . . .' The big man smiled and tilted his head to one side. It was a childish posture that looked bizarre, surreal, on a man of his stature. The stretching of his neck rippled the words that looped around the base of his throat.

'What? My name isn't Hans. You know that. It's Max . . .'

'Clever Hans . . .' repeated the big man, tilting his head the other way.

'Max – I'm Max. Look, big guy, I don't know what you're on. You take a little something tonight? I think you'd better come back when—'

The big man stepped forward and slammed both hands simultaneously on either side of Max's head, clamping it and squeezing hard.

'Oh . . .' he said. 'Clever Hans, Clever Hans . . .'

'My name isn't Hans! My name isn't Hans!' Max was screaming now. His entire world had filled with a white, electric fear. 'I'm Max! Remember me? Max! The tattoo guy!'

Behind the stretched, grotesque mask, the huge features of the big man's face suddenly melted into sadness and his tone was pleading, plaintive. 'Clever Hans, Clever Hans . . . why don't you cast friendly eyes on her?'

Max felt his cheeks being pushed into his teeth. The vice that closed on his head crushed and twisted his features.

'Clever Hans, Clever Hans . . . why don't you cast friendly eyes on her?'

Max's scream became a high-pitched animal shriek as his attacker's huge thumbs pressed into the flesh beneath his eyebrows, just above the bulge of his eyelids. The pressure increased and became pain of incredible intensity. The thumbs pushed deeper. Into the sockets. Max's shriek became a blubbering gurgle as his eyes were forced from his head and the gorge rose in his throat.

Now blind, Max hung limply in the inescapable grip of his immensely strong assailant. His universe now flashed and sparked, and he even thought he could again see the outline of his attacker, as if etched in neon, as his optic nerves and brain tried to make sense of the sudden absence of his eyes. Then darkness. The vice grip was removed. But before Max could slump to the floor, he felt a single hand grab him by the hair and yank him upright. There was a moment of silence in Max's darkness. Again all he could hear was the even, deep, resonant breathing of the giant who had blinded him. Then he heard the sound of metal being drawn from something. As if from a leather sheath.

Max gave a little jump of surprise as he felt the blow across his neck and throat. A tiny sliver of time, in which he puzzled why the man hadn't hit him harder, stretched into an infinity. By the time he realised that his throat had been slashed and the warmth he felt splashing spasmodically on to his shoulder and chest was his blood, Max was already slipping into death.

The last thing he heard was the bizarre mix of the deep, resonant voice and childlike tone of his attacker.

'Clever Hans, Clever Hans . . . why don't you cast friendly eyes upon her?'

CHAPTER 42

7.40 p.m., Friday, 16 April:
St Pauli, Hamburg

What was that smell? It was an unclean smell. Faint, diffuse and impossible to identify, but unpleasant. Pungent. It was like the odour he would sometimes smell in his home. But it was here too, as if it were following him. Haunting him.

Bernd had taken the S-Bahn. It was difficult to park in the Kiez and he enjoyed the anonymity of public transport whenever he went off on one of his excursions. Anyway, he would probably have a few drinks. Afterwards.

A young woman sat opposite him on the S-Bahn train. She was in her early twenties, with blonde hair cut boyishly short and with a streak of pink through it. Her coat was Afghan style and mid-calf length, but lay open. Her figure was full, verging on plump, and her T-shirt was pulled tight across her breasts. He focused on the band of pale, smooth skin that lay exposed below the bottom of her T-shirt and the low waistband of her hipster jeans. The bared flesh was punctuated by the dimple of her pierced and studded navel.

Bernd gazed at her, at her youth and her ripeness, and felt himself stiffen. Again. The girl looked over and their eyes met. He smiled what he had intended to be a mischevious smile but it formed on his lips as nothing short of a leer. The girl mimed a nauseated shudder, pulled her coat closed and placed her shoulder bag on her lap. He shrugged but kept his smile in place. After a few minutes in which he sought with his eyes to trace out again the delightful but now concealed curves of her young body, the S-Bahn stopped at the next station, Königstrasse. The girl rose to her feet as the automatic doors opened. As she did so she glared at him.

'Piss off, you creep . . .'

Bernd rode the train until the next stop. His anticipation rose as he climbed the stairs from the station and exited out into the night. He took a deep breath and was aware that the odour was still there, not a strong smell this time, but insinuated between the damp evening air and the traffic fumes. And all around him, St Pauli glittered.

The S-Bahn station was at the extreme west end of Hamburg's Sündige Meile – sinful mile. The Reeperbahn stretches long and wide through the heart of the St Pauli district. This was once Hamburger Berg, in the days before they had given the area the name of the local St Paul's church. It had been a no man's land between two neighbouring, competing cities: German Hamburg and Danish Altona. It was a low, sodden marshland into which both cities had dumped their waste. And their unwanted. The lepers were sent here to live, shunned by each municipality, down by the river, in the least hospitable part of an already inhospitable bog. Then those who were not permitted to be articled as tradesmen in Altona or Hamburg were told they could ply their trades here, including the ropemakers, who made Reep, as they called it in Low German, and who gave the Reeperbahn, the Ropers' Way, its name. All these tradesmen were free to follow their previously unlicensed occupations, and the area's second most famous street took the name Grosse Freiheit: Great Freedom.

But other trades had been attracted by this great freedom and had found their way into the area, where they had flourished. And those had been the trades of the prostitute and the pornographer.

Now the Danes were long gone and Altona was part of Hamburg. But the area between remained a half-world of libidinousness and raucous vulgarity. In recent years, St Pauli had sought to cover her immodesty with trendy bars, nightclubs, discos and theatres, but in the narrow streets that radiated out from the Reeperbahn desire, flesh and money were still traded.

And this was where Bernd had found his own great freedom. Something had happened to him recently that he could not explain. A liberation. A cutting-free of all of the moral restraint that had been heaped upon him since childhood. Now he stalked the night and expressed every dark desire.

This was his favourite spot – his starting point – standing outside the mouth of the S-Bahn with the Reeperbahn stretched before him in one direction, and the Grosse Freiheit rascally flashing and twinkling invitations from across the street. This was more than a place. It was a time: the bright, delicious moment that lay between anticipation and fulfilment. But tonight, Bernd's need was even more urgent than before and he had no time to savour the moment. The tingle of dark lust that had started on the U-Bahn had become, as it always did, an unpleasant discomfort, like a pressure needing to be released. A boil that needed to be lanced.

Bernd strode purposefully along the Reeperbahn, ignoring the windows filled with impossibly proportioned sex toys and brushing aside the importunate invitation of a 'video lounge' doorman. He turned into Hans-Albers-Platz. The pressure in his groin and the churning in his chest reached a new level of intensity, and he could have sworn he smelled that smell even more acutely, as if the two things were connected; as if the odour combined an aphrodisiac element with repulsion. He was nearly at his goal. He strode straight through the screen baffles that shield Herbertstrasse, the hundred-metre-long brothel street, from the rest of Hamburg.

★　★　★

Afterwards, Bernd crossed the Reeperbahn and made his way to the small pub in Hein-Hoyer-Strasse. It was a typical St Pauli Kneipe. Schlager pop music shouted from the jukebox and the walls were decked out with fishing nets, model ships, Prinz-Heinrich caps and the obligatory cluster of photographs of visitors of various degrees of celebrity. A picture of Jan Fedder, the St Pauli-born star of the long-running TV police series *Grossstadtrevier* had been cut out of a magazine and stuck on the wall, next to a faded photograph of St Pauli's most famous son, Hans Albers. Bernd shouldered his way through to the bar, ordered an Astra beer and leaned against the counter. The barmaid was overweight, with bad skin and hair that was an unconvincing blonde, yet he found himself considering what his chances would be. Again he thought he smelled that same smell.

It was then that Bernd became aware of the huge man who loomed beside him at the bar.

CHAPTER 43

11.20 a.m., Sunday, 18 April:
Norddeich, Ostfriesland

'I really don't know why you're so down on this place.' Susanne held her face up to the sun and to the breeze that played unimpeded by shadow or obstacle on the vast levels of Wattenmeer mudflats that stretched, unbroken, from horizon to horizon. They walked where the sandy beach began to smudge into the glossy black of the mudflats. The wet, muddy sand seeped between the toes of Susanne's naked feet as she walked. 'I think it's wonderful.'

'And it has so much to offer.' Fabel's smile and tone were mock-enthusiastic. 'Maybe this afternoon we can all go to the tea museum, or to the "Ocean-Wave Wellenpark" for a swim.'

'Well, both sound good to me,' she protested. 'There's no need to be so sarcastic. I think, deep down, you don't hate this place as much as you pretend.'

Another group of Wattwanderer passed them and there was an exchange of 'Moin, Moin' greetings.

These were more serious mudflat explorers, led by a local guide, and they wore shorts above naked legs that were sleek and black with the rich mud of the Watt. Susanne looped her arm through Fabel's and drew him closer, resting her head on his shoulder as they walked.

'No,' answered Fabel. 'I don't hate it. It's just the thing we all have about the place where we grew up, I suppose. A need to escape. Especially if it was provincial. I always felt that Norddeich was as provincial as you can get.'

Susanne laughed. 'All of Germany is provincial, Jan. Everyone has their Norddeich. Everyone has their Heimat.'

Fabel shook his head and the stiff breeze ruffled his blond hair. He was barefoot too, dressed in an old denim shirt, a faded blue windcheater and chinos that he'd rolled up above his ankles. His pale blue eyes were shaded by a pair of sunglasses. Susanne had never seen Fabel dressed so casually. It made him look boyish. 'Maybe that's why fairy tales have endured in Germany longer than elsewhere – because we heeded the warnings never to wander far from the known and easy and comfortable . . . from our Heimat. But, anyway, this isn't my Heimat, Susanne. That's Hamburg. Hamburg is where I truly belong.' He smiled and steered her gently around in a wide sweep until they faced the shore, where the colour of the sand changed from glossy brown to white-gold, and where the horizon was defined by the thin green ribbon of the dykes. 'Let's head back.'

They walked in contemplative silence for a while. Then Fabel pointed to the dyke ahead.

'When I was a boy, I used to spend hours up there, looking out to sea. It's amazing how much the sky and sea change here, and how quickly.'

'I can imagine that. I see you as a very earnest little boy.'

'You've been talking to my mother.' Fabel laughed. He had been anxious, for reasons he couldn't define, about bringing Susanne here; about her meeting his mother. Especially as he had decided to combine it with his weekend with his daughter. But, like the evening with Otto and Else, Susanne's beauty, easy manner and charm had been as winning as ever; even when Susanne had commented to his mother that she still had a hint of a charming British accent. Fabel had flinched inwardly: his mother liked to think that she spoke perfect, accentless German and, as kids, Fabel and his brother Lex had learned not to correct their schoolteacher mother when she got an article wrong. But, somehow, Susanne had managed to make his mother feel as if she'd received a compliment.

They had driven here together from Hamburg. Susanne and Gabi had spent most of the journey making good-natured jokes at Fabel's expense. The journey, and the weekend here in Norddeich, had pleased and disturbed Fabel in equal measure:

for the first time since his divorce from Renate he had experienced a sense of something like a family again.

That morning, Fabel had got up first, leaving Susanne to sleep on. Gabi had headed off early into Norden, Norddeich's 'parent' town. He had made breakfast with his mother, watching her carry out the same kitchen routines that she had when he'd been a boy; but now, despite her fast and almost complete recovery, she moved more slowly, more deliberately. And she looked frailer. They had talked about Fabel's dead father, about Lex, his brother and his family and then about Susanne. Resting her hand on Fabel's forearm, she had said: 'I just want you to be happy again, son.' She had spoken to him in English, which, since his childhood, had been the language of intimacy between himself and his mother. Almost as if it were their secret language.

Fabel turned to Susanne and confirmed her observation. 'You're right, I was an earnest little boy, I suppose . . . Too earnest. Too serious, as a boy and as a man. Last time I was here, my brother Lex said the very same thing: "always such a serious kid". I used to sit up there on the dyke behind the house and look out across the sea, imagining the Angle and Saxon longships sail out towards the Celtic British coast. For me, that defined this place, this coast. I would face the sea and be aware of the vastness of Europe behind me and the open sea before me. I suppose having a British mother had something to do with it too. So much began here. England was born here. America. The whole Anglo-Saxon world from Canada to New Zealand. They gathered here, the Angles, the Jutes, the Saxons . . . all the Ingvaeones . . .' He stopped, as if what he had said had taken him by surprise.

'What is it?' asked Susanne.

He gave a bitter laugh. 'It's just this case. This "Grimm" thing. I can't seem to get away from it. Or, more precisely, I never seem to be far away from one or both of the Grimm brothers.'

'I hope we're not drifting into shop talk.' Susanne exaggerated the warning tone in her voice.

'It's just what I was saying, about the Ingvaeones: "the people of the sea", the children of Ing. I suddenly remembered where it was that I first read about them . . . *Teutonic Mythology* by Jacob Grimm. You scrape anywhere on the surface of German linguistics or history and you expose a Grimm connection.'

Fabel made an apologetic gesture. 'I'm sorry. This isn't really shop talk. It was just that I was talking to the author, Gerhard Weiss. He says we all think we're unique, but we're all just variations on a theme; and that's why fables and fairy tales have a constant resonance and relevance. But I can't help feeling that the Grimm tales are so . . . so *German*. Even if some have origins and parallels outside Germany. Maybe it's like the way the French and the Italians have an instinct for food. Maybe we have an instinct for myths and legends. The Nibelungenlied, the Grimm Brothers, Wagner and all that stuff.'

Susanne shrugged and they fell into silence again. Once on the wide swathe of white-gold sand and dunes, they made their way to the enclosed wicker Strandkorb double seat where they had left their towels and shoes. They sat down in the shelter from the breeze and kissed.

'Well,' said Susanne, 'if you're not going to take me to the wonderful water world of the Wellen-park, or to appreciate the cultural riches of the Teemuseum, then maybe we should go back and take your mother and Gabi out somewhere nice for lunch.'

CHAPTER 44

10.20 p.m., Sunday, 18 April:
Ottensen, Hamburg

M aria Klee leaned her back against the door of her apartment, as if adding her weight to the barrier between her inner space and the world beyond. The food had been great; the date had been a disaster. They had met for dinner at the Restaurant Eisenstein, a stylishly converted former ships'-propeller factory. It was one of Maria's favourite places to eat and, being in Ottensen, it was handy for her. Her date had been Oskar, a lawyer she had met through mutual friends. Oskar had been intelligent, attentive, charming and attractive. In fact, as a prospective boyfriend he couldn't have been better qualified.

But whenever she had felt that he was invading her personal space, she had recoiled. It had been like this every time since she had been stabbed. Every date. Every encounter with a man. Her boss, Fabel, did not have a clue about it; could not be allowed to know about it. She knew herself that there was a real danger that it could affect her effectiveness as a police officer. And whatever the bastard who stabbed her had taken away from her, he wasn't going to take away her career. Now that Werner was on sick leave recovering from Olsen's attack, Maria was Fabel's sole number two officer. And she wasn't going to let him down. She *couldn't* let him down.

But deep in her gut a dark fire of dread burned remorselessly: what would happen when it came to it? What would happen when she was again faced with a dangerous offender, which was almost certain to happen sooner or later? Would she ever be able to hack it again?

In the meantime, with each new date, Maria had to fight down the panic that any threat of intimacy with a man brought. Oskar had been polite right up to the end, when at last the time came when they could bring the evening to an end without it being obviously and embarrassingly premature. He had driven her home and dropped her at the door to her apartment building. They had kissed briefly as she said goodnight: she had not suggested he come in for coffee and he had clearly not expected it.

Maria slipped off her coat and threw her keys down into the wooden bowl next to the door. Absent-mindedly her hand fiddled with the shoulder strap of her dress before it found its way to her chest, just below the sternum, and her fingers rubbed against the silk of her dress. She could feel nothing through the fine silk but she knew it was there. Her scar. The mark he had made on her when he had sunk the blade into her abdomen.

Maria gave a small jump when there was a knock at the door. Then she gave an irritated sigh. Oskar. She thought he'd taken the hint. She put the door on the chain before opening it. She felt almost disappointed when she saw that it wasn't her date. Unhitching the chain, she held the door wide to admit Anna Wolff and Henk Hermann.

'What's up?' she asked, but she was already reaching into the drawer of the cabinet by the door where she kept her service SIG-Sauer.

'Our literary friend has been busy again. We've got a male victim. This time in Sternschanzen Park – under the water tower there.'

'You notify Fabel?'

'Yep. But he's in Ostfriesland. He told me to get you out to the locus right away to start things moving. He's heading back now and will meet us at the Präsidium later.' Anna smiled as she watched Maria, her SIG-Sauer in one hand as she gazed down at her black evening dress, as if it would suddenly come to her where she could clip the holster. 'Nice dress. We'll wait while you get changed.'

Maria smiled her thanks and headed towards the bedroom.

'Oh, and Maria,' said Anna, 'This one's sweet – the bastard's gouged his eyes out.'

The Schutzpolizei and the Spurensicherungsteam had already put up a white screen barrier fifty metres out from the murder scene. The body itself was protected by a second ring of forensic screens. The scene was lit up by arc lights and the low hum of the mobile generator that powered them buzzed in the background. Sternschanzen Park remained an ongoing battleground between the young, upwardly mobile families who were moving into the increasingly trendy area, and the drug dealers and users who haunted the Park after dark. Tonight, the arc-light-illuminated trees loomed menacingly above the scene and, beyond the trees, the red-brick Wasserturm water tower thrust upwards into the night. It was, Maria noted, an almost identical set-up to the last death scene, in the Winterhuder Stadtpark, in the shadow of the Planetarium: also originally a water tower. The killer was trying to tell them something. Maria cursed the fact that she didn't share Fabel's ability to interpret the perverse vocabulary of the psychotic.

The duty SpuSi forensic team leader wasn't Brauner, but a younger man she had not met before. Maria forced the thought that this was the night for deputies from her head. As she entered the protected scene, her hands sheathed in latex gloves and her feet encased in forensic overshoes, she and the forensic team leader exchanged businesslike nods and he introduced himself as Grueber. He wore glasses behind which large, dark eyes glittered; he was almost boyish-looking with a pale complexion and very dark hair that flopped carelessly over his high, broad brow. Maria mentally christened him 'Harry Potter'.

In the centre of the protected scene a man lay, as if laid out by an undertaker, in a pale grey suit, white shirt and gold-coloured tie. His hands were folded across his chest and a large lock of blonde hair had been placed between them, just as the rose had been left between Laura von Klosterstadt's hands. Beneath the folded hands, Maria could see a small bloom of dark red on the white shirt.

The eyes were gone. The bruised lids sagged into the sockets, not fully covering them. Blood had crusted around where the eyes had been, but not as much as Maria would have expected. Maria found that she was drawn to the eyeless face. It was as if taking away the eyes had taken away the humanity. Even if he had been lying with his eyes closed, there would have remained something human about the corpse.

'Shot?' she asked Grueber, indicating the blood-stain under the hands. There were no other obvious wounds on the body to suggest a struggle or a frenzied knife attack.

'I haven't examined it yet,' Grueber, the forensic chief said; he moved round the body and knelt down beside it. 'Could be a bullet, or it could be a single stab. But whatever removed the eyes wasn't sharp. My guess is that they were forced out by the killer's thumbs. You've got a real "hands-on" killer here.' He stood up and turned to face Maria fully. 'The victim is about thirty-five to forty, male, obviously, one metre seventy-seven tall, and I'd say he's somewhere about seventy-five kilos. There's capillary rupture around the nose and lips as well as the obvious strangulation trauma to the neck, so that looks like our cause of death.'

'The thing with the eyes. Pre- or post-mortem?'

'Difficult to say at the moment, but the relative lack of blood would suggest it was done after death or immediately before. Although there wouldn't be masses of blood anyway.'

Anna Wolff came into the canopy with Henk Hermann. She winced as she looked at the eyeless face. Hermann knelt down by the body.

'I'll bet analysis will prove that this is the missing section of Laura von Klosterstadt's hair.' He turned to Grueber. 'Is it okay to move the hands? I'm guessing we'll find a note from our killer under one of them.'

'Let me do it,' said Grueber. 'Like I said, I reckon your killer is very "hands on". Maybe the victim got his hands on the killer in return. We could have skin cells under the fingernails.' He carefully eased up one hand and laid it slightly to one side, then removed the hair and put it into an evidence bag. He lifted the second hand. A small slip of yellow notepaper lay beneath it.

'That's it,' said Hermann. Grueber used tweezers to lift the slip and place it in a clear plastic evidence bag. He handed it to Hermann who turned it to the arc light and peered at it.

335

Rapunzel, Rapunzel, Lass mir dein Haar herunter.
Again the writing was small, tight and in the same red ink.

'Rapunzel, Rapunzel, let down your hair.' Hermann read it out loud.

'Great,' said Maria. 'So he's chalked up number four.'

'Number five,' said Anna, 'if you include Paula Ehlers.'

Grueber examined the shirt front, carefully easing open a button and looking at the wound below. He shook his head. 'Weird . . . he wasn't shot. Looks like a single stab wound. Why didn't he defend himself?'

'And what's the thing with the eyes?' Henk Hermann. 'It looks like our guy is collecting trophies now.'

'No,' said Maria, looking up at the water tower. 'He's not taken them as trophies. This –' she indicated the corpse with a slight movement of her head '– is meant to be the Prince. In the Rapunzel fairy tale, the Princess is locked away in a tower by her enchantress stepmother. When she finds out that Rapunzel and the Prince are having secret trysts, the enchantress tricks the Prince and, as he falls from the tower, his eyes are pierced by thorns and he is blinded.'

Anna and Henk made impressed faces.

Maria smiled a bitter smile. 'Fabel's not the only one who's been reading up on his fairy tales . . .'

★　★　★

336

By the time Fabel made it to the Präsidium, they already had an identity for the eyeless man in Sternschanzen Park – Bernd Ungerer, a catering-equipment salesman from Ottensen – and photographs of the body and the scene had been processed and were up on the inquiry board. Fabel had called Maria on his cell phone and asked her to assemble the whole team, including Petra Maas, Hans Rödger and Klatt, the Norderstedt KriPo officer.

It was two in the morning when everyone was gathered in the Mordkommission's main office. Everyone looked as if they were under the influence of the same cocktail of tiredness, adrenalin and coffee. All except the newest team member, Henk Hermann, who couldn't have looked fresher, or more eager.

Once Maria had gone through all they knew about the victim and the forensic details to date, Fabel scanned the incident board. He moved back and forth between the von Klosterstadt murder scene and the Sternschanzen images, then to the other scene-of-crime images from the Naturpark Harburger Berge and the Martha Schmidt body on Blankenese beach. There was what seemed like an interminable silence, and then he turned to the team.

'Our killer is trying to tell us something,' he said at last. 'I couldn't work out what it was, and then the water towers gave it away. He's linking the murders. Not just with the Grimm fairy tale theme. He's telling us what he's going to do next . . . or at least he's dropping hints.' Fabel moved over to the

Martha Schmidt images. He slammed his hand against the image of the dead girl. 'We've always suspected that he killed Paula Ehlers. Well, now I'm convinced of it. That's why he used the changeling story for Martha Schmidt. He chose Martha because she looked so much like Paula Ehlers and themed the death with "The Changeling" Grimm fairy tale . . . to show us that there's a body we haven't found. He used Martha's face as an advertisement that he'd killed Paula.' Fabel paused and laid his hand on a second picture: a general shot of the Elbstrand beach where Martha had been found. 'But he wasn't just being retrospective in his confessions, he was being predictive.' Fabel pointed to the background of the shot, where the terraces of Blankenese rose steeply from the shore. Part of a building jutted out above the trees and bushes. 'This is the swimming-pool annexe to Laura von Klosterstadt's villa. He had already chosen Laura as a victim and posed Martha's body in sight of Laura's house. Laura was already his Sleeping Beauty, sequestered from the likes of poor Martha, the "underground people" changeling – elevated above her by wealth and by social standing.' He moved over to the von Klosterstadt murder section of the board. 'And here we have a victim that is posed beneath an icon from two Grimm fairy tales, the tower. He's mixing his metaphors here, but in a controlled way. The Planetarium in Winterhuder Stadtpark doubles as Rapunzel's tower and Dornröschen's castle . . .' He moved to the close-up image of where Laura von Klosterstadt's hair had been cut. 'And then he places her hair in the hands of his next victim, and gouges out his eyes to fit with the Rapunzel tale.'

'What about the double murder in the Naturpark Harburger Berge? How is that connected?' asked Anna.

Fabel rubbed his chin, thoughtfully. 'It could be that the connection is confined to the location. Two murders, one place: two characters, one story. The link is the story, "Hänsel und Gretel". But I don't think that's it. To begin with, I actually thought that the killings in the Naturpark sat removed from the other murders; that they were inspired by Olsen's sexual jealousy. But that's not it either. I believe that the Naturpark murders are a single act and that they are connected to another or others – but not with the murders to date. The link is with some murder still to be committed, and I believe that there will be a cross-reference – another fairy tale link – back to one or more of the killings we've already seen. And I have a feeling that the link we shall see emerge has something to do with the missing eyes.'

After the briefing, Fabel sat in his office alone. The only illumination was his desk lamp, which cast a bright disc on to the desktop. Into this pool of light, Fabel placed the sketchbook on which he had already replicated the inquiry board, adding his own, more subjective comments.

Everything else was shut out. His entire consciousness telescoped down into this small, bright focus. Fabel updated the sketchbook with the details of the latest killing. More would emerge about this newest victim over the coming days, but for now they knew that Bernd Ungerer was a forty-two-year-old salesman for a catering equipment company based in Frankfurt. Ungerer, apparently, was the company's sole representative for Hamburg and the North of Germany. He was married, with three children, and lived in Ottensen. Fabel stared at the bald facts he had laid out: in what kind of world did a middle-aged salesman end up stabbed in the heart and with his eyes ripped from his head?

Fabel gazed long and hard at the bright white page with its black felt-tip pen notations and its red felt-tip pen lines, connecting names, locations, comments. He started to write the bizarre formulae of the investigation: Paula Ehlers + Martha Schmidt = *The Changeling*; Martha Schmidt 'placed beneath' + Laura von Klosterstadt 'placed above' = *The Changeling/Sleeping Beauty*. Hanna Grünn + Markus Schiller = *Hänsel und Gretel*; Bernd Ungerer + Laura von Klosterstadt = *Rapunzel*.

There was at least one equation missing. He stared at the page, willing it to come out at him. He wrote down: Grünn/Schiller + Bernd Ungerer? = ? He scored it out and wrote Grünn/Schiller + ? = ?; Ungerer + ? = ? No matter how hard Fabel stared at it, the page refused to yield more. He felt an anxiety clench tight in his belly: the pieces that were not yet there would come in the form of more deaths. Someone else would have to pay in fear, in pain and with their lives for Fabel's inability to see the full picture.

Olsen. Fendrich. Weiss. Was there another equation there? Was Fabel wrong to think that this was a solo killer? Was it Olsen plus Fendrich, Weiss or another? He opened his desk drawer and took out a copy of Weiss's book. He had read *Die Märchenstrasse* from cover to cover; but now his focus was specific. Weiss had titled a chapter *Rapunzel*. Again, the narration was in the voice of the fictively elaborated Jacob Grimm.

Within Rapunzel, as within each of these tales, there lies an articulation of elemental Good and Evil; an understanding of the forces of Creation and Life; of Destruction and Death. I have found within these ancient fables and tales such commonality of theme as to suggest that their origins lie not simply in our un-lettered pagan past but in the earliest articu-lations of the most elemental of forces. The nascence of some of these tales must, indeed, lie deep in some early community of man, when and where our numbers on the Earth were few. How, otherwise, are we to explain why the tale of Cinderella exists in almost iden-tical forms not only throughout Europe but also in China?

341

Of these elemental forces, I have found that Nature, at her most bountiful and at her most destructive, is most commonly given human form. The Mother. The maternal and the natural forces are so often seen as in parallel, and in the old folk tales and fables the Mother embodies both. Nature gives life, nourishes and sustains; but She is also capable of fury and cruelty. This dichotomy of Nature's character is solved in these tales by the dual (and sometimes triple, if one counts the motif of the Grandmother) representation of Motherhood. There is the image of Mother herself, who commonly represents the hearth and home and all that is good and wholesome: she is Safety and Protection; she nourishes and succours; she gives Life. The motif of the Stepmother, on the other hand, is often employed to represent the negation of normal maternal impulses. It is the Stepmother who persuades her husband to abandon Hänsel and Gretel in the woods; it is the Stepmother, driven by insane envy and vanity, who seeks the death of Snow White. And in the form of the wicked Enchantress, we see the Stepmother as the abductor and tormentor of Rapunzel.

In the city of Lübeck there was a beautiful and wealthy widow, whom I shall call Frau X. Frau X had herself borne no child, but found herself the guardian of Imogen, her late husband's daughter by a previous marriage.

Imogen was every inch a match for her step-mother's beauty but, of course, possessed a wealth that in her stepmother diminished daily: youth. Now it must be made clear that not I nor anyone else had the slightest reason to believe that Frau X was envious of Imogen, or was in any other way ill-disposed towards her. Indeed, Frau X seemed to be most solicit-ous and affectionate towards her ward and treated her as if she were her own child. But this is an inconsequence: it sufficed that I had found a beautiful stepmother and daughter, one of the most common motifs in the fairy tale. As Imogen was not dark of hair, I could not use her to re-enact Snow White, but she did have lustrous golden hair about which I believe she was quite vain. I had found my Rapunzel! I ensured that I had no contact with either Frau X nor Imogen which might incrim-inate me in the future and set about planning the execution of my re-enactment.

Over the preceding months, I had acquired large quantities of laudanum, which I obtained in small increments by visiting various physi-cians on my travels with a specious complaint of sleeplessness. I again noted my subject's movements and selected the best opportunity to strike. Imogen took a walk each day in the wooded park to the north of the town. Being a young lady of some breeding, she was always accompanied by a female companion. I neither know nor care about the identity of Imogen's chaperone, but she was the type of dull, homely companion that women of beauty habitually choose to contrast with their own pulchritude. I found myself loathing the companion for the preposterousness of her headgear: a ridiculously cheerful bonnet which, one can only assume, she chose in the mistaken belief that it mitigated the homeliness of her features.

There was a stretch of path where the two walkers were temporarily concealed from others in the park (on this particular day, the unpromising sky had deterred many from promenading) and which fortuitously allowed an exit from the park completely concealed by trees. I approached the women from behind and let swing, with some relish, at the companion's ludicrously ornamented head with a heavy iron bar I had secreted in my cloak. I was in such a rush to subdue Imogen that I could only take the most passing satisfaction in the manner in which I had forced the ridiculous bonnet of the companion through her smashed skull. Imogen began to scream, however, and I was forced to deliver a sharp jab to her jaw. This concerned me greatly, because any damage to her beauty would compromise the success of my re-enactment. I picked her up and carried her into the trees, just far enough to be out of sight. Then I dragged the dead companion into the woods.

A pool of blood had gathered about her ugly head and smeared on the paving as her bonnet separated from her shattered cranium and grey matter spilled forth. I am thoroughly ashamed to admit that I uttered a rather foul curse as I dragged her from view. Gathering some well-leaved branches, I returned to try to sweep up the mess, but succeeded only in spreading the stain further. I knew I could not avoid discovery of the companion's body – most likely imminent discovery – but that concerned me not: what I had to achieve was the swift removal of Imogen from the park without detection. I had left a hansom carriage at the far side of the woods and I hoisted Imogen over my shoulder and carried her with what haste my burden and the terrain would permit. Imogen had begun to stir by the time I placed her in the interior of my carriage and I quietened her by forcing some laudanum down her throat.

I had dressed as a coachman and, after securing Imogen in the cabin, I climbed atop the hansom and made my departure from the scene in an unhurried manner. I had succeeded with my abduction without being observed. Indeed, it was by great fortune that the companion's body was not found within minutes, as I had feared, but much later that day, when a search had been undertaken by townsfolk concerned for the safety of the missing ladies.

345

Prescient of the need for a place of some concealment, I had secured separate lodgings in Lübeck from those of my brother: a small house on the outskirts of the city. After darkfall I bundled Imogen, to whom I shall henceforth refer as 'Rapunzel', into the house and carried her down to the basement. There I bound her securely, applied some more laudanum, and gagged her lest she rouse sufficiently in my absence to alert some passerby with her screams.

I then joined my brother for a rather splendid meal of vension 'direkt von der Jagd'. I allowed myself a moment of amusement at the idea of consuming flesh 'straight from the hunt' when I had come 'straight from the hunt' myself. I found, however, that when I thought of the bounty of flesh my chase had yielded, I experienced a manly disturbance and placed the thought from my mind.

On returning to the lodgings, I found my beautiful Rapunzel had stirred from her slumbers. Rapunzel or Sleeping Beauty? The quandary had occurred to me before: these tales are essentially variations, rather than separate stories. In both, my brother had insisted we 'civilise' the account somewhat, having Sleeping Beauty awoken by a kiss. In the original we had found, she is actually discovered deep in her hundred-year slumber by a married King, not a Prince, who knows her carnally, several times, while she sleeps. It is only after she gives birth to twins and one, attempting to suckle, sucks the splinter from her thumb that she is awoken from her enchanted slumber. Again, with the Rapunzel tale, the young Princess in her tower is not so chaste as later versions, including that which we recorded, would suggest. A veil is again drawn over how Rapunzel comes by two children after her trysts with the Prince. Therein lies a morality of an earlier time, when Christian values held less or no sway. Both Rapunzel and Sleeping Beauty, in their original forms, bear children from liaisons non-marital . . .

Fabel put the book down. He remembered what Heinz Schnauber had said about Laura von Klosterstadt's secret pregnancy and abortion. If the killer was following either authentic, original versions of the fairy tales or Weiss's book, then it added to her 'suitability' as a victim. But it had been a closely guarded secret: if the killer knew about it then he must have had some intimate knowledge of the von Klosterstadt family. Or he must have been the father. Fabel read on.

In the interests of verisimilitude to the fable, I therefore was compelled to violate my Rapunzel, but only once she was asleep. She looked at me with pleading eyes which made her singularly unattractive. When I removed

347

her gag she began to plead for her life. I found it interesting that, being a woman of breeding, she did not seek to plead for her virtue, which I sensed she would have surrendered freely were it to assure her survival. I made her drink more laudanum and the tranquillity and beauty of her face and form were restored. Once I had removed her clothing I became intoxicated with the beauty of her body and I admit to having indulged in her flesh several times as she slept. I then placed a silk cushion gently over her face. There was no bitter last struggle for life and she gave up her spirit.

Again Fabel broke from the book, this time to pull out the von Klosterstadt autopsy report: far from exhibiting any signs of sexual trauma, there were indications that Laura might have been celibate for some time. He returned to *Die Märchenstrasse*.

The following night I returned to the park and laid my Rapunzel beneath the ornamental tower at its centre. The moon shone brightly and illuminated her beauty. I brushed out her lustrous hair, which shimmered like white gold in the moonlight. I left her there, my Rapunzel, for others to find and recall the old tales.

I had considered my re-creation complete, and was well satisfied with it. It came as a great and welcome surprise when it emerged

348

some days later that Frau X had become the subject of rumour and speculation about her role in her stepdaughter's death. Such was the suspicion – though none was felt officially – that not only was her social standing amongst the elite of Lübeck completely destroyed, the woman was often assaulted with jeers from the common folk when she appeared on the street. Proof positive not only that the prejudice of the peasant lives on in the so-called civilised world, but also of the essential truth of these old tales.

Fabel closed the book, leaving his hand to rest on its cover as if he expected it to yield more through osmosis. He thought beyond the glossy cover, the publisher's commercial product beneath his hand, to the moment of creation. He imagined the menacing bulk of Weiss hunched over his laptop, the too-black eyes glittering, in that light-absorbing study of his. He pictured the wolf/werewolf sculpture, probably crafted by Weiss's insane brother, caught in its silent snarl as Weiss committed his serial murders on paper.

Fabel stood up and pulled on his Jaeger jacket, switching off his desk light. Hamburg sparkled at him through his office window. Out there one and a half million souls slept, while others explored the night. Soon. The next killing, Fabel knew, would be soon.

CHAPTER 45

11.00 a.m., Monday, 19 April:
Altes Land, south-west of Hamburg

Fabel waited.

He was beginning to feel that almost drunk sensation that comes with too little sleep. He could have done without the early-hours drive back to Hamburg from Norddeich. Susanne had decided to stay with Gabi and his mother, making the most of her two days off before taking the train back on Wednesday.

The killer was stretching them. They now had so many concurrent murders to deal with, forensics to process and interviews to conduct that Fabel had given Maria total control of the Ungerer murder inquiry. It was not a decision that had sat easily with him. He valued Maria above all the members of his team, perhaps even above Werner. She was a startlingly intelligent woman who combined a methodical approach and an eye for detail with speed. But he still was not convinced she was ready for this. Physically, she was fit. She had even been given a clean bill of health psychologically. Officially. But Fabel could see something in Maria's eyes that he hadn't seen before. He couldn't specify it, but it bothered him.

Unfortunately, at the moment, he had no choice but to hand the Ungerer case file over to Maria. There were lots of compromises being made: he had Anna back on duty, even though she could no longer hide the winces of pain if something rubbed against her injured thigh; he had Hermann working full-time in the Mordkommission, despite him not being fully KriPo-trained; and he had two Sexual Crime SoKo members drafted in to bolster his team.

Still Fabel waited. There were two things that he could have predicted on his drive to the Altes Land: the first was that the von Klosterstadts weren't the type to answer their own door, the second was that they would keep him waiting. The last time he had been here, the rawness of Laura's death had ensured him an immediate audience. This time, the blue-business-suited butler who answered the door conducted him to a reception hall in which he had now sat for twenty minutes. Half an hour was his limit. Then he would go looking for them.

Margarethe von Klosterstadt emerged from the drawing room that Fabel had been in during his last visit. She closed the doors behind her: clearly, this interview was going to be conducted in the hall. He stood up and shook hands with her. She gave a polite smile and apologised for keeping him waiting; the smile and the apology both lacked sincerity. Frau von Klosterstadt wore a dark navy suit which emphasised her narrow waist. The expensive, high-heeled cream court shoes tensed her calf muscles and Fabel again had to push from his mind how sexually attractive he found her. She indicated that he should sit again and she took the seat next to him.

'What can I do for you, Herr Kriminalhauptkommissar?'

'Frau von Klosterstadt, I have to be frank with you. There are elements to this inquiry that lead us to believe that your daughter's death may have been the work of a serial murderer. A psychotic. Someone who has a twisted, perverted perspective. Part of that perspective means that details of his victims' lives – specifics that may seem remote or insignificant to us – take on an especial meaning.'

Margarethe von Klosterstadt arched one of her perfectly shaped eyebrows inquisitively, but Fabel could detect nothing more than patient politeness in the glacial eyes. Fabel paused for a heartbeat before continuing.

'I have to ask you about your daughter's pregnancy and subsequent abortion, Frau von Klosterstadt.'

The patient politeness disappeared from the pale blue eyes; an Arctic storm welled up somewhere deep within them but did not, yet, break through.

'What, might I ask, leads you to ask such an offensive question, Herr Kriminalhauptkommissar?'

'You don't deny that Laura had an abortion?' Fabel asked. She did not answer but held him in her steady gaze. 'Listen, Frau von Klosterstadt, I am making every effort to deal with these matters as discreetly as possible, and it would be much easier if you were to be direct with me. If you force me to, I will get all kinds of warrants to go stomping about in your family's affairs until I get to the truth. That would be, well, unpleasant. And it could be more public.'

The Arctic storm now raged and rattled against the panes of Margarethe von Klosterstadt's eyes, yet still did not break through. Then it was gone. Her expression, her perfect poise, her voice remained unchanged, yet she had surrendered. Something she was clearly not used to. 'It was just before Laura's twenty-first birthday. We sent her to the Hammond Clinic. It's a private clinic in London.'

'How long before her birthday?'

'A week or so before.'

'So it was almost exactly ten years ago?' Fabel's question was more to himself. An anniversary. 'Who was the father?'

There was an almost imperceptible tensing of her posture. Then a smile flickered across her lips.

'Is that really necessary, Herr Fabel? Do we really need to go into all of this?'

'I'm afraid so, Frau von Klosterstadt. You have my word that I will be discreet.'

'Very well. His name was Kranz. He was a photographer. Or rather he was an assistant to Pietro Moldari, the fashion photographer who launched Laura's career. He was a nobody then, but I believe he's done rather well for himself since.'

'Leo Kranz?' Fabel recognised the name immediately. But he didn't associate it with fashion shoots. Kranz was a well-regarded photojournalist who had covered some of the world's most dangerous war-zones over the last five years. Margarethe von Klosterstadt read the confusion in Fabel's face.

'He gave up fashion photography for press work.'

'Did Laura have anything to do with him? Afterwards, I mean.'

'No. I don't think they had been particularly involved. It was an unfortunate . . . episode . . . and they both put it behind them.'

Did they? wondered Fabel. He remembered Laura's austere, lonely villa in Blankenese. He doubted very much if Laura von Klosterstadt had left anything of her sadness behind her.

'Who knew about the abortion?' he asked.

Margarethe von Klosterstadt didn't answer for a moment. She regarded Fabel silently. Somehow she managed to sprinkle just enough disdain into that look to make Fabel feel uncomfortable, but not enough for him to actually confront her. He thought idly of Möller, the pathologist, who always tried to achieve this level of arrogant haughtiness: in comparison, he was a clumsy amateur; Frau von Klosterstadt was world-class at it. Fabel wondered if she practised on the servants.

'We're not in the habit of sharing details of our family affairs with the outside world, Herr Fabel. And I am certain that Herr Kranz had absolutely no interest in making his involvement widely known. As I say, it was a family matter and it was kept within the family.'

'So Hubert knew about it?'

Another frosted silence, then: 'I didn't feel that was necessary. Whether Laura told him or not, I don't know. But I'm afraid they were never close as brother and sister. Laura was always distant. Difficult.'

Fabel kept his expression blank. It was clear who had been the favoured child in this family. He remembered the contempt with which Heinz Schnauber had spoken about Hubert. Two things had become clear to him: first Heinz Schnauber really was the closest thing Laura had known to family, and second, this interview was going to yield nothing. And it was going to yield nothing because, once again, he was asking questions of an acquaintance, not a mother. He looked at Margarethe von Klosterstadt: she was elegant, classically beautiful and one of those women whose age only seemed to intensify their sexiness. In his mind, he overlaid the image of Ulrike

Schmidt, the prematurely aged occasional prostitute and regular drug user, whose skin and hair had dulled. Two women who were so different they could have belonged to different species. But one thing united them: their profound lack of knowledge of their own daughters.

Something dull and heavy dragged at Fabel as he made his way back to his car: a leaden, gloomy sadness. He looked back at the vast, immaculate house and thought of a little girl growing up there. Isolated. Dislocated from any sense of real family. He thought of how she had escaped this gilded prison merely to build one of her own, high on the Blankenese banks of the Elbe.

Fabel had to admit that her killer could not have made a more appropriate choice for his fairy tale princess. And he felt certain now that her killer, at some point, must have had some kind of contact with her.

CHAPTER 46

1.15 p.m., Monday, 19 April:
Ottensen, Hamburg

Fabel had given Maria the task of interviewing the wife of the latest victim, Bernd
Ungerer. And she would still be his wife,
not his widow. Maria knew she was about to meet
with someone whose grief was as raw as burned
flesh; someone who would be struggling to come
to terms with a new, absurd, but permanent reality.

Ingrid Ungerer's eyes were inflamed with the
tears that she had shed before Maria had arrived.
But there was something more there. A bitterness.
She conducted Maria into the sitting room, where
they were alone, but Maria could hear subdued
voices from an upstairs room.

'My sister,' Ingrid explained. 'She's helping me
with the kids. Please . . . sit down.'

A pine shelving unit lined one wall. It was filled
with the usual careless mix of books, CDs, orna-
ments and photographs that typify a family
home. Maria noticed that most of the photographs
were of Ingrid and a man whom Maria took to

357

be her husband, Bernd, although his hair looked lighter, more grey, than it had on the dead man found in the park. And, of course, unlike the body in the park, the man in the picture had eyes with which to look at the camera. In all the photographs there were two boys, both of whom shared their mother's dark hair and eyes. As families always do in these photographs, they all looked happy. Ingrid's smile looked natural and relaxed, but, as Maria looked at the woman before her, she realised that happiness was now a permanently alien concept to Ingrid Ungerer; and Maria had the feeling that it had been so for some time. Bernd Ungerer's face also beamed a smile at the camera. Again the smile looked genuinely happy. Contented.

'When will I be able to see the body?' Ingrid Ungerer's expression was one of a forced, spiritless composure.

'Frau Ungerer . . .' Maria leaned forward in the chair. 'I have to warn you that your husband sustained certain . . . injuries . . . that could be distressing for you to see. I think it would be best—'

'What type of injuries?' Ingrid cut Maria off. 'How was he killed?'

'As far as we can tell, your husband was stabbed.' Maria paused. 'Listen, Frau Ungerer, the person who killed your husband is clearly a deranged individual. I'm afraid to say that he removed your husband's eyes. I really am very sorry.'

Ingrid Ungerer's expression remained composed, but Maria noticed that she trembled as she spoke.

'Was it someone's husband? Or a boyfriend?'

'I'm afraid I don't understand, Frau Ungerer.'

'Was my husband caught with another woman? Or was it a jealous husband who caught up with him? Then I could understand the thing with the eyes. He was always staring at other women. Always.'

Maria looked hard at Ingrid Ungerer. She was unremarkably attractive, of medium height and build, with short chestnut hair. A pleasant face, but not one you would notice; but if you did, you would see that a sadness continually lurked behind her expression. Maria could see that it was an established sadness; a melancholy that had made temporary house-room for Ingrid's new grief, but whose own tenancy was of a much longer, and now permanent, standing.

'Your husband saw other women?' Maria asked.

Ingrid gave a bitter laugh. 'Do you like sex?' She asked the question as if she were asking the time. Maria, naturally, looked stunned, but the question bit deeper than Frau Ungerer had intended. Fortunately, she didn't wait for Maria to answer. 'I used to. I'm a very physical person. But you know what it's like, after you've been married for a while, the way the passion fades, the way kids exhaust you and kill your sex drive . . .'

'Sorry, I don't. I'm not married.'

'But you have a boyfriend?'

'Not at the moment.' Maria kept her tone even. It was an area of her life that she did not feel like discussing with a stranger, even if it was a bereaved woman.

'Things cooled down a bit after Bernd and I got married. As they do. A bit too cool for me, if I'm honest, but Bernd had a demanding job and was often dead tired when he got home. But he was a wonderful husband, Frau Klee. Faithful, supportive, caring, and a great father.' Ingrid stood up, taking a set of keys from her handbag. 'I'd like to show you something.' She led Maria out into the hall, through an archway and down some stairs. Once in the basement she switched on the lights. There was the usual collection of items that found no place in the main dwelling of a family home: bicycles, storage boxes, winter boots. Ingrid stopped in front of a large chest, resting her hand on it but making no effort to open it.

'It started about six months ago. Bernd became more . . . attentive, shall we say. I was happy to begin with, but we seemed to go from one extreme to the other. We made love every night. Sometimes twice in one night. It became more and more . . . *urgent*, I suppose. Then it stopped being like we were making love. He would do it to me and it was like I wasn't there. And then, one night when I said I wasn't in the mood . . .' Ingrid stopped. She looked down at the set of keys and fumbled through them, as if they were a rosary. 'It was that night that he made it very clear that he didn't care whether I was in the mood or not.'

Maria placed her hand on Ingrid's arm but felt her pull slightly away. 'It was about then that I started to find out about the other women. He was working for a different company then. He'd been with them for years, and he suddenly had to make a move to the firm he's with now . . .' She shook her head as if annoyed with herself and corrected her statement. 'I mean, the company he was working for until now. It wasn't until recently that I found out a couple of the women at his old company had made complaints about him.'

'I'm sorry, Frau Ungerer. So that's why you think it might have been a jealous husband? I don't think that's the case. We have reason to believe that your husband's murder was committed by someone who has killed a number of unconnected people before.'

Ingrid Ungerer stared blankly at Maria, then continued as if she hadn't heard what she had said. 'There were half a dozen women that I know about over the last six months. And countless more who rejected him. He had no shame. It didn't seem to matter to him that he was embarrassing himself . . . or me and the children, for that matter.' She laughed her small, bitter laugh once more. 'And it wasn't as if he left me alone. All the time he was with other women I still had to perform for him. He became insatiable.'

She took the keys she had taken from her bag and unlocked the chest, swinging the lid up to reveal its contents. It was packed with pornography. Hard-core pornography: magazines, videos, DVDs. 'He told me never to come down here. Never to open this chest, if I knew what was good for me.' She looked at Maria beseechingly. 'Why did he do that? Why did he threaten me? He'd never threatened me before.' She nodded at the contents of the chest. 'There's more on his computer upstairs. Do you understand it? Why would he change like that? Why would a caring, loving man turn into a beast? So suddenly? Everyone knew about it. That's what made me so sad. Neighbours and friends would smile and chat to me and I could see they either felt sorry for me or were trying to find out more dirty details. Not that we had many friends left. Any couple we knew fell out with us because Bernd was always trying to get into the woman's pants. Even the people at his work joked about it . . . had a nickname for him. His customers too, apparently. I'm telling you, Frau Klee, I can't believe his murder hasn't got anything to do with the way he's been behaving recently.'

Ingrid shut and locked the chest and they went back up to the lounge. Maria tried to concentrate on getting details from Ingrid about her husband's movements over the previous week. But the more Maria tried to focus on his movements, the more the locked chest in the basement, the secret life bothered her. In any case, it was a diffi-cult and thankless task because, alongside his sudden lasciviousness, it appeared that Ungerer had become increasingly secretive and defensive. He had gone out more in the evenings to 'see clients socially', and that was where he'd said he had been going the night he was killed. When he had not returned that night, Ingrid had not been concerned. Upset, but not concerned: it was quite common for Bernd to stay out all night. There had been credit-card slips hidden, which Ingrid had found, but she had put them back where she had found them, without comment. They had all been made out to escort agencies, clubs and saunas in St Pauli.

'It was clear that there was something wrong with Bernd,' Ingrid explained. 'He became a different person. There were other strange things about him. Sometimes he would come home and complain that the house smelled dirty. It never did, but I would have to clean the house from top to bottom, even if I'd already done it that day, just to keep him happy. Then I would get my "reward", as he put it. I thought he was having some kind of breakdown, so I suggested that we went to see our family doctor, but Bernd wouldn't have any of it.'

'So you never got any kind of professional opinion on his behaviour?'

'Yes. Yes, I did. I went to see Herr Doktor Gärten myself. I told him what was happening. He said that there is a condition called "satyriasis" – it's the male form of nymphomania. He said that he was very concerned about Bernd and wanted him to come in to see him, but when I told Bernd that I'd been to see the doctor without him, behind his back, as he put it . . . well, things started to get even more *unpleasant.*'

The two women sat in silence for a moment. Then Maria started to explain the kind of help that was available to Ingrid, and went through the procedures that would be followed over the coming days and weeks. Then Maria got up to go. She was almost at the door when she turned to say goodbye to Ingrid Ungerer, and repeated her condolences.

'May I ask you one last question, Frau Ungerer?'

Ingrid nodded lifelessly.

'You said his colleagues and customers had a nickname for him. What was it?'

Ingrid Ungerer's eyes welled with tears. 'Bluebeard. That's what they called my husband . . . Bluebeard.'

CHAPTER 47

3.00 p.m., Monday, 19 April:
Krankenhaus Mariahilf, Heimfeld, Hamburg

The nurses were delighted. Such a lovely thought – to have brought in a huge box of the most delicious pastries for them to have with their coffee. It was a small 'thank you', he had explained, to the Oberschwester and all of her staff for the wonderful care they had taken of his mother. So nice. So considerate.

He had been in with the Chefarzt, Herr Doktor Schell, for almost half an hour. Doktor Schell was going over, once more, the essentials of his mother's care once she was home with him. Schell had the report that the social services had provided on the apartment the son had prepared to share with his sick mother. According to the report it had been equipped to the highest standard and the chief doctor complimented him on his commitment to providing his mother with the best possible care.

When he came out of the Doktor's office, the big man beamed a smile at the nurse's station. He was so obviously delighted to be taking his mother home. Again the chief nurse found herself doubting that any of her ungrateful brood would make a quarter as much effort for her in her old age.

He sat again by the old woman's bed, pulling his chair in tight, drawing in to their confined, exclusive, poisonous universe.

'Do you know what, *Mutti*? At the end of this week we will be together. Alone. Isn't that wonderful? All I'll have to worry about is the odd visit we'll be getting from a District Nurse, to see how we're getting on. But I can work around that. No, it won't be a problem at all when the Gemeindeschwester comes to call. You see, I've got this wonderful little apartment all fitted out with stuff that we'll never use – because we'll hardly ever be there, will we, *Mutti*? I know that you'd much rather be in our old house, wouldn't you?'

The old woman lay, as ever, motionless, helpless.

'Do you know what I found the other day, mother? Your old costume from the Speeldeel. Remember how important that was for you? German traditions of dance and song? I do believe I might find a use for it.' He paused. 'Do you want me to read to you, *Mutti*? Do you want me to read the Grimm stories to you? I will when we get home. All the time. Like before. Do you remember how the only books you would allow in the house were the Bible and the Brothers Grimm fairy tales? God and Germany. That's all we needed in our household . . .' He paused. Then his voice fell to a low, conspiratorial whisper. 'You hurt me so much, *Mutti*. You hurt me so much that sometimes I thought I was going to die. You beat me so hard and you told me all the time that I was worthless. A nobody. You never stopped. When I was a teenager and then a grown man, you told me I was useless. Unworthy of anyone else's love. You said that was why I could never form a lasting relationship.' The whisper became a hiss. 'Well, you were wrong, you old bitch. You thought we were always alone when you beat the crap out of me. Well, we weren't. He was always there. My Märchenbruder. Invisible. He didn't speak for such a long, long time. Then I heard him. I heard him; you couldn't. He saved me from your beatings. He gave me the words for the stories. He opened up a new world. A wonderful, shining world. A truthful world. And then I found my true art, with his help. Three years ago, remember? The girl. The girl you had to help me bury because you were terrified of the scandal, the disgrace of having a son go to prison. You thought you could control me. But he was stronger . . . *is* stronger than you can ever imagine.'

He leaned back in his chair and scanned her body, from head to toe. When he spoke, his voice was no longer a whisper, but flat, cold, menacing.

'You will be my masterpiece, mother. My masterwork. It will be for you, more than anything else I have done, that I will be remembered.'

CHAPTER 48

Noon, Tuesday, 20 April:
Polizeipräsidium, Hamburg

The dressing on the side of Werner's head was small and the side of his face was no longer swollen, but there was still a smudge of bruising around the area of the wound. Fabel had only agreed to let him back if he stayed in the Mordkommission and helped with the processing and collation of the evidence that the active team gathered. And then only if he restricted his hours. Werner's methodical approach was ideally suited for sifting through the oddball correspondence and e-mails that Weiss's theories had attracted. So far, wading through this junk had tied up Hans Rödger and Petra Maas. And, because of its very nature, it had turned up a pile of crackpots who needed to be checked out, and there was a mounting backlog of interviews to be done.

The truth was, Fabel was as glad to see Werner return to the team as he had been to see Anna back. He did, however, feel irresponsible at having allowed two injured officers to return to duty prematurely. Fabel decided to make it up to them by negotiating some extra paid leave for Werner and Anna after this case was over.

He took Werner through the inquiry board. Running through the progress, or lack of it, of the case so far was a frustrating experience. Fabel had been forced to turn the media spotlight generated by Laura von Klosterstadt's murder to his own advantage: Olsen's picture now appeared on news bulletins and in papers as the person to whom the Polizei Hamburg wanted to speak in connection with the murders. He had put Anna and Henk Hermann on to interviewing Leo Kranz, the photographer who had been involved ten years ago with Laura von Klosterstadt: but Kranz was on assignment, covering the Anglo-American occupation of Iraq. His office had been able to confirm that he had been in the Middle East throughout the time when the murders had been committed. Fabel went through his meeting with Weiss, which Werner had prompted, and explained that Fendrich remained on the edge of the investigation.

'The thing that bothers me most about Fendrich,' said Fabel, 'is that his mother died six months ago. In her psycho-profile of the killer, Susanne reckoned that the gap between the first and the second killings could indicate that some kind of restraint was exerted on the killer by a dominant figure, a wife or a mother, who may have since died.'

'I don't know, Jan.' Werner turned a chair from a nearby desk to face the inquiry board, then eased himself into it. His face looked grey, tired. For the first time, Fabel became aware that Werner was getting older. 'Fendrich has been put through the mill at least twice. He just doesn't fit. I don't like the sound of this guy Weiss, though. You reckon we've got another high priest and acolyte? Weiss pulling the strings and Olsen doing the killing? We've been there before, after all.'

'Could be.' Fabel gazed at the inquiry board, with all the pictures and time-lines laid out on it. 'But does Olsen strike you as someone who would be inspired by fairy tales, or Weiss's half-assed literary theories?'

Werner laughed. 'Maybe we're trying too hard. Maybe we should just be looking for someone who lives in a gingerbread house.'

Fabel smiled grimly, but something snagged in his brain. A gingerbread house. He shrugged. 'You could be right. About trying too hard, I mean. Maybe Olsen is our guy. Let's just hope we close in on him soon.'

It was about three p.m. when Fabel's wish was answered. A SchuPo unit reported that someone matching Olsen's description had been seen entering a squat in a disused block overlooking the harbour. The uniformed officers had had the good sense to hold back and call up a plain-clothes Mobiles

Einsatz Kommando to keep the building under surveillance. The report hit the Mordkommission like a missile. Fabel had to calm everyone down before giving them their orders.

'Listen, people. This is our capture. I've already told the MEK commander that *we*'re making the arrest. *We* take him. No one else.' He looked across to Maria; as usual, her expression was hard to read, but she gave a decisive nod. 'When we get there we'll work out a game plan. I want Olsen alive and in a condition to talk. Is that clear? Okay, let's go.'

Fabel had to stop Werner in his tracks as he donned his black leather jacket and made his way out with the rest of the team.

'Just an observer?' Werner smiled meekly. 'Please, Jan, the bastard split my head open. I just want to see him get taken.'

'Okay, but you stay back where I put you. Maria's my number two on this.'

It had, at one time, been a working community. A place where the workers in the Hafen came home to; where families lived; where their children played. But now it lay empty, awaiting the inexorable forces of development and gentrification that seemed to be taking hold of all the former working-class districts of Hamburg. Even Fabel's beloved Pöseldorf, the home of Hamburg's trendy, wealthy *Schickeria*, had been known as the Arme Leute Gegend – the poor people's area – until the

1960s, when it had been transformed into the trendiest part of Hamburg to be seen in.

But this area down by the harbour had yet to acquire any such desirability. Architecturally, the area seemed frozen in time, with its cobbled streets and huge tenements. The only incursions of the twenty-first century were found in the ugly graffiti that defaced the buildings and the silent, hulking form of a container vessel that could be seen sliding by through the gaps between the tenements. All the officers were tense.

The building where Olsen had been spotted sat on the fringes of the Hafenstrasse Genossenschaft, the area of Hamburg that, since December 1995, had been owned and administered by a tenants' commune 'Alternativen am Elbufer'. Politically and socially, this part of the city had been a battleground. Literally.

In the autumn of 1981, the apartment blocks along Hafenstrasse and in Bernhardt-Nocht-Strasse had become systematically occupied by squatters. Alfons Pawelczyk, who was Innensenator at the time, had ordered the police in to clear them out. The result had been total anarchy and mayhem. A decade-long war between the squatters and the Polizei Hamburg had followed, and German TV screens had been filled with scenes of burning barricades, vicious hand-to-hand street battles and hundreds of injured police officers and squatters. Ultimately it had cost the then Erster Bürgermeister, Klaus von Dohnanyi, his job. It had only been with the compromise deal struck in 1995 that the unrest had ended. Nevertheless, the area around Hafenstrasse had continued to simmer, and it was not a place the police could enter and operate in without care.

The MEK team had therefore positioned itself a block back all round the building, which sat on a corner, where Olsen had been sighted. The MEK commander was glad to see Fabel. In an area like this, it would have been impossible to keep their presence a secret much longer. He informed Fabel that Olsen was believed to be in the squat, which sat one floor up in the tenement. It was certainly his motorbike that was parked outside, and one of the MEK team had sneaked in to disable it, in case Olsen tried to make a run for it. Because it had been so badly vandalised, the ground floor was unoccupied. It made things easy. Basically, there was one way in, one way out.

Fabel divided the team in two. Maria was in charge of Anna and Henk Hermann. They would secure the outside of the building. Fabel, Hans Rödger and Petra Maas would go in for Olsen, taking two MEK officers with them in case any of the other occupants of the squat gave them trouble. He asked the MEK commander to use the rest of his team to support Maria in sealing off any possible escape route.

They split up into the MEK van, Fabel's BMW and Maria's car. They pulled up simultaneously outside the building, vehicle noses inwards.

Maria and her team were out and deployed in seconds. Fabel and his group took the front door. The two MEK men slammed a door-ram into the centre of the double doors which splintered and flew open. Fable drew his pistol and led the team in. The hallway stank of urine and some other unclean odour that Fabel could not place. There was the sound of a commotion upstairs and Fabel moved swiftly and silently up the stair-well, flattening himself against the flaking pale green paint and keeping the bead of his pistol lined up on the uppermost point he could see. The door of the squat was open, and Fabel waited until the others could give him cover before going in.

He scanned the room. It was large and surprisingly bright. It was also empty. There were three large windows facing out on to the street and it took a second for Fabel to register the shape of a man just outside one of them, sitting on the ledge outside, poised to jump. Fabel had just shouted 'Olsen!' when the figure was gone.

'He's jumped!' Fabel shouted into his radio. 'Maria, he's jumped!' He had no sooner made the report when he realised that he had been in this situation before: him inside, Maria outside and a suspect fleeing.

'Shit!' he shouted and nearly knocked Petra Maas and an MEK officer over as he burst back out of the squat, taking the stairs three at a time.

★   ★   ★

374

Outside on the street, Maria could hardly believe what she had seen. Olsen had not only dropped a full floor's height on to the street, but he had immediately picked himself up and started sprinting down towards the water. By the time she had heard Fabel's shouts on the radio, she was already running. This was it. This was her time. Now she would find out if she still could hack it. She screamed into her radio that she was heading for the Hafen and she knew that Anna and Henk wouldn't be far behind her, but she also knew that she would be the one to get to Olsen first. And they didn't come bigger or badder than Olsen.

Up ahead, Olsen made a sudden turn into another disused building. This time its history had been more industrial than residential and Maria found herself in a large, wide, pillared factory space. The rusting chains and the pulleys in the ceiling from which they hung hinted at some kind of heavy engineering past. Olsen was nowhere to be seen and the huge workbenches that had at one time obviously supported heavy equipment offered a dozen places for him to have hidden. Maria stopped dead and drew her SIG-Sauer from its holster, snapping her arms out in front of her. She strained her ears, trying to hear over her own laboured breathing and the pounding in her chest.

'Olsen!' she shouted.

Silence.

'Olsen! Give it up. Now!'

She felt an intense pain as something flashed

before her face and slammed into her wrists. Her gun flew from her grasp and she bent double, clutching her right wrist with her left hand. She turned to see Olsen to her right, an iron bar raised above his head, like some oversized medieval executioner wielding an axe, ready to bring it down on to her neck. Maria froze. For a split second she was somewhere else, with someone else who had a large knife rather than an iron bar. A feeling that went beyond any fear she had felt before surged up in her. It coursed through her like cold electricity, locking her in her bent-over position. Olsen let go a deep, animal cry as he swung the iron bar, and suddenly Maria's fear became something else. She threw herself forward like a swimmer taking a dive and rolled on the filthy floor of the factory. Olsen's rage and the viciousness of his attempted blow threw him off balance. Maria was up on her feet and she slammed her foot into the side of Olsen's head.

'You fuck!' she screamed. Olsen scrabbled to get to his feet. Maria, clutching her injured wrist, jumped up and forwards, ramming the sole of her boot into his neck. Olsen's head snapped forward and smashed into the concrete floor. He moaned and his movements became slower. Maria searched the floor for her gun, found it and snapped it up with her good hand. She aimed it at Olsen's head as he rolled on to his back. He placed his hands above his head.

Maria examined her wrist. It was bruised but

not broken and the pain was already beginning to ease. She looked down her gun barrel at Olsen and hissed.

'Big man. Big fucking scary XYY man. Like hitting women, do you, you fuck!' She swung her boot once again into the side of Olsen's face. By now Anna Wolff was running across the factory floor towards them.

'Are you okay, Maria?'

'I'm okay.' Maria didn't take her eyes from Olsen. Her voice was tight. 'You like scaring women? Is that it? You like hurting them?' She slammed the heel of her boot into Olsen's cheek. It split and blood started to flood from the wound.

'Maria!' Anna was now beside her and levelled her SIG-Sauer at Olsen's bleeding face. She looked across at Maria. 'Maria . . . we've got him. We've got him. It's okay. You can back off now.' Henk Hermann was suddenly there too, and Maria could hear Fabel and the others running towards them. Hermann dropped beside Olsen, rolled him on to his belly and, twisting his arms behind him, cuffed him.

'You okay?' Fabel put an arm gently around Maria's shoulders and eased her back from Olsen.

Maria smiled a broad, warm smile. 'Yes, *Chef*. I'm fine. I really am fine.'

Fabel gave her shoulder a squeeze. 'Good work, Maria. Really good work.' When Henk Herman rolled Olsen back over so he faced up, Fabel saw the gash on his face.

'He fell, *Chef*,' Maria said, trying to sweep away her smile. By this time, Werner and the rest of the MEK team had arrived. Werner looked down at Olsen's battered face, touching the dressing on his own head. He turned to Maria and grinned.

'Fucking excellent!'

CHAPTER 49

6.00 p.m., Tuesday, 20 April:
Polizeipräsidium, Hamburg

Some things were predictable in police work. Olsen refusing to talk until he had access to a lawyer was one of them. He had been taken to the hospital for treatment to the wound on his face. Fabel had asked him if he had any complaint to make about the injuries he had sustained during the course of his arrest.

Olsen had laughed bitterly. 'Like the lady said, I fell.'

What was not expected was that Olsen's lawyer would emerge from a twenty-minute meeting with his client to declare that Olsen wanted to cooperate totally with the police and that he had extremely important information to give them.

Before going in to conduct the interview, Fabel gathered his senior team together. Anna Wolff, spike-haired and red-lipped, was dressed in her usual leather jacket and jeans, but her injured leg was still causing her obvious discomfort. Werner was sitting at his desk, the bruising still blooming from under the white dressing on his head. Maria leaned against her desk, in her usual pose of elegant composure, but her grey trouser suit was scuffed and torn and her right wrist and hand were bound in the strapping they had applied at the hospital.

'What's up, *Chef*?' asked Anna.

Fabel grinned. 'I need one of you to do the Olsen interview with me . . . I was just trying to make up my mind as to which of you is least likely to fall off their chair and break something.'

'I'll do it,' said Maria.

'Under the circumstances, Maria, I think that Olsen may be more forthcoming with someone he hasn't had such a *physical* relationship with.'

'That excludes me, then,' said Werner, bitterly.

'Anna?' Fabel nodded in Kommissarin Wolff's direction.

'My pleasure . . .'

Olsen sat sullenly across the table from Anna and Fabel. His lawyer was a state-appointed Anwalt: a small, mouse-like man who, for some odd reason, had chosen to wear an insipid grey suit that emphasised the colourlessness of his complexion. He was small and, next to Olsen's bulk, looked as if he belonged to another species. Olsen's face was badly bruised and swollen. The flesh seemed puffed up around where the gash on his cheek had been stitched and dressed. The mouse-man spoke first.

'Herr Kriminalhauptkommissar, I've had a

chance to talk to Herr Olsen at length and in depth on the matter about which you wish to question him. Let me get straight to the point. My client is innocent of the murder of Laura von Klosterstadt – or, for that matter, the killing of anyone else. He admits to taking flight when he should have been providing the police with information central to their investigation, but, as will become clear, he had good reason to fear that his account would not be treated credibly. Furthermore, he admits to assaulting Kriminaloberkommissar Meyer and Kriminaloberkommissarin Klee during the commission of their duties, but we would ask that some leniency is shown here, considering that Herr Olsen does not wish to pursue any complaint regarding the, shall we say, *enthusiasm* of his arrest by Frau Klee.'

'That's it?' Anna snorted. 'Three police officers have been injured trying to nail the Incredible Hulk here, we have absolute forensic proof that places him at the double-murder scene, as well as first-hand experience of his psychotic temper, – and you seriously expect us to negotiate with you because he got a scrape while violently resisting arrest?'

Olsen's lawyer did not reply but looked pleadingly at Fabel.

'Okay,' said Fabel. 'Let's hear what you've got to say, Herr Olsen.'

The Anwalt nodded. Olsen leaned forward, resting his elbows on the interview table. His hands were still handcuffed and he made an open gesture with them. Fabel noticed how huge and powerful his hands were. Like Weiss's. But they also reminded him of someone else whom he couldn't, at that moment, place.

'Right. First of all, I didn't kill nobody.' Olsen turned to Anna Wolff. 'And I can't help my temper. It's a condition. I've got a kinda genetic disorder. It makes me lose it sometimes. Big time.'

'XYY syndrome?' asked Fabel.

'It's always got me into a lot of trouble. Someone gets me angry and I go fuckin' ape. Nothing I can do about it.'

'Is that what happened with Hanna Grünn?' asked Anna. 'Did you lose it "big time" with her and Markus Schiller?' Before Olsen could answer, Anna slipped some photographs from a SpuSi forensics envelope. She placed a series of four of them on the table before Olsen, as if she were dealing cards. They showed the bodies of Hanna Grünn and Markus Schiller. Together and apart. Fabel watched Olsen's face as Anna laid out the images. He winced and Fabel noticed the huge handcuffed hands begin to shake.

'Oh, fuck.' Olsen's voice seemed to tremble. 'Oh, fuck. I'm sorry. Oh God, I'm sorry.' His eyes glossed with tears.

'Is there something you want to tell us, Peter?' Fabel's voice was calm, almost soothing. 'Why did you do it?'

Olsen shook his head violently. A tear escaped

from the corner of his eye and made a run for the dressing on his cheek. To see Olsen weep was a disturbing sight. It looked so incongruous with his massive bulk and heavy features. 'I didn't do it. I didn't do this.'

Anna laid out another two images. They were forensic comparisons of a boot print and a tyre mark. 'Your boots. Your bike. You were there. You did it all right. You couldn't forgive Hanna, could you? She wanted to trade up, so she dumped the oversized grease-monkey for an oversized wallet. You couldn't stand that, could you?'

'I got so jealous. I loved her, but she was just using me.'

Anna leaned forward eagerly. 'You must have stalked them for weeks. Watching them screw in that fancy car of his. You hiding in the shadows, in the trees. Watching and planning and fantasising about how you would give them both what was coming. Am I right?'

Olsen's huge shoulders slumped. He nodded his head, wordlessly. Anna didn't allow a heartbeat to pass.

'Then you did it. Then you really did give them what was coming. I understand that. I really do, Peter. But why the others? Why the girl on the beach? The model? Why the salesman?'

Olsen dried his eyes with the heels of his hands. Something harder, more determined swept across his face. 'I don't know what you're talking about. I didn't kill nobody. Everything you said about

383

Hanna and that prick Schiller is true. I wanted to scare them. Beat the crap out of them. But that was all.'

'But you got carried away, right?' said Anna. 'You've admitted you can't control your temper. It's not your fault. You meant to give them a scare but you ended up killing them. Isn't that about the size of it?'

No, thought Fabel. That isn't it. The killings didn't show rage or loss of control, they showed premeditation. He glanced across at Anna and she picked up the signal, reluctantly sitting back in her chair.

'If you didn't kill them, or even get a chance to beat them up,' said Fabel, 'then what exactly is it that you're sorry for?'

Olsen seemed fixed on the image of Hanna Grünn, her throat slashed open. When he tore his gaze away and looked at Fabel, his eyes were pained and pleading. 'I saw it. I saw it. I saw him and I didn't stop him.'

Something tingled the skin on the nape of Fabel's neck. 'What did you see, Peter? Who are you talking about?'

'I didn't kill them. I didn't. I don't expect you to believe me. That's why I went on the run. I don't even know what you're talking about with these other murders. But yes, I was there when Hanna and Schiller got killed. I saw the whole thing. I saw it and I did nothing.'

'Why, Peter? Did you want them to die?'

'No. Christ, no.' He locked eyes with Fabel. 'I was scared. I was terrified. I couldn't move. I knew if he knew I was there he'd come for me too.'

Fabel looked at Olsen. At the huge hands. At the bulk of his shoulders. It was difficult to imagine anything or anyone scaring him. But Fabel could tell that he had been frightened. Frightened for his life. And he was reliving that fear, right here, in front of them. 'Who was it, Peter? Who killed them?'

'I don't know. A big man. As big as me, maybe bigger.' He looked again at Anna Wolff. 'You were right. Everything you said was true. I watched them. I was waiting to scare the shit out of them and give Schiller a real hiding. But I wasn't going to kill no one. I don't know, maybe if I lost it I could've killed Schiller. But never Hanna. No matter what she'd done to me. Anyway, I had something better planned. I was going to tell Schiller's wife. She would have fixed him good and proper and Hanna would have seen just how serious he'd been about leaving his wife for her. I wanted Hanna to feel used. I wanted her to feel the way she made me feel.'

'Okay, Peter, tell us what happened?'

'I hid in the woods and waited for them. She turned up first and then he arrived. But before I could do anything I saw something come out of the woods. I didn't think it was a man to start with. He was really fuckin' big. All dressed in black with some kind of mask on. It was like a kid's party mask.

385

Some sort of animal . . . a bear, or a fox. Maybe a wolf. It looked really small on him. Too small. And all stretched out of shape and that made it even scarier. Even the way he moved was scary. He just seemed to take shape out of the shadows. He simply walked up to the car – they were both in Schiller's car by then – and knocked on the window. Schiller opened it. I couldn't hear too good, but it sounded like Schiller got angry and started shouting. Obviously didn't like being interrupted. Then it was like he saw the big guy, with the mask on and everything. I couldn't make out what Schiller was saying, but he sounded scared. The big man in black just stood and listened. He didn't say nothin'. Then it happened. I couldn't believe what I was seeing. The big man's arm shot up above him and I saw the moonlight flash on something. Like a big blade. Then he brought it down through the open car window. I heard Hanna screaming but I couldn't do nothin'. I was afraid. Scared shitless. I can take just about anyone, but I knew if he knew I was there this big guy would have done me too.' He broke off. Tears glazed the eyes again. 'He was so calm. Slow, even. What's the word? Methodical. He was methodical. Like he'd got all the time in the world. He just walked around the car, calm as you like, opened the door and dragged Hanna out. She was screaming. Poor Hanna. I didn't do nothing. I was rooted to the spot. You've got to understand, Herr Fabel, I knew I'd die. I didn't want to die.'

Fabel nodded, as if he understood. Olsen was

afraid of no man, but there was something more than human, or less than human, about the figure he described.

'He had her by the throat.' Olsen's lower lip trembled as he spoke. 'With one hand. She was crying and begging and begging him not to hurt her. Not to kill her. He just laughed at her. It was a horrible laugh. Cold and empty. Then he said, "I'm going to kill you now" – just like that – "I'm going to kill you now", quietly, not like he was angry or like he hated her or nothing. He pushed her down on to the bonnet of the car, almost gently. Then he drew the blade across her throat. Real slow. Deliberate. Careful. After that he stood for a while, just looking at the bodies, again as if he was in no hurry, like he wasn't afraid of someone coming along. He just stood and looked at them. Then he'd move a little to one side and look at them some more. After that, he dragged Schiller's body away into the woods.'

'Didn't you go over to check if Hanna was alive?' asked Anna.

Olsen shook his head. 'Too afraid. Anyway, I knew she was dead. I waited until the big man in black had gone into the woods with Schiller's body. Then I crept back to where I'd hidden my motorbike. I pushed it down the track for a hundred metres or so. I didn't want him to hear me start the engine. Then I sped off as fast as I could. I didn't know what to do. I knew that none of you would believe my story, so I decided just to carry on like nothing had happened. Christ knows how, but I thought that was the best way of staying out of it. But on the way back I stopped at an Autobahn service station and made the call to the police. I thought there might be a chance you could catch him still there – he didn't seem to be in any hurry. I thought that if you did catch him there, that would put me in the clear.'

Anna placed a tape in the cassette player and pressed the play button. It was the recording from the call received by the Polizeieinsatzzentrale. The voice on the end of the line was stretched tight by shock, but it was clearly Olsen's. It told the police where to find the bodies.

'You confirm that's your voice?' she asked.

Olsen nodded. He looked pleadingly at Fabel. 'I didn't do it. I swear I didn't do it. What I've told you is the truth. But I don't expect for a minute that you believe me.'

'Maybe I do,' said Fabel. 'But you've got a lot more questions to answer, and we've still got charges against you.' He looked across to Olsen's mouse-like lawyer, who nodded. 'Kriminalkommissarin Wolff will ask you about the other killings, where you were, what you know of the victims.' Fabel stood up and leaned on the interview table. 'You're still in a great deal of trouble, Herr Olsen. You're still the only person we can identify at the scene, and you have a motive. I suggest that you answer all Frau Wolff's questions fully and truthfully.'

★   ★   ★

As Fabel was leaving, Anna said, 'Excuse me a moment . . .' to Olsen's lawyer and followed Fabel out into the corridor.

'You believe him?' she asked Fabel when they were alone in the corridor.

'Yes. Yes, I do. There was always something about Olsen that didn't gel. These killings weren't crimes of passion. Someone is meticulously planning and living out these horrific psychotic fantasies.'

'You really believe that Olsen would be scared of another man? He took Werner on, and Werner's no lightweight.'

'True. But, there again, I think Olsen has more to fear from Maria than Werner.' There was a hint of disapproval in Fabel's smile. 'I hope she's not been taking lessons from you, Anna.'

Anna regarded Fabel with a blank expression, as if she hadn't understood. It gave her, beneath the short, spiky black hair and the make-up, a schoolgirl innocence. Fabel had already cautioned her twice about her aggressive conduct. 'Anyway,' she continued, 'I'm not so sure that Olsen's big-spooky-man story is enough to put him in the clear. We only have his word for it.'

'I tend to believe him. He was afraid out there in the Naturpark – afraid for his life. Our killer is obsessed with *Grimms' Fairy Tales* . . . well, that's what Olsen was afraid of – not a man, not just another big-built bruiser with whom Olsen could slog it out. Olsen was alone, in the dark, in the woods, and he saw something come out of the darkness of the woods that didn't look entirely human. That's what he was scared of – the bogeyman, the ogre, the werewolf. I couldn't work out why Olsen was too scared to act, but the truth is that, out there, he wasn't the hulking thug we've got sitting in the interview room: he was a little boy having a bad dream after hearing a scary story. That's what our killer wants. That's why he succeeds: he turns his victims into frightened children.' Fabel paused. He nodded his head in the direction of the closed interview door. 'Anyway, we'll find out soon enough if he's telling the truth, Anna. In the meantime, just see what more you can get out of him.'

Anna went back into the interview room and Fabel headed towards the Mordkommission office. There was something nagging at the back of his mind. It lay in some half-lit corner, just beyond his reach.

He sat in his office. He stayed still and quiet, looking out of the window towards Winterhuder Park. Hamburg stretched herself low and wide across the horizon. Fabel tried to empty his mind of all the clutter of detail, of the thousands of words heard and read about this case, of inquiry boards and Tatort – scene-of-crime – photographs. He watched the blue-white silk sky slide over the city. Somewhere, he knew, there was a central truth waiting to be uncovered. Something simple. Something pure and crystalline and defined in sharp clear, edges.

Fairy tales. It was all about fairy tales and two brothers who had collected them. Two brothers gathering philological research material and seeking 'the true and original voice of the German-speaking peoples'. They had been driven by a love for the German language and a fervent desire to keep the oral tradition alive. But more than that, they were patriots, nationalists. They set out on their researches at a time when Germany was an idea, not a nation; when the Napoleonic overlords sought to extirpate local or regional cultures.

But the Grimms had changed direction. When the first set of tales had been published, it hadn't been German academia that had responded with over-whelming enthusiasm and bought the collection in vast quantities: it had been the ordinary folk. It had been the very people whose voice the brothers had sought to record. And, most of all, it had been children. Jacob, the seeker after philological truth, had acquiesced to Wilhelm's wishes and they had sanitised the tales for the second edition, often embellishing them until they doubled in length. Gone was Hans Dumm, who could impregnate women simply by looking at them. No longer did the pregnant but naive Rapunzel ask why her clothes no longer fitted her. No longer was Dornröschen or Sleeping Beauty raped as she lay, unwakeable, in her bewitched slumber. And sweet Snow White, made queen at the end of the original story, would no longer order that her evil stepmother be forced into shoes of red-hot iron and made to dance to death.

The truth. The Brothers Grimm had sought the true voice of the German people and had created their own quasi-fictions. And was it an authentic German voice anyway? As Weiss had pointed out, French, Italian, Scandinavian, Slavic and other tales all echoed in the stories and fables that the Grimms had collected. Was that what the killer was seeking? The truth? To make the fiction true, like Weiss's fictitious Jacob Grimm?

Fabel stood up, went over to the window and watched the clouds. He couldn't get to it. The killer wasn't just trying to talk to Fabel, he was screaming into his face. And Fabel couldn't hear him.

There was a knock and Werner came in, carrying a folder. Fabel noticed that he was wearing a pair of forensic latex gloves. Fabel looked at the file questioningly.

'As well as the stuff you got from Weiss, I've been wading through sackfuls of fan mail from his publishers. The stuff they sent goes back nearly a year and I've worked my way back to about six months ago. I've been coming across more than a few nutcases who I'd like to have a chat with,' Werner said. He opened up the folder and carefully caught the edge of a single sheet between his gloved forefinger and thumb. 'Then I found this . . .' He pulled the single-sheet letter from the file, still holding it by one corner.

Fabel stared at it. Hard. The letter Werner held up

392

was written, in a tiny hand and in red ink, on a sheet of yellow paper.

Holger Brauner had confirmed that the paper was exactly the same as the small strips, all cut from a single page, that had been found in the hands of each victim. Brauner had also stated that his initial hunch had been right and that the paper was from a generic mass-market brand that was sold in supermarkets, office supply and computer stores throughout the country. It was impossible to get any kind of trace on where and when it had been bought. The handwriting too was a match, and chemical analysis of the red ink was expected to hold no surprises. What had most excited Fabel about Werner's find was that it was a letter. Fan mail. It wasn't a leave-behind at a murder scene. And that might mean that the killer would not have taken so much care to avoid leaving forensic traces on it. But Fabel was to be disappointed: Brauner had confirmed that there were no DNA traces or fingerprints on the letter or anything else with which they could trace its writer.

When he had written to Weiss, he had known he was going to kill. And he had also known that the police would eventually find this letter.

Brauner had sent over four copies of a photograph of the letter, blown up to two and a half times the size of the original. One of these was now pinned to the incident board.

Lieber Herr Weiss,

I just wanted to contact you to say how delighted I am with your most recent book, Die Märchenstrasse. I looked forward, with very great eagerness, to reading it; and I was not to be disappointed. I feel that this is one of the greatest, most profound pieces of modern German literature.

As I read your book, it became so clear to me that you speak with the authentic voice of Jacob Grimm, just as Jacob sought to speak with the authentic voice of Germany: our stories, our lives and our fears; our good and our evil. Did you know that W. H. Auden, the British poet, wrote, at a time when his country was locked in mortal combat with ours, that the Grimm Fairy Tales, alongside the Bible, represent the foundations of Western culture? Such is their power, Herr Weiss. Such is the power of that true, clear voice of our people. I have heard that voice, so many, many times. I know that you understand this; I know you hear the voice as well.

You have spoken much about how people can become parts of stories; do you believe that stories can become people? Or that we are all a story?

I am, in my own way, a creator of tales. No, I arrogate my role: I am more a recorder of tales. I lay them out for others to read and understand their truth. We are brothers, you and I. We are Jacob and Wilhelm. But where you, like Wilhelm, edit, embellish and elaborate on the simplicity of these tales to appeal to your audience, I, like Jacob, seek to present their raw, bright verity. Imagine Jacob, concealed outside the woodland home of Dorothea Viehmann, listening to the tales she would tell only to children. Imagine the wonder of it: centuries-old, magical tales passed down through the generations. I have experienced something similar. That is what I will lay out before my public; and they will be in awe.

With the love of one brother to another,
Dein Märchenbruder

Fabel reread the letter. It said nothing. It wouldn't even have aroused Weiss's suspicion or that of his publishers. It sounded like some loopy fan talking about their own writing, not like a killer laying out his plans to re-enact Grimm fairy tales with real corpses.

'Who's Dorothea Viehmann?' Werner stood beside Fabel, looking up at the enlarged image of the letter.

'She was an old woman whom the Grimms found – or, more correctly, whom Jacob found,' answered Fabel. 'She lived outside Kassel. She was a famed storyteller but refused to relate any of them to Jacob Grimm, so he sat outside a window and eavesdropped as she told the stories to the children of the village.'

Werner made an impressed face. Fabel turned to him and smiled.

'I've been improving my mind.'

The rest of the team had, by now, assembled and there was a buzz of chatter as they gathered around the new piece of evidence. Fabel called for their attention.

'This tells us nothing we don't already know. The only additional information we will be able to get from this is whatever further psychological insight Frau Doktor Eckhardt can gain from its content.' Susanne would not be back from Norddeich until the next day, but Fabel had already arranged to send a copy over to her at the Institut für Rechtsmedizin, and he planned to call her later at his mother's to read the contents to her and get an initial reaction.

Henk Hermann put his hand half up, as if in a classroom. Fabel smiled and nodded and Hermann self-consciously withdrew it. 'He's signed himself "Märchenbruder",' Hermann asked. 'What does that mean: Fairy Tale Brother?'

'He obviously feels strongly connected to Weiss. But there may be some other significance. And I know the ideal person to call to find out.'

'The ideal person,' said Werner, 'would be the killer himself.'

'And that,' said Fabel grimly, 'might just be exactly who I am going to ask.'

★   ★   ★

Weiss answered the phone after two rings. Fabel assumed that he must have been in his study, working. Fabel explained how they'd discovered a letter sent to Weiss through his publishers, and that it had clearly come from the killer. Weiss had no recollection of having seen the letter and listened in silence as Fabel read its contents to him.

'And you're convinced he's talking about these killings?' Weiss asked when Fabel was finished.

'I am. It's the same person, all right. Is there anything in what he says that may be significant? The mention of Dorothea Viehmann, for example?'

'Dorothea Viehmann!' Weiss's tone was cynical. 'The font of German folkloric wisdom at whose feet Jacob Grimm worshipped. And so would your misguided psycho, obviously.'

'And he shouldn't?'

'What is it about we Germans? We're constantly searching for an identity, to find out who we are, and we invariably end up with the wrong bloody answer. The Grimms venerated Viehmann and took her versions of German fairy tales as gospel – almost literally. But Viehmann was her married name. Her maiden name was Pierson. French – Dorothea Viehmann's parents were expelled from France for being Protestants, Huguenots. The stories she told were, she claimed, German stories she'd heard from travellers on the road to and from Kassel. The truth is that many of the stories she passed on to the

Grimms were French in origin from her own familial background. The same stories that Charles Perrault recorded in France a century or more before. And she wasn't the only one. There was the mysterious "Marie" who was credited with passing on Snow White, Little Red Riding Hood and Sleeping Beauty. Wilhelm's son claimed that it was an old family servant woman. It turned out to be a wealthy young society lady called Marie Hassenpflug, also from a French family, who had been told the stories by her French nannies.' Weiss laughed. 'So the question is, Herr Fabel: is Sleeping Beauty Dornröschen or is she *la belle au bois dormant*? And is Red Riding Hood Rotkäppchen or is she *le petit chaperon rouge*? Like I say, we continually seek the truth about our identity and, without fail, we totally screw it up. And we usually end up relying on foreign observers to define who we are.'

'I don't think this psycho is going to split patriotic hairs over this.' Fabel didn't have time for another sermon from Weiss. 'I just want to know if you think there is any significance in him mentioning Viehmann's name.'

There was a short silence at the other end of the phone. Fabel imagined the massive author in his study, with its rich, dark wood absorbing the light. 'No. I don't think there is. His victims have been of both sexes, right?'

'Yes. He seems to be an equal-opportunity killer.'

'The only significance I can see in him mentioning

Dorothea Viehmann is that the Grimms really did see her as an almost unique source of ancient wisdom. And they seemed to think that women were the flame-keepers of the Germanic oral tradition. If your killer was focusing on women, especially old women, then maybe I might have seen some connection.' Again there was a short silence at the other end of the phone. 'There is one thing about the letter that does bother me. Really bothers me. It's the way he signed himself off.'

'What – "dein Märchenbruder"?'

'Yes . . .' Fabel sensed an unease in Weiss's voice. '"Your Fairy Tale Brother." As you probably know, Jacob died four years before Wilhelm. Wilhelm gave an impassioned eulogy at Jacob's funeral. He called him his Märchenbruder . . . his Fairy Tale Brother. Shit, Fabel, this maniac thinks he and I are in this together.'

Fabel drew a deep breath. There had been a partnership behind the killings all along. And Weiss had been the other partner. The only thing was Weiss hadn't known about it.

'Yes, Herr Weiss. I rather think he does.' Fabel paused. 'You know how you have your theory of making fiction real? About allowing people to "live" in your stories?'

'Yes – what about it?'

'Well, it looks as though he's written you into his.'

CHAPTER 50

9.45 a.m., Wednesday, 21 April:
Institut für Rechtsmedizin,
Eppendorf, Hamburg

F abel hated the mortuary.
He hated being present at autopsies. It was not so much the natural physical revulsion to gore, although that played its part by churning nauseatingly somewhere between his stomach and his chest; it was more the inexplicability of how a human being, the centre of its own vast and complex universe, suddenly became just so much meat. It was the very inanimateness of the dead – the sudden, total and irrevocable destruction of personality – that he hated to face. In every murder case, Fabel sought to keep something of the victim alive in his mind, as if he or she were still living but in some other, distant room. To him they were wronged people for whom he sought some kind of justice, as if it were a debt to the living. Even visiting the scene of death, or reviewing photographs of the fatal injuries didn't seem to detract from that sense of a person. But,

for Fabel, watching someone's stomach contents being soup-ladled into a weighing dish turned a person into a corpse.

Möller was on form. As Fabel entered the post-mortem exam room, Möller regarded him with his practised disdainful expression. He was still in his blue autopsy coveralls and the disposable pale grey plastic apron had traces of smeared blood on it. The stainless-steel autopsy table was empty and Möller was almost absent-mindedly hosing it down with its attached spray head. Something hung in the air, however. Fabel had discovered long ago that the dead haunt not with their spirits, but with their odours. Möller had clearly only just concluded his journey through the mass and matter of what had once been a human being called Bernd Ungerer.

'Interesting,' Möller said, idly watching the water swirl pink as it washed away the traces of blood towards the drain. 'Very interesting, this one.'

'How so?' asked Fabel.

'The eyes were removed post-mortem. The cause of death was from a single knife blow to the chest. Classic, really – under the sternum at an upward angle and straight into the heart. Your gentleman gave the knife a twist, clockwise, almost forty-five degrees. That, effectively, devastated the heart and the victim would have been dead within seconds. At least he didn't suffer much and wouldn't have known anything about the eyes being removed. Which was done manually, by the way. No evidence of an instrument having been used.' Möller switched off the spray and leaned on the edge of the table. 'There were no defensive wounds. None whatsoever. No nicks or cuts on the hands or forearms and there is no other evidence of trauma. Or of a pre-mortem struggle or fight.'

'Meaning that our victim was taken totally by surprise or that he knew the murderer, or both.'

Möller straightened up again. 'That's your area, Herr Hauptkommissar. I report the facts, you draw the conclusions. But there are quite a few other things about this gentleman that you may find interesting.'

'Oh?' Fabel smiled patiently, resisting the temptation to tell Möller to get on with it.

'For a start, Herr Ungerer was prematurely grey and dyed his hair dark – unlike our own dear Chancellor, of course. But it was what I found under the scalp that interested me more. Your killer didn't exactly cut Herr Ungerer's life short. He merely beat the grim reaper to it by a few months.'

'Ungerer was ill?'

'Terminally. But he may well have been unaware of it. There was a large glioma in his cerebrum. A brain tumour. Its size would suggest that it had been growing for some time and its location would lead me to think that the symptoms could have been misleading.'

'Can you tell if he was he being treated for it?'

'No, not that I can see. There was no evidence of anti-cancer treatment in the system – nor of cortisone, which is normally prescribed in such cases to relieve the swelling of brain tissue. Most importantly, there was no evidence of surgery, and that is the first line of defence against this type of tumour. I need to get a full hystology on the glioma, but it looks to me like an astrocytoma – a primary tumour. And because it was a primary tumour, there would have been nothing elsewhere in the body to flag up to his doctor that there might be a problem. Brain tumours are more often secondary to cancers elsewhere in the body, but not this baby. And, here's a scary thought for you, he was the right age for it. Middle-aged men are the most likely to get these high-grade aggressive primary tumours.'

'But surely he must have had symptoms . . . headaches?'

'Probably, but not necessarily. Brain tumours have nowhere to go. It's the one part of the body totally encased by bone, so as the tumour grows so does the pressure inside the skull and on the healthy brain tissue. It can cause severe headaches that get worse when one lies down, but not always. But, as I told you, the position of Herr Ungerer's tumour, despite it being reasonably fast-growing, was such that the damage was being done gradually. And that means the symptoms may have been more subtle.'

'Such as?'

'Personality changes. Behavioural changes. He might have lost his sense of smell – or suddenly have smelled pungent odours that were not there. He might have had pins and needles down one side of his body, or frequently felt nauseated. Or, conversely, another common symptom can be sudden vomiting without any warning nausea beforehand.'

For a moment Fabel thought over what Möller had told him. He remembered what Maria had said about her conversation with Frau Ungerer, how she had described Ungerer's change of personality. About how his sexual appetite had become insatiable; how a faithful, loving husband had become a lascivious lecher and serial adulterer. How he had become 'Bluebeard'. When Fabel had heard that, along with Maria's description of the 'forbidden' basement and the chest within, he had felt ice crystals form in his veins. Another fairy tale link, except 'Bluebeard' was a Perrault story, French, but it did have a German, Grimm equivalent in 'Fitcher's Bird'. This killer knew Ungerer. Or, at least, he knew enough about him to recognise him as a perfect choice to fit with his insane Grimm-story-driven theme.

'Could it have manifested itself in the victim's sexual behaviour?' He outlined to Möller what they knew about Ungerer's dramatic change.

'It could have,' said Möller. 'If there was a change as dramatic as that which you've described, then I would say it isn't coincidental with the tumour but almost certainly consequential. We think that sex is a physical thing. It's not. In the human animal it's all up here.' Möller tapped his temple with his forefinger. 'Change the brain's structure or chemistry – and the victim's tumour would have most likely changed both – and all kinds of personality and behavioural changes take place. So yes, it is entirely possible that it turned your sexually moral, married, family-orientated man into a lecherous wolf.'

As he drove back to the Präsidium, the April sun shone cheerfully upon Hamburg. The city looked bright and fresh and eager for the summer to come. But Fabel saw none of this. All he was aware of was the dark, menacing presence of a psychotic who killed and mutilated in a search for some kind of twisted literary or cultural verity. He was close. So close, Fabel could almost smell him.

CHAPTER 51

9.30 p.m., Thursday, 22 April:
Altona, Hamburg

Lina Ritter decided, as she struggled into the costume, that she was getting too old for this. She *was* too old for this. It had been her career for nearly fifteen years now and, at thirty-four, enough was enough. After all, this was a game for younger women. She was being forced more and more to 'specialise': to cater for the more bizarre and exotic tastes of specific clients, and the role of a dominatrix had suited her age better. And anyway, there was no fucking involved most of the time: you got to order some fat businessman about for half an hour, whack him on the arse if he was too slow following your instructions and then tell him how bad he was and how angry you were as he jerked himself off. It paid reasonably well, the health risks were fewer and her clients, as their punishments, often did all her housework for her. Tonight would be harder work, however. The guy who had booked her had given her a wad of cash in advance. Then he had made his appointment for tonight, with precise instructions that she must wear the outfit he brought for her. She knew, from this ridiculous bloody costume, that she wasn't going to be the dominant partner this time and had resigned herself to having to fuck the big guy.

He had arrived bang on time, and now he waited for her in the bedroom, while she squeezed into the outfit he had brought. It had clearly been meant to fit someone a size or two smaller than Lina. The things a girl had to do to make a living. Lina had forgotten just how big her customer was. Big, but quiet. Almost shy. He wouldn't give her any trouble.

Lina walked into the bedroom and twirled around. 'You like?' She stopped mid-twirl as she saw him. 'Oh . . . I see you've got a special costume too . . .'

He was standing by the bed. He had switched off all but the small bedside lamp behind him and he stood in half-silhouette. Everything in the room seemed dwarfed by his dark bulk. He was wearing a small rubber mask, like a child's mask, in the shape of a wolf's face. The wolf's features were distorted as the tiny mask had been stretched across the too-big face. Then Lina realised that he wasn't wearing some kind of skintight costume, as she had first thought, but that his entire body, from his ankles to his throat and down his arms to his wrists, was covered with tattoos. All words. All in the old pre-war script. He stood massive and silent, with that stupid mask and his tattoo-covered body, the light behind him. Lina realised that she was, now, afraid. Then he spoke.

'I've brought you a present, Gretel,' he said, his voice muffled by the rubber mask.

'Gretel?' Lina looked down at her costume; the one he had asked for. 'This isn't a Gretel outfit. Have I got it wrong?'

The head behind the too-small rubber wolf mask shook slowly. He stretched out his hand, holding a bright blue box tied with a yellow ribbon.

'I've brought you a present, Gretel,' he repeated.

'Oh . . . oh, thank you. I like presents.' Lina performed what she considered a coquettish curtsey and took the box. She did her best to conceal that her fingers trembled as she undid the ribbon. 'Now . . . what have we here?' she said as she lifted the lid from the box and looked in.

By the time Lina's scream hit the air, he had already crossed the room to her.

CHAPTER 52

9.30 p.m., Thursday, 22 April:
Polizeipräsidium, Hamburg

Fabel stood facing the inquiry board, leaning on the table in front of it. He was looking at the board but wasn't seeing what he wanted, what he needed to see there. Werner was the only other person in the office and sat on the corner of the table. His wide shoulders were slumped and his face was pale, exaggerating the vividness of the bruising on his head.

'I think you should call it a day,' said Fabel. 'First day back and all that.'

'I'm okay,' said Werner, but without much conviction.

'I'll see you tomorrow.' Fabel watched Werner leave and then turned back to the inquiry board. The killer had referred to Jacob Grimm gaining folkloric wisdom from Dorothea Viehmann. That he had had a similar experience. With whom? Who had passed on the tales to him?

Fabel scanned the images of Weiss, Olsen and Fendrich he had placed on the board. Old women.

Mothers. Weiss had an influential Italian mother. He didn't know anything about Olsen's parentage, but Fendrich clearly had had a close relationship with his mother until she had died. And she had died shortly before the killings took place. Weiss and Olsen now seemed to be out of range of Fabel's suspicion, so all that left was Fendrich. But as soon as you took a closer look at him, it didn't make any sense. Fabel looked at the three men. Three men as different from each other as it was possible to be. And it looked like none was the right man. Fabel became aware that Anna Wolff was now by his side.

'Hi, Anna. You finished with Olsen?' he asked. Anna shook her head impatiently. She held up the photograph of the latest victim, the eyeless Bernd Ungerer.

'There's a link,' Anna's voice was tensed with controlled excitement. 'Olsen recognised Ungerer. He knows him.'

Olsen was still sitting at the table in the interview room but his demeanour, his whole body language had changed. It was eager, almost aggressive. His lawyer, however, looked much less chipper. After all, they had been cooped up with tenacious little Anna Wolff for nearly four hours.

'You realise, Herr Kriminalhauptkommissar, that in trying to help you with your inquiry my client is risking incriminating himself further.'

Fabel nodded impatiently. 'Let's just hear what

Herr Olsen has to say about his relationship with Herr Ungerer.'

'I didn't have no relationship with Ungerer,' said Olsen. 'I only saw him a couple of times. He was a salesman. A smarmy prick.'

'Where did you see him?' asked Anna.

'The Backstube Albertus. He sold this really fancy Italian bakery equipment. State-of-the-art shit. He had been hanging around Markus Schiller for months, trying to persuade him to buy new ovens. He and Schiller got on really well – two smarmy bastards together. Ungerer was always taking Schiller out for expenses-paid lunches and that sort of thing. He was barking up the wrong tree, though. It was Schiller's wife that had all the say, all the cash and, from what I can gather, all the balls.'

'Exactly where and when did you say you saw him?'

'I just saw him a couple of times when I was picking Hanna up from the bakery.'

'You seem to have picked up a great deal of information about him, considering you only saw him in passing.'

'Hanna told me all about him. He was always making eyes at her. Every time he came into the place. He was married and everything but he had a reputation for chasing skirt. A sleazeball, was how Hanna described him.'

'You never spoke to him directly?'

'No. I would have . . . had a quiet word, if you

411

know what I mean. But Hanna told me to leave it be. She'd already complained to her boss about Ungerer, anyway.'

'But Hanna had nothing to do with him, in or outside work?'

'No. She said he gave her the creeps, the way his eyes were never off her. Mind you, I can't for the life of me see the difference between Ungerer and Markus Schiller. Both slimy creeps. But Hanna saw something, I guess.'

Fabel, who had let Anna do all the talking so far, leaned forward in his chair. 'Peter, you are the link between three out of five murder victims . . .' He sifted through the photographs on the table and placed the images of Paula Ehlers, Martha Schmidt and Laura von Klosterstadt in front of him. 'Do any of these people mean anything to you?' He put names and locations to the faces.

'The model. I know her. I mean, I know *about* her, her being famous and everything. But no. I don't know any of them other than that.'

Fabel watched Olsen as he spoke. He was either telling the truth or he was a clever liar. And Olsen wasn't that skilled. Fabel thanked Olsen and his lawyer and had Olsen returned to the holding cells.

Fabel remained in the interview room with Anna. They had a link. At last there was a line they could follow. The frustration lay in not being able to find a further link: that next connection which would take them closer to their quarry.

Fabel phoned his mother. After talking to her for a minute he asked to speak to Susanne. He explained that he had sent a copy of the letter over to the Institut für Rechtsmedizin, but he took her through it on the phone, stressing the Dorothea Viehmann mention and the Märchenbruder signature, explaining what Weiss had told him about both.

'There is a possibility, I suppose,' said Susanne. 'It could be that a mother or some other older woman is or was a dominant part of the killer's background. But, equally, the Märchenbruder reference could suggest that a brother has played a big part of his life and he's now transferring this on to Weiss. I'll have a proper look at the letter when I get back on Wednesday, but I don't think I'll get much more out of it.' She paused. 'Are you okay? You sound tired.'

'It's just the drive and too little sleep catching up on me,' he said. 'Are you having a good time?'

'Your mother's great. And Gabi and I are really getting to know each other. But I miss you.'

Fabel smiled. It was nice to be missed. 'I miss you too, Susanne. I'll see you on Wednesday,' he said.

After Fabel hung up he turned back to Anna, who was grinning in a way that said 'Aw . . . sweet.' Fabel ignored her smile.

'Anna . . .' His tone was contemplative, as if the question was only half-formed as he began to speak. 'You know how Fendrich's mother is dead?'

'Yep.'

'How do you know?'

'Well . . . because he told me. I didn't check officially – I mean, why would he lie?' Anna paused, as if processing the thought. Then something sharp glinted through the tiredness in her eyes. 'I'll check it out, *Chef.*'

CHAPTER 53

7.30 a.m., Friday, 23 April:
Ohlsdorf, Hamburg

Fabel had been late home from the Präsidium the night before. He had been tired: that irritable, restless overtiredness that takes you beyond the point where you can sleep. He had stayed up late and watched television, something he very rarely did. He had watched Ludger Abeln deliver news reports in fluent Plattdeutsch on the Low German version of *Hallo Niedersachsen*, part of broadcaster Norddeutscher Rundfunk's promotion of the ancient language. Abeln's Emsländer voice had soothed Fabel: it reminded him of his home, of his family, of the voices he had grown up with. He thought back to how he had protested to Susanne that Hamburg was now his Heimat; that this was where he belonged. Yet now, dispirited and tired beyond sleeping, the language and accent of his birthplace wrapped itself around him like a comfort blanket.

After the report was over, Fabel had flicked

aimlessly through the channels. 3-SAT was showing *Nosferatu*, F.W. Murnau's silent expressionist horror classic. Fabel had sat and watched as the flickering black and white of the screen fingered its light across the walls of his apartment and Max Schreck's vampire, Orlok, advanced menacingly towards him. Another fable. Another scary story of Good and Evil that had been elevated to a German masterpiece. Fabel remembered that this, too, was a borrowed tale that Germans had made their own: Murnau had shamelessly plagiarised the story from an Irish author, Bram Stoker. Stoker's tale had been entitled *Dracula*, and Stoker's widow had succeeded in getting an injunction against Murnau. All copies of the film had been destroyed as ordered. All except one print. And a classic had endured. As he watched the sinister Orlok infect an entire North German city with his vampire plague, Fabel recalled the lyrics of the Rammstein song he had read in Olsen's apartment. Grimm, Murnau, Rammstein: different generations, the same fables.

Weiss was right. Everything stayed the same. We still needed fairy tales to frighten us, imagined horrors and real fears. And we always had.

Fabel had gone to bed about two.

He was aware that he had dreamt throughout his fitful night. As Susanne had said, his constant dreaming was a sign of stress, of his mind's frantic struggles to resolve problems and issues in both his personal and professional life. But what Fabel hated most was when he knew he had dreamt but couldn't remember the dream. And the night's dreams had veiled themselves the instant he awoke to answer Anna Wolff's call at five-thirty.

'Good morning, *Chef.* I'd skip breakfast if I were you. The bastard's done another one already.' Anna had spoken with her usual directness that often bordered on the disrespectful. 'By the way, I think I've found Bernd Ungerer's missing eyes. Oh – and I've got a spare pair, just in case . . .'

More than half of Hamburg's Ohlsdorf area is devoted to a park. A park that is the largest green area in Hamburg: more than four hundred hectares dense with trees, lovingly tended gardens and magnificent examples of the sculptor's art. A place where many Hamburg residents and visitors come to soak up its verdant tranquillity. But the Friedhof Ohlsdorf is a park with a very specific function. It is the largest cemetery in the world. The Friedhof Ohlsdorf's beautifully crafted sculptures are there to adorn the mausolea, tombs and headstones of Hamburg's dead. Nearly half a million graves mean that almost every Hamburg family has a member interred in the vast Friedhof.

The brightening sky was reasonably clear of cloud and was already streaked by the red fingers of the approaching morning by the time Fabel arrived at the scene. An Ohlsdorfer SchuPo unit led Fabel along the Cordesallee, the main thoroughfare that cuts through the massive Friedhof and past the Wasserturm to a large area that seemed to have its own integrity, as if it was a graveyard in its own right. It was fringed with broad-leaved trees that had already almost completely filled out with their spring foliage. White marble, bronze and red granite figures stood silent watch over the graves as Fabel made his way across to where the body had been discovered. Anna was already there, as were Holger Brauner and his forensics team who had secured the locus. Everyone exchanged grim, early-morning murder-scene greetings as Fabel approached.

A woman lay on her back as if asleep, her hands folded across her breast. At her head a vast sculpture of a female angel looked down with one hand extended, as if regarding the dead woman and reaching out to her. Fabel looked around. All of the sculptures were female, as were the names on all the headstones.

'This is the Garten der Frauen,' Anna explained. A graveyard exclusively for women. Fabel knew that the killer was trying to tell them something even in his choice of venue. He looked back to the dead woman. Her pose was almost identical to that of Laura von Klosterstadt. The differences were that this woman was darker-haired and did not possess Laura's beauty. And she wasn't naked.

'What kind of outfit is that?' asked Anna.

'It's a traditional Northern German woman's costume. The kind of outfit worn by women in a

Speeldeel,' said Fabel, referring to the numerous Plattdeutsch folkloric dance societies in Hamburg. 'You know, like the Finkwarder Speeldeel.'

Anna looked none the wiser. 'And there are your eyes.' She pointed to the woman's chest, on which four masses of white and red tissue lay scattered. 'We seem to have an embarrassment of riches here. Specifically, we have an extra pair of eyes'

Fabel examined the body, working his way from the dead woman's head to her feet. She wore a bright red traditional bonnet, trimmed in white lace and tied beneath her chin. There was a gaily coloured shawl over her shoulders and her wide-sleeved white blouse was gathered in by a black bodice decorated with gold and red threadwork. The bodice was stained with the viscous globs of the eyeballs. Her red ankle-length skirt was all but concealed beneath an embroidered white apron. She also wore thick white stockings and low-heeled black shoes. A small wicker basket had been laid beside her, in which sat a bloomer of bread.

'It looks like the real deal,' said Fabel. 'These outfits tend to be made by Speeldeel society members, or passed down from mother to daughter. Do we have an identity?'

Anna shook her head.

'Then I think we should circulate a photograph of her, as well as the details of the costume. Someone in a Speeldeel society will recognise her or it.'

'You see the colour of the bonnet?' Anna handed Fabel a transparent evidence bag. In it was another slip of yellow paper. Fabel peered at the tiny writing in the pale morning light: 'Rotkäppchen.'

'Shit – Little Red Riding Hood.' Fabel thrust the bag back at Anna. 'The bastard's going to work his way through the whole collection if we don't get him soon. The space between killings is getting shorter, but his little bloody tableaux aren't getting any less elaborate. He's had this whole thing planned out for some time.'

'The eyes, *Chef*,' said Anna. 'What about the eyes? We have a pair we can't account for. That means there's another victim we don't know about.'

'Unless they're Paula Ehlers's eyes, and he's kept them frozen or something.'

'Nope, I don't think so.' Holger Brauner had joined them. 'Two pairs of eyes. Both human, both removed by force, rather than surgically. As far as I can see, both pairs are in the process of desiccation, but one pair has dried out more than the other. It would suggest that they were taken some time before the second pair. But I see no signs of any attempt to preserve them, by pickling or freezing.'

'So why haven't we found another body?' asked Anna.

Fabel snapped his fingers. 'Clever Hans . . . dammit – that's it: Clever Hans.'

Anna looked confused.

'I've been poring over these bloody fairy tales for days,' said Fabel. 'There are so many of them that he could hit us with any one of a couple of hundred tales to base his killing on, but I remember Clever Hans. I don't know if he's meant to be the same person as in "Hänsel und Gretel" but the girl in the "Clever Hans" story is called Gretel. Anyway, Clever Hans is sent to Gretel by his mother several times, each time with a simple task to perform, basically to give Gretel a present. Each time he screws it up – he fails to give Gretel her present and ends up coming back with something that *she* has given *him*. On the final trip, his mother gives him the simplest of tasks. She says to him "Clever Hans, why don't you cast friendly eyes on Gretel?" In other words, look at her kindly. Be nice to her. But Clever Hans takes his instruction literally: he goes into the field and into the barn and cuts out all the eyes from the cows and the sheep. Then he goes to Gretel and throws them on her.'

'Shit . . .' Anna looked at the body. 'So that's the link you were talking about. Just as he linked Sleeping Beauty to Rapunzel through von Klosterstadt, he's linked Rapunzel to Clever Hans through Bernd Ungerer.'

'Exactly. And now we have Little Red Riding Hood.'

Fabel gazed down at the dead woman's face. It was heavily made-up. An unnatural look that clashed with the traditional costume. He turned to Brauner, the forensics chief. His tone was almost pleading. 'Holger, anything. Please. Give me something that will give me an angle on this guy.' He sighed. 'Anna, I'll head back to the Präsidium. Come to my office as soon as you get back from processing this.'

'Okay, *Chef.*'

Fabel headed back towards the exit on to the Cordesallee. The birds were now singing full tilt. He remembered reading somewhere that the Friedhof Ohlsdorf had a stunning range of otherwise quite rare birds, as well as colonies of bats who used the mausolea as nesting places. In fact, the Friedhof was a protected nature zone. So much life in a place designed to receive the dead. The thought was shattered by Anna's shout behind him.

'*Chef*! *Chef* – come and see this . . .' She beckoned vigorously for Fabel. He half-ran back to the body. They had eased it from where it had lain and into a body shell. The female angel still gazed and pointed downward, but no longer at a murdered women in traditional North German Tracht. Instead the angel's extended finger indicated a white marble slab on which was inscribed a name.

Emelia Fendrich. 1930–2003.

CHAPTER 54

10.15 a.m., Friday, 23 April:
Hamburg Hafen, Hamburg

Maria, Werner, Henk Hermann and the two officers seconded from the Sexual Crimes SoKo turned up about ten minutes after Fabel and Anna arrived at Dirk Stellamanns's Schnell-Imbiss snack stand down by the docks. The sky had dulled and the air felt thick and heavy, as if in a mood that could only be relieved by the explosive temper of a storm. Around the immaculately kept snack cabin and its handful of parasol-sheltered tables, a forest of shipyard cranes loomed into the steel grey sky. Dirk, himself an ex-Hamburg SchuPo, was, like Fabel, a Frisian and the two chatted briefly in their native Frysk before Fabel ordered coffees for his team.

They stood huddled around a couple of the chest-high tables and briefly discussed the unpromising state of the sky and whether they would finish their coffees before the storm broke. Then Fabel got down to business.

'What does this mean? We clock up another victim, killed in the same way. But we find her lying on the grave of the mother of one of our suspects – albeit a lukewarm suspect. I'd like some opinions.'

'Well,' said Anna. 'At least he's saved me from chasing up the records office to check if Fendrich's mother really is dead. The Friedhof authorities confirmed that Emelia Fendrich was, indeed, interred six months ago and the address listed for her is the same as her son's, in Rahlstedt.'

Henk nodded. Rahlstedt was close to the Friedhof, bordering on Ohlsdorf. 'So what do we do?' he asked. 'Do we bring Fendrich in for questioning about this latest killing?'

'On what grounds?' Anna made a face as she sipped the too-hot coffee. 'That his mother really is dead and that he didn't lie to us?'

Henk shrugged off Anna's sarcasm. 'Well, I suppose it could be a coincidence. But you do the arithmetic: two hundred and eighty thousand possible graves on which to dump the body, and it lands on one occupied by the mother of one of three suspects. And we know this guy is talking to us through every element he puts together in these scenes.'

'We at least have to talk to Fendrich,' said Maria. 'We need to check out his whereabouts once we have ascertained the exact time of death.'

'Holger Brauner squeezed an estimate out of our esteemed pathologist, Herr Doktor Möller, when he arrived on the scene,' said Fabel. 'Sometime between eight p.m. and midnight last night. And yes, we need to know where Fendrich was at that time. But we need to be extremely diplomatic about it. I don't want him crying harassment again.'

'I'll deal with it,' said Anna. Everyone stared at her. 'What? I can be diplomatic.'

'Okay,' said Fabel, deliberately ladling uncertainty into his tone. 'But don't wind him up.'

'Why not?' asked Henk. 'Fendrich's got to be top of our list now. I mean, placing the body on his mother's grave . . .'

'Not necessarily,' said Anna. 'Paula Ehlers's disappearance was widely reported. It was no secret that Fendrich was interviewed by police. We've got to remember that our killer more than likely abducted and killed Paula. So he'll have followed developments after he took her. Anyway, I can tell you now, Fendrich won't have an alibi.'

'Why?' asked Fabel.

'Because he doesn't know he needs one. And because he's a loner.'

Fabel sipped his coffee and looked up at the sky. The sheet of steel grey was bruised with darker clouds. He could feel the pressure of the air, as he always could before a storm, manifest itself in a dull pain in his sinuses. 'You really don't think Fendrich did this, do you, Anna?'

'I don't think his relationship with Paula Ehlers was entirely straightforward. But no. He's not our guy.'

425

Fabel massaged his sinuses with thumb and fore-finger. 'I think you're right. I think we're being deliberately diverted. Everything this guy is doing is connected. Each killing links one fairy tale with another. He's dancing with us. But he's taking the lead. There's an order in what he's doing. He's as organised as he is creative, and he's had this all worked out well in advance. I get the feeling we're nearing the end. He started off with Paula Ehlers, where he gave us nothing but used her identity for his second murder, three years later. Then, with Martha Schmidt, the girl in Blankenese, all he gave us was the false identity. It was only after the Laura von Klosterstadt killing that we saw that he had placed Martha Schmidt "beneath" Laura. As he's gone on he's given us more and more. He wants us to guess what he's going to do next, but he needs time to do it. That's why he's trying to point us towards Fendrich.'

'What if you're wrong, *Chef*?' Werner leaned his elbows on the Schnell-Imbiss table. 'What if Fendrich *is* our guy and he wants us to stop him? What if he's telling us that he's the killer?'

'Then Anna will get the truth when she and Hermann question him.'

'I'd rather go alone, *Chef*,' said Anna. Henk Hermann didn't look either surprised or annoyed.

'No, Anna,' said Fabel. 'Fendrich is still a suspect and you're not going into his house alone.'

'Don't worry, Frau Wolff,' said Henk. 'I'll let you do all the talking.'

'In the meantime,' continued Fabel, 'we need to analyse the messages this guy is sending us.' The sky flashed behind the cloud, somewhere to the north. It took several seconds for the hard rumbling wave of thunder to roll over them. 'I think we should get back to the Präsidium.'

The first thing that awaited Fabel on his return to the Präsidium was a summons to the office of Kriminaldirektor Horst van Heiden. It wasn't unexpected. The media was now running head-lines and lead stories about the 'Fairy Tale Killer' and Fabel knew that reporters and photographers were starting to circumvent the Presseabteilung and were harassing van Heiden directly. One TV crew had gone so far as to doorstep the Kriminaldirektor on his way from the Präsidium: something unthinkable even ten years before. The 'Anglo-Saxon Model' seemed to be taking an ever greater hold on Germany, moving it away from its traditions of courtesy and respect. And, as always, the media was at the vanguard of the change. Van Heiden was unhappy and needed someone to blame. As he entered the Kriminaldirektor's office, Fabel braced himself.

As it turned out, van Heiden was more desperate for a morsel of good news than he was angry. He reminded Fabel of himself at the last scene of crime, almost pleading Holger Brauner to turn up some clue. Van Heiden was not alone in his office when Fabel arrived. Innensenator Hugo Ganz was there, as was Leitender Oberstaatsanwalt Heiner Goetz, the state prosecutor for Hamburg. Goetz stood up and smiled warmly as Fabel came in and shook his hand. Fabel had crossed swords with Goetz on many occasions, mainly because Goetz was a tenacious and methodical prosecutor who refused to cut corners. Despite Fabel's occasional frustration with Goetz they had between them secured a great many sound convictions and they had built up a strong mutual respect and something approaching friendship.

Ganz also shook Fabel's hand, but with significantly less warmth. Aha, thought Fabel, the honeymoon is over. He guessed that his visit to Margarethe von Klosterstadt had ruffled aristocratic feathers and Ganz had received a call. He was right.

'Herr Hauptkommissar,' Ganz got in before even van Heiden could speak. 'I believe you took it on yourself to re-interview Frau von Klosterstadt?'

Fabel didn't answer but glanced questioningly at van Heiden, who didn't respond.

'I'm sure you appreciate,' Ganz continued, 'that this is a most distressing time for the von Klosterstadt family.'

'It's also a distressing time for the Schmidt and Ehlers families. I take it you don't have a problem with me re-interviewing them?'

Ganz's scrubbed pink face became pinker. 'Now listen, Herr Fabel, I have already told you that I am a friend of the von Klosterstadt family of some standing—'

Fabel cut him off. 'And I have to tell you that that is of absolutely no interest to me. If you are here in your capacity as Hamburg's Innensenator and you wish to discuss this case objectively and in its entirety, then I'd be delighted to do so. But if you've been sent here because Frau von Klosterstadt's nose is out of joint because I had to ask a few personal questions about her daughter, then I suggest you leave now.'

Ganz stared at Fabel with something approaching fury in his eyes. Impotent fury, because he couldn't deny what Fabel had said. He stood up, turned towards van Heiden and blustered: 'This is outrageous. I will not sit here and be lectured on protocol by one of your junior officers.'

'Herr *Erster* Hauptkommissar Fabel is hardly a junior officer,' was all van Heiden said. Ganz snatched up his briefcase and stormed out of the office.

'For God's sake, Fabel,' said van Heiden, once Ganz was gone. 'You could at least try to make my life a little bit easier. It doesn't do the Polizei Hamburg any favours if you make an enemy of the Innensenator of Hamburg.'

'I'm sorry, Herr Kriminaldirektor, but what I said is true. Ganz has been sent here because I found out that Laura von Klosterstadt had an abortion ten years ago, arranged by her, to be honest, cold-hearted bitch of a mother. She became pregnant by Leo Kranz, the photographer. But before he was famous, so he didn't register on Margarethe von Klosterstadt's social radar.'

'Is that relevant, do you think?' asked Heiner Goetz.

'Not directly. It may, however, suggest that the killer had an intimate knowledge of the von Klosterstadt family. It's just that the whole "Rapunzel" thing involves pregnancy and illegitimacy. And I reserve the right to pursue all and any leads.'

'Understood, Herr Fabel,' said van Heiden, gloomily. 'But you could perhaps try to distinguish between suspects and senior Hamburg politicians when it comes to your approach. Anyway, what do we have on this latest killing? This is fast becoming the number one Hamburg news story.'

Fabel ran through what they had to date, including the killer's choice of grave and why Fabel thought it was a deliberate smokescreen.

'I think you're right not to pursue Fendrich too aggressively,' said Heiner Goetz. 'I checked up with the Schleswig-Holstein Staatsanwaltschaft. They never had anything more than a police officer's suspicion against Fendrich. I don't want to end up with him pursuing us through the courts for harassment.'

Van Heiden sat back in his chair and placed his hands, fingers splayed and arms locked, on the vast cherrywood expanse of his desk. It was an intense posture, as if he were prepared for some dynamic physical action. He looked at Fabel, but it was as if he were somewhere and some time else.

'When I was a child, I used to love the Grimms' fairy tales. "The Singing, Ringing Tree", that kind of thing. I think the thing I liked most was that they were always much darker than the usual children's tales. More violent. That's why kids liked them.' Van Heiden leaned forward. 'You've got to find him, Fabel. And soon. At the rate this maniac is killing, we don't have the luxury of weeks or months to track him down. He's escalating far too fast.'

Fabel shook his head. 'No . . . He's not escalating, Herr Kriminaldirektor. This is no feeding frenzy. All these killings have been worked out in detail – maybe years in advance. He's working to a pre-planned timetable.'

Fabel stopped speaking, but his tone suggested he hadn't said all he had to say. Van Heiden picked up on it.

'Okay, Fabel – let's hear it.'

'It's just a feeling I've got. Another reason we have to get him quickly. I think what we've seen so far is the prelude. I have this feeling that he's building up to something big. A finale. Something spectacular.'

Once he was back in his own office, Fabel took out his sketch pad again. He turned over from the page on which he had summarised the inquiry to

431

date and took a fresh, blank page. It looked up at him, inviting him to commit some new thought process to paper. Along the top he wrote the names of each of the fairy tales so far imitated by the killer. Underneath he wrote down words he associated with each tale. As he predicted, the closer he came to the most recent murder, Little Red Riding Hood, the more he wrote down: themes, names, relationships. Grandmother. Stepmother. Mother. Witch. Wolf. He was still still working his way through the tales when his desk phone rang.

'Hello, *Chef*. It's Maria. Could you meet me at the Institut für Rechtsmedizin? The Wasserschutzpolizei have just pulled a body out of the Elbe. And *Chef*, I'd cancel any plans for lunch.'

Everyone who dies in Hamburg without an appointment ends up in the mortuary of the Institut für Rechtsmedizin. All sudden deaths for which a doctor will not issue a death certificate are brought there. A body that had been weighted down and thrown into the Elbe was a prime candidate for accommodation.

As soon as Fabel entered the mortuary, he felt the usual leaden swell of revulsion and dread. There was always that smell. Not just the smell of death, but of disinfectant, of floor cleaner: a nauseous cocktail that was never overpowering, but it was always there. An attendant led Fabel, Maria and the Kommissar from the Wasserschutzpolizei patrol boat that had found the body through into the chill mortuary, lined with steel cabinets. Fabel noted with unease that the harbour policeman looked decidedly reluctant as they headed towards where the attendant had stopped, resting his hand on the handle of the appropriate cabinet. The harbour cop had, of course, already seen the body when it was fished out of the river and was clearly not too happy about coming face to face with it again.

'This one's a bit stinky.' The mortuary attendant gave his warning a moment to sink in; then he turned the handle, opened the door and slid out the metal tray that held the body. A stench washed over them in a nauseating wave.

'Shit!' Maria took a step back and Fabel was aware of the Wasserschutz Polizeikommissar tensing beside him. For his part, Fabel fought to keep control of his disgust; and of his stomach, which lurched heavily at the sight and smell of the corpse before him.

A naked man lay on the body tray. He would have been about one metre seventy-five tall. It was difficult to tell what his build, or even ethnicity, had been, because his body had distended and discoloured in the water. Most of his swollen torso was covered in ornate tattoos that had paled slightly as they had been pulled across the stretched, blotched skin. The tattoos mainly consisted of intricate patterns and designs, rather than the usual naked women, hearts, skulls, daggers and dragons. A deep indentation ran all around the bloated torso, like a massive crease, and the over-tight skin had ruptured. The dead man had long, greying hair that had been pulled back from the face and tied into a ponytail.

His throat had been cut. Fabel could see vestiges of the straight lateral slash, but elsewhere along the cut the skin and flesh looked torn.

But it was in the devastation of the face that the true horror lay. The flesh around the eye sockets and the mouth was ripped and ragged. Bone gleamed through flaps of empurpled skin and pink flesh. The victim's teeth grinned a lipless grin.

'My God . . . What the hell has happened to his face?' asked Fabel.

'Eels,' said the Wasserschutz Kommissar. 'They always go for wounds first. That's why I'm guessing that his eyes had been removed before he was dumped. The eels did the rest. Simply found the easiest way into the head and a prime source of protein. Same with the throat wound.'

Fabel recalled reading *The Tin Drum* by Günter Grass: the description of a fisherman using a dead horse's head to fish for eels, pulling the head from the water, its eye sockets writhing with eels. Fabel imagined the dead man being hauled up, the eels clinging on to their precious source of food; Fabel's nausea intensified. He closed his eyes for a moment and focused on forcing back the rising feeling in his chest before speaking again.

'The deformation around the torso. Any idea what caused it?'

'Yes,' said the harbour Kommissar. 'There was a rope tied tightly around the body. We retrieved quite a bit of it. Our guess is that a weight was attached before he was thrown into the water. It looks as if the rope broke or the weight separated from it somehow. That's what brought him up to the surface.'

'And he was like this? Naked?'

'Yep. No clothes, no ID, nothing.'

Fabel nodded to the mortuary attendant who slid the corpse back into its cabinet and slammed the door shut. Its ghost still haunted the mortuary in the form of the stench of putrefaction.

'If you don't mind,' he said to the other two officers, 'I think we should step outside.'

Fabel led Maria and the harbour policeman out into the fresh air of the car park. No one spoke until they reached the open, and only then after they had each taken a deep, cleansing breath.

'God, that was bad,' said Fabel at last. He snapped open his cell phone and phoned Holger Brauner. He explained about their find and asked if Brauner could do a DNA check to see if the spare pair of eyes they'd found in the Friedhof matched the body from the river. After he hung up, he thanked the harbour policeman for his time. When they were alone, he turned to Maria.

'You know what the rope and the weight means?'

'Yes,' she replied. 'We weren't supposed to find this one.'

'Exactly. Let's assume for a moment that we do get a match between this body and our spare pair of eyes. It makes this victim nothing more than a donor – he was killed simply for his eyes.'

'I suppose that's possible.'

'Maybe. But does having a second pair of eyes to "cast on Gretel" enhance the tableau that much? Why not just use Ungerer's eyes? Or, if you're going to have more than one pair of eyes, why add just one more pair? Why not half a dozen?'

Maria frowned. 'What's your point?'

'Simply this. I'm right back to where I was when we had Olsen as our prime suspect – when we had a motive for him killing Grünn and Schiller, but for none of the others.' He indicated the Institut für Rechtsmedizin with a nod of his head. 'That man in there didn't just die for his eyes. He was killed for a reason. He's a diversion that our guy was forced to take. And that's why he didn't want – or need – us to find the body.'

'Why?' Maria's frown still didn't lift. 'Why did he have to kill this guy?'

'Maybe he knew who was committing these murders. Or maybe he simply had a piece of information that the killer didn't want us to get to.' Fabel rested his hands on his hips and turned his face up to the grey sky. He closed his eyes and rubbed at his sinuses again. 'Get the SpuSi guys to see if they can get a decent fingerprint and arrange for some photographs of his tattoos. I don't care if we visit every tattooist in Hamburg . . . we have to get an identity for him.'

As they drove back to the Präsidium, the storm, which had lurked broodily all day in the heavy air, broke.

CHAPTER 55

3.00 p.m., Monday, 26 April: St Pauli, Hamburg

As Anna had predicted, Fendrich had been unable to offer any kind of solid alibi for his whereabouts on the night the last murder had taken place. He hadn't even been able to say that he had been watching television and give an account of the evening's programmes. Instead, he had spent the evening reading and doing some preparation for the following day's class work. It was clear that Anna now felt sorry for Fendrich. He had, apparently, been totally distraught at the violation of his mother's grave. Fabel had suspected that Anna had perhaps gone further than she should in putting his mind at rest by letting him in on Fabel's theory that he was being used as a diversion by the real killer.

At least they knew to whom the eyes belonged. DNA tests had confirmed that one pair belonged to Bernd Ungerer, while the second pair matched the body fished out of the Elbe. Holger Brauner had also run tests on the river body's hair. They confirmed that the tattooed dead man was a drug user, but did not suggest recent heavy use. Möller, the pathologist, confirmed that the cause of death was the single, wide cut to the throat and that no water had been present in the lungs. The victim was dead before he was dumped in the water.

And now they had secured Durchsuchungsbeschluss entry and search warrants for two premises. The first was for the apartment of Lina Ritter, a known prostitute who had been reported missing by her sister. Ritter's files had been accessed and had revealed that she was, indeed, the woman whose body had been posed, dressed in a traditional Tracht costume, in the Garten der Frauen in Ohlsdorf cemetery.

The second warrant was for this place, a tattoo studio in a seedy part of Sankt Pauli. It hadn't taken them long to find it. The SchuPo in each of Hamburg's Stadtteile city divisions had been told to check out every tattoo parlour in their area, and to show the images of the tattoos around to see if anyone recognised them. A sharp young Obermeister had decided not to shrug off the fact that this particular studio seemed always to be closed and did some asking around in the neighbourhood. No one knew where Max Bartmann was, but it was unusual for him not to be open. His business seemed to be his life, and, anyway, he lived over the shop.

The studio was tiny. A single room with a window that would have looked directly out on to the street, had it not been covered by the photographs and illustrations pasted to it, displaying to passers-by the talents of the tattooist within. Hardly any natural light managed to squeeze past the collage of examples and Fabel had to switch on the naked ceiling bulb to see clearly. He thanked the SchuPo and asked him to wait outside, leaving Fabel and Werner in the cramped studio. There was a couple of old, battered leather armchairs, arranged on either side of a small side table with some magazines scattered on it. A padded physiotherapy table was pushed up against one wall and a swivel stool sat next to it. An anglepoise lamp was fixed to the edge of the table. A tangle of wires hung from a wall socket, leading to a metal box with a switch and a dial, then to an aluminium tattoo machine. Three other machines lay on the table. A wall-mounted cabinet held rows of tattoo inks in a vast range of colours, tattoo stencils, needles, a box of surgical gloves and sterile swabs.

Before touching anything, Fabel took a pair of forensic gloves from his jacket pocket and snapped them on. Like the window, the walls were lined with sample tattoo patterns and photographs of satisfied customers. It would take an age to sort through all these images to see if any of them matched the tattoos on the dead man. A large poster, showing a vista of mountain and sea, captioned in large capitals NEW ZEALAND, was one of only two non-tattoo-related wall decorations. The other was a notice, handwritten in felt pen, which laid out the rules of the studio: no smoking, no kids, no drink or drugs, no disrespect.

Fabel examined the photographs more closely. They were not all close-up flash images of vivid new tattoos: some showed two or more people grinning at the camera, turning a shoulder or a hip towards the lens to display their bodies' artworks. One person featured in all of the pictures: a thin man with dark hair, going grey, tied back in a ponytail. His face was pinched and the cheeks sunken and he had the look of a drinker. Fabel focused on one picture in particular. It was summer and the man with the ponytail wore a black vest as he was photographed with a fat woman who had obviously just had a floral motif tattooed on the fleshy breast she exposed for the photograph. Fabel could see that the man in the picture was, himself, covered in tattoos. But they weren't as colourful as those of his customers. And they consisted of designs and patterns.

'Werner . . .' Fabel called him over, without taking his eyes from the picture. 'I think we may have found our guy. Not a customer; the tattooist himself.'

There was a doorway from the studio. The door had been removed, obviously to maximise the meagre space, and had been replaced with a curtain of multicoloured plastic strips. Werner continued checking the studio while Fabel explored the rest

441

of the premises. He parted the plastic strips and stepped into a tiny square hall. To the right was a cupboard-sized room that contained a toilet and hand washbasin. Directly ahead of Fabel was a steep stairwell that snapped sharply right, then right again, taking him to the upstairs level. There were three tiny rooms. One combined a kitchen and sitting room and was furnished with a sofa and a leather armchair. The armchair matched those in the studio, but was in much better condition. There was also an ancient-looking TV and a stereo system. The second room was the bedroom. It was so small that the only furniture was the bed, a bookcase along one wall, and a lamp that sat on the floor next to the bed.

The tiny flat depressed Fabel. It was dingy but clean, and Bartmann had obviously kept it tidy. But it was the kind of functional, soulless space of a man living alone. Fabel thought about his own apartment, with its smart furnishings, beechwood floors and stunning views over the Alster. It was in a different league. But there was something about this space that had encapsulated Bartmann's life that was depressingly similar. As he stood there, in a dead man's dead apartment, Jan Fabel made a decision about his own life.

Fabel checked beneath the bed and found a large, flat portfolio case. He pulled it out and laid it on the bed before opening it. It contained pen-and-ink drawings, charcoal sketches and a couple of paintings. They were of uninspiring subjects – trees, buildings, still lifes – and were clearly studies set to test and stretch the technical abilities rather than the imagination of the artist. Fabel recognised that the artist's craftsmanship was excellent. Each study was initialled 'M.B.'

Fabel left the portfolio on the bed and moved over to examine the bookcase. This was clearly Bartmann's library of all things relating to the tattooist's craft. There were scholarly texts on the history of body art, books on semi-pornographic 'fantasy' art, and manuals for tattooing equipment. But there were three books that didn't fit. And one of them caused Fabel to feel a small current of excitement tingle across his scalp. *Gebrüder Grimm: Gesammelte Märchen*. The collected tales of the Brothers Grimm. Next to the fairy tales, Fabel found two books on the old German gothic scripts: Fraktur, Kupferstich and Sütterlin.

Old German type and script; a copy of Grimms' fairy tales. It wasn't what you would expect in a tattooist's apartment. Another murder with a Grimm connection and another body, but one they had not been meant to find.

Fabel removed the three books from the shelves and put them to one side to be placed in evidence bags later. He stood in the dingy bedroom for a moment and gazed down at the books. He knew he was still to unravel their exact significance; he also knew he had just taken a large step closer to his killer. He snapped open his cell phone and hit a pre-set dial button.

'Anna – it's Fabel. I have a strange request. I want you to phone Fendrich and ask him if he has any tattoos . . .'

CHAPTER 56

2.10 p.m., Tuesday, 27 April:
Neustadt, Hamburg

Weiss had been polite and cooperative on the phone when Fabel had called him at home, but had managed to squeeze the tiniest hint of tested patience into his tone. He explained that he was tied up most of the following day doing book signings and some research for a new book he was writing. He was going to be in the Neustadt area and Weiss suggested that they meet there, about eleven-thirty.

'As long as you don't mind doing your interrogation alfresco,' Weiss had said.

Fabel arrived, as usual ten minutes early, and sat on a bench in the pedestrianised Peterstrasse. The sky had wiped the last smudges of cloud from its face and presented itself in a flawless bright blue and Fabel cursed having worn his heavier Jaeger jacket. Being dressed appropriately for the ever-changing weather was a problem Fabel shared with the rest of Hamburg's population. He couldn't slip his jacket off because his service automatic was clipped to his belt, so he chose a bench shaded by a rank of trees that punctuated the cobbled street. Peterstrasse was flanked by five- and six-storey Baroque town houses, their façades crowded with windows and rising to Dutch-style gables.

Slightly after eleven-thirty, Weiss's huge frame emerged from the imposing doorway of number thirty-six, which sat on the corner of Peterstrasse and Hütten. Fabel knew the building: as a student he had visited it frequently. He stood up as Weiss approached and the two men shook hands. Weiss's gesture suggested that they should sit down on the bench.

'I take it your new book follows a similar traditional literary theme?' said Fabel.

Weiss raised one of his heavy brows questioningly and Fabel indicated the building from which Weiss had just come. 'The Niederdeutsche Bibliothek – I take it you've been researching older Low German literature. I used to spend quite some time in there myself . . .'

'What can I help you with, Herr Kriminalhauptkommissar?' Weiss's intonation still nursed a hint of impatient indulgence. It rankled with Fabel, but he let it go.

'There are more coincidences in this case than I'm comfortable with, Herr Weiss,' said Fabel. 'I suspect that the murderer has read your book and that it is influencing his actions.'

'Or it could be that your killer and I simply use

the same source material, if in a radically different way. By which I mean the original Grimms' *Children's and Household Tales.*'

'I have no doubt that is the case, but I also feel that there is a . . .' Fabel struggled for the best form of words '. . . well, a *freestyle* element to both. An interpretative element, if you like.'

'By which I take it that you mean he doesn't stick strictly to the book?'

'Yes.' Fabel paused. An elderly woman walked past with a dog on a lead. 'Why didn't you tell me that the sculptor was your brother? That he created the wolf sculpture in your study?'

'Because I didn't think it was any of your business. Or that it had anything to do with what we were talking about. Which leads me to ask why you feel that it *is* your business. Am I a suspect, Herr Fabel? Do you want a full accounting of my whereabouts?' Weiss's eyes narrowed and the heavy brows shaded the first sparks of a dark fire. 'Oh, I see your logic. Maybe madness runs in the family.' He leaned his massive head towards Fabel. 'Maybe I am moon-mad too.'

Fabel resisted the temptation to back away and held Weiss's gaze. 'All right, let's say that I have grounds for suspicion. Your book comes out and all of a sudden we have a series of murders that follow the same specific themes as your novel. Added to that, these murders are placing you in the public spotlight, increasing interest in – and sales of – your book. That, at least, legitimises my interest in you.'

'I see . . . So I'm in the police searchlight as well as the public spotlight?' The smile that stretched Weiss's lips lacked any form of warmth. 'If you could provide me with a list of dates and times you want me to account for, I'll supply the information you need.'

'I've already prepared that.' Fabel took a folded sheet of paper from his inside pocket. 'The times and dates are all there. And, wherever possible, it would be useful if you could give details of anyone who can corroborate your whereabouts.'

Weiss took the paper and placed it in his jacket pocket without looking at it. 'I'll attend to it. Is that all?'

Fabel bent forward, leaning his elbows on his knees. He watched the woman and her dog as they turned the corner into Hütten. 'Listen, Herr Weiss, you are clearly a very intelligent man. The coincidences between your book and these murders are not the main reason I'm here. I suppose you're the nearest thing I've got to an expert on what drives this killer. I need to understand him. I need to understand what it is he thinks he sees in these tales.'

Weiss eased back on the bench and spread his large hands on his knees. He looked at the cobbles at his feet for a moment, as if contemplating what Fabel had said.

'Okay. But I don't know what I can do to help. I can't claim to have any special insight into what motivates him. It's his reality; not mine. But, if you ask my opinion, it has nothing to do with the Grimm Fairy Tales. What he's doing is his own invention. Like my book . . . *Die Märchenstrasse* has nothing to do with Jacob Grimm, really. Nor the Grimm Fairy Tales. It's just, well, a *background* to that which I have freely invented.' Weiss paused. He indicated the Baroque Bürgerhäuser before them. 'Look at this. We're sitting here surrounded by history. In high season Peterstrasse – and Hütten and Neanderstrasse around the corner – is filled with tourists, particularly Americans, soaking up the late-medieval splendour of these buildings. But, as I'm sure you know only too well, it's all a lie. These splendid Baroque town houses were built in the late 1960s and early 1970s. There were never buildings like these here. They're not even reconstructions – they're inventions, fabrications. Admittedly they were built according to genuine historical plans for such buildings, but they don't belong here, in this place, in this time. At any time.'

'What's your point, Herr Weiss?'

'Just that you and I and anyone who knows about Hamburg history are aware of that. But the majority of people don't have a clue. They come here, and sit on these benches, just as we are now, and soak up a sense of their history, of German history. And that is what they experience. What they feel. It is their reality, because they believe it. They don't see a sham because there is none to see.'

Weiss rubbed the heels of his hands on his knees, frustratedly, as if he was struggling still to give form to his thoughts. 'You asked about my brother. The reason I didn't mention that he was the sculptor of that piece in my study was because it is all still too real for me. Too raw. I was glad when Daniel killed himself, and I still find that difficult to deal with. He was so tortured towards the end that I was relieved when he ended it. I explained how Daniel believed himself to be a lycanthrope, a werewolf. The fact is that he really did believe it: it was an absolute, unquestionable, hideous reality to him. He was my older brother and I loved him dearly. He was everything I wanted to be. Then, when I was about twelve and he was seventeen, he started to have these episodes. I saw it, Herr Hauptkommissar. I witnessed my brother in the grip of some invisible force that tore at him. It wasn't just mental anguish that made him scream and howl, it was intense physical agony. What we watched was a teenage boy having a seizure. But what Daniel experienced, what he truly felt physically, was every sinew twist and stretch, his bones bend, his body racked with unbelievable pain as he changed shape. My point is that he felt it all. It was all real to him. Even if it wasn't to us.' Weiss broke off the intense gaze with which he had locked Fabel. 'That's where I got the idea for my *Wahlwelten* novels. I wrote about Daniel in the very first one. I made him a wolf. Not a werewolf, but a wolf-king who was master of all the world's wolf packs. I made him happy and free – free from pain – in my story. And that became my reality for him.' Again Weiss paused. Fabel could see pain in the dark eyes. 'That's why you're wrong to say that your killer isn't sticking to the book, to the authentic tales. He is . . . because it's his book. It's his reality.'

'But the Grimm Fairy Tales, and maybe even your book, are his inspiration?'

'Obviously. But it's *how* he interprets them that is hard to second guess. Listen – do you remember I showed you my collection of illustrations?'

Fabel nodded.

'Well, think how many highly individual artistic interpretations of the Grimms' tales they represented. And they are only a fraction of the paintings, drawings, book illustrations and sculptures that the tales have inspired. Take the Humperdinck opera . . . the Sandman comes along and sprinkles magic dust in Hänsel's and Gretel's eyes to make them sleep. Something that has nothing to do with the original tale at all. Your killer's interpretation – because he clearly sees himself as an artist – is as subjective and personal as these others. And such interpretations can be twisted. The Nazis appropriated Grimms' Fairy Tales just as they did anything else in our culture that they could twist and corrupt to suit their own purposes. There is a particularly nasty, notorious book illustration of a very "Aryan" Gretel pushing the old witch into the oven. And the old witch has stereotypical Jewish features. It is a repulsive piece of work and, when you think about it, a pretty chilling presage of the horrors that were to come.'

'So what you're saying is that all we have is a theme, rather than a plan?'

Weiss shrugged. 'What I'm saying is that there is no way of telling what he will do next or how he sees his work evolving. But the material he is working with gives him a terrible scope and choice of tale to twist to his particular agenda.'

'Then God help us,' said Fabel.

CHAPTER 57

9.00 p.m., Thursday, 29 April:
Othmarschen, Hamburg

The skies above Hamburg had stayed clear after another cleansing storm and now glowed with the late evening. Fabel's apartment was flooded with the warm, gentle light. He felt absolutely exhausted. He threw his jacket and his gun clip on to the sofa and stood for a moment, taking in his apartment. His little realm. He had furnished it well, even expensively, and it had become an externalisation of his personality. Clean, efficient, almost too organised. He absorbed the view and the furnishings, the books and the pictures, and the expensive electronics. But was it, at the end of the day, any less lonely than Max Bartmann's seedy Sankt Pauli apartment above his studio?

Before stripping and stepping into the shower, he called Susanne. They hadn't arranged anything for this evening and she was surprised to hear from him: surprised, but happy.

'Susanne, I need to see you tonight. Your place, my place, in town – it doesn't matter where.'

'Okay,' she said. 'Is there anything wrong?'

'No . . . Nothing at all. It's just that I need to talk to you.'

'Oh, I see . . .' she said. She clearly had assumed it was about the case. 'Why don't you come over here? Stay the night.'

'I'll be there in half an hour.'

Susanne's apartment was in a grand Wilhelminische-era building in the Övelgönne part of Hamburg's Othmarschen district. Övelgönne sat down by the Elbe, on the Elbechaussee, and was on the way to Blankenese, both in terms of geography and desirability. Fabel had often stayed the night at Susanne's, but they had somehow fallen into the custom of her sleeping over at his apartment. Fabel suspected that Susanne sought to protect her own space more consciously than he did. But she had given him a key and, after parking off the main street, he let himself in.

Susanne had seen him arrive and waited for him at the door to her flat. She was in the oversized T-shirt she wore to bed. Her glossy, dark hair tumbled down to her shoulders and her face was naked of make-up. There were times, unexpected times, when Fabel felt overwhelmed by her beauty. As he looked at her now, on the threshold of her apartment, this was one of them.

Her apartment was much larger than Fabel's and tastefully decorated, but there was a hint of tradition in the style that was absent from the Nordic minimalism in Fabel's place.

'You look tired,' Susanne said, and stroked his face. She led him into the living room before going into the kitchen, re-emerging with a glass of white wine and a bottle of beer.

'There you go, a Jever.' She handed him the bottle. 'I got a stock in especially for you.'

'Thanks. I need this.' He sipped the chilled, sharp Frisian beer. Susanne sat down on the sofa next to Fabel, folding her legs under her. The T-shirt rode up and exposed the silky skin of her thigh.

'What is it you wanted to talk about so urgently?' She grinned. 'Not that I'm not delighted to see you. But it sounded like you wanted to discuss this case and you know how I feel about talking shop . . .'

Fabel silenced her by pulling her towards him and kissing her long and hard on the lips. When he released her, he held her gaze.

'No,' he said at last. 'I didn't come here to talk about the case. I've been doing a lot of thinking. Thinking about us.'

'Oh . . .' Susanne said. 'This sounds ominous.'

'We don't seem to be going anywhere with this relationship. I suppose that's because we're both contented, in our different ways. And maybe you don't want any more than we have.' He paused, searching her eyes for any reaction. All he could read in them was her patience. 'I took a kicking

455

over my marriage. I don't know what I did wrong, but I guess it was maybe that I just didn't do enough to keep it alive. I don't want that to happen to us. I really care about you, Susanne. I want this to work.'

She smiled and caressed his cheek again. Her hand was cool from the wineglass. 'But Jan, things are fine. I want this to work too.'

'I want us to live together.' Fabel's tone was decisive, almost curt. Then he smiled and his voice softened. 'I would really like it if we lived together, Susanne. What do you think?'

Susanne arched her eyebrows and let out a long breath. 'Wow. I don't know. I really don't know, Jan. We both like our own space. We're both very strong-willed people. That's not an issue now, but if we lived together . . . I don't know, Jan. Like you say, we've got a good thing going here, I don't want to screw it up.'

'I don't think it would. I think it would strengthen it.'

'I was in a relationship before.' Susanne swung her legs down from the couch. She leaned forward, resting her elbows on her knees and cradling her wineglass in both hands. 'We lived together for a while. I didn't see it at first, but he was a very controlling person.' She gave a bitter laugh. 'Me . . . a psychologist, and I couldn't recognise a control freak when I saw one. Anyway, it wasn't good for me. I felt belittled. Then I felt worthless. I stopped believing in myself, stopped trusting my own judgement. I got out before he destroyed any self-esteem I had left.'

'You think I'm like that?'

'No . . . of course I don't.' She took his hand. 'It's just that I've spent a long time creating a sense of, well, *independence* for myself.'

'God, Susanne, I'm not looking for some kind of Hausfrau. I'm looking for a partner. I'm looking for someone to share my life with. And the only reason I'm looking for that is because of you. Before I met you I hadn't given it any thought. Will you at least think about it?'

'Of course, I will, Jan. I'm not saying no. I'm not saying that at all. I just need time to think about it.' She smiled broadly. 'I tell you what: you take me to Sylt, the way you've been promising for ages. To stay at your brother's hotel. You do that and I'll give you an answer.'

Fabel smiled. 'It's a deal.'

They made intense, eager love before falling asleep. A feeling of contentment nursed Fabel into a deep sleep. A deeper, sounder sleep than he had known for weeks.

His awakening was sudden. Something had reached down to find him and hauled him suddenly up to the surface. He lay, his eyes wide, watching the shadows on the ceiling. Susanne slept beside him. Something, somewhere in a dark, small room in a distant corner of his mind, was hammering to get out. He swung his legs around and sat on the edge of the bed. What was it? Something that had been said? Something he had seen? Or both? Whatever it was, he knew it had to do with the murders: some link that had registered on the fringes. He stood up and walked through to the living room and looked out through Susanne's windows. Her apartment couldn't compete with Fabel's in terms of its outlook. Susanne's view extended over the park and down to the Elbe, but it was heavily framed by the other buildings. A couple of cars passed by, heading towards Liebermann Strasse. A solitary dog wandered across the street and Fabel followed it with his eyes until it disappeared from view.

Something he had heard. Something he had seen. Or both. His exhausted, sleep-deprived brain refused to give it up.

Fabel went through to the kitchen and squinted his eyes against the dazzle as he switched on the lights. He made himself a cup of tea. As he took the milk from the fridge he saw three bottles of Jever chilling. He smiled at the thought of Susanne buying them in for him and placing them in her fridge. Fabel always thought of people's fridges as an intimate area: the contents of someone's fridge were as personal as the contents of their wallet or purse. Whenever he was at a murder scene, he would examine the fridge to get an impression of the person or people who lived there. And now his beers shared that personal space with Susanne's yogurt, with her favourite Southern German cheeses and with the pastries she had a weakness for.

He took his tea over to the breakfast bar. He took a sip of it. It was too hot and he set it down to cool. Susanne walked into the kitchen, rubbing her eyes.

'You okay?' she asked sleepily. 'Bad dream again?'

He stood up and kissed her. 'No. Just couldn't sleep . . . sorry if I disturbed you. Do you want some tea?'

'That's okay – and no, thanks.' She talked through her yawn. 'I just wanted to check you were okay.'

Fabel froze as a dark energy coursed through him. His tiredness was gone and he was now as fully awake as it was possible to be. Every sense, every nerve had come alive. He stared blankly at Susanne.

'Are you okay?' Susanne asked. 'Jan, what's wrong?'

Fabel crossed the kitchen and opened the fridge door. He stared at the pastries. They were delicate: baked apple encased in a light, flaky crust. He closed the door and turned back to Susanne.

'The Gingerbread House,' he said. But he wasn't talking to Susanne.

'What?'

'The Gingerbread House. Werner said to me that we should be looking for someone who lives in a Gingerbread House. Then I saw the pastries in the fridge, and that's what reminded me.'

'Jan, what the hell are you talking about?'

He took her by the shoulders and kissed her cheek. 'I've got to get dressed. I've got to go back to the Präsidium.'

'What on earth for?' she asked, following Fabel into the bedroom, where he hastily pulled on his clothes.

'I've heard him, Susanne. All this time he's been trying to tell me something and now I've heard him.'

Fabel phoned Weiss from his car.

'Christ, Fabel – it's nearly five in the morning. What the hell do you want?'

'Why do baked goods feature so much in the Grimm fairy tales?'

'What? What the hell . . .'

'Listen, Herr Weiss, I know it's late – or early – but this is important. Vitally important. Why are there so many references to baked goods – to bread and cakes, to gingerbread houses and the like – in the Grimm fairy tales?'

'Oh, God . . . I don't know . . . it symbolises so much.' Weiss sounded confused, as if being forced to search through mental files when still half asleep. 'Different things in different tales. Take 'Rotkäppchen', for example: Little Red Riding Hood's freshly baked bread for her grandmother is a symbol of her uncorrupted purity while the wolf represents corruption and rapacious appetites. It isn't the bread he wants, it's her virginity. Yet Hänsel and Gretel, despite being innocents lost in the darkness of the woods, succumb to their appetites and greed when they come across the gingerbread house. So, in that case, it represents the temptation to sin. Baked foods can represent so many different things. Simplicity and purity. Or even poverty – the meagre breadcrumbs that Hänsel secretly stores to use to guide him and his sister back to safety. Why?'

'I can't explain right now. But thanks.' Fabel hung up and immediately redialled. It took some time for the phone to be answered.

'Werner, it's Fabel . . . Yes, I know the time. Can you get to the Präsidium right away? See if you can get hold of Anna and Maria as well.' Fabel checked himself. For a moment he was about to ask Werner to call Paul Lindemann in: the lateness of the hour and the force of habit obscuring, for a second, the fact of Paul's death a year ago while on duty. 'And get Anna to contact Henk Hermann.' He hung up.

So much death. How did he ever end up surrounded by so much death? History had been his overwhelming love and he had felt drawn to the life of the historian as if his very genes had predestined his path. But Fabel didn't believe in destiny. Instead he believed in the cruel unpredictability of life: a life where a chance encounter between a young girl student, Fabel's girlfriend at the time, and a nobody with a severe psychotic disorder resulted in a tragedy. And that tragedy had set in train a sequence of unforeseen events that ended in Fabel's career becoming that of a murder-squad policeman, instead of a historian, or an archaeologist, or a teacher.

So much death. And now he was closing in on another killer.

It was nearly six before everyone was assembled in the Mordkommission. No one complained about being summoned from their beds, but everyone had the bleary-eyed look of the barely awake. But not Fabel. Fabel's eyes burned with a cold, dark determination. He stood with his back to them, moving his searchlight gaze along the images on the inquiry board.

'There have been times I thought that we weren't going to get this guy.' Fabel's voice was quiet, deliberate. 'That we were going to see several weeks of intense activity and a pile of corpses, and then he would disappear. Until his next spree.' There was a heartbeat's pause. He turned to his audience. 'We have a busy, busy day ahead of us. By the end of it I intend to have our killer in custody.'

No one spoke, but suddenly everyone looked more alert. 'He's clever. Mad – but clever,' Fabel continued. 'This is his life's work and he has thought it through to the tiniest detail. Everything he does is significant. Every detail is a link to another. But there was one link we missed.' He slammed his open palm against the first image. 'Paula Ehlers . . . this is the picture taken the day before she disappeared. What do you see?'

'A happy girl.' Werner stared hard at the picture, as if the intensity of his gaze could squeeze more from it that he could currently see. 'A happy girl at her birthday party . . .'

'No . . .' Maria Klee moved closer. Her eyes scanned the sequence of images, just as Fabel had. 'No . . . that's not it . . .' Her eyes locked with Fabel's. 'The birthday cake. It's the birthday cake.'

Fabel smiled grimly but did not speak, inviting Maria to take it forward. She stepped up and pointed to the second image.

'Martha Schmidt . . . the girl found on the beach at Blankenese. A stomach empty of anything other than the remains of a meagre meal of rye bread.' She moved to the next image and her voice became tighter. 'Hanna Grünn and Markus Schiller . . . the breadcrumbs scattered on the handkerchief . . . and Schiller was part-owner of a bakery . . .'

As Maria spoke, Fabel nodded across to Anna. 'Get me the Vierlande Detention Centre. Tell them it's urgent that I speak to Peter Olsen . . .'

Maria moved to the next image. 'Laura von Klosterstadt?'

'Another birthday party,' answered Fabel. 'A glitzy one organised by her agent, Heinz Schnauber. It would have been catered. Schnauber told me he always wanted Laura to feel that it was still her personal birthday party and not simply some promotional event. He said he liked to arrange little surprises for her: presents . . . and a birthday cake. We need to know who the catering company was.'

'Bernd Ungerer.' Maria moved along the inquiry board as if she and it were alone in the room. 'Of course, catering equipment. Bakery ovens . . . And here . . . Lina Ritter, posed as Little Red Riding Hood, with a freshly baked loaf of bread in her basket.'

'Fairy tales,' said Fabel. 'We're dealing in fairy tales. A world where nothing is what you think it is. Everything has a meaning, a symbolism. The big, bad wolf has nothing to do with wolves and everything to do with us. With people. The mother is everything bountiful and good in nature, the stepmother is the other side of the same coin, everything in nature that is malicious and destructive and evil. And baked goods: the simple, honest wholesomeness of bread; the lustful temptation of baked delicacies. It is a motif that runs throughout all the Grimm tales.'

'*Chef,*' Anna called over to Fabel, her hand shielding the mouthpiece of the phone. 'The custody officer wasn't happy about it, but I've got Olsen on the line.'

Fabel took the handset.

'Olsen, this is your chance to put yourself completely in the clear for these killings. You remember we talked about Ungerer, the equipment salesman?'

'Yeah . . .'

'What was it that Hanna said about the way he looked at her?'

'What . . . I dunno . . . oh yeah, that his eyes were all over her.'

Yes, thought Fabel, and those eyes were gouged out and ended up all over someone else.

'Was there anyone else in the bakery who was attracted to Hanna?'

Olsen laughed. 'Most of the male staff, probably.'

'But was there anyone in particular?' Fabel's tone was impatient. 'Someone who might have made a nuisance of himself?'

There was a silence at the other end of the phone.

'Please, Herr Olsen. This is very important.'

'No . . . no, I think that her boss, Herr Biedermeyer, the Chief Baker, was very strict about that kind of thing. She even complained to him about Ungerer. He said he would have a word with Frau Schiller.'

It was Fabel's turn to fall silent.

'Is that what you want to know?' Olsen said uncertainly. 'Does that put me in the clear?'

'Perhaps . . . probably. Let me get back to you.' Fabel hung up. 'Get on to the Kassel KriPo,' he told Anna 'Find out if Martha Schmidt had been to any kind of birthday party or catered function in the few weeks immediately before she was abducted.'

'Okay, *Chef*, but given her family background that would seem unlikely. I don't see her junkie parents being organised or interested enough to accept an invitation and take her to a party.'

'The sad thing is, Anna, Martha maybe took care of that kind of thing herself. She was probably the closest thing to a responsible adult in her family.' Fabel sighed. The image of a shabby Martha Schmidt arriving, alone and without a present, at a birthday party stung him. 'The other thing I'd like you to do is contact the Ehlers family – they know you – and find out where Paula's birthday cake came from.' He called over to Maria Klee. 'Maria, I want you to get in touch with Heinz Schnauber, Laura von Klosterstadt's agent, and find out who he got to do the catering for her party. Again I want to know where the cake came from.'

CHAPTER 58

10.00 a.m., Friday, 30 April:
Backstube Albertus, Bostelbek,
Heimfeld, Hamburg

Fabel had the answers he needed. Or enough of the answers he needed. The Kassel police had been, so far, unable to confirm whether or not Martha Schmidt had been at a birthday party before she was abducted. Anna had also found out that Martha's mother had never returned home from her visit to identify her daughter. It annoyed Fabel that the Mordkommission had to find out from a distant police force that Ulrike Schmidt had committed suicide while still in Hamburg: information that he should have received from the Polizeidirektion involved. Once the annoyance that there had been such a communications breakdown within the Polizei Hamburg subsided, Fabel remembered how Anna had been so hard on Ulrike Schmidt, simply taking her for a heartless, self-centred junkie. She had been a mother after all, in her own way.

Anna had contacted the Ehlerses, who had

confirmed that Paula's cake had been supplied by the Backstube Albertus. Maria's check revealed that Heinz Schnauber had arranged for a vast, ornate cake to be custom-made for Laura von Klosterstadt. It hadn't, however, come from the caterers: he had organised it himself with a specialist bakery who had delivered the cake directly. The bakery had been the Backstube Albertus.

The girl behind the reception desk in the Backstube Albertus was clearly unsettled by the sudden presence of so many police officers. When Fabel held out his oval Kriminalpolizei disc and asked if Frau Schiller was in she simply nodded.

Fabel had stationed uniformed SchuPo officers at the main entrance of the bakery, as well as at its fire exits and the delivery bay. Anna Wolff and Henk Hermann waited down on the bakery floor. The air was rich with the odours of dough and warm bread, but when Fabel, Werner and Maria entered Vera Schiller's office it still had the hard, functional feel of industrial administration. And Markus Schiller's desk still had the look of recent abandonment. Vera Schiller stood up, an incandescent fury in her eyes.

'What is the meaning of this? I demand to know why you have barged into my premises . . . into my office . . .'

Fabel held up a hand, and when he spoke it was with a quiet, calm, authority. 'Frau Schiller, we have some very important questions for you and your staff. I know this has been a distressing time for you. Please don't make things any more difficult than they have to be.'

Vera Schiller sat back down, but her pose remained tight, rigid. The dark fire still burned in her eyes.

'Do not presume that you know the slightest thing about me, Herr Kriminalhauptkommissar. You don't know anything about me at all.'

Fabel sat down opposite her. 'That's as may be. But there is something I do know: seven murders have been committed . . . perhaps even eight. Each of them the most horrific murder, including your husband's. And each of them is connected to the Backstube Albertus.'

'In what way connected?' Vera Schiller looked as if a sharp jolt of electricity had passed through her. 'What do you mean?'

'Laura von Klosterstadt. You must have read about her murder. Yet you didn't think to advise us that you had supplied the cake for her birthday celebrations.'

'I don't know what you're talking about. We didn't supply a cake for her. I would have remembered.'

Fabel gave her the dates. A computer sat, slightly off to one side, on her desk. She punched some keys on her keyboard.

'No, nothing. You can see for yourself.' She swivelled the screen towards him.

'That's it.' Fabel pointed to an entry on the table

displayed on the screen. 'It's in the name of Heinz Schnauber. He's Laura von Klosterstadt's agent.'

Vera Schiller peered at the entry. 'Oh yes, a large cake. A special. Plus a full delivery of bread rolls and pastries. I remember that order, but he didn't tell me it was for the von Klosterstadts.'

'Who didn't?' asked Fabel. But already he had in his mind the image of huge hands working with incongruous delicacy.

'Herr Biedermeyer, of course. Our Chief Baker.' She opened her desk drawer and pulled out a heavy ledger. She flicked through the pages, checked the computer screen again, then ran a red-varnished fingernail down a column. 'Yes . . . here it is . . . Herr Biedermeyer delivered the order himself. He's very thorough.'

Fabel looked over his shoulder to Werner and Maria.

'May I look at your delivery ledger?' he asked Frau Schiller. She held his gaze for a moment, but the anger had subsided. She turned the ledger around so that it faced Fabel. He took his notebook from his pocket and checked the date of Martha Schmidt's disappearance. Then he flicked back through the pages and found the date he sought. The moment seemed to stretch and an electric current now arced in the nape of his neck. 'Herr Biedermeyer takes time out from his supervisory duties to make deliveries like this?' He pointed to the entry in the ledger.

'Yes. Well, in cases like this, he does. The

Konditorei Wunderlich is a very big customer of ours. Herr Biedermeyer ensures that they feel they're getting attention from a senior level.'

'And the Konditorei Wunderlich is in Kassel?' Fabel heard Werner and Maria already moving towards the door before he received an answer.

'Yes. Why?'

'Does Herr Biedermeyer use one of your panel vans to make his deliveries?'

'Sometimes. Yes. Why are you asking about Herr Biedermeyer?'

Fabel ignored the question. 'Is Herr Biedermeyer here just now?'

'He's on the production floor—'

Before Frau Schiller had time to finish her answer, Fabel had risen from his seat and was following his officers down the stairs.

Just as Fabel remembered from the first time he had seen him, Biedermeyer was leaning over, placing a small floral decoration on a cake. Again it seemed an impossibly delicate operation for his huge, heavy hands and the icing flowers looked tiny and fragile between his massive forefinger and thumb. As he saw the group of police officers approach him, he straightened up and his good-natured features broke into a broad grin. Anna and Henk broke off from the advancing group and started to usher the other workers out of the production hall. Biedermeyer watched with amusement.

'Hello, Herr Kriminalhauptkommissar. Excuse me a moment, I just have to put the last two flowers on this cake.' Again the forefinger and thumb picked up a decoration from the palm of his other hand and placed it on to the cake. He repeated the operation with the final flower. Straightening up his huge frame, Biedermeyer took a step back to survey his handiwork and said, 'There!' He turned back to Fabel. 'Sorry to keep you, but I had to finish that.' The smile across his big face remained friendly, warm almost, and the creases around his eyes deepened. 'I like to do things just right. Get them finished properly. Perfectly. With something like this, I always feel that the detail is everything.' He looked at the other officers and then back to Fabel. 'But, there again, I think I've already proved that, haven't I? Did you like my work, Herr Hauptkommissar? Did it amuse you?'

Fabel's hand moved to his hip and he took his pistol from its holster. He didn't raise it, but kept it at his side, ready. Biedermeyer looked at the gun and shook his head, as if disappointed.

'There's no need for that, Herr Fabel. No need at all. I have finished my work. I have done all I set out to do.'

'Herr Biedermeyer—' Fabel began to say, but Biedermeyer held up a hand, like a traffic cop stopping oncoming vehicles. He kept smiling, but his size, his sheer bulk was more threatening than any expression.

'Now, Herr Fabel, you know that is not my real name, don't you? After all that you've seen?'

'Then what *is* your name?'

'Grimm . . .' Biedermeyer laughed as if being forced to explain something dazzlingly obvious to a child. 'I am Brother Grimm.'

Fabel heard the sound of firearms being drawn from their holsters.

'Franz Biedermeyer, I am placing you under arrest for the suspected murder of Paula Ehlers, Martha Schmidt, Hanna Grünn, Markus Schiller, Bernd Ungerer, Lina Ritter and Max Bartmann. Any statement you make may be used as evidence.' Fabel reholstered his gun, first checking over his shoulder that Werner and Maria had Biedermeyer covered. He removed the pair of handcuffs from his belt pouch and grasped Biedermeyer's wrist, turning him round to hand-cuff him. Taking hold of Biedermeyer made Fabel even more aware of his bulk and potential power. The wrists were thick and solid. But, to Fabel's relief, Biedermeyer offered no resistance.

As they took the Chief Baker out to the waiting cars, they passed Vera Schiller. Her dark gaze held Biedermeyer as he was led up the stairway and along the hall to the exit. He stopped, and Fabel and Werner became aware that they had hold of an immovable object. The smile faded from Biedermeyer's face.

'I'm sorry,' he said to her in a quiet voice. She snorted, as if dismissing something contemptible.

Biedermeyer moved on. Frau Schiller placed a hand on Fabel's arm and he signalled for Henk and Anna to join Werner as Biedermeyer's escort. When he turned to Vera Schiller, there was something like defiance in her eyes. Her voice was cold and sharp-edged.

'I loved my husband, Herr Fabel. I loved Markus very, very much.' Her expression remained hard, but a tear seeped from the corner of her eye and ran down her cheek. 'I wanted you to know that.'

They put Biedermeyer in the back of Fabel's car. He was hunched over in the confines of the rear seat and looked as if he had been carelessly folded to fit into its inadequate space. Werner sat next to him and, despite his height, looked small in comparison to the baker.

Before he started the engine, Fabel turned round to face Biedermeyer.

'You said your work is finished. Why did you say that? I know you haven't done all you planned. I've followed the links – the tales . . . you have at least one more to do . . .'

Biedermeyer grinned and the wrinkles around his eyes again folded into creases. And again it reminded Fabel of the way his brother Lex smiled and the thought chilled him.

'Be patient, Herr Kriminalhauptkommissar. Be patient.'

CHAPTER 59

1.30 p.m., Friday, 30 April:
Polizeipräsidium Hamburg

Fabel, Maria and Werner waited in the interview room. They had discussed their interrogation strategies before coming in and now sat in an unwilling silence. Each tried to think of something to say. A joke, even, to break the quiet. But none could. Instead Fabel and Werner sat at the table with the tape recorder and the microphone at its centre, while Maria leaned against the wall.

And they waited for a monster to be brought into their midst.

They heard footsteps approaching. Fabel knew that it was medically impossible but he could have sworn he felt his blood pressure rise. There was a tightness in his chest: excitement, dread and determination blended into an emotion without a name. The footsteps paused and then a SchuPo officer swung open the interview room door. Two more SchuPos led the handcuffed Biedermeyer into the room. They seemed insignificant next to his bulk.

Biedermeyer sat down opposite Fabel. Alone. He had refused the right to a legal representative. The two SchuPos stood silent watch behind him, against the wall. Biedermeyer's face still looked relaxed, amiable, pleasant. A face you would trust; someone you would chat to in a bar. He held out his hands, folding them back from his wrists to expose the handcuffs. He tilted his head slightly to one side.

'Please, Herr Fabel. I think you know that I represent no danger to you or your colleagues. Nor do I have any desire to escape your custody.'

Fabel signalled to one of the SchuPos, who stepped forward and unlocked and removed the cuffs before taking up his station by the wall again. Fabel switched on the tape machine.

'Herr Biedermeyer, did you abduct and murder Paula Ehlers?'

'Yes.'

'Did you abduct and murder Martha Schmidt?'

'Yes.'

'Did you murder—'

Biedermeyer held up his hand and smiled his disarming, good-natured smile. 'Please. I think, to save time, it would be best if I made the following statement. I, Jacob Grimm, brother of Wilhelm Grimm, recorder of the tongue and soul of the German peoples, took the lives of Paula Ehlers, Martha Schmidt, Hanna Grünn, Markus Schiller, Bernd Ungerer, Laura von Klosterstadt, the whore Lina – I'm sorry, I never knew her surname – and the tattooist Max Bartmann. I killed them all. And

I enjoyed each and every second of each and every death. I freely admit to killing them, but I am guilty of nothing. Their lives were inconsequential. The only significance each had lay in the manner of his or her death . . . and those universal, timeless truths that they expressed through their deaths. In life they were worthless. By killing them, I made them worthy.'

'Herr Biedermeyer, for the record, we cannot accept a confession in any name other than your real one.'

'But I have given you my real name. I have given you the name on my soul, not the fiction that exists on my Personalausweis.' Biedermeyer sighed, then smiled, again as if he were indulging a child. 'If it makes you happier: I, Brother Grimm, known to you by the name Franz Biedermeyer, admit to killing all of these people.'

'Did you have any help in carrying out these murders?'

'But of course I did! Naturally.'

'From whom?'

'From my brother . . . Who else?'

'But you have no brother, Herr Biedermeyer,' Maria said. 'You were an only child.'

'Of course I have a brother.' For the first time the amiability of Biedermeyer's expression dissolved and was replaced by something infinitely more menacing. Predatory. 'Without my brother I am nothing. Without me *he* is nothing. We complete each other.'

'Who is your brother?'

Biedermeyer's indulgent smile returned. 'But you know him, of course. You've met him already.'

Fabel's gesture was one of incomprehension.

'You know my brother, Wilhelm Grimm, by the name of Gerhard Weiss.'

'Weiss?' Maria spoke from behind Fabel. 'You're claiming that the author Gerhard Weiss committed these crimes with you?'

'To begin with, these are not crimes. They are creative acts – there is nothing destructive about them. They are the embodiments of truths that stretch back generations. My brother and I are recorders of these truths. He *committed* nothing with me. He *collaborated* with me. Just as we did nearly two hundred years ago.'

Fabel leaned back in his chair and regarded Biedermeyer: the amiable, smile-worn face that contrasted with the threat implicit in his huge frame. That's why you wore the mask, Fabel thought. That's why you hid your face. He imagined the terrifying figure that the masked Biedermeyer must have presented; the raw terror his victims must have experienced before they died. 'But the truth is, is it not, Herr Biedermeyer, that Gerhard Weiss knows nothing of this. Apart from the letter you sent to his publishers, there has been no real, tangible contact between you.'

Again Biedermeyer smiled. 'No, you don't understand, do you, Herr Kriminalhauptkommissar?'

'Perhaps I don't. I need you to help me

understand. But first, I have an important question to ask you. Perhaps the most important I shall ask today. Where is Paula Ehlers's body?'

Biedermeyer leaned forward, resting his elbows on the table. 'You will get your answer, Herr Fabel. I promise you that. I shall tell you where to find Paula Ehlers's body. And I shall tell you today . . . but not yet. First I will tell you how I came to find her and why I chose her. And I will help you to understand the special bond between my brother Wilhelm, whom you know as Gerhard Weiss, and myself.' He paused. 'May I have some water?'

Again Fabel nodded to one of the uniformed officers who filled a paper cup from the water dispenser, then placed it before Biedermeyer. He drank all the water down, and the sound of his swallowing was amplified in the otherwise silent interview room.

'I delivered the cake to the Ehlers residence the day before her birthday party, two days before I took her. Her mother hurried away with with the cake because she wanted to hide it before Paula came home from school. I was just driving away when I saw Paula come around the corner and head towards her house. I thought to myself: "That was lucky! I delivered that cake just in time, she very nearly saw her surprise." It was then that Wilhelm spoke to me. He told me that I had to take the girl and end her.'

'Wilhelm was in the car with you?' asked Werner.

'Wilhelm is always with me, wherever I go. He had been silent for such a long, long time. Since I was a child. But I always knew he was there. Watching me. Planning and writing out my story, my destiny. But I was so glad to hear his voice again.'

'What did Wilhelm say to you?' asked Fabel.

'He told me that Paula was pure. Innocent. She was yet unsullied by the corruption and filth of our world. Wilhelm told me that I could make sure that she stayed that way: that I could save her from corruption and ruin by putting her into a sleep that would last forever. He told me I had to end her story.'

'Kill her, you mean?' asked Fabel.

Biedermeyer gave a shrug that made clear the semantics of murder were unimportant to him.

'How did you kill her?'

'Most days, I begin work very early in the morning. It is part of being a baker, Herr Fabel. For half my life I have watched the world around me slowly awake while I prepared bread, that most ancient and most central to life of foods, for the coming day. Even after all this time, I still love the combination of morning's first light and the smell of freshly baked bread.' Biedermeyer paused, temporarily lost in the magic of a recalled moment. 'Anyway, depending on the shift I'm working, I often finish early and have much of the afternoon to myself. I made use of this freedom and studied Paula's movements the next day, which were atypical, because it was her birthday and offered no chance for me to take her. But the following day was a school day, and I found that, during my watching of her, an opportunity presented itself suddenly as she crossed the main road from her school to her home. I had to make a decision. I was very afraid of being caught, but Wilhelm spoke to me. He said: "Take her now. It's all right, you'll be safe. Take her and end her story now." I was afraid. I told Wilhelm I was afraid that what I was about to do was wrong and that I would be punished for it. But he said he would give me a sign. Something that would prove it was the right thing to do and that everything would be all right. And he did, Herr Fabel. He gave me a true sign that he was in control of my destiny, of her destiny, of us all. It was in her hand, you see. She held it in her hand as she walked: a copy of our first volume of fairy tales. So I did it. It was so quick. And so easy. I took her from the street, then I took her from the world and her story was ended.' A wistful expression drifted across the huge features. He snapped back to the here and now. 'I won't go into unpleasant details, but Paula knew little about what happened. As I hope you know, Herr Fabel, I am no pervert. I ended her story because Wilhelm told me to. He told me to protect her from the evil of the world by taking her from it. And I did so as quickly and with as little pain as was possible. I suppose, even after all this time, the details will become clear to you when you recover the body. And I stand by my promise that I will tell you exactly where to find her. But not yet.'

'Wilhelm's voice. You said you hadn't heard it for a long time. When had you heard it before? Have you killed before? Or hurt anyone before?'

The smile faded again. This time a pained sadness filled Biedermeyer's expression. 'I loved my mother, Herr Fabel. She was beautiful and she was clever and she had rich, red-blonde hair. That's about all I can remember of her. That and her voice when she sang to me as I lay in bed. Not speaking. I can't remember her speaking voice, but I remember her singing. And her lovely long hair that smelled of apples. Then she stopped singing. I was too young to understand, but she became ill and I saw her less and less. She sang to me less and less. Then she was gone. She died of cancer when she was thirty and I was four.'

He paused, as if waiting for comment, for commiseration, for understanding.

'Go on,' said Fabel.

'You know the story, Herr Fabel. You must have read the tales while you pursued me. My father married again. A hard woman. A false Mother. A cruel, evil woman that made me call her *Mutti*. My father did not marry out of love but for practicality. My father was a very practical man. He was a first officer on a merchant ship and spent months away from home, and he knew that he could not look after me alone. So I lost a beautiful mother and gained an evil stepmother. You see? You see already? It was my stepmother who brought me up, and as I grew so did her cruelty. Then, when *Papi* had a heart attack, I was left alone with her.'

Fabel nodded, inviting Biedermeyer to continue. Already he was aware of the scale of Biedermeyer's insanity. It was monumental. A vast yet intricate edifice of elaborately constructed psychosis. Sitting there, in the shadow of a huge man with a huge madness, Fabel felt something not far removed from awe.

'She was a fearsome, terrible woman, Herr Fabel.' Biedermeyer's face too revealed something like awe. 'God and Germany were all she cared for. Our religion and our nation. The only two books she allowed in the house were the Bible and *Grimms' Fairy Tales*. Everything else was pollution. Pornography. She also took away all my toys. They made me idle, she said. But there was one I kept hidden: a present my father had bought me before he died . . . a mask. A play wolf-mask. That little mask became my only, secret rebellion. Then, one day, when I was about ten, a friend let me borrow a comic book to read. I sneaked it into the house and concealed it, but she found it. Thankfully it wasn't in the same hiding place as my wolf-mask. But that was the beginning. It was then that she started. She said that if I wanted to read I would read. I would read something pure and noble and true. She gave me the volume of *Grimms' Fairy Tales* that she had had since she was a girl. She told me to start by memorising "Hänsel und Gretel." Then she made me recite it. I had to stand, with her next to me, and recite the whole thing, word-perfect.' Biedermeyer looked pleadingly at Fabel and there was something of the child in his big face. 'I was only a boy, Herr Fabel. Only a boy. I got things wrong. Of course I did. It was such a long story. Then she beat me. She beat me with a stick until I bled. Then, every week, I was given a new story to learn. And every week I took a beating. Sometimes it was so bad that I passed out. And, as well as the beatings, she would talk to me. Never shout, always quiet. She would tell me that I was no good. That I was a freak: that I was growing so big and so ugly because there was a big badness within me. I learned hate. I hated her. But much, much more than that, I hated myself.' Biedermeyer paused. His face was sad. He held up his water cup questioningly. It was refilled and he took a sip before continuing.

'But I started to learn from the tales. I began to understand them as I recited them. I learned a valuable trick to make memorising them easier . . . I looked beyond the words. I tried to understand the message within and to see that the characters weren't really people, but that they were symbols, signs. Forces of good and evil. I saw that Snow White and Hänsel and Gretel were just like me, hopelessly trapped by the same evil that my own stepmother represented. It helped me remember the stories and I made fewer and fewer mistakes.

It meant that my stepmother had fewer excuses to beat me. But what she lost in frequency, she made up for in severity . . .

'Then, one day, I got something wrong. A single word. A sentence out of sequence. I still don't know what it was, but she beat me and beat me. Then the whole world seemed to shake. It was like an earthquake in my head and everything shuddered from side to side. I remember thinking that I was going to die. And I was glad. Can you imagine that, Herr Fabel? Eleven years old and happy to die. I fell to the floor and she stopped hitting me. She told me to get up, and I could tell she was afraid that she'd gone too far this time. But I tried to be a good boy. I really did. I wanted to do what I was told and I tried to get up, but I couldn't. I just couldn't. I could taste blood. It was in my mouth and in my nose and I felt it hot in my ears. Now, I thought. Now I'm going to die.' Biedermeyer leaned forward. His eyes were eager and intense. 'It was then that I heard him. It was then that I first heard his voice. I was scared at first. I'm sure you can imagine. But his voice was strong and kind and gentle. He told me that he was Wilhelm Grimm and that he had written the stories with his brother. "You are not alone now," he told me, "I am here. I am the storyteller and I will help you." And he did, Herr Fabel. He helped me with the stories I had to recite to my *Mutti* as a punishment. After that, after the first time I heard him, I never got a single word wrong, because he would tell me what to say.'

Biedermeyer gave a small laugh, as if he was privy to a joke that no one else in the room could ever understand.

'I grew too big for *Mutti* to beat me. I think she might even have grown afraid of me. But her cruelty continued, except now she used words instead of the stick. Every day she told me how worthless I was. How no woman would ever have me, ever want me, because I was a big, ugly freak and because I was so bad. But all the time Wilhelm's voice soothed me, helped me. For every insult she threw at me, he reassured me. Then he stopped. I knew he was there, but he simply stopped talking to me and I was left alone with my stepmother's vicious, evil poison.'

'And then he came back to tell you to kill Paula Ehlers?' asked Fabel.

'Yes . . . yes, exactly. And I knew that he would keep talking to me if I did what he told me. But she was too strong. My stepmother. She found out about Paula. She told me that they would lock me away. That she would have to live with the shame of it all. So she made me dispose of Paula before I could use her . . . before I could relive a story through her.'

'Shit . . .' Werner shook his head in disbelief. 'Your stepmother knew about you abducting and murdering a schoolgirl?'

'She even helped me hide the body . . . but, as

I said, we'll get back to that later. For the moment, I want you to understand that I had a calling, and she frustrated it. She stopped me following what Wilhelm told me to do. Then he stopped talking again. For nearly three years. Then my stepmother was silenced for good, about three months ago.'

'She died?' asked Fabel.

Biedermeyer shook his head. 'A stroke. It shut the old bitch up. Shut her up and paralysed her and put her in hospital. It was over. She could no longer hurt me or insult me or stop me doing what I was meant to do. What I had to do.'

'Let me guess,' said Fabel. 'The voice in your head came back and told you to kill again?'

'No. Not then. Wilhelm stayed silent. Then I saw Gerhard Weiss's book. As soon as I began to read it I knew that he was Wilhelm. That he didn't need to talk to me in my head. It was all there, in the book. In the *Märchenstrasse*. It was the road we had travelled together a century and a half before. And it was the road we were to travel along again. And the very same night I began to read, Wilhelm's soft, sweet voice came back to me, but through those beautiful pages. I knew what I had to do. But I also knew that I had to play the part I had played before: the voice of truth, of accuracy. Wilhelm, or Gerhard Weiss, if you will, was forced to alter things to suit the audience. But not I.'

'So then you killed Martha. You ended her story,' said Fabel.

'I was free from my stepmother and I was

reunited with my Märchenbruder, with Wilhelm. I knew it was time. I had my masterwork all planned: a sequence of tales leading up to fulfilling my destiny. To the happy end of my story. But other stories had to end first. And the girl from Kassel, Martha, was first. I was making a delivery there and I saw her. I thought that she was Paula – that she had been awoken from an enchanted sleep. Then I realised what she was. She was a sign from Wilhelm. Just like the copy of the tales that Paula had carried. It was a sign for me that she was to be ended and would play her part in the next tale.'

'You kept her alive. You hid her for a couple of days before "ending her story". Why?'

Biedermeyer looked disappointed in Fabel; as if he had asked an obvious question. 'Because she was to be an *Underground Person*. She had to be kept beneath the ground. She was very afraid, but I told her that I wasn't going to do anything to her. There was no point in her being afraid. She told me all about her parents. I felt sorry for her. She was like me. She was trapped in a tale of parents who had abandoned her in the darkness. In the woods. She didn't know what love was like, so I ended her story by making her *The Changeling* and giving her to parents who would love her and care for her.'

Werner shook his still-bruised head. 'You are mad. Insane. You do know that, don't you? All those innocent people that you murdered. All that pain and fear you caused.'

Biedermeyer's expression suddenly darkened and his face twisted with contempt. It was like a sudden, unpredicted storm gathering and Fabel glanced meaningfully across at the two SchuPos at the wall. They straightened themselves in readiness.

'You just don't get it, do you? You're too stupid to understand.' Biedermeyer's voice was raised only very slightly, but it took on a deep, menacing resonance. 'Why can't you understand?' He waved his hands about him, casting his gaze around to encompass his environment. 'All this . . . all this . . . you don't think it's *real*, do you? It's only a story, for God's sake. Can't you see that? It's only a myth . . . a fairy tale . . . a fable.' He gazed wildly at Fabel, Werner and Maria, his eyes frustratedly searching theirs for understanding. 'We only believe it because we're in it. Because we're in the story . . . I didn't really kill anyone. I realised everything was just a story when I was a child. No one could really be as unhappy as me. No one could be as sad and lonely. It's ridiculous. That day, the day my stepmother was beating me, and my whole world started to shake, Wilhelm didn't just help me remember the stories I had to recite – he explained that it wasn't really happening to me. None of it. That it was all a story and he was making it up. Remember? He told me he was the storyteller? You see I am his brother because he wrote me into his story as his brother. This is all simply a Märchen.'

Biedermeyer nodded knowingly, as if everyone at the table should have felt monumentally enlightened. Fabel thought back to what Otto had said about the premise that the author Gerhard Weiss had laid out: the pseudo-scientific babble about fiction becoming reality across the universe's dimensions. Crap. Utter crap, but this sad, pathetic monster of a man had believed every word of it. Had lived it out.

'What about the others?' Fabel asked. 'Tell us about the other killings. Let's start with Hanna Grünn and Markus Schiller.'

'Just as Paula represented all that was good and wholesome in the world, like fresh-baked bread still warm from the oven, Hanna represented everything which has gone stale and foul . . . she was a loose, promiscuous, vain and venal woman.' There was pride in Biedermeyer's smile: the pride of a craftsman displaying his best work. 'I saw that she hungered for something more. Always something more. A woman driven by lust and greed. She used her body as a tool to get what she wanted, yet complained to me about the salesman, Ungerer, leering at her and making lascivious remarks. I knew her story had to be ended, so I watched her. I followed her, just as I had Paula, but for longer, keeping an exact diary of her movements.'

'And that's how you found out about her relationship with Markus Schiller?' asked Fabel.

Biedermeyer nodded. 'I followed them to the

woods on several occasions. Then it became so clear. I read *Die Märchenstrasse* again – as well as the original texts. Wilhelm had given me another sign, you see? The woods. They were to become Hänsel and Gretel . . .'

Fabel sat and listened as Biedermeyer outlined the rest of his crimes. He explained how he had planned to take the salesman, Ungerer, next, but there had been a mix-up over the Schnauber party cake and Biedermeyer had delivered it personally. It was then that he had seen Laura von Klosterstadt. He saw her haughty beauty and her long blonde hair. He knew he was looking at a princess. Not just any princess but Dornröschen – Sleeping Beauty. So he had put her to sleep for ever and taken her hair.

'Then I ended Ungerer. He was a lecherous, filthy swine. He was always leering at Hanna and even at Vera Schiller. I followed him for a couple of days. I saw the filth and the whores he wallowed in. I engineered it so that I bumped into him in St Pauli. I laughed at his filthy, disgusting jokes and his lewd remarks. He wanted to go for a drink, but I didn't want to be seen with him in public so I pretended to know of a couple of women whom we could visit. If the tales tell us anything, it's how easy it is to tempt others from the path and into the darkness of the woods. He was easy. I took him to . . . well, I took him to a house that you will soon visit yourself, and I told him the women were there. Then I took a knife and I twisted it in his black, corrupt heart. He wasn't expecting it and it was easy and all over in a second.'

'And you took his eyes?'

'Yes. I cast Ungerer as the king's son in "Rapunzel", and ripped out those leering, lecherous eyes.'

'What about Max Bartmann, the tattooist?' Fabel asked. 'You killed him before you killed Ungerer and he played no part in any of your tales. And you tried to hide the body for good. Why did you kill him? Just for his eyes?'

'In a way, yes. For what his eyes had seen. He knew who I was. I knew that now I had become free to start my work, he would see reports on the television or in the papers. Eventually he would have made the connection. So I had to end his story too.'

'What are you talking about?' Werner's tone was impatient. 'How did he know who you were?'

Biedermeyer moved so fast that none of the officers in the room had time to react. He shot to his feet, sending the chair he had been sitting on flying backwards towards the wall and the two SchuPos behind him jumped sideways. His vast hands flew up and ripped at his vast chest. The buttons flew from his shirt and the cloth tore as he struggled to free himself from it. Then he stood, a colossus, his body huge and dense in the interview room. Fabel held up a hand and the SchuPos who had lunged forward held back. Werner and Fabel were both on their feet and Maria had rushed forward. All three stood in the shadow of Biedermeyer's enormous frame. Everyone stared at the huge man's body.

'Holy fuck . . .' Werner said in a low voice.

Biedermeyer's torso was completely covered in words. Thousands of words. His body was black with them. Stories had been tattooed on to his skin in black Fraktur lettering, as small as the medium of human skin and the skill of the tattooist would allow. The titles were clear: *Dornröschen, Schneewittchen, Die Bremer Stadtmusikanten . . .*

'My God . . .' Fabel couldn't take his eyes from the tattoos. The words seemed to move, the sentences to writhe, with every single movement, with every breath Biedermeyer took. Fabel remembered the volumes in the tattooist's tiny flat: the books on old German Gothic scripts, on Fraktur, and Kupferstich. Biedermeyer stood silently for a moment. Then, when he spoke, his voice had the same deep, menacing resonance that it had had before.

'Now do you see? Now do you understand? I *am* Brother Grimm. I *am* the sum of the tales and the Märchen of our language, of our land, of our people. He had to die. He had looked upon this. Max Bartmann helped create this and had looked upon it. I couldn't let him tell anyone. So I ended him and I took his eyes so that he could play a part in the next tale.'

Everyone remained standing, tense, waiting.

'Now it's time,' said Fabel. 'Now you must tell us

where Paula Ehlers's body is. It doesn't fit. The only other body you hid was Max Bartmann's, and that was because it wasn't really part of your little tableaux. Why haven't we found Paula's body yet?'

'Because we have come full circle. Paula is my Gretel. I am her Hänsel. She still has her part to play.' His face broke into a smile. But it wasn't like any smile Fabel had seen before on Biedermeyer's normally amiable, friendly face. It was a smile of a terrible, bright coldness and it locked Fabel in its icy searchlight. 'It was "Hänsel und Gretel" more than any other tale that my stepmother would make me recite. It was long and it was difficult and I would always get it wrong. And then she used to beat me. She used to hurt my body and my mind until I thought they were broken for ever. But Wilhelm saved me. Wilhelm brought me back into the light with his voice, with his signs and then with his new writings. He told me the very first time I heard him that one day I would be able to exact revenge on my evil witch of a stepmother, that I would be liberated from her grasp, just as Hänsel and Gretel took revenge on the old witch and freed themselves.' Biedermeyer leaned his massive frame forward and the words stretched and warped on his skin. Fabel fought the instinct to draw back. 'I baked Paula's cake myself,' Biedermeyer continued in a dark, cold, deep voice. 'I baked and prepared Paula's cake myself. I do some freelance work for smaller functions and parties, and I have a fully equipped bakery in the basement, including a professional oven. The oven is very, very big and it needs a concrete floor to support it.'

Fabel's confusion showed on his face. They had sent a SchuPo unit to secure Biedermeyer's home. It was a ground-floor apartment in Heimfeld-Nord and the uniformed officers had confirmed that it was empty and that there was nothing unusual about it, except that one of the two bedrooms looked like it had been converted to accommodate an elderly or disabled person.

'I don't understand,' Fabel said. 'There is no basement in your apartment.'

Biedermeyer's cold grin broadened. 'That's not my home, you fool. That is merely the place I rented to convince the hospital authorities to release *Mutti* to my care. My real home is where I was brought up. The home I shared with that poisonous old bitch. Rilke Strasse, Heimfeld. It's by the Autobahn. That's where you'll find her . . . That's where you'll find Paula Ehlers. In the floor, where *Mutti* and I buried her. Bring her out, Herr Fabel. Bring my Gretel out of the darkness and we will both be free.'

Fabel gestured to the SchuPos who grabbed the unresisting Biedermeyer's arms and placed them behind his back, handcuffing them once more.

'You'll find her there . . .' Biedermeyer called to Fabel as he and his team left the room. Then he laughed. 'And while you're there, could you turn off the oven? I left it on this morning.'

CHAPTER 60

4.20 p.m., Friday, 30 April:
Heimfeld-Nord, Hamburg

T he house sat on the fringe of the Staatsforst woodland, near where the A7 sliced through it. It was large and old and presented a depressing prospect. Fabel guessed that it had been built in the 1920s but it lacked any feeling of character. It was set in a large garden that had been left to grow wild. The house itself looked as if it had been unloved for some time: the exterior paint was dull, stained and flaking, as if its skin was diseased.

Something about it reminded Fabel of the villa in which Fendrich and his late mother had lived. This house, too, looked lost, displaced; as if it now sat in surroundings and in a time that no longer suited it. Even its position with the swathe of woodland to its rear and the Autobahn hard by its side seemed incongruous.

They had taken two cars, and a SchuPo unit accompanied them. Fabel, Werner and Maria went directly to the front door and rang the bell.

Nothing. Anna and Henk Hermann were behind them and they beckoned to the SchuPos who brought a door-ram from the boot of their green and white Opel patrol car. The door was solid: made from oak that had stained almost black over the years. It took three swings of the ram before the wood splintered from the lock and the door slammed in against the vestibule wall.

Fabel and the others exchanged a look before they entered Biedermeyer's home. They all knew they were on the threshold of an exceptional madness and each prepared him or herself for what lay within.

It started in the hall.

The house was dark and gloomy inside and a glass door separated the vestibule from the hall beyond. Fabel pushed the door open. He did so cautiously, even though no danger waited for him. Biedermeyer was now safely locked up in his cell: yet he wasn't; his colossal presence was here, too. It was a large, narrow hall with a high ceiling, from which hung a pendant light with three bulbs. Fabel switched the lights on and the hall was filled with a bleak, jaundiced glow.

The walls were covered. It was a patchwork of pictures and printed and handwritten pages. Sheets of yellow paper had been pasted to the plaster; each was covered with tiny red-ink hand-writing. Fabel examined them: all Grimms' fairy tales were here. All written out in the same, obsessive hand and all free of a single error. A perfect madness. Between the handwritten sheets there were printed pages from editions of the Grimm Brothers' writings. And pictures. Hundreds of illustrations of the stories. Fabel recognised many of them from the originals that Gerhard Weiss had collected. And there were others, from the Nazi time, similar to those that the author had described. Fabel noticed that Anna Wolff had stopped to examine one: it was from the 1930s and the old witch was depicted with caricature Jewish features, bent-backed and stoking the fire beneath the oven while casting a greedy, short-sighted eye over the blond, Nordic Hänsel. Behind her an equally Nordic Gretel was poised to shove the witch into her own oven. It was one of the most nauseous images Fabel had ever seen. He couldn't begin to imagine how it made Anna feel.

They moved down the hall. Several large rooms led off it and a staircase ran up one side. All the rooms were empty of furniture, but Biedermeyer's insane collages had spilled into them and up the side of the staircase, spreading across the wall like damp or rot. There was a smell. Fabel couldn't quite place what it was, but it lurked in the house, clinging to the walls, to the clothes of the police officers.

Fabel took the first room on the left and beck-oned for Werner to take the one opposite. Maria headed along the hall and Anna and Henk went up the stairs. Fabel examined the room he was in. The dark wooden floor was dusty and, like the other rooms, there was no furniture nor any sense of habitation.

'*Chef* . . .' Anna called. 'Come and see this.' Fabel climbed the stairs, followed by Werner. Anna stood by an open doorway which led into a bedroom. Unlike the other rooms, this one clearly had been occupied. The walls, like the ones in the hallway, were thick with handwritten pages, pictures and extracts from books. There was a camp bed in the middle of the room, along with a small side table. But none of these were the focus of Fabel's attention. Two walls of the room had been lined with shelving. And the shelves were filled with books. Fabel stepped closer. No. Not books. *A* book.

Biedermeyer must have spent years, and practically all his money, buying editions of *Grimms' Fairy Tales*. Antiquarian copies sat alongside brand-new paperbacks; gold-embossed spines sat next to cheap editions; and next to the hundreds of German editions from nearly two hundred years of publication sat French, English and Italian copies. Titles in Cyrillic, Greek, Chinese and Japanese lettering were interspersed with those in the Roman alphabet.

Fabel, Werner, Anna and Henk stood speechless for a moment. Then Fabel said: 'I think we had better find the basement.'

'I think I've found it, or at least the way into it.' Maria was behind them at the doorway. She led them back down the stairs and along the hallway. The room at its far end was, or had been, the kitchen of the house. It was a vast room with a cooking range against one wall. Its comparative cleanliness and the faint electric hum from the large, new-looking refrigerator suggested that, like the bedroom/library above, it was the only other functioning living space. There were two doors, side by side. One was open and led into a pantry. The other was padlocked.

'I reckon this will lead us to the basement,' said Maria.

'And to Paula . . .' Anna stared hard at the door.

Werner left the kitchen and headed to the front door, where the two SchuPos were standing guard. He came back a minute later with a crowbar.

'Okay.' Fabel nodded towards the padlocked door.

As soon as the lock had been prised and the door opened, Fabel became aware that the smell he'd noticed before intensified significantly. Steps led down into the darkness. Werner found a light switch. When he turned it on, there was the sound of strip lights fizzing into life below them. Fabel led his team down into the basement.

It was a bakery. A proper, working bakery. Just as Biedermeyer had said, he had installed a vast Italian baking oven. The tray-trolley outside it would have been capable of holding dozens of loaves. In contrast to the house above, everything down here was clean. A preparation table, its surface of burnished stainless steel, gleamed under the strip lights, as did the pastry machine next to it. Fabel looked at the concrete floor. Paula was under there.

That smell. The smell of something burning. Fabel remembered Biedermeyer telling him to switch the oven off, because he'd left it on in the morning. Fabel had thought he'd been joking, but he obviously had put something in to bake before going to work in the Backstube Albertus, thinking he would have been back mid-afternoon.

Fabel's world slowed down.

The adrenalin that surged up within him stretched every second and he travelled a greater distance in that moment than he had throughout the whole investigation. He turned to look at his colleagues. They were standing, looking down at the concrete floor as if trying to see through it to where Paula lay. Not Paula, Gretel. Fabel looked back at the tray-trolley that should have been inside the oven, not outside it. And nothing bakes for a whole day.

'Oh, Jesus . . .' he said as he reached for the cloth that lay on the preparation table. 'Oh, Christ, no . . .'

Fabel wrapped the cloth around the handle of the oven and turned it. Then he swung the door open.

A tidal wave of heat and a sickening stench rolled over Fabel and into the basement bakery. It was the clinging, suffocating stench of roasted flesh. Fabel stood back, holding the cloth over his nose and mouth. His universe folded in a thousand times upon itself until there was nothing in it but himself and the horror before him. He did not hear Henk Hermann retching, Maria's stifled cry or Anna Wolff's sobbing. All he was aware of was that which lay before him. In the oven.

There was a large metal tray sitting in the bottom of the oven. On the tray, trussed up in a foetal position, lay the naked and half-cooked body of an elderly woman. The hair was all but gone and just a few frazzled balls clung tight to the roasted scalp. The skin was blackened and split. The heat had desiccated and drawn tight the tendons and the body had pulled even tighter in on itself.

Fabel stared at the corpse. This was Biedermeyer's masterpiece: Brother Grimm's final tale that brought everything full circle.

The conclusion of Hänsel and Gretel: the old witch cast into her own oven.